Oracle

The Prophesy Fulfilled

by

Katherine Greyle

LionHearted Publishing, Inc.
Zephyr Cove, NV, USA

This book is a work of fiction. Names, characters, places and incidents are products of the author's imagination or are used fictitiously. Any resemblance to actual events or locales or persons, living or dead, is entirely coincidental.

LionHearted Publishing, Inc.
P.O. Box 618
Zephyr Cove, NV 89448-0618
admin@LionHearted.com

Visit our website: **http://www.LionHearted.com**

Copyright © 1998 by Katherine Grill

Cover model Cherif Fortin
Cover photo and art by Lynn Sanders
Computer artist Julie Melton

ISBN: 1-57343-022-6

Printed in the U.S.A.

Dixie, Allison, and Reverend Gaffron:
You kept me going when I would have quit.

Elisabeth:
You pushed me to levels I never imagined.

David:
You are the best hero a woman could ever love.

This book is dedicated to you all.

Thank you.

Prologue

◆ ◆ ◆

October 31, 2012

Jane Deerfield's hand hovered over the on/off switch, but she couldn't press it down. Turning off a computer always seemed a little like murder to her. Stopping access to millions of gigabytes of information was criminal, especially since she'd just spent five hours repairing the system, reloading the software, and making sure everything networked perfectly for the people who used it.

Jane stood up, hating to leave the dancing lights of the monitor's screensaver, even to stretch. She straightened, rolling her shoulders a bit before looking around. Except for the soft glow of the computer's monitor, the library was completely dark. Glancing at the clock in the upper corner of the screen, Jane gasped at the time.

Damn. Not only had she missed Mary's Halloween costume party, but federal curfew too. By a good two hours, no less. She hoped any police she met understood the importance of her mission. The rest of the world might view her as a lowly computer nerd and perpetual student, but she knew in her heart she was a warrior bravely fighting to keep alive one of the last free centers of knowledge available to all.

Information was getting harder to come by in this information age. With the electrical black-outs and restricted net sites, not to mention the New Cold War eating up electronic products like candy, even big universities were finding it hard to keep their systems up and running.

But that, of course, was her job. Jane ran Boston University's computers. Well, she didn't run them in terms of being head of the department. They had pencil-pusher Dr. Beavesly doing that. She did all the work; maintaining the software and the machines, and keeping each and every terminal shining bright against the darkness of ignorance.

Jane straightened her shoulders, laughing at herself as she mentally added a stiff breeze, the right lighting, and of course super-hero music. She was Jane Deerfield, a.k.a. Oracle, defender of truth and justice and computer integrity throughout cyberspace. All she needed now were the bat-boots to go with her costume, because her orange high-tops just didn't seem to fit the image. Course, it didn't matter anyway, she thought sourly, since no one would ever see her awesome black leotard with the neon bat on the front this Halloween.

"Damn terrorists and their fragging homebody bombs," she muttered. "They can't blow-up some munitions dump. No. They have to go for *my* computers."

She should have expected it, she knew. The psychos had been out in force ever since those last Dustmaker satellites went up. It seemed like every megalomaniac and his government was buying the latest and greatest weapons of destruction whether they understood the technology or not. It was getting hard to see the sun for all the satellite shadows.

No doubt about it. Some mutant virus had destroyed everyone's common sense.

Sighing, Jane slipped her backpack on feeling depression settle in as well. She was a computer jockey, not a comic book heroine—more's the pity. All she could do was her job, fighting ignorance in her own special way. She'd leave global politics to the mental cases in power.

Jane hunched her shoulders against the New England fall and started walking to the door.

There was no warning. Just a loud sound, felt more than heard. But Jane knew instantly that something awful had happened. She tensed to run, but didn't know where. Should she go back to the library computer, the core of stored knowledge, making sure to save it? Or should she run to the central net hoping she could keep the whole system up?

She couldn't decide. And in that moment of indecision, she was caught.

There was no sound, just a blackness, like a rip in the air. Around its jagged edges everything was distorted, as though space shriveled, curling backwards like a paper slowly eaten by flame.

Then it was on her. The rip stretched and tore, as though reaching for her.

She ran, but it was too fast. One minute her feet were pounding on the stone floor. The next, she was suspended in a nightmare.

Nothing was around her, but that nothing was black and so very cold. She twisted, trying to keep her balance, but there was no up or down. Only incredible coldness. And the weight of ages pressing against her, choking her lungs, squeezing her body into a tiny pinprick of existence.

Her mind fought with the impossibility of it all, desperately scrambling for a logical handhold for escape. Then she had no thoughts at all.

Only pain.

She was dying.

Chapter One

◆   ◆   ◆

Forty-first day, Warming season,
Thirteenth year of the Seef

Cold.
Ice cold.
Warmth. Blessed warmth, spreading like hot fudge on ice cream throughout her system. Starting at her forehead, sliding into her mind, it heated the tiny nooks and crannies of her body.

Jane sighed with delight and opened her eyes, then winced at the glaring sunlight. She felt a hand glide low over her forehead, shielding her from the glare. The hand was large and calloused, but gentle as it caressed her skin.

"Yyi cquiness mnansirul?" The voice was deep and lilting, like a magical river in an animated vid. It was beautiful. And insistent. *"Mnansirul?"*

"Huh?" One syllable was all she could force through her raw throat.

The hand slid away, and she blinked rapidly trying to sort shape from shadow. A man was beside her, gently sliding his arm behind her shoulders. His touch was almost painful. Wherever he pressed against her, she felt tiny pinpricks, like electricity shooting minute bolts of lightning through her skin.

This must be how a recharging battery feels, she thought. She knew the man was bringing her back to life in slow, torturous inches. He revitalized her cell by cell, but God, if this was living, maybe being a dead battery wasn't so bad.

Her head lolled back against his arm, and she felt his energy pulse through her with the beginnings of a first class headache.

Something wet pressed against her lips and before she realized what was happening, hot water seared across her tongue, thawing as it slid past.

She swallowed, waiting greedily for more. It came in patient mouthfuls, swallow by swallow. She drank it all, only vaguely realizing the water wasn't hot. It was probably tepid at best, but she was so very, very cold it burned as it went down.

Then he lay her back down on the grass, and she was able to see him clearly for the first time.

Wow. He was gorgeous; just how she'd create a leading man for some computer game. Somewhere in his thirties, his face was cut into hard planes and strong lines. His eyes were an intense dark blue swirled with mesmerizing gold flecks that were the sexiest things she'd seen in a considerable career of guy watching. Add to that his golden brown hair and a sweet smile, and she was in love.

"Wh—" Her throat closed up, but she swallowed away the pain. "What happened?"

He shook his head, indicating he didn't understand.

"Where am I?" she asked, her words slow and deliberate. She had a vague impression of grass, trees, blue sky, and clean air, all of which meant she wasn't in Boston.

He settled her back down in the grass. She felt his fingertips run over her eyes again, closing them with a firm insistence. Despite her growing confusion, she felt herself succumb to their gentle urging.

Rest, his fingers seemed to say as they traveled across her cheek, stopping against her lips. He seemed to be holding back her questions, keeping her from speaking until she at last surrendered to his soothing caress.

Sleep, he urged.

She slept.

✦   ✦   ✦

Jane moaned, rolled over and covered her ears against the sound of the oddest car alarms she'd ever heard. There must have been another explosion because a whole slew of them were going off at once. Why weren't they the piercing electronic wails that she could tune out without a second thought? These were lyrical, shifting notes and tones like a bird call, except there were so many.

Bird call? A vague sense of dread stole over her, and she opened her eyes.

She saw a bug. A big black bug with red spots and long furry antennae ambling across her arm toward her face. She jumped up with a squeal, shaking her arm and fighting the nausea. Fortunately, the startled thing flew away. Unfortunately, the nausea was caused by her sudden movement, not the sight of a strange new member of the beetle family.

She dropped her head into her hands and took deep, painful breaths, her chest muscles fighting the movement. Suddenly she felt him beside her. His hands held her lightly across the shoulders. She didn't move. Gradually she felt a warmth spreading from his hands, through her shoulders, gently sinking into her body. She vaguely remembered hot fudge over ice cream, but this heat was different, deeper. Like frozen popcorn in a microwave, she felt herself pop awake, cell by cell as she heated from the inside out.

Then he stopped, slowly withdrawing while she was still half done. Disappointed, she opened her eyes and turned to say something, but the words never formed. Instead, her jaw went slack as she took in her environment.

She was at the edge of a meadow ringed with trees and birds. Lots of real birds, like in an aviary. There wasn't a carport in sight. Reaching down, she touched soft, springy grass that hadn't been mowed in months. A cool breeze caressed her tongue, and she shut her mouth with a snap. Gone was the familiar scent of exhaust, the acrid tang of pollution. In its place was a sweetness both fresh and laden with the heavy scents of a garden.

"Ugh. What is that smell?" She wrinkled her nose, trying to adjust to the faint electric pulse of the air.

"Yyi stransve hrenvivr?"

She looked at her gorgeous hero. He seemed the same today as yesterday, his soft white shirt alternately flaring or flattening against his broad chest according to the capriciousness of the wind.

"Svenetrins? KVanteke? Gronta?" He was asking her something, his voice changing slightly with each word. She knew her expression was one of complete stupidity, but she was still in reboot and couldn't think of a thing to say.

He sighed. It was a masculine sigh, full of rippling chest muscles and frustration with the female sex. She'd seen it a thousand times from her father, her brother, even her boss.

He leaned backward, neatly snatching his pack from the grass by a low campfire. Hers rested right beside his.

"What's going on? Where am I?" she demanded. But he was focused on his backpack and ignored her, and soon she began watching him, her curiosity piqued. His pack was an odd thing made out of leather with none of the neon colors or lightweight synthetic materials she favored. In fact, now that she looked closely, everything about him seemed natural—no bright colors, all natural fiber cloth, even a leather thong to tie back his wavy hair.

"Are you some sort of naturalist?" she asked. "It's not that I mind, but you must be incredibly rich to afford such stuff." She bit her lip in frustration. Why did she always say the stupidest things? Taking a deep breath, she ordered her questions and started with the most pressing one. "My name's Jane. What's—"

Her words stopped cold as he pulled a filthy baggie filled with fireflies out of his pack and pushed it toward her.

"Ugh! Get that away from me!"

She tried to slide away, but he caught her wrist. Even if she'd been at full strength, he would have been stronger. He was relentless as he drew her closer to it, firmly placing her hand on top of what she now saw was some sort of bloated animal gut.

"Yuck!"

It felt warm and squishy and strangely tingly, all of which was very much like putting her hand on living sheep intestines. She was thoroughly repulsed, but that was nothing compared to the fear that sliced through her when her companion drew out a very sharp, very wicked looking dagger.

"Steemanti. Steemanti!"

He couldn't really want her to eat that, could he? "Look, I'm not very hungry. Please feel free to eat your sheep guts without me. Hey!"

She tried to jerk away as he brought the knife closer. Her fingers curled into a fist as she twisted against him, but his grip was like durosteel bands, and she was trapped in it.

Then she watched in horror as he nicked the fleshy edge of his hand, the one holding her wrist. His blood welled dark red, then slipped down the edge of his hand onto her arm.

"Okay," she whispered. "I'll eat the sheep gut. Whatever you want."

"Steemanti."

He lifted her hand, twisting it until he exposed the same fleshy part beneath her left pinkie.

"No. No way are you going to cut me." She let her hand go lax. Then suddenly, she put her back into it, bracing her legs and wrenching away. She didn't care if she pulled her arm out of its socket, she would get away from Mr. Psychotic with the knife.

She made it, though from the pain in her shoulder, she'd probably dislocated it. Then she scrambled to her feet and started running. Although not athletic, she'd always been able to cut and run whenever needed. But she was weak, her movements off balance, and her head still felt three times too big for her neck. Even with the adrenaline boost, she felt like she moved in slow motion.

She heard a muttered oath behind her. Amazing, she thought, swear words are identifiable in all languages. Then she literally flew through the air as her hero tackled her.

She landed on her side and was rapidly pushed onto her back while her hero sat on top of her. Her breath came in painful gasps, and her head pounded like a techno band, but terrified as she was, a part of her still recognized the sheer thrill of two hundred pounds of muscle grinding into her with a power as exciting as it was swift and sure.

He straddled her hips. Then he leaned forward, supporting himself on his knees as he twisted his feet behind him to hook over her legs. It was probably to keep her from kneeing him in the back, which was exactly what she'd intended to do when she caught her breath. His hardened chest stretched across her, giving her a close up view of sleek, tan skin lightly brushed with golden brown hair. Then he caught her wrists, neatly subduing her while he grumbled nonsense into her ear.

For annoyed, irritated male grumbling, it sounded remarkably erotic.

She looked up and caught the flash of something in his eyes. If this were an anima novel, she would have labeled it passion, but this was real life. Still, their gazes locked for a moment and despite her position, the nearby knife, and his blood trickling onto her wrist, she felt reassured.

He smiled—a wry twist to his lips, and she smiled back. She couldn't help it. Then she gasped as he wrenched himself to sit upright, his thickening groin pressing deeply against her as he lifted up his torso and her wrists.

"Yyi jaggenwa martense. Steemanti. Steemanti."

He looked so serious, so intense with his blue eyes burning down at her that she knew she had no hope of fighting him.

"Do you really have to?" she asked. Her brief fight had exhausted her from head to toe. A vague sort of fatalism washed through her as she watched him twist her hand. "Guess that means you have to."

The incision was quick, like a deep paper cut, but it was over in an instant, then his lips, soft as neovelvet, brushed over the wound. She smiled weakly at his sweet gesture, but it faded quickly at his next move. Stretching behind him with his cut hand, he grabbed the sheep gut.

"I told you, I'm not really hungry." She knew the firefly sheep gut wasn't food, but it made her feel better to pretend it was.

He pressed it against her wound, wrapping the tube around her palm and holding it there with his own bloody hand. It was still warm and tingly, and she tried to flinch away, but he kept her firmly in place. Then he slid the knife between them and neatly cut the bag.

It was the oddest sensation. The fireflies escaped the bag and tickled her palm, buzzing against her skin before zipping away to her hero. No, not fireflies. Static. As though they'd caught electrical sparks between their palms.

Then one tiny point of energy found her wound, sliding right in and up her bloodstream. She jerked, but he held her fast, keeping their hands pressed together.

Bit by bit, the static wormed its way in, swarming through her wrist, creeping up her arm until she trembled with the horror of it. He said something, crooning nonsense syllables meant to reassure her, but she couldn't focus.

Then suddenly it burst on her. It was as though the energy dancing up her arm hit a major artery and went straight for her brain. She screamed as her vision faded into a wash of white. Her thoughts spun in the dizzying vortex of energy that swarmed through her mind.

From somewhere above her, she heard his grunt of surprise, but she was still dealing with the reeling, pounding electricity throbbing through her consciousness. In the end, she gave herself up to it, letting it flood her senses on the wildest sensory trip virtual reality sci-fi had yet to create.

Then it faded, and she was left sweetly energized, her thoughts sparkling like Christmas lights gone berserk. "Wow! That's better than coffee. Even my coffee!"

Her hero still sat on her, his expression dazed and confused. "That was unusually intense," he said, his voice hushed and lyrical.

"Intense? It was great! What was that stuff? And how come you're suddenly speaking English?"

He looked down, his face slowly spreading into a Hollywood sex god smile. "I'm not. That's what that was."

Jane blinked. "You've lost me."

"You are right with me. My companions are never lost." He sounded vaguely insulted.

She struggled onto her elbows, propping herself up so she could peer into his dreamy eyes. Unfortunately, he immediately lifted himself off of her, politely settling onto the grass beside her.

"I don't mean physically lost like geographically. I mean—"

"I know, woman," he cut in. "I was testing the magic. Language is a tricky thing, and we're supposed to be able to understand each other completely."

"Huh?"

"That was a spell. Permanent. I am sorry I used it on you, but it was necessary." From his expression, it was clear he meant "waste" it on her.

"Well, excuuuse me." She rubbed her hand, staring at the fleshy part, now completely healed over.

"No need to apologize," he said. She peered at him, wondering if he was teasing or serious. "I needed to know if it worked."

Jane took a deep breath and tried to sort through the confusion while keeping panic at bay. "You mean, we're both talking in our own language, but I hear English and you hear...uh—"

"Svenetrins."

Jane sat up. "Really? So I'll always understand sene— Svenet—"

"Svenetrins. And no. It's a personal spell between two people. You will only understand me. And I, you."

"Oh." Then she shrugged. "Still, that's better than a secret decoder ring. Where'd you get it?" She tried to act casual as though magic sheep guts were normal.

He looked at her oddly. "A bard sold it to me for thirty doleens."

"Thirty doleens?" What were doleens?

"I know. Exorbitant. But she was...entertaining. And she had the most stunning blond hair, like the color of sunlight on Nansar's pond." His eyes grew abstract as he focused on some pleasant memory, and Jane felt the first stirring of annoyance.

"A little hair dye, and they all go on a testosterone high," she grumbled. Then she stood up, moving slowly in case the dizzies came back. "Well, this has been fun, but would you mind directing me toward the nearest phone? Preferably without working video." She self-consciously tugged at her mousy brown locks, matted now with bits of grass.

He stared at her, his face registering disappointment. "The spell must not have worked well. I don't understand your words."

"Oh. I need a phone." She mimed putting a receiver to her ear. "Or a computer. Actually a computer would be better. Then I can hook into the University Net and get a lock on the damage." She looked around, studying the meadow as her memories slowly jumbled into a strange order. "Exactly how did I get here? In fact, where is here? The last thing I remember is the library."

Her gaze was caught by a strange purple flower, and she approached it slowly. It was a pretty thing, with some spiked petals, some curved. They dotted the meadow grass the way the letter "i" dotted a printed page. She'd never seen one before. Never, ever in a whole childhood of helping her father, a botanist.

"What is this?"

"The mansara flower? It's a common plant. They're all over the place."

"Uh-huh. And that?" She pointed to one of the tall trees lining the meadow. Its bark was like smooth concrete, and its leaves looked like a marijuana plant.

"An oant tree."

"Right." Jane turned slowly, anger building within her like a Georgia heat wave. She put her fists on her hips and fixed her hero with her ice queen glare. "Okay, I want to know just where I am, and how do I get from here to Boston."

"Boston?"

"Big city. Streets that used to be cow paths."

Blank. His face was completely blank. She bit her lip and started pacing off her energy.

"I didn't ask before. Denial, I guess. But it's over now. Tell me what's going on." She waited for him to speak, but all he did was settle more comfortably on the grass and give her his complete attention. It was as if he were studying her, and that only increased the burn within her. Still, she took a deep breath and decided to start slowly.

"Where am I?"

"The Plains of Eacost, south of the Great Forest."

She stared at him, worrying her lower lip until it started to feel bruised and swollen. Then suddenly her spirits lightened. "I'm sorry." She was proud of how level her voice sounded. "Your secret decoder gizmo isn't working right."

"It's working perfectly. You are on the Plains of Eacost, south—"

"South of the Great Forest. I heard." Still, she shook her head, wondering if her ears were clogged.

"What is the last thing you remember?" he asked.

"I . . ." She thought back, finding her mind slow and difficult. She remembered her morning shower. The power had been cut again during the night and domestic energy was on lowest priority, so the water had been ice cold. Her memories leaped forward through a normal work day. Then she'd put on her costume intending to go to the party just after stopping at the library.

Glancing down, she groaned in real horror. Yes, she was indeed pacing agitatedly in front of her computer hero still wearing a billowing cape, a leotard with a huge bat outline on her breasts, black leggings, and neon orange sneakers—she hadn't been able to afford the stylish boots.

Of course, she realized as she peered closer at her hero, he was in costume too. Sort of an eighteenth-century pirate outfit. Soft flowing shirt, dagger sheathed in the belt of his leather breeches. He even wore the softest pair of boots she'd seen in her life. And to complete the outfit, a huge, two-handed, bastard sword lay strapped on his back. It didn't look in the least bit fake either.

She stared at it until he brought her back to the present.

"Are you hungry?" he asked.

"I was working in the library."

He must have taken that as a "no" because he reached into his pack and pulled out what looked like beef jerky. Thank heaven he didn't offer her any because the very sight of it made her think of dried caterpillar. Rather than watch him eat it, she went back to her confusing memories.

"I had to reload a system. The last brown-out zapped everything, but I can't remember anything after that."

"I came upon you two nights ago," he said between bites. "You were lying face down, so cold I thought you were dead."

Jane stared at him. "I was just lying there? In the grass?"

He nodded.

"How the hell did I get there?" she yelled.

He shifted nervously, his broad shoulders rippling as he moved. "I don't know," he said, his eyes dark with sympathy.

She took a deep breath, trying to recall the zen-calming chant she'd told her friend was stupid. "This is too bizarre. It's like one of those bad comic books when…" Her voice trailed off, a sick feeling churning in her gut. Comic books often showed some innocent bystander sucked into a vortex, transported across space and time as a result of the villain's manipulations. Usually the nameless slob died before the next page.

She glanced at her hero, wondering if he could possibly be the product of another planet or dimension. He looked human. She clenched her fists, ordering herself to stop being silly. She had not stepped into a comic book. She was simply disoriented.

"What day is it?"

"Forty-third day, Warming season, Thirteenth year of the Seef."

Her knees wobbled, but she persevered, determined to face the truth. "What…" She couldn't say it. She cleared her throat and tried again. "What planet?"

He hesitated only a second. "Urta."

Her knees went out. Her legs went out. In fact, her whole body and brain went out to lunch. She fell to the ground, landing hard on her tush.

She didn't see him move, but suddenly he was beside her, his large hands warm on her shoulders. Instinctively, she asked for the one thing that always made everything easier to handle.

"Chocolate?"

He deftly pressed the beef jerky into her hands.

She moaned, but decided anything was better than thinking. Grabbing the brown stick, she closed her eyes and bit.

She was wrong. There was something worse than facing reality. And she was chewing it.

Gagging, she spit it out on the ground, simultaneously reaching for his water bag to wash the taste out of her mouth.

"Ugh! What is that stuff?"

He opened his mouth, but she raised her hand to stop him. "No. Don't tell me. I don't want to know. Ugh." She took another swig. "Have you got any toothpaste?" At his blank look she tried again. "Something to clean your teeth?"

His eyes widened. "You clean your teeth?"

"No, I like foul breath, a brown smile, and pain when I chew. Of course I—" She cut off her words at his stunned expression. "You don't clean your teeth?" From his whitewash smile, she'd have guessed they were plastic coated.

"Of course I clean my teeth. I am a king." He sounded insulted. As her emotions seesawed between outrage and hysteria, he rooted through his pack and came up with a box of brown powder.

"What's that?"

"Tooth powder."

At her hesitant expression, he dipped his finger in the powder, rubbed it along his teeth, then spit. The stream of expectorant looked totally gross, but he offered it to her and flashed his poster boy smile. It was either try it or be totally rude to the man who had probably saved her life.

Difficult decision.

Finally, she imitated him and nearly gagged. It felt like rubbing sandpaper across her teeth and tasted about as appetizing. She spit, managing a weak smile.

"Vile?" he asked.

She nodded. They both drank some water.

Then he turned to her, his expression curious, if a little wary. "Where do you come from where tooth powder is not a chore?"

"Boston. The United States. And it's not powder, it's a…" She gave him a vapid smile as though she were in a commercial. "A minty, fresh gel." He looked at her like she was moldy spaghetti. She sighed. "Oh, never mind."

"I don't know about Bos-ton. Or the U—"

"United States. And what do you mean you don't know about it? Everybody knows about the U.S. Those we haven't annoyed are actively trying to terrorize us. There isn't a soul on the planet that doesn't know about us." She stopped talking, once again feeling sick to her stomach. "That's the problem, isn't it? I'm not on Earth anymore."

Her companion was silent, oddly accepting of her strange comments. "I don't know."

She stared at him. His sexy body was relaxed, his expression calm. Everything she wasn't. And that really annoyed her. Her fragile mental health broke, and she rounded on him in fury. "You don't know? Well, that does me a whole lot of good. I'm lost. I've got five bucks, no food, I'm talking to every woman's fantasy, and I'm in a stupid comic book costume!" She towered over him, shaking with frustration and fear, and all he did was gaze back at her, the gold in his eyes sparkling in the sunlight.

"My name is Daken," he said softly. "King Daken of the house of Chigan. I am pleased you think me every woman's fantasy."

She stared at him. "So glad I could be of service," she said dryly. Then she collapsed back onto the ground and dropped her head into her hands.

Daken sighed, then reached out to her, wishing he could do more for her as he absently brushed her short curls from her face. "I don't know how to help you," he said softly. Her fear was like a tidal wave, swamping his thoughts. He could feel her frustration like a raving beast, and it left him feeling very exposed.

He had to leave. His people were dying, and his first priority was to them. But even knowing that, he felt horrible guilt at abandoning this woman when she was at her most vulnerable.

He clenched his jaw. He had done his duty. He healed her, even used his very expensive language spell. He couldn't afford to waste any more time or resources on her. But still, he stayed.

She stood, pacing back and forth in front of him, rubbing her arms as though she were cold. He would have offered her his jacket, but he knew she didn't feel chill. Her movements betrayed her fear. And that she didn't often feel afraid.

"You can remember nothing else?" he asked.

She shook her head. "It's all a blur."

Healing her would be a mistake. His healer skills would absorb her terror like a sponge, and then he'd spend the next hour steadying the trembling in his own limbs. Against his will, he found himself in front of her, gradually enfolding her in his arms, giving her what comfort he could.

She was stiff against him, fighting herself more than him. He could tell she wanted to drop into his arms, but her pride kept her away. He waited, demanding nothing of her until she decided. Then to his joy, she softened against him, melting into his arms like a child burrowing into her parent's embrace, or a woman nestling into the cradle of her lover's arms.

It was a sweet moment, at odds with his warrior's soul, but still he clung to it, sheltering her in his arms while his mind told him he should be leaving.

"I must go," he whispered into the sweet scent of her hair.

She jerked as if he'd slapped her, but he held her tight, forcing her to hear the rest of his words. "This is a safe land with generous people. Find a farm house and offer your help. They will pay you honest wages for honest work."

"But—"

"Your memory will return in time." He didn't know if it was true, but he knew she needed to believe it. Then he broke the embrace, feeling the emptiness in his arms like an ache, but he suppressed the emotions and turned away. He couldn't stay with her any longer.

He began to close camp.

"You can't leave me, hero, uh, I mean Daken." She said it flatly, as though he had no choice in the matter. "I'm completely lost. All I need is to get to a phone."

He glanced up, and she shook her head to stop his next words.

"I know. You don't know what a phone is. How about the nearest city? Maybe I can get my bearings there." She reached out, pulling him around to face her, desperation making her brown eyes luminous. "Please, I'm begging you. Don't abandon me."

He twisted away to break their physical contact. He couldn't think when she touched him. Her emotions bled through to him too easily, running riot over his own thoughts.

"Daken?"

He swallowed, knowing she wouldn't like hearing this any more than he liked saying it. "I am going to Bosuny, and I have tarried too long already."

She stepped forward. "Let me come with you."

He shook his head. "You are still weak. You'll

walk too slowly, and I can't lose any more time. I'm sorry." He kicked some dirt on the dying embers, then grabbed his pack. "There is a farmhouse a half day's journey that way." He pointed. "Tell them a king has sent you to them. They will help you." Then he started walking, his long stride quickly eating up the distance to the edge of the clearing.

"Wait a minute," she called, running behind him like a lumbering tekay.

He grumbled out a curse and stopped. She was too weak to sustain his pace, but from the sound of it, she wasn't about to stop until she'd said her peace.

"You can't just leave me here."

"I can't do anything more for you. Perhaps a better healer, but I—"

"I'm not crazy," she interrupted. "I've lost some of my memory, not my mind."

"Woman—"

"Just listen to me. I don't know what's going on here, but I'm not going to find out at some farmhouse where I can't even speak the language. Take me with you to Bo... to Bosu—"

"Bosuny is a long, long way, and you are too weak—"

"Please." Her entire soul seemed poured into her eyes as she pleaded with him. He should have been unmoved by such a display. As a king, he'd seen it many times for one reason or another, and he'd been able to ignore it then.

But with her it was different. He sensed this woman didn't beg. Not without great need. He reached out, touching the wetness on her cheek, stroking it between his fingers.

"I'm not crying," she said, clearly trying to hold

back her tears.

It happened so fast, as though an Old One pushed him into something he never would have done on his own. One moment he was thinking about the odd puzzle she was, and the next second he was kissing her, her lips warm and sensuous against his own. She gasped in surprise, and he dipped lower, deeper into her mouth.

He stroked her tongue, feeling a passion build within her that had nothing to do with her confusion. She responded to him as a woman, and he felt himself curl around and within her, instinctively protecting that which he wanted to possess.

Her arms wrapped around his neck, and he let his hands trail down her back, pulling her deep against his thickening heat. She groaned into his mouth, and he felt his blood surge within him.

This was wrong. She was ill. He was late. Reasons crammed into his brain, all telling him with perfect logic to leave her alone. She was a distraction he couldn't afford right now.

But still he held her, possessing her mouth as he slowly wedged his knee between her legs.

Then his conscience won. He pulled away from her with a curse, slamming his fist into a tree trunk, using the pain to clear his fogged brain.

"Daken?"

"I'm sorry," he said stiffly, his voice rough and coarse. "I should not have done that."

"Hey, I didn't object."

He ran his hand through his hair, unable to face her. "You are ill."

"I told you, I've just lost some of my memory. That's all."

He turned to look at her, feeling tormented by conflicting responsibilities and desires. "You are ill," he said softly. "I am the one who cares for you. I cannot use someone I am responsible for."

"Oh, it's a doctor-patient thing." He saw understanding light in her eyes, like a garnet held before a flame.

He blinked, not following her strange words. "You are ill, and I am a king."

"King. Not a doctor. A king who can't kiss peasants." He heard the outrage in her voice, but he didn't understand its cause.

"A king is a doctor," he said.

She leaned forward, her eyebrows pulled together as she struggled to communicate with him. "What do you mean a king is a doctor? Kings lead people. Doctors heal people."

Did she know nothing? "Kings lead because they can heal."

"So it *is* a doctor-patient thing."

Unable to stop himself, he reached out, trailing his fingers across her full, red lips. How could he explain to her something he didn't understand himself? "Your kiss is a wonder to me—full of magic and power." His voice was low and hoarse, and he saw her passion flare again in her eyes. Rather than give in to the promise he saw there, he turned away, looking east to Bosuny. "But I must go."

"Take me with you."

"I can't."

"Please."

He groaned, knowing he was lost long before he said the words. "Very well. I will slow my steps for you."

"Thank you—"

"But we must not kiss again."

She watched him, her eyes so incredibly open and vulnerable. "I told you, I'm not sick. And I didn't mind—"

"I can't afford the distraction." He shook his head, turning his gaze to the distant horizon. "I am a fool to let you slow me down at all."

"You mean I'm a burden and an annoyance." He heard the bitterness in her voice, but would not allow himself to soften more.

"My mission is urgent."

She straightened her shoulders, and he caught a flash of defiance in her eyes. "Then I guess we better get going."

Chapter Two

♦   ♦   ♦

"So, you're a king." Jane watched him closely, but Daken's face remained impassive, his thoughts hidden beneath his calm facade.

"Chigan is a territory to the northwest."

Jane nodded, cudgeling her brain trying to remember any small third world country named Chigan. She wasn't surprised when she drew a blank. Geography had never been her strong suit. "Don't you want to know my name?" she asked.

He raised an eyebrow at her. "I assumed you would tell me if you knew it."

"Of course, I know it! It's Jane. Jane Deerfield."

He smiled, lifting the harsh planes of his face until he looked almost young. "Jane Deerfield is a beautiful name. I understand now why you wished to keep it a secret since it describes your home. I am honored that you shared it with me. Do you claim the deer or the field?"

She opened her mouth, but couldn't phrase the questions filling her mind at his odd question. Finally, "I'm confused," was all she managed.

"Yes. I know," he said gently, and she nearly ground her teeth in frustration. "Perhaps you were joined with a deer, and the creature died. That would explain your illness."

"What do you mean 'joined with a deer'? I..." She struggled to push all her questions into a coherent form, but he looked at her so oddly that she gave up.

Over the last twenty-four hours they'd had many conversations like this, each more frustrating than the last. Despite his secret decoder trick, they obviously communicated on two very different levels.

"Perhaps the mages in Bosuny will be able to help you," he offered.

"The mages?" She bit her lip, deciding to take things one step at a time. "What's a mage?"

"A wizard. One who uses the Power in other ways."

"Other than healing."

He nodded. Jane sighed. Wizards, mages, and some unknown power. She had the horrible feeling her life was about to get a lot more complicated. They'd been traveling for over a day, walking east through meadows, fields, and a few farms. The area reminded her of what America looked like in the history vids about settlers. It was wide open, the land green and lush, if a bit odd to the daughter of a botanist.

Everywhere she looked, she saw plants she thought she recognized, but then again didn't. This tree looked like a maple, except its color was off. There seemed to be a blue tint to the leaves, not to mention the strange strings that almost looked like hair. Even the water tasted different. She'd expected non-chlorinated, unpolluted water from a crystal clear stream to taste different, but not with an almost electric tingling as it slid down her throat.

At least last night she'd been able to see the stars. Much to her relief, there was only one moon and it seemed very familiar. Of course, one moon looked pretty much like another to her, and this one was just a quarter full. She thought she recognized the Big Dipper, but who could tell? She'd seen more stars last night than ever before in her life. The sky seemed littered with them, like glitter dust spilled by a careless child. She'd been enchanted, even more so when Daken gave her a lesson in constellations. The names were unfamiliar, but she listened to his lyrical voice and watched where he pointed, feeling almost at peace.

They talked late into the night, and she found unexpected depths in her normally taciturn companion. She also discovered things were very different in this strange world. Fortunately, Daken was a gracious host when he wanted to be. He told her the legends of his people, and thankfully, he didn't press for information about hers.

With all the good will of the night before, one would think she'd wake up in a chipper mood. But without coffee, a good doughnut, or even normal toothpaste, much less her favorite minty fresh gel, she stomped and grumbled about. Now they were breaking for lunch, and her mood had deteriorated. She felt tired, sore, and completely at odds with the world.

Then she spied a stream through the trees and hit on a wonderfully delightful thought.

"I'm going swimming," she declared, daring him to argue. "I know you've got a schedule, but I'm going to be a miserable person until I wash this grime off of me. Please, please say you don't mind." She was half begging, half threatening him, and given the tight set to Daken's jaw, he didn't appreciate her attitude.

"Ask for permission," he said.

"Permission? Like I'm supposed to go down on one

knee and ask you if I can bathe?" She hated herself for the sarcasm that dripped like acid from her tongue. She wasn't normally this caustic a person, but this whole world threw her into a deep regression.

"You don't need *my* permission," Daken answered slowly, his dark gaze burning into her. "That's someone's home."

"Well, the fish can share today." And with that she stomped off to the water.

She didn't want to waste time any more than necessary, so she stripped as she walked, peeling off her belt, leotard, and leggings as quickly as possible. She was already naked and about to step into the water when she thought to glance behind her.

Sure enough, he was watching. But not with the lurid, peeping Tom, behind-the-bushes type stare. No, he was out in the open, legs spread, hands on his hips, scowling at her. Scowling! Like washing was some mortal sin!

Well, to hell with him. She wanted a bath.

She eyed the stream. It was a little muddy, a little dirty, generally healthy, but not exactly crystal clear mountain water. Still, it was cleaner than she was, so she stepped into the stream, ignoring his strange comment about asking permission.

At first it tingled, the tiny stabs of electricity a sensory delight when combined with the cool water as it rushed by her. She released a sigh of pure pleasure, then dropped down to her knees, intending to arch backwards to trail her hair in the stream.

She never got the chance. She started to sink, and then the stream turned on her. There was no other way to describe it. What started out as a cheerful, bubbling brook became a roiling, seething mass. What once was a cool tingle became tiny needles of pain which then became slashes of agony. Her body was suddenly on fire, and she screamed, clawing at the bank as she scrambled to get out.

To her horror, the feeling lingered long after she'd achieved dry land. Wherever she was wet, wherever a drop of water clung to her body, it felt like a boil burning into her. She swiped at her skin, her imagination creating insects or creatures burrowing through her body leaving corrosive trails in their wake. But in truth, there weren't any bugs. The water was eating her.

She turned her tormented gaze on Daken who sighed and knelt by the stream.

"I am sorry for the intrusion. The woman is ill and meant no harm. I am Daken, King of the western land of Chigan, and she is in my care. I did not realize she was so ignorant." He turned his head on his last comment and shot her a look of fury.

Jane was still wiping away the water when slowly the pain lessened. Everywhere her skin burned red and raw, but at least it wasn't getting worse.

"It doesn't hurt anymore," she said softly.

Daken nodded and turned back to the stream. "Thank you for your patience. I beg permission to wash her wounds. Afterward, I will bless your home to cleanse her stench from you."

To her surprise, the stream slowly calmed. The churning subsided to waves and soft gurgles. It was once again a happily, bubbling brook.

She stared at Daken, her thoughts running back through everything that just happened, stumbling over his last comment.

Jane lifted her chin. "Cleanse my stench?"

"Yes," he said, coming over to roughly inspect her raw skin. "Stench."

"That's why I was trying to bathe in the first place."

"Too bad stupidity doesn't wash away. I told you it was someone's home. What else did you expect?" He started pulling her back to the water.

She dug in her heels. "I'm not going back in there. It's dangerous."

"Weren't you listening? We have permission now."

"Permission?" she repeated. "I'm getting a little confused about this permission business. To me a home is where someone lives. Like a house or an apartment building. A stream is not a home, and so why would I need permission to enter it?"

He looked up at her, his eyes wide with shock. "Do you know nothing?"

"I know a hell of a lot," she snapped, losing her patience with a world gone mad. "I know water isn't alive, and it can't give permission for someone to walk into it. Water is a combination of hydrogen and oxygen, and it can't suddenly turn acidic and eat my skin off."

"Then what happened to do this?" He deftly twisted her wrist to reveal an especially raw patch.

Jane bit her lip, staring at the damage with a horror bordering on panic. "I don't know," she breathed. "Nothing makes sense anymore."

"Come on, little fool," he said gently. "Let me tend to your skin."

"I'm not a fool," she grumbled, feeling very much one.

He sat down on the edge of the stream and started stripping off his clothes. "It is not an insult. It means one who is innocent. Who does not understand the ways of the world."

"Then call me innocent. Don't call me a fool."

He nodded to her. "As you wish." Then he stood. He'd taken off his shirt and boots, dropping them with his weapons onto the ground. But he kept his breeches on as he stepped into the stream. "Come, innocent. You are in a great deal of pain. Even without touching you, I can feel your burning."

She nodded. Her entire body seemed to throb like an exposed nerve, which in essence, she was. She stepped nervously into the water, her eyes trapped by Daken's gaze, and he drew her in firmly, inexorably, one step at a time.

This time the tingling hurt, and she winced as she moved, but then he touched her, his own skin reddening as he brushed his hands over her body. His touch was heated. It spread through her like good coffee, barely cool enough to drink, soothing and vitalizing every inch, every ache, every cell.

His hands brushed through her hair first, lingering over her face and lips. Then he caressed her shoulders, moving past them to stroke her breasts which puckered at his touch, thrusting forward into his palm. He hastily skipped away to her hand, rolling her fingers between his, before moving up her arm.

Everywhere he touched, the skin cooled and healed. She watched amazed as raw welts faded, slowly disappearing into healthy, pink flesh.

He repeated the process with her other arm before turning her away from him, smoothing her back, then spanning her waist. Jane flushed, acutely conscious of her extra pounds there, but he didn't seem to mind, running his hands along the slight indent above her hips, then turning her around again so he could lightly brush her belly. She sighed, letting her body and mind relax, enjoying the sensation as her muscles quivered beneath his touch.

This was wonderful.

When he reached around her to cup and mold the swell of her buttocks, she leaned into his embrace, lifting her lips for his kiss. But he drew away, shifting her to lie on her back against the shore while he held her feet. He spent his time there, washing away the blood and blisters, tenderly kneading her shins and knee. By the time he pressed against her thighs, her breathing was thick with desire, her body heavy and languid.

He continued up her thighs, and she moaned once beneath his feathery brush, arching against him, silently begging him to deepen his touch. He did, rubbing and kneading her thighs before spreading her legs. Then with a firm stroke, he probed her deepest core. She cried out in ecstasy, climaxing over his hand while he continued to stroke and brush her pulsing flesh.

She was in heaven.

Gazing up at him, she reached out, pulling him down to her for a deep, sensuous kiss, but he evaded her to brush his lips against her forehead.

"That was great," she said, her voice still husky with desire.

"That was healing," he countered softly. "Your body is free of sores now."

She looked down, her mind slowly clearing. He was right. Her skin was pink and healthy and flawless. Even her moles were gone. She stared back at him.

"But I… I mean you…" She couldn't put her mind around what just happened, much less express it in words.

"It was a completely natural reaction given your

injuries. I had to touch you everywhere the water burned you. The process can be quite stimulating."

"The process? Quite stimulating!" She sat up. "You mean this had nothing to do with…" She stopped, feeling suddenly naked. She twisted out of the stream, reaching for her cape to wrap around her. "You weren't even…" She look down at his breeches, partly submerged in the stream. Nothing. No bulge. No telltale bump. Just flat, flaccid nothing, which pretty much summed up just how she felt.

"I am a King," he said, his bland expression failing to cover how awkward he clearly felt about this whole thing. "A doctor. I healed you."

"You healed me." She said the words, but only now began to understand their meaning. "That's it. A few swipes of your hand, and I'm fine."

"Essentially, yes."

Jane climbed out onto the bank. "Essentially, yes," she mimicked, appalled at how blind she'd been.

"Jane, why does this upset you?"

She rounded on him, feeling her fury burn through her like poison. "Let me tell you something, Buster. Next time you feel like healing someone, you might mention you're doing it as a scientist. That it will be a… a simple clinical procedure."

"Jane!"

"Save it, King Daken." She practically spat out his name. "I'm perfectly healthy now. Maybe I'll come back for a check-up later. Like when hell freezes over." She grabbed her clothes and stomped away.

"Jane!" She heard him step out of the water, and she hurried away faster. "Jane! Leave your clothes. They must be washed. Your skin is still too new to abrade it with dirt."

She rounded on him, her fury seething through every pore. "Oh! You do laundry too! Well, bully for you!" She threw her clothes at him, feeling a surge of satisfaction as the fabric landed splat on his face. "Have a ball!"

Then she whirled around and ran to the edge of the trees, not bothering to stop the tears that streamed down her face.

❖   ❖   ❖

Daken watched Jane run away and felt each of her tears as a slap on his face. Beneath him, he could almost hear the laughter of the stream, which, thank the Father, at least had a sense of humor.

Grumbling in frustration, Daken threw the woman's odd clothing into the water, weighted it with rocks, and let the old soul in the stream wash it clean. Meanwhile, he stripped off his own breeches and began the irritating task of washing those.

The Crones of Fate must be truly laughing today. How could they land him with a moonling of a fool? Not only did he have the new responsibilities of the kingship, but also a war to fight. A war! Yet here he sat, wasting his time and energy on a witless woman.

He flipped his breeches inside out and dropped it into the water, washing away his seed and his shame at the same time. For years, he'd been a healer. Years. Yet he'd never lost his distance before now. He'd started to heal her skin, but the luster in her eyes, the sweet openness of her reaction to his touch, even the honesty of her desire drew him in. He'd known he was stroking her passion. By the Father, her hunger had danced along his skin like a thousand firelings twisting within him.

So he'd lost his distance, and when she'd reached her release, he joined her, exploding into his breeches like a boy in his first dream.

"Why, Old One?" he asked the stream. "Why now?" He didn't get an answer, though he felt the stream's sympathy lap around him as he worked out his frustration on his poor breeches.

The whole thing was one more example of how unfit he was to rule. His brother would never lose himself, but Daken had spent his whole life on self-gratification rather than the discipline that had been Tev's daily lot.

And now with Tev dead, Daken's lacks were more than apparent.

He glanced down at his breeches. If he scrubbed them anymore, he would rub a hole right through, then his shame would hang free for all to see. Daken sighed and pulled them on, then turned his attention to the stream and his promise to heal it. Crouching in the center where the current was strongest, he drew on his inner strength. Like a candle burning in his heart, he felt heat and power pulse within him. It was dimmer than usual because of what he'd done for the woman. It would grow darker still as he spread his power throughout the stream.

He envisioned his inner flame burning white hot, filling his body then spreading out into the water. The current swirled about him, carrying his energies throughout the stream's course. He felt the power leave him, its heat searing through his fingertips, radiating out of his limbs until it filled the water, enriching, empowering, and redeeming the stream.

He held the image for as long as he dared, his

consciousness expanding as he purified the water, annihilating the corruption as a hammer pulverizes a seed. Then his thoughts returned to his mind, leaving his energy behind to bless and maintain the stream.

It took hours. It took seconds. But when it was done, he felt limp and used, his energy drained, his soul barely flickering. He had given his healing power to the stream as promised. Animals and birds would thrive here for a time.

It would take him a week at least before his healing energy would be at full strength.

He felt the water surround him, cradling him as it urged him to the bank where he collapsed, his lower half still trailing in the tingling stream.

He slept.

✦ ✦ ✦

It took an hour before she registered his absence. After an hour and a half, she started to get concerned. After two hours, she sighed, rewrapped the blanket around her, and walked slowly to the stream.

She saw him immediately. He was stretched out on the bank, half in and half out of the suddenly clean water. It looked as though he had been tossed there like a discarded doll.

She made it to his side before her cry of alarm faded from the trees. Rolling him over, her nervous fingers felt for a pulse. His skin was ashen, his body clammy and damp, but his heart was strong where it beat in his throat.

Relieved, she dropped her head, pressing her forehead to his. "Geez, Daken, I get huffy all the time. That's no reason to go into a decline."

She took a deep breath, calming her own thready pulse before evaluating the situation.

"First, let's get you out of this water." She knelt down at his head, ignoring the blanket as it peeled away from her skin. She angled her arms under his shoulders and pulled. No go. It was as if something held him back, keeping him in the water.

Looking down, she realized she would have to lift his legs out of the stream. That meant entering the dreaded thing again. She clenched her jaw. She would do it for Daken, even if he was cold and arrogant, and had the annoying ability to be right just when she most wanted him to be wrong.

"All right, Daken. Let's get you out of here." She grit her teeth and stepped toward the water. So far, this stream had caused her nothing but pain and humiliation. "Uh, I guess I should ask for permission. I'm just gonna get him out, so I'm assuming it's okay with you."

She wasn't sure what she expected when she finally did step in. The tingling she remembered, but not the caressing warmth that swirled about Daken. It was like a soothing whirlpool bath, and she felt the energy suffusing each drop.

He needs to rest.

She added to the thought out loud. "Well, Daken, looks like you're gonna hang up your walking shoes for a day or two."

He will recover his strength by morning. His power will take longer.

"Upsy-daisy," she lifted his left leg and pushed it toward the bank. "I hope you really do get better by morning because I'm not nearly as good as you at catching and skinning rabbits. And believe me, neither of us is going to be very happy with your dried caterpillars."

She leaned down to grab his other leg, submerging herself up to her shoulders.

You have pained him deeply, fool. Learn quickly, so you can help each other.

Jane froze. Her gaze darted around the bank, both sides, but she couldn't see anything out of the ordinary. Sometimes, she had conversations with herself, both silently and aloud. That was, in fact, exactly what she thought she was doing.

Except that last comment definitely had not come from her own brain. It was from someone else.

I am an Old One. I have lived in this stream since the world ended and began again. I was one of the first to lose my body, joining with the water.

Jane didn't dare breathe. She didn't understand anything of what the voice said, but the losing your body stuff didn't sound like anything she wanted to do.

"Okay, Daken. Here's what we're gonna do. We're gonna get you out of here if I have to make a bulldozer out of sticks. So I want you to help me. Come on." She lifted Daken's other leg, pushing it as far as she could up the bank.

You, little fool, are even older than I.

Jane jumped out of the water, shook every drop off of her, then used the blanket as a towel. Her hands trembled, her heart beat like a freight train, and all she could think of was she'd lost her mind. This entire crazy world was one big hallucination left over from the one designer drug she'd taken at a party when she was fifteen.

Of course, crazy or not, she couldn't just abandon

Daken. She bent down again, planting her feet and lifting him from the shoulders. This time he slid right out, not easily, but certainly without the resistance she'd felt before. He came so quickly, she didn't have time to adjust her feet, and she landed flat on her butt with his head in her lap.

"Well, I suppose there are worse positions to be in," she muttered.

She stopped a moment to catch her breath, then she lingered a little longer. In sleep, Daken's features relaxed, becoming less blank, less rigidly polite. His face took on character, and she finally noticed the laugh lines around his eyes and mouth. God, he was gorgeous.

"Okay, Daken. Enough beauty rest. Help me dry you off."

He didn't respond, so she gently settled his head on the grass while she ran the blanket over his body and breeches.

Even lax, he was chiseled perfection. Golden skin dusted with dark brown hair, he was a study in contrasts. He said he was a doctor, but she saw the scars on his skin—cuts from swords or knives. And there was no fat on his body, just taut cords of muscle, honed to flawless precision.

This man was no doctor. He was a warrior. Yet, she couldn't dismiss the healthy pink of her own skin where this morning had been raw burns and welts. Neither did she understand how he could talk to a stream or fill it with the sparkling purity now glistening in the noontime sun.

But he had, and she was learning to live with her questions, accepting the impossible where before she would have shut it out with disbelief.

"Pretty soon, Daken, we're going to have to have a heart to heart talk because I need some real answers."

He didn't respond, but she wasn't worried. Now that he was dry, his body warming in the sun, she felt easier about him. He was not ill, just sleeping heavily, deeply, regaining his strength while she watched over him.

Looking around, she found her costume. It was underwater, but she managed to retrieve it with a minimum of fuss and hung it out to dry. Then, she settled on the grass next to Daken and absently brushed a damp curl from his forehead. It took less than a minute for her to give in to temptation. Scooting around, she lifted his head onto her lap, then relaxed against a tree.

Who said fantasies couldn't come true?

✦   ✦   ✦

"Good morning."

Daken looked up into the most beautiful pair of brown eyes he'd ever known. They were soulful eyes, innocent yet mischievous, constantly surprising him.

"Well, actually," she continued, "it's evening, but good night didn't seem to fit, not with you just waking up."

Daken glanced around, noting with chagrin that they were sitting completely exposed beside the stream. Not only had they wasted the day, but who knew what had happened to their gear while he was napping.

He started to sit up. "We must be going. We have tarried too much already."

"Not so fast, Buster." She pressed down on his chest, her expression determined. He struggled against her for a moment, then dropped back into her lap, his self-discipline won over by his delightful pillow and the beautiful view.

Still, he put up token resistance. "I've wasted so much time. And we're very exposed here. Anyone could come on us."

"Your sword's right there."

He followed the motion of her chin and saw his grandfather's sword within reach. He pulled it closer, his gaze uneasy.

"Relax. There's been no one here all day. Or shall I say no people."

"We are outside of the normal trade routes, and these are peaceful lands. Still, we can't let down our guard."

She smiled with a wry twist to her lips. "I'd say our guard, namely you, needs to lie down for a while and recover. In the meantime, you can answer a few questions."

He suppressed a tiny shiver of panic. Exactly what questions did she mean? She couldn't possibly know his intentions, could she?

"Don't look at me like that—"

"Like what?" Could she read even the smallest expression on his face?

"Like a clam. Like you're a robot that can't be threatened into talking. I just have a few basic questions."

He still didn't relax, but he schooled his features into an expression of uneasy patience.

"Humph," she snorted, clearly not fooled. "Let's start with the most immediate concerns." She looked up and to his right, the opposite direction of his sword. He turned to follow her gaze and his breath caught between his teeth.

A sleek, black pantar lay in the grass near them. She

was half asleep, her eyelids closed, her tail twitching every few moments.

"What do you call that in your language?" Jane asked.

"A black pantar."

"Close enough. I call it a black panther. He came—"

"She."

"She? It's a girl?"

He nodded.

"How can you tell?"

He shrugged, not entirely sure himself. "I'm a healer. Some things I just know."

Jane stared at the pantar, then she turned to glare down at him. "I have so many questions, I don't know where to begin."

"You were saying she came…?"

"Oh, yeah. She came to the river late in the afternoon. She was limping from a big gash in her shoulder that went down to her side. I… I think she was dying."

He nodded, then he curled on his side to get a better view of the sleek cat and the new fur on her side.

"She sort of stumbled to the water to take a drink. Then she fell in."

"How long did it take?"

"Hmmm?"

"How long until her wound healed over?"

Jane looked down into his face, her eyes almost luminescent in the evening shadows. "Twenty minutes. Maybe less. I was frozen. I know you're supposed to stay still and hope she can't see you, but—"

"The pantars are peaceful creatures. They eat rabbits, small dogs, maybe a few thruns. They won't hurt you if you don't bother them."

"That's sort of what I was counting on."

"So she healed in the stream, then climbed out to rest in the shade over there."

"Yes." Jane returned to watching the cat.

Even from this distance, he could hear the animal's purr. He smiled and snuggled deeper into his warm pillow. Much to his chagrin, his motion brought Jane's scattered attention back to her questions.

"Er, no. I mean, she did go rest but only after she…" Her voice trailed off.

"She what?"

"She came up to you and licked your face. I swear I was about to cleave her head in two with your sword."

"More likely, you'd have missed her and gotten me," he said dryly.

"Well, yes. Your sword is rather heavy."

"But you didn't."

"No. I waited, terrified out of my skull. If it weren't for you, I think I would have bolted when the creature first showed up."

He grinned, inordinately pleased she would stay with him, even in terror. Then the thought hit that he had received homage from the pantar. This was turning out to be a great morning-night. Tev used to get homage all the time. Cats, dogs, bears, they'd all stop by to bow regally to him. But this was Daken's first.

"Quit grinning, Daken. It's not funny. I was really scared."

"I'm grinning because I feel good. I'm rested. I'm lying in a beautiful woman's lap. And a pantar paid me homage. Why shouldn't I be grinning?"

Jane gazed down at him. "You really think I'm beautiful?"

His grin grew even wider. Even his odd little fool was a woman at heart after all. "Yes, I do."

She blushed and shifted restlessly beneath him. Then her expression changed, slipping into slight irritation. "You're trying to distract me."

"Not at all."

"You're much nicer this morning," she said. "Or rather tonight."

"I'm allowing myself to be distracted. But not for much longer. I'll give you five more minutes, then we must go."

"Go? Go where?"

"I already told you. To Bosuny." He was losing his patience. Not with her, although from the look on her face, she certainly thought so. He was losing his temper with himself. How much time had he lost to dally with this Jane? How many people were dying on his home lands? Were there any left at all?

"We're not going anywhere until you answer my questions," she said firmly.

"You cannot stop me, woman, so I suggest you ask quickly."

With his ear pressed into her stomach, he felt her grumbled oath more than heard it, but still the sound made him smile. She was so different from all the women he knew. She didn't attempt to hide herself— her irritation or her passion. She was open and free, and so very vulnerable because of it.

"Okay. Question number one: How can a soul inhabit a stream? And how can it talk to me?"

He rose up on one arm. "It talked to you?"

"I'm not sure." She pressed him back down into her lap.

"What did he say?"

"I'm not sure." She glanced down in irritation. "And I'm asking the questions here."

He sighed, wondering how she could have lived so long without knowing the most simple things. "A soul lives in the stream because that is its home. I don't know how it spoke to you, only that it sometimes happens."

"Great. A non-answer."

Daken folded his arms across his chest. "If you don't like my answers, then perhaps we could start walking."

"Not yet. Question two: How can a cat give homage to you? And why?"

"That was two questions—"

"I don't care, Daken. My sanity's slipping by the second, so just answer me, okay?"

She was so beautiful when agitated. It was as though she had no artifice in her. It struck him that she was perhaps the most honest person he'd ever met.

"Daken!"

"Hmmm? Oh. The pantar gave me homage because she knew I healed the stream which in turn healed her. It's really very simple."

"But how can you heal a stream?"

"I'm—"

"A healer. I know."

"A King."

"I thought they were the same thing."

"They are."

She groaned.

"The healing skill runs through the royal line. That is how you know royalty. My father was a King, but he was killed. My brother then became King, and he too, was killed."

"Which leaves you."

"Which leaves me." He tried not to let the pain seep

through his words, but she was smart. She heard it in his voice or saw it in his features. Before he could sit up or stop her, she bent down, dropping a kiss on his forehead.

"I'm sorry," she whispered against his skin. "It must have been very hard."

"Don't be sorry," he grumbled, pushing her away as he struggled to stand. "Help me get to Bosuny."

She sighed. "You are a moody creature today."

"I am an anxious creature who should be in Bosuny by now."

She folded her arms across her chest, watching him with the exact same expression his old tutor used to have. "One last question. What are you going to do in Bosuny?"

He felt himself grow cold, his insides freezing into the old patterns of anger and suspicion. He would not be stopped or deterred from his course.

"That is none of your concern," was all he said.

Chapter Three

✦ ✦ ✦

"She's following us." Jane worked hard to keep the nervousness out of her voice.

"Who's following us?"

"The panther."

Daken turned around, his scowl sour enough to curdle water. Jane pointed behind them, knowing the gesture was unnecessary. He could hardly fail to see the large black cat walking silently behind them. She wanted to say the animal was stalking them, except the cat's stride was slow, almost lazy, as she moved in their wake.

"What should we do?" Jane kept her voice low.

"Do? We walk to Bosuny. If she wants to come along," he shrugged. "Let her."

"But aren't there people there?"

He stared at her like she'd just sprouted green antennae.

"I mean, won't those people get a little upset when we walk in with a black panther on our heels?"

He glanced back at the cat, then bent down to grab his gear. "She's a smart cat. I'm sure she can take care of herself."

"That's so reassuring. Especially since I, too, am

following you."

Daken spun to face her, his expression dark and forbidding in the murky light. "I didn't ask for your company or hers. If you want to follow me, fine. If she wants to follow me, fine too. But don't expect me to delay my task just because you don't know an inhabited stream from a dead one."

"Well, excuuuse me. And here I thought I'd just spent the day taking care of you. Far be it for me to expect a little gratitude."

He advanced on her, his fists tight against his sides. "You wouldn't have had to take care of me if you hadn't walked into the stream without asking permission!" He threw up his fists and stalked away. "By the Father! Why did I get saddled with a lackwit?"

Jane bit her lip, annoyed and hurt, but still very aware he was right. She was a fool, and in more ways than one. Throughout their time together, he had made it abundantly clear she was a burden to him. A fool he did not suffer gladly. But still, her romantic heart wanted to believe they were starting to get along. That maybe he could like her a little.

Clearly, she was wrong. Jane squared her shoulders. Fine. If that's the way he wanted it. This wasn't the first time she'd bottled up her pride, swallowed her self-esteem, and generally humiliated herself in order to accomplish a larger goal. First it had been with a boyfriend, but she quickly realized the futility of that. Then it had been on the job with pencil-pusher Dr. Beavesly. Getting him to approve the latest protective hardware had been like begging for crumbs from a rich man's table, but eventually she had won.

And assuming she ever made it back to Boston to find out, she would bet her next paycheck that her special hardware was the only thing keeping the computer running after that tremendous explosion.

Jane stopped in her tracks. When had she remembered the explosion? She saw it clearly in her mind, replayed in sharp detail like a new video. She heard the boom, then saw herself poised in front of a rip in space that sucked her in.

She *had* been transported through space. She'd thought about it, toyed with the idea, but she hadn't really believed it. Not until now.

She pressed her hand against her mouth, holding in a scream. Was she really in a completely different world? Panic clutched at her throat. Her scream pushed through her mouth and slid through her fingers, but only as a terrified whimper.

"Jane?" Daken turned around, his expression shifting from frustration into concern. "Are you well?"

She stared at him, unable to fathom that he was a person from another place, a totally different planet. They didn't have magic translator spells or inhabited streams on Earth.

Then suddenly she realized—in this land, he wasn't the alien. She was. She was the stranger thrown here by some quirk of fate. Her friends and family lost to her forever unless she could find a way to get back.

Assuming she could get back. She didn't even know where she was. What if she was in a totally different galaxy? Or universe? Hell, what did it matter? She could be on Moon Colony, but without a spaceship how could she get home?

She moaned softly against her hand.

Daken stepped to her side, his movements stiff and awkward as he tried to apologize. "I'm sorry, Jane. I shouldn't have yelled at you. My people are in trouble, and I…"

She shook her head, the panic still pulsing in her veins. She knew if she tried to talk, it would come out as a hysterical scream. So she held her hands over her mouth, squeezed her eyes shut, and tried not to remember.

"Jane?"

She felt his hand brush her forehead, and she jerked away. She didn't know if a healer could read minds, but she certainly didn't want to find out now. He'd made it clear what he thought of her. His little fool.

Well, this little fool was rapidly wising up. She stamped down the panic within her as she remembered who and what she was. Jane took a deep steadying breath, slowly letting her hands fall from her face.

Okay. She was a stranger in a strange land who was probably vulnerable in countless ways. But she was smart, capable, and a quick study. From now on she would dedicate herself to learning everything she could about this new world. Even in the enlightened United States, an outer space alien would have turned the world upside down. Nutcases and legitimate scientists alike would have sold their souls to exploit an alien.

She wouldn't allow that to happen to her. She would not be victimized. She sure as hell wouldn't tell her secret to Mr. Kingly Arrogance. It wasn't that he'd abuse her. He'd actually been quite kind, in a gruff, macho sort of way. But how would he react to a space being?

No, it was much safer if he thought her crazy.

Later, after she found a way to get home, then she would explain it all to him.

"Jane?"

"Uh." She swallowed. "Sorry. I… I'm okay now.

We can go on."

"Are you ill?"

She couldn't look directly into his eyes and lie. So she watched the panther, pretending to be entranced by the cat cleaning a paw. "I'm fine. Just a little tired." She tried to smile. "You may have gotten a nap, but I didn't."

Daken was silent, clearly waiting for her to look at him. She didn't. She watched the panther. Then he twisted abruptly toward the horizon. "We should make it to the main road soon and an inn soon after. Can you make it another hour?"

"Yeah. Sure. Lead on."

"You feel healthy?"

"I'm fine." She could sense the heavy intensity of his gaze, and she slowly faced him, giving him her version of a blank stare. The gold in his eyes reflected the moonlight with an eerie glow. Then, abruptly, he spun on his heel and walked. She followed directly after him, a couple paces behind, needing the space to think.

To their right, the panther slipped in and out of the trees, her steps silent and stealthy.

✦   ✦   ✦

The inn was quiet, but not deserted. Jane judged it a little after midnight. Most of the patrons had already left. It had been eerie walking down the road, her footsteps echoing through the deserted street. The black panther had long since disappeared into the shadows surrounding the sleepy village.

Daken pushed his way into the inn, and Jane followed, squinting as they stepped into a cozy main room with tables and a bright fire. The whole setting reminded her of a pub at a Renaissance fair she'd once been to. There were a few people around—a woman and her daughter cleaning tables, two patrons who looked very drunk, and a young boy singing softly while plucking a tune on a crude guitar.

In short, all was peaceful as the innkeeper bustled forward. He spoke in a language Jane didn't recognize, but true to the spell, Daken's words came clearly to her as English. From his half of the conversation, she gathered he was haggling over the price of a room and dinner.

Jane wandered to the fire, extending her hands to the warmth while she studied the people. They looked humanoid. They had short, squat bodies with dark skin and black eyes. Definitely human-like, except for some reason, they reminded her of small burrowing animals. They appeared quiet and alert, small and earthy. Both Jane and Daken towered over these people, and she felt the urge to sit down to feel less like a giant. She settled into a booth, and Daken soon joined her. They hadn't spoken since the return of her memory, and from all appearances, he was perfectly content with the status quo.

A few minutes later, the woman placed two thick bowls of stew and a loaf of black bread in front of them. Daken dug in with a vengeance. Jane too, tucked into her meal, surprised at how very hungry she was and how very, very good the food was. Even the black bread was tasty, if a bit hard. Then the woman returned, dropping two mugs of thick black liquid in front of them. It looked like her favorite type of coffee, except it was cold and crumpled green leaves floated on top.

She picked up the mug and sniffed. It had a faint herbal scent, like expensive shampoo. "What's this?"

"Pinnan."

"Uh, yeah. Do you think they have some water? I'm not—"

"Drink it." His words weren't loud or angry, but they held the definite tone of command. Jane sighed, knowing better than to argue with a man in a Macho Mood. She hefted her mug, took a deep breath, then sipped at her drink.

To her shock, it tasted great. Sort of like cocoa and rum mixed with water, as if that were possible. It wasn't carbonated, but it still tingled as it went down. It refreshed like water, tasted like chocolate, and wet her insides like a much needed lubricant. She drained the mug.

"Wow! This is wonderful!"

Daken didn't respond. He didn't speak until after he'd finished his second bowl of stew. "I've gotten us a room for the night. It's too late for a bath, but the mistress can clean your clothes by morning."

Jane looked down at her costume. It was certainly worse for wear, but after this morning's escapade at the stream, it was relatively clean. "No, thanks. But if you can afford it, I would like some new clothes." The mistress and the girl both wore loose-fitting tunics. She wondered if she looked as ridiculous to them as she felt.

"The clothes they have here won't fit you. Wait until Bosuny."

Jane nodded and kept her tongue. She'd been watching Daken pay the innkeeper. Up until that moment, she'd held out some vain hope that her U.S. dollars would be of some value here. But the coins

Daken used were nothing like her money, and she didn't want to expose her alienness by trying to use her credit card with holographic ID photo.

That meant she was living off of Daken. Completely and totally. And the thought of that dependence scared her more than the black panther.

With sudden resolve, she decided to live as cheaply as possible. Intending to show him just how amenable she could be, she glanced up and said sweetly, "One room will be fine."

"They didn't have any more." His voice was curt, as though he were insulted that she thought they ought to have two rooms.

"No... I mean, whatever arrangements you make are fine. I'm happy to sleep on the floor if you like."

"There's a bed." He practically growled into his *pinnan*.

"That's fine," she repeated, wondering how she'd managed to insult him while trying to show how flexible she could be. Truth was, she didn't really care what the arrangements were. They'd been sleeping next to each other on the ground since she arrived in this crazy world. What difference did it make inside or outside?

Unless, perhaps, he meant they'd be in the same bed? Her spine tingled at the thought, and she looked down, staring awkwardly at her food.

"As soon as you're done, ready yourself for bed. I'll be up later."

She looked at him, completely at a loss. When her brother had been like this, she'd just stayed clear. So she nodded her understanding to Daken and didn't say a word.

"Don't open the door to anyone but me," Daken

continued, pointing his spoon at her like a sword.

She felt her eyes widen in alarm. "You don't think we're safe here?"

He shrugged, then waved for another bowl of stew. "There are thieves everywhere. It never hurts to be cautious."

She nodded. He was being the imperious lord, ordering her around like a child. But given that she knew nothing of this world, his advice was probably for the best. She finished her meal, sopping up the last of her stew with the black bread and feeling like a regular Renaissance serf without a knife or fork. Then, she gave the mistress a warm smile and went to the room.

It was sparsely furnished with one chair, a table with a basin of tepid water, and a bed barely large enough for two small people. She washed up, shook out her short hair, then lay down.

She didn't want to think about Daken joining her. She didn't want to imagine him settling into the bed next to her, the heat from his body merging into hers, his breath tickling the fine hairs of her back. But lying in the dark on a straw tick bed, she could hardly think of anything else.

Her eyes drifted closed, and she dozed in and out of fantasies that were both satisfying and infinitely frustrating. But she was comfortable with them, having dreamed the same dreams in various combinations since she first met Daken.

Forget Daken, she told herself sternly. She was tired. Still, she didn't actually sleep until she felt his weight settle against her.

✦   ✦   ✦

"SQUAWK! SQUAWKAWK!"

Jane sat bolt upright in bed, her head pounding from all the noise. Beside her, Daken muttered something in his sleep, then settled back into his low, rumbling snore.

Rubbing her eyes, Jane slid out from bed, stumbled to the window, and threw open the shutters. Then she cringed from the light and covered her ears against the clatter.

It would seem last night's sleepy village had woken up to what must be market day in the front courtyard. She recognized just over half the animals milling about and only some of the wares loudly pushed by hawkers in a strange, lilting language.

She glanced back at Daken. He lay sprawled across the mattress. Her belly and right leg tingled with remembered warmth, and she knew he had slept holding her, his arm resting casually across her belly, one leg draped neatly over hers.

Odd how even with all the cluttered emotions, arguments, and growing secrets between them, their sleep time was still as comfortable as that first night he had told her about the stars. Even last night in a bed. It had felt so natural, so wonderful, so...she swallowed hard...erotic.

Too bad he'd made his opinion on that subject perfectly clear. Sex was fine if it happened as part of a medical procedure, but she clearly wasn't what he wanted as a recreational bed partner. No man was that restrained unless he was completely uninterested.

With that depressing thought, Jane pulled the chair up to the window and settled down to watch the show.

What better way to learn about this strange world than to watch the comings and goings in the courtyard outside her window?

✦   ✦   ✦

Daken woke to an odd sense of loneliness. Jane had left their bed. Turning, he saw her perched half in and half out of the window, the morning sun dancing in her short curls, her face a mixture of delight and confusion as she gazed at the courtyard. As always, she wore her bizarre clothes that covered all, yet left nothing to the imagination. Yesterday, she had asked for some new clothes, and he had lied about being unable to find any here. An outright lie, and he a King no less. But the thought of her changing out of her delightful attire left him surly.

He was fortunate the inn had only one room or he might have lied twice just to keep her with him.

Oh Jane, his little fool. Since she was completely absorbed with the scene out the window, he had the luxury of studying her at some length. What was it about her that drew him so deeply? She wasn't exactly beautiful. He had known women far more stunning in every way; women who used their charms to set men on fire. The bard who sold him the language spell had been such a woman. Yet once she left his lands, he had thought less about her than about his boots.

Perhaps the Father intended Jane as his wife. Daken was King now, and he should continue his parents' lineage, not only for his name, but because Chigan needed more healers. It would be irresponsible to allow his healing seed to die out.

Daken grinned at the idea of getting Jane with his

child. The image of her body, ripe and heavy with his babe, set his groin tightening with hunger. He had stayed apart from her because she was ill, and he could not take advantage of a lackwit. But his blood still burned with desire every time he looked at her.

He no longer cared that she was a peasant and he a King. His parents and brother were gone. They could not object to the mismatch. He would marry Jane despite the gossip. The look of gratitude in her eyes would more than make up for any social discomfort.

Bosuny would be an excellent place to woo the naive girl. She would be confused and frightened by the large city and would naturally turn to him for guidance. It would take little effort to have her melting in his arms as she had in the stream.

They would marry in the city, and then he could return home triumphant with not only an army to defend his lands, but a wife to grace his bed and bear his children.

Sometimes, he thought, grinning into his pillow, life could be very, very good.

❖   ❖   ❖

"Have you ever been to Bosuny before?"

"Every year when I was young, we went for the Grand Fair. The last time was nine years ago when I was introduced to the Elven Lord."

Jane nearly choked on the hard buttered bread that was her breakfast. "An *Elven* Lord?"

"Yes. He nurtures the land. My family and the other kings owe allegiance to him. Bosuny is his capitol."

"Elven lord," she repeated, still not quite believing the title, even knowing that whatever the word was in his language, it translated to "elf" in English. "You mean, like a little guy with pointy ears, a thick beard, and a green cap?" Or was that a leprechaun?

"No," he said with obvious confusion. "A tall, slim man with silvery hair and no beard. The dwarves have the pointy ears and thick beards."

"And sing hi-ho all day, no doubt." She didn't know if she was being sarcastic or not. The whole thing was too incredible to believe.

"I do not know what they sing. They mine precious metals in the dark ridges to the southeast. Their craft is highly prized."

She nodded weakly, feeling the blood drain from her face. "Of course, I should have known." She hadn't really been transported through space to another planet. She'd just disappeared into a fantasy creation of Earth archetypes. Or maybe it was just a fairy tale come to life. "Don't they worry about dragons?"

"The big lizards that breathe fire? I don't know. I have heard of them, but never seen one. You needn't be afraid. There are no dragons in Bosuny."

Jane choked back a hysterical laugh. "Of course. They're too big to feed, even in a city. Do they hoard gems?"

"So they say, but I think it is just children's tales."

Jane giggled. Not a normal giggle, but a high-pitched nervous noise that made her sound like a sick hyena.

"Jane? Are you well?"

"Just fine," she whispered, afraid to say more for fear she'd go completely berserk.

He continued to study her, so she kept her face blank while she forced herself to swallow her bread. Apparently satisfied that she was not about to self-destruct in front of him, Daken gobbled the last of his bread and pushed away from the table. "Come. I've found us a ride to Bosuny."

"A ride?" The thought of not having to walk down miles of road broke her out of her suppressed hysterics.

"Yes. A fur merchant is carrying his wares to market. We will drive one of his wagons."

"No more walking?" She wiggled her bruised and blistered toes, delighted at the thought of a prolonged rest.

Much later, after her backside was black and blue from the wagon bench, she wondered if walking might be better. Or riding, though she'd never ridden a horse in her life. That thought led her to another question that had hovered in the back of her mind since this morning.

Just before Daken had risen, she'd seen a clearly wealthy youth rush in on a tall, shaggy steed, stop for breakfast, then ride off. He was exactly how she'd pictured Daken in his younger days—a handsome young man dashing about with speed and flair.

Then it struck her that Daken was on foot.

Now, bouncing painfully on a buckboard, Jane got the courage to ask the potentially insulting question. "Daken, how come you don't have a horse? I mean you're a King and all. I'd think you'd travel in style."

Daken was driving a covered wagon, just like on a vid about the open prairie, except the horses were more of those squat, shaggy things that smelled like a garbage dump in summer. But even with her complete ignorance about horses, she could see Daken stiffen, unnecessarily jarring the horses, which caused them to hit a rather large rut, which in turn jostled Jane painfully on their bench seat.

Criminy, she cursed silently as she tried to adjust to

a less bruised position. Hadn't these people ever heard of pillows? Cushions? A rock would feel better than this bench.

Perhaps if she'd been less interested in finding a distraction from her rear end, she would have been smart enough to avoid the topic. But she was looking for a diversion, and this was close enough.

"I mean," she continued. "You're King of Chigan, right? So why don't you have a carriage to take you to court? Or at least a horse. A king shouldn't have to walk, should he?"

"My lands are very rich and fertile. I am a wealthy man," he said stiffly.

She blinked at his huffy tone. "Well of course you are. I never meant to imply—"

"I owned a horse and a carriage. But my stallion was killed during the last Tarveen raid."

"The last what?"

"It is planting season. It seemed ridiculous to take two much needed horses from the plowing just to plod their way to Bosuny."

"I didn't mean to imply—"

"I am a fast walker and quite adept at catching rides."

"I'm sure you are—"

"And as you could see from the inn, I am a quite wealthy man."

"Geez, Daken. Relax. I was just curious."

"Now you know."

"Yeah. Now I know that you're real touchy about the silliest things."

"You think my wealth is silly?" If he sat any straighter in his seat, his back would break.

"Heck, no. Look, Daken, I think it's great you'd

walk however many miles to Bosuny rather than take away some horses. I think it's noble of you. Many kings wouldn't do that."

His shoulders relaxed just a bit. "You think so?"

"Of course. You're obviously a king who cares about the well-being of your people over your own comfort. I think that's admirable."

He lifted an eyebrow and allowed his head to turn a little in her direction. "Truly?"

"Truly." Good God, no matter what the planet, men's egos were the same.

"I was not always so concerned," he said, his face shifting into a rueful quirk of his lips. "In fact, I was incredibly reckless. But as second son, I was never supposed to inherit the kingship. When I did…" He shrugged. "Being king makes one reevaluate one's own comfort."

His little speech could have sounded pompous, but Jane found it endearing. It must have been difficult for him, first dealing with his parents' death, then his brother's. Add to that the sudden burden of a kingship, and it was no wonder he wanted some time to walk peacefully to Bosuny. Too bad she'd forcibly imposed herself on his solitude.

And no wonder he wished her anywhere but with him.

"It must have been very hard on you," she said softly, an apology in her voice.

He didn't appear to notice. Instead, his thoughts seemed turned inward as he stumbled over his words. "These last two years have been…sad and difficult."

She reached out and squeezed his right hand. It was meant to be a quick gesture, one of comfort and friendship, but he wouldn't let it end. Shifting the reins to his left hand, he captured her fingers, drawing them up to his lips. He kissed her knuckles with a courtliness that made her cheeks heat.

She searched for something to say, but his gaze captured hers. His eyes, a brilliant royal blue and gold, sparkled with a happiness she'd never seen before. They seemed full of a promise that left her breathless with excitement. Then they hit another rut, and Jane's hand flew out of his to keep herself from bouncing out of the seat.

Daken too, had to steady himself. With a muttered curse, he redirected his attention to the horses.

"That one hurt," she grumbled as she tried to ease forward off her more tender parts. "How much further is it?"

"Another day."

Jane groaned and wondered how she could possibly want such torture to continue indefinitely. But she did.

❖   ❖   ❖

"So are you at war or something?" They were sitting alone beside a fire after dinner, the fur trader gone to check his wares. Jane was once again intent on learning as much as possible about this world.

"I haven't seen any soldiers," she continued, "but everyone seems to carry weapons." She glanced uneasily at the bastard sword strapped to Daken's back. Even the fur trader wore a long sword and dagger. "I almost feel naked without a knife." She was teasing when she said it, but he gave her a long, considering look that took in her body from top to bottom.

"You are not naked."

No, she wasn't, but the way he looked at her made

her feel like she was.

"And we are not at war," he said. "Aggression is forbidden by the Elven Lord. We carry weapons to defend ourselves against...beasts." She saw his jaw muscles clench over the last word, and that told her he was holding something back.

"Beasts?" she pressed. "Like the panther?" Their silent shadow had not shown herself since the village, but she sensed the cat's presence almost as surely as she sensed Daken's current emotional withdrawal.

"This is the heart of the Elven Lord's lands. It is relatively safe with few beasts. If you look closer, many of the weapons are for show or to eat with."

Jane nodded, remembering that yes, most people carried small daggers used more to cut their dinner bread than to defend themselves.

"The trader and I both live in lands on the edge of the Elven Lord's influence. The animals there are much less tame."

He covered well, his tone almost conversational. But Jane hadn't spent the last few days studying him without recognizing when Daken was being evasive.

"Is that how your family was killed?" she pressed. "Beasts?"

Daken sat very still, his gaze lost in the depths of the campfire. "The Tarveen attacked and killed my family."

"The Tarveen?"

"A race of monsters in the eastern region of my lands." He spit out the words like bad caterpillars.

"I take it they aren't pacifists?"

He glanced up, repeating himself as if he were impressing the basics on a witless child. "They are monsters who do not bow to anyone, much less the

Elven Lord. They are animals that know only how to kill and eat."

Jane shivered at the implacable hatred in his voice. "So they raid your lands, and you're forbidden to fight?" That seemed rather stupid to her, even in her most anti-violence moments.

"We can defend ourselves, but it's hard against their relentless raids."

Raiding parties didn't sound like her definition of mindless animals, but she didn't press the point. "They killed your parents and your brother?"

His nod was a short, brutal slash of his chin.

"Is that why you're going to Bosuny? To ask for help against these Tarveen?"

He turned to her, his head lifted in surprise while the firelight flashed in the dark pools of eyes. "You are a quick innocent. I didn't think you would understand."

"You'd be surprised what I know about violence," she muttered. "So what is it you need? More weapons? Better defenses? What?"

Slowly he shifted his gaze from her, seemingly drawn to the pure heat of the fire. His mask of placidity, of gentle politeness fell away. What was left of his expression was a stark hatred that shocked her. It was a twisted thing that matched the tortured heat of the fire. His skin glowed red, and his eyes became flickering coals ready to incite violence.

"You misunderstand. In this land of sheep farmers and soft women, I am going to Bosuny to raise an army." His words were cold and low, and she knew with sudden shock that his whole being was focused on his private war with the Tarveen.

"An army? But I thought the Elven Lord forbid aggression."

"With or without the Lord's help, I will get men and arms. Then I will attack the Tarveen, and I will slaughter every one of them like the monsters they are."

"But," she stammered, still trying to absorb this new and violent side of Daken. "You'd exterminate an entire race of people? Men, women, and children? All?"

"I will kill every one of them." Then he turned his dark intensity on her, showing her the unshielded hatred within him. "And I will kill anyone who tries to stop me."

Chapter Four

✦ ✦ ✦

Jane expected Bosuny to be a congested mass of people and animals fighting for a living among filth and degradation. After all, that was how she sometimes thought of modern day Boston, so how much worse would a city of this world be without sanitation, social security, or a solid police force? She prepared herself to be mobbed by beggars, choked by the stench, or even lynched as a witch for her odd clothing.

She couldn't have been more wrong.

Bosuny was a beautiful place of brilliant flowers in green fields, fat babies, and well-kept houses. The roads were made out of a cheery-bluish brick with sidewalks on either side in front of quaint little stores, cafes, and even what might be an office building or two. Looking down, she realized the streets were cleaner than downtown Boston and, as far as she could tell, free of homeless beggars or drunken derelicts.

By the time they reached the marketplace, Jane had fallen in love with the city. Even the central market square, which was indeed teeming with people, wares, and every sight, sound, or smell she could imagine, was clean, joyful, and a sheer delight to watch.

And the best part of all was the citizenry. She had

worried that people would think her odd or worse, evil. As if the words "space alien" were tattooed on her forehead somewhere. But here, she fit right in. As far as she could tell, people of every race, breed, and color milled about the marketplace. Skin tones alone, whether natural or dyed, went through all the colors of the rainbow. Similarly, hair color and styles varied wildly. She had seen some of these races at the village inn, but nothing prepared her for the riot of human-type people and colorings that abounded.

Fashion generally consisted of tunics and trousers or leggings, although she saw a few sumptuous dresses with matching head gear on women. The well-dressed man appeared to wear fancy shirts and ties that seemed more like scarves.

She couldn't make out any of the languages spoken, although even her untutored ear could distinguish several different ones. By the time they had helped the trader unload his wagons at a fur booth, Jane felt a little shell-shocked from trying to see everything at once.

Then she heard a familiar voice and a very unfamiliar belly laugh. Turning, she saw Daken, laughing for the first time since she'd known him.

"What's so funny?" she asked, craning her neck around a very fat woman to see the yo-yo type toy her son played with.

"You are, little fool. Your eyes are bigger than a full moon. Haven't you ever been to a market before?"

"Not like this I haven't."

She glanced back at him, as surprised by his happy, carefree expression as she was by anything in the market.

He grabbed her hand, pulling her along with him as he started for an exit. "It is rather overwhelming, isn't it?" His voice softened with sympathy. "Come on. I'll find us some place a little quieter."

The moment she realized he intended to leave, she dug in her heels, drawing him back to her and the fair. Then, she let a slow smile pull up her lips as a delightfully wicked thought sneaked past her prudish defenses. "Daken, didn't I just see the trader pay you for driving the wagon?"

Daken nodded, his face growing more wary by the second.

"Well," she said, her head tilting as she pretended to think of something. "It seems to me that some of the money belongs to me."

"What?" He seemed more shocked than upset by her audacity.

"I did help you drive the wagon."

"You sat and complained about your backside."

"I kept you from falling asleep."

"On a buckboard?"

"I helped unload the furs."

"You carried one fur."

"I watched the horses."

He didn't argue that one, though his expression told her clearly that they hadn't needed her services there either.

"So you want to be paid for your...work." He toyed with his purse, letting the coins clink and rub together. "Exactly how much do you think you're worth?"

"More than you can afford, that's for sure," she shot back. Then she smiled. "Exactly how much did you get paid?"

He grinned at her joke. "Tell me what you want to buy, Jane, and I'll get it for you."

"No way. I want my share to spend as I will."

The dark slash of his eyebrows suddenly lowered. "Do you really want to go into the fair?"

"Of course, I do!" She laughed at his stunned expression. "I absolutely *love* shopping. It's almost more fun than paging through the Rumornet."

"The what?"

She started to answer but was distracted by a delicious scent wafting toward her from a large brown man carrying a tray of what looked like meat pies. "Mmmm. Can you smell that?" She turned around. "Come on, Daken. Give me my share and let me loose."

He stared at her for a moment, his jaw slack with astonishment.

"Please. I'm starved." Her gaze followed the man with the meatpies while she inhaled deeply, trying to hold onto the heavenly scent.

Then Daken laughed, his face lit with amusement mixed with a wry self-mockery. "So much for you being overwhelmed. Very well."

He dropped three large coins into her hand. They were perfect gold circles stamped with a tree on one side and something like a blunt-tipped maple leaf on the other. She glanced up at Daken, but his face betrayed nothing.

"Are these doleens?"

"Yes."

"And how much were you paid by the trader?"

"That's a fair share, little fool," he said, his voice dropping.

"The hell it is." Jane glanced back at the trader who was bartering with a customer. "You didn't get any three doleens from that guy. I saw smaller coins—silver and copper. No gold."

Suddenly, Daken grinned, even though his voice

was serious. "You do learn fast. But perhaps you've forgotten the day you cared for me by the stream."

"But—"

"Consider that payment for protecting me from the pantar."

"The panther? She didn't do anything."

"But you didn't know that at the time, did you?"

Jane didn't argue. For whatever reason, Daken wanted to give her money to spend at the fair, and she felt overwhelmed with gratitude. She couldn't understand any of the prices listed, but she was sure Daken had just been very, very generous.

Jumping up, she planted a wet, loud kiss on his cheek. "Thank you." Then she started to run after the meat pie man.

"Hold on," he said, grabbing her arm to keep her with him. "There's a condition."

"I knew there was a catch," she grumbled, but she waited for his terms.

"You must stay with me at all times. And don't spend a sora without my help."

She cocked her head. "Well, of course. How else would I do it? I don't speak a word of the language."

He chuckled, the sound a teasing pulse along her spine. "You will find these merchants don't require anything but your money. The last thing they want to do is talk."

She echoed his laughter, her own voice high and free for the first time since she'd arrived in this strange world. "I guess merchants aren't that different wherever you go."

She started to run off again, but he tugged her back, his hand a warm band of steel around her wrist.

"What now?"

"Nothing," he said, dropping a light kiss on her lips. "Only that I will pay for our meal."

She gazed up into his eyes, more golden now than blue, and felt joy slide through her veins. Could he really like her? Maybe a little?

Then they were jostled from behind and the moment was broken. "Come on," he said. "I find myself ravenous for meatpie."

She pulled back, and he turned, his expression questioning.

"He's long gone. Besides, who wants meat pie when you can have lasagna?" She pointed at another booth where a woman ladled red sauce over what she hoped was dough and cheese. She turned back to Daken who promptly threw up his hands.

"Lead on. But be careful of your stomach. Red *canatas* are hotter than you think."

Red canatas, or whatever he called them, were definitely not lasagna. They were more like hot peppers wrapped in spicy dough covered with chile sauce. They were delicious.

Daken ate a meat pie. Jane stole a bite from him and decided she liked those too.

In fact, she tried a whole lot of foods. It seemed the worst thing about the marketplace was that there were so many things to taste, she didn't have enough room in her stomach to fit them all. Although she definitely tried.

"Aren't you full yet?"

She had just finished the first thing that had actually tasted like what she thought it ought to—a delicious, New York hot dog.

"I'm still looking for a hot fudge sundae."

"A what?"

"Dessert."

He groaned, weighing his purse, pretending it was very, very light. "Had I known you could eat more than a Zenian levon, I wouldn't have been so generous with my offer to feed you."

She turned, her laughter floating around her. "Too bad, King. You can't go back on your word."

He stopped, gently pulling her back from another food stand. "Where did you ever get that idea?"

She blinked. "Aren't kings supposed to be honorable? Never lie, cheat, or steal? Always follow through on their promises, that sort of thing?"

"Yes."

"Well, then," she turned back to the stand, but he pulled her back again.

"Who said I was a good king?"

She knew he was just teasing her, but his eyes darkened and the laugh lines around them dropped away until they looked more like pain etched in a face too young to bear the scars. A part of him, she realized, really doubted he was a good king.

"You're a good king, Daken. I said you were, remember? When you told me about leaving your carriage behind, after your horse was killed." She playfully tapped the end of his nose.

He smiled and caught her finger in his mouth. Blushing, she withdrew it and captured his hand as she looked around for her next destination.

They'd been doing a lot of that today—touching whenever and wherever they could. None of it was sexual, not even the brief kisses they'd given each other. They walked holding hands, or he brushed crumbs off her face, or she tugged on his arm. They were practically inseparable, which was just how she liked it.

She might enjoy shopping, but wandering alone through a fair this large when she didn't speak the language was too daunting a task for even her. So they ran through the marketplace together, or rather, she ran dragging him, and they laughed like children unexpectedly released from school.

Then she saw it. They'd been wandering about for over an hour before she spotted it. It hung in the corner of a booth in the chaotic center of the marketplace. It was a dark blue tunic with threads of gold shot through the sleeves and neck. It had a V-type collar and a soft texture like worn denim. And it was perfect for Daken.

She bought it when he wasn't looking. He was busy haggling over a dagger, so she slipped away, dropped all three of her coins into the vendor's hand, grabbed both the shirt and a couple plain tunics for herself, then ran back before Daken was any the wiser. She knew she should somehow hide the shirt. The surprise would work better if she gave it to him tomorrow morning, but she'd always had trouble waiting to give her gifts. He was right here with her, and she was so happy that she just threw it over his head, laughing as a sleeve flopped wildly over his right ear.

"Surprise!"

He fumbled his way out of the tunic. "What?"

"Hey, careful!" She pulled the shirt off of him before he ripped it, then smoothed out the folds before presenting it to him. "A tunic fit for a king." She held it up to his eyes. It wasn't a perfect match, she noted with chagrin. His eyes were a bit more vibrant, the gold flecks a little richer. But it was close enough.

He didn't take it.

"Hey. It's a gift." She leaned forward. "You're

supposed to say thank-you."

He stared at the shirt. "You bought this?"

"No, I stole it. Of course, I bought it."

"You paid for it," he repeated, his mouth still struggling to form words.

"Yes. Probably way too much, but," she smiled up at him, "it was worth it to see your face." His expression was torn between surprise, pleasure, and horror. "Yes," she giggled, spinning away. "It was definitely worth it."

He grabbed her, turning her back to face him. "Why would you spend your coins on me? On this?"

"Because it's your money, silly. Who else should it be spent on?"

"But—"

"Criminy, Daken. You act like this is some big deal. It's just a shirt."

He shook his head, clearly searching for the right words. "This is not just a shirt."

"Well, of course, it is," she teased. "It's got fabric, front and back, two sleeves for your arms, and a collar. That's the big hole in the middle for your head. Boy," she shook her head with mock horror. "And you call me a fool."

"Little fool..."

She glanced up, her expression sobering at the sudden intensity in his eyes. "What? What's wrong?"

"This is a bridegroom's tunic. Are you proposing to me?"

"Proposing what?" Finally his words sunk in. "Proposing? As in marriage proposing?"

He reached out and lifted her chin. She felt the rough texture of his fingertips as well as the heat his smallest touch always aroused within her.

"I would be very pleased if you wished to marry me," he said, his voice low and sincere.

"Marry you?" Her voice came out as a squeak.

"You would be my queen." His lips quirked in a half smile. "A wealthy queen of a fertile land. Your heirs would be healers and as their mother, you would be revered. Your every wish fulfilled."

"Heirs? As in children? Babies?" Her voice cracked on the last word. Her thoughts spun and suddenly, her stomach felt much too small for her chest, especially given that her heart was beating so fast she thought it had climbed into her throat.

"We would have beautiful children, you and I," he continued. "They would have a laugh like their mother and have their father's physique."

"Physique?"

He tilted his head, trying to explain. "Body. Form. Strength."

She cleared her throat. "I know what it means," she said, slowly backing out of his arms as she struggled for rational thought. But it was hard when his gaze seemed to heat her entire body, mesmerizing her even as she tried to stop the dizzy buzzing in her head.

"Jane?"

"Daken." She took one last steadying breath before facing him. "Look, I didn't know that was a...that it was for a...you know. For marriage."

She watched his face change. She couldn't say exactly what part of him shifted or when the transformation was complete. She only knew that with each word, his face became stiffer and colder, hidden behind his mask of polite civility.

"Does this mean you do not wish to marry me?" His words were filled with kingly hauteur.

"I don't wish to marry anyone." She tugged on her hair, pulling a curl to almost below her ear. "Try to understand. I don't belong here."

His eyebrows drew together. "Here? In the marketplace or Bosuny?" He looked around at the milling sea of people pushing past them on all sides.

"Here, as in this world."

His attention refocused on her. "I don't understand."

"Join the crowd, buddy," she muttered. "Let me try to explain. I'm from out—" Fortunately, she was jabbed from behind by a pushy customer, and her next impulsive words were swallowed. Once she regained her balance and her senses, she started on a different tack. "Can we go somewhere quiet and talk?" She saw the cold anger in his eyes. "Please, Daken. Let me try to explain before you cast me off."

That seemed to break through his cold facade. She started to move toward a road, but he stopped her, turning her to read the truth in his face as he spoke. "I would never cast you off, Jane. Never. Do you understand?"

Jane nodded, afraid she did. Like it or not, this man was proposing to her. His intentions couldn't be clearer if he'd broadcast it from the nearest booth. Suddenly, she wasn't afraid he'd abandon her to find her way alone, but that he wouldn't let her go once she finally found a way back to her own world.

She shivered at the thought, even as a small voice whispered in her head. *"Would it be so bad?"* it asked. She'd be a queen. Her children would be healers. She'd be married to her own personal fantasy man, for goodness sake. What more could she want?

Except she'd be abandoning Earth, her home. It wasn't that she'd miss her parents. She loved them, but they'd long since deteriorated to making polite phone calls at Christmas. As for her brother, she thought she had his address written on an old receipt, lost somewhere in her nightstand.

No, what she'd be abandoning was much more obscure than her family, much larger and at times more immediate than her friends. She would be leaving Earth. Her skills weren't all that great, but she counted her computer training as a valuable asset. Her job at the university was simple and specific. She kept the flow of information open to the public. Maybe there were others who could do her job as well or better than she. But the point was, it was her job, and she did it well.

On Earth, she was a single person working to keep the light alive in a world of increasing darkness. And the church had taught her that the loss of one candle, no matter how small, was a loss to all.

Jane watched the swirling mass of people as she and Daken ducked and twisted through the stands. What was she to these people? She didn't even speak their language, didn't understand the most basic things about their customs or bridal gear. Didn't even recognize the food they ate.

On Earth, she was a competent computer technician. Here, she was just a fool.

By the time they escaped the marketplace and found the relative peace of an inn, Jane had reaffirmed her decision. Tempting as it might be to be Daken's queen, she was at heart a computer technician. It may not be much, but it was who she was. She couldn't leave it behind just for a life of luxury.

She shook her head, knowing now that she was indeed a fool.

"I'll get us a room. Then we will talk in private," Daken said in her ear.

Jane turned, suddenly nervous about being alone in a room with him. "Are you sure?" she stammered. "I mean, we could talk right here—" She gestured to an empty booth near a large glass window. But the moment she looked back at Daken, her spirits plummeted. He would have it out with her, and it would be on his terms, on his turf.

And that meant in a private room.

Jane sighed. "Whatever you want is fine with me."

Daken nodded. "We will talk in our room."

Five minutes later, they were ushered into a large, luxurious suite with rich furnishings, thick fur skin rugs, and a large bed.

"This," Daken declared, "is an apartment fit for a king and his mate."

"You mean queen," she said dryly, her feminist soul noting the subordinate position he would relegate her to.

Daken's eyebrows drew together. "Of course. My mate will be a queen." He dismissed the innkeeper with a curt nod of his head. "This is the best room in the best inn in Bosuny. But your room in my home is even larger than this."

Jane sat down heavily on the bed, feeling her shoulders droop almost to her knees. "You can't buy me, Daken. I don't care if you own a palace inlaid in gold, with a thousand servants. I can't marry you. I can't marry anyone."

"Then why did you give me this?" He held up the shirt in his fist, shaking it at her as if it were a dead animal he'd just killed for her.

"Because I didn't know what it meant."

He shifted to stand directly in front of her, his legs spread, his hands on his hips. The shirt drifted to the bed beside her as he casually tossed it aside. "You are not," he paused, struggling with his words, "as innocent as you seem."

"And you're not this stupid," she shot back, her anger suddenly bursting through. She stood up, facing him eye to eye. Or rather, eye to collarbone until she tilted her head to glare up at him. "You're being deliberately obtuse, and it's making me real uncomfortable."

Daken drew himself up even taller. "Refusing a king is not supposed to be comfortable."

Jane balled her fists in frustration. "Damn it, Daken. You haven't even proposed. I did, and you know I didn't mean it."

Suddenly his face lightened. "Is that what you need?" He swiftly drew out his sword. She squeaked in alarm, springing backward onto the bed as the bright blade flashed before her eyes. Then he flattened the blade across his palm and set it down before her.

"Cripes, Daken. Warn a body—"

"Mistress Jane Deerfield," he said in solemn tones as he dropped to one knee.

Jane groaned. "Oh, God—"

"Will you do me the greatest honor—"

"Daken, wait—"

"—of becoming—"

"Daken—"

"—my queen?"

He lifted his bowed head, his eyes on level with her knees given her position perched on the bed. She waited, her breath coming in quick, short bursts.

"Jane?"

"Are you finished? Are you willing to listen now?"

"Do you wish me to say more?"

"No!"

Suddenly, she jerked forward and shoved hard on his shoulders. He wasn't prepared for the surprise attack and tumbled backwards onto his rear end. She immediately followed him, jumping down from her perch to stand over him, her position as domineering as his had been just moments before.

"Now you listen to me, you big galoot, and listen good. I am honored more than I can say. I'll be your friend. I'll even maybe be your—" She cut off her breath before the word could spill out, but it came anyway, slipping through on a breath of a sigh. "—your lover, if you like. But I can't marry you. I don't belong in this world. As soon as I can find a way, I'm going back to my home."

He looked up at her, his eyes hard, his face blank. "I don't want a lover. I want a wife."

"That'll make for a fun honeymoon," she said dryly.

His forehead wrinkled in confusion. "What is a hon-E-moon?"

Jane sighed, suddenly stepping away to drop down beside him, her legs crossed Indian style, her hands on her knees. "Daken, we can't even communicate on the basics. Don't you see? I don't belong here."

"You belong anywhere you wish to be."

"Maybe I don't wish to be here."

He lifted his chin. "You mean, you don't wish to be with me."

Jane bit her lip, wondering how he could look so haughty and so hurt at the same time. "I have a life, a home, and a job somewhere else. Somewhere far from here, and that is where I belong. Can't you see that?"

Daken sat up. In one lithe move, he faced her, crossing his legs until he mirrored her position exactly. "Do you have a...a husband at your home?"

Her laugh was almost bitter. "I can't even keep a goldfish, to say nothing of a man."

"Then keep me."

She smiled at his awkward phrasing, knowing what he said and what he meant were worlds apart. Daken would never be anyone's pet.

"I don't belong here, Daken. You know that as well as I."

He shook his head, his dark hair falling into his eyes. "I don't know that. And I don't think you do either."

She started to argue, but he pressed his fingers to her lips.

"You do not wish to marry me. I accept that. For now. But I will keep the wedding tunic for when you change your mind."

"You mean *if* I change my mind."

He just grinned, refusing to amend his statement, and she was forced to admire his grace and determination, even in the face of her refusal.

Then, before she could think of anything else to say, he pulled a small dagger and sheath out of his belt and offered it to her, hilt first.

"What's this?"

"A dagger. For you."

She took the weapon, drawing it out, extending the bright blade to the sunshine. "It's beautiful."

It was a fine dagger. Its hilt was iron inlaid with silver. The blade was razor sharp, and its point deadly. But most incredible to her was the way, even in the sunlight, that the edge seemed to dance with its own fire. A bright copper flame seemed to skate along the tip, burning up the edge until it slipped through the silver designs on the hilt and into her fingers.

"Uh..." She glanced up nervously, wondering if the tingling that spread through her body was supposed to happen. She tried to drop the knife, but she couldn't make her fingers release it. "I feel strange," she said, her voice a thready whisper.

"It is linking with you. Now it is your blade, and it will help you to use it better."

"Great." She giggled. It was her sick hyena laugh because she still had trouble accepting the magic he seemed to think was common. The tingling stopped, and she fumbled in her rush to sheathe the strange weapon.

He steadied her hands, his grip gentle as he guided her nervous movements, helped her stand, then tied the sheath about her waist. Only after it was fixed to her side did Jane say the things uppermost in her mind.

"Thank you, Daken. It's a beautiful gift, but..."

He raised an eyebrow.

She swallowed. "But is there some, uh, special meaning to this?" After all, she'd just given him a wedding tunic. For all she knew, this dagger meant she was part of some tribe that was in a death feud with everyone else. Or worse yet, that wearing it made her his woman somehow. "I, uh, just need to know."

He smiled, his eyes suddenly darkening to a mesmerizing navy. "It means, little fool, that I don't want you to feel naked."

That threw her until she remembered her earlier comment about everyone having weapons but her. She'd said she felt naked without a knife.

A slow smile spread across her face, but before she

could speak, he turned her around, untying the sheath and dropping her dagger on the floor next to his sword.

"I don't want you to feel naked with anyone but me."

She felt her eyes widen at the implication. Up until that moment, they had skated around the edges of sexuality. Now, it appeared, Daken was changing the rules of the game. Suddenly she was very aware of him and of the very big bed right behind them. His hands came up to frame her face, and she tingled from the electric intensity of his eyes.

Sunlight on glacier ice. The image flashed through her mind. His eyes were just like sunlight on blue glacier ice, sometimes as brilliant as the noontime sun, sometimes, like now, as dark as the night shadows, but always beautiful, possessing an elemental power that awed her, excited her, and in general made her knees go very weak.

"You know," he said casually, his voice like the low throb of a purring cat. "I think I was wrong. I want *both* a wife and a lover."

"Daken..." She pushed his name through the tightening in her throat. Her mouth was suddenly very dry as she tried to retreat from his advance. But she bumped straight into the bed. Slowly his hands framed her face, drew it upward to meet his gaze. "I...uh... I'm not sure—"

"I know," he said, and then he lowered his mouth to hers, capturing her slight gasp of alarm and molding it with his lips into a sigh of delight.

His kiss was warm and wet and wonderful. She'd expected him to be harsh, almost brutal in his possession of her. Instead he was gentle and disarming.

"Wait a minute." She pushed him away, only succeeding in separating them by an inch. "Two days ago, I was less appealing than rat bait. What happened?"

"You have always been appealing, Jane. I merely waited until I was sure of your good health."

Jane felt her heart lurch into double time. "You mean you don't think I'm crazy?"

He glanced away, his expression nervous.

Her pulse dropped with a disappointed ka-thunk.

"You *do* think I'm crazy."

"I think you are different. And," he looked back at her, his face suddenly open with his surprise. "I like it. I like you."

Then he caught her face again, and she tensed, wanting to wait until she sorted out her conflicting desires. Did she want to go to bed with him now? Yes! said her body, but her mind wasn't entirely convinced, especially since she liked to carefully weigh pros and cons before committing to a decision. But Daken wasn't to be deterred. He pulled her closer, stroked her lips with his tongue, and his delicate persuasion pushed away her arguments, leaving no room for thinking at all.

Her mouth slipped open on a sigh, but he didn't enter. Instead, his tongue teased her lips, alternately stroking and sucking the tender flesh until she was dizzy from the new sensations. It wasn't until her jaw relaxed in invitation that he finally ventured inside to taste her.

She would do it, she thought dizzily. She would become his lover. It was what she'd dreamed about nightly. It was what she'd dreaded as an awkward complication. It was something, everything, she'd secretly longed for.

He played with her, teasing his tongue along her

teeth, brushing the inside of her lips, tickling the roof
of her mouth. The myriad sensations flooded her mind
until her knees went slack, pressing her whole body
against him. She felt his hands run down the length of
her back until he cupped her buttocks, pressing her
intimately against his hardness.

Her body heated, and her belly began to tense. She
lifted her arms, sliding them up his until she twined
her hands in his long hair, feeling for the first time the
silky dark brown strands as they seemed to melt
around her fingers.

It was at that moment that he changed. Where
before she had been aware of his gentleness, now she
learned the warrior strength of him. Cradling her head
in one hand, he bent over her, deepening his kiss until
he thrust into her with a battle fire she quickly matched.
They dueled, the two of them, dancing in and out of
each others mouths with the precision of accomplished
campaigners and the awe of awkward youths.

It was impassioned, and it stoked the fire in her
blood until she panted for breath, her hands grasping
his shoulders for support against the dizzying vortex of
desire.

He broke from her mouth, his breathing as ragged
as her own, but unlike her, his hands were not still. He
ran them up and down the length of her, following
every curve, sinking into every valley, and molding
every peak. She moaned as both his hands found her
breasts, grasping and teasing the soft mounds through
the thin Lycrasheen material.

He pressed her backwards, pushing against her
until she lowered onto the bed. He came down on top
of her and possessed her mouth again. This time his
kiss was harsh and brutal, but she reveled in it, eagerly

urging him to take more, arching into his weight as he ravished her mouth.

Then suddenly he rolled away, and his absence was as sharp as his presence had been only seconds before.

She lay there, slowly bringing her breathing under control as beside her, he too struggled with harsh gasps. Later, when her body's tingling abated enough for her to think, she levered up on one elbow and looked at him.

He sat next to her, but his face was averted, his shoulders taut and high around his bowed head.

"Daken?" She reached out and touched one muscled shoulder. He flinched as if she'd burned him. She drew back, her heart sinking within her as she realized the source of his disgust. "Women here aren't nearly as aggressive, are they? They're not so," she finally pushed the words out, filling them with her disappointment in herself. "Not so loose?"

He twisted, his dark eyes shadowed by his hair. "Loose?"

"Amoral. Sexually free." She bit her lip. "A slut."

He twisted some more on the bed, his eyes slowly clearing as he reached out to stroke her face. "I don't understand these words, but I don't think you know what...what I have to do."

She dropped her head on her arm, staring into the pillow, seeing only the hard edge of his shoulder in her peripheral vision.

"Daken, I lost my virginity behind the bleachers when I was fourteen. He was a football star, and I was a nerd. He was big and hard, and it hurt like hell. Five years later, I tried again with somebody nicer. He was gentle in a fumbling sort of way." She turned to meet his eyes, knowing she was babbling, but unable to stop herself. "I know what we're doing. I'm not afraid. Or at least I wasn't." She looked away. "I guess I'm sorry I can't be an innocent for you. I mean, given the quality of my sex life, I'd have been just as happy to skip it altogether." She closed her eyes, wishing it didn't matter. "I'm not a virgin."

He was silent a long time before he moved. And when he did, he lowered himself on the bed so they faced each other, almost but not quite touching, their gazes locked and even.

"You misunderstand me. I don't wish you to be a virgin. I would not take a...an innocent."

She almost smiled at his quaint sense of honor. "You mean it's okay to have sex with me because I'm already damaged goods."

His eyes opened in alarm. "You're hurt?"

"No. No, that's not what I meant."

He settled back down on his arm, his gaze caressingly warm. "You mean you are mature."

"Uh, yes. I guess."

"I don't like taking virgins. They are skittish, frightened, and it is easy to accidentally pain them."

"I'm sure they appreciate your forbearance," she said dryly.

"Why are you angry with me?"

"Because you've just rejected me, and I'm hurt." She almost rolled away to put her back to him, but he stopped her, holding her shoulder still until she relaxed. Slowly, he began to caress her arm, then gently slid his hand up to touch her face.

"I stopped for two reasons. First, I must know if you are a virgin. It was too fast, and I didn't want to hurt you."

"Well, I'm not."

He grinned. "So you've told me."

"And the second reason?"

His hand became slower, more sensual in its movements as he returned to her arm, rubbing closer and closer to the tight peak of her breast.

"I must present myself to the Elven Lord today. Before the evening meal, which means I should leave very soon. When we make love," his hand lowered, pushing her onto her back before capturing her breast. "When we make love," he continued, following her over, the hunger deepening in his eyes as she gasped, arching into his caress. "I want it to be a long, lingering night of passion, not a stolen moment when my thoughts should be on what I must say to the Lord."

It felt so wonderful, his hot words brushing past her ear, his hand, large and possessive, stroking her breast until she moaned his name.

He kissed her one last time. She felt his hunger in his weight on her body, the deep, penetrating thrusts of his tongue, and the hot, swollen rod he pressed into her thigh.

"I want you, Jane Deerfield. And I will take you tonight until we scream out our ecstasy," he stroked her breast, "again," he pressed hard into her with his groin, "and again," a deep thrust that he punctuated with a kiss. She shuddered, too filled with lust to speak.

Then he rolled away to the edge of the bed while he watched her with heavy-lidded sensuality, his own desire smoldering in his gaze.

All she could do was watch him until eventually she laughed, a short exhale of passion that held as much awe as humor.

"Wow. You're good."

He grinned, his smile pure male satisfaction.

She threw a pillow at him then pulled herself upright.

"Okay, Casanova. You win. Now exactly what should I wear to meet this Elven Lord? Or do I wait here counting the seconds until you return?" Jane glanced at the floor. She wasn't exaggerating with that last bit. If she was left behind, she'd go crazy, probably pacing the room like a caged animal until he returned.

"You come with me."

Her breath came out in a gust of relief. At least now, she'd have something to do while waiting for tonight.

"And don't change your clothes."

She glanced up. "I can't meet an Elven Lord in a comic book costume!"

He turned to her, his head tilted slightly to one side. "What does this," he said the word slowly, "com-ic book mean?"

"Mean? Oh, nothing really. Just, well, they are stories about people who fight for truth and justice in their own special, renegade-type way."

"And you wear this to honor them?"

"Uh, yeah, sort of." How could she explain Halloween?

"Then it is honorable attire for the Elven Lord."

She stared at him, wondering how she got cornered into this one. Then she felt him tie her dagger in place, sliding his hands over her hips with a laziness that was slow torture.

Thank God that days of walking and a diet of dried caterpillar had shed the last of her unwanted pounds. For the first time in a long while, she could be really proud of her body.

"You just like the way it shows off my legs," she accused.

He grinned. "Don't change."

She blushed, pleased that he might think her sexy. "I won't. Just don't abandon me to the lascivious gazes of anyone else, okay?"

He growled, a low sound he magnified for her benefit. "You will stay within my reach every moment of the next...the next...," he paused, clearly trying to think of an appropriate time frame. "The next hundred years."

She laughed, suddenly feeling very young and very beautiful. "I promise I won't leave your side tonight."

He reached up, stroking her cheek while his eyes darkened again to a smokey haze. "I accept your promise. Remember that there is a penalty if you go back on your word."

She lifted her chin, intrigued by the implied threat even as a shiver of anticipation slid down her spine. "Oooh," she breathed. "A challenge. Hmmmm, what shall I do? The possibilities are endless." Then she lifted up on her toes, dropped a quick kiss on his lips, and danced out of the room.

"Jane!" His roar surprised her, but it didn't stop her. Or at least not until he grabbed her arm and pulled her back against the hard length of his body. "The court is a confusing and sometimes dangerous place. Don't be foolish."

She leaned back, luxuriating in the hard planes of muscle that shifted beneath her weight. "Never threaten a modern woman, Daken. She'll do the exact opposite of what you want just to prove she can." She twisted in his embrace until they once again faced each other. "A modern woman doesn't take orders from anyone."

"You will obey me in this, Jane." He sounded serious, but no more than she.

"I don't take orders, Daken. Even from a lover." And with that she sailed out of his embrace and the room.

Daken stared after her, his head slightly tilted as he mentally reviewed the conversation. By the Father, what kind of woman was this "modern" type? It sounded damned inconvenient to him.

He sighed heavily, settling his sword on his back. Perhaps it was time to rethink marriage to this "modern" woman. The last thing he needed was another problem.

As he readjusted his trousers for the third time, he realized it was too late to change his mind. Inconvenient or not, he wouldn't release her. And modern or not, she would have to bend to his will because she was his fool and he was the King.

And that would never change.

Chapter Five

◆   ◆   ◆

The palace was nothing like Jane expected.

Over the last week, Jane had learned this world was different in many ways, but the palace grounds were downright weird.

It started out a little odd. She pictured the Elven Lord in a castle, a defensible structure as a power base that gradually became a simple show of strength as his influence expanded. However, royalty was often eccentric and their royal structures sometimes reflected their oddities.

When the front entrance to the "palace" looked more like a California beach house than a royal home, she took it all in stride. Maybe the Elven Lord was a beach bum at heart. Not that there were any beaches around that she'd seen, but plenty of verdant gardens, brilliant flower beds, and even a very large park-like area reminiscent of an arboretum.

In short, everything was very lush, very green, and very open. Jane grinned. This was her kind of palace.

That's when things started to get weird.

They approached what could have been front doors if there were any doors. It was really a huge open square in a wall through which people came and went as they pleased. Daken took her arm, and as they stepped through, Jane suddenly felt a tingling along her spine.

"Daken?"

"The Lord knows we are here. He will come find us when he has a moment."

"But how?"

Daken glanced down, a soft smile playing about his lips as he explained what, apparently, was supposed to be obvious. "He has spelled the door, Jane. He knows all who enter or leave by it."

Jane nodded. "Sort of a security alarm. Does it detect weapons and bombs and stuff?"

"Of course." Daken nodded congenially at a group of people lounging on couches just to their left. "The spell no doubt tells the Lord everything we carry."

"Everything? Like clothing, hairpins, exact change?"

Daken nodded.

"Is that it? Or does it read minds too?" She was only half joking. Just how much of herself had she exposed by coming here? She glanced nervously around her, wondering if a dozen guards would soon come running down the hallway screaming "Space alien!"

Nothing happened. Just people chatting in loose groups. Some read thin linen-like papers, others seemed absorbed in contemplating the scenery.

Jane relaxed until Daken spoke. "The doorway would not read your mind, although there are spells to do that. It is more likely it can recognize an intent to do evil or the like."

"Oh. Is that all?" she asked weakly.

Daken gave her a quick piercing look, but Jane didn't elaborate. They continued to stroll through the palace which was really two floors of open rooms for people to lounge in.

That's when things changed to bizarre.

They left the front building to enter the back courtyard, and Jane felt her jaw go slack. Surrounding a well-trafficked field were dormitories, two large classroom buildings, and what seemed like a cafeteria. At least that was what it looked like to Jane.

"This looks more like a university than a palace," she said as much to herself as to Daken. Even the people constantly milling around looked more like students and faculty than courtiers.

"A un-i-ver—?"

"University. A center of knowledge. Where people come to learn and to teach."

"Yes. This is Bosuny, the Elven Lord's capitol."

Jane stopped, turning to watch Daken's face as she spoke. "You mean people come here to study and learn? The Elven Lord's home is really a school?"

"Yes. Knowledge is strength. Why does this surprise you? How else would it be?"

How else indeed? The Elven Lord zoomed up several notches in her esteem. "You mean there are no heavy political games, no big gun lobbies, little clerks wrapping everything up in red tape?" Jane stalled out. What exactly had she expected? Her image of the doings in Washington D.C. was fed primarily by glitz and glamour vids of well-meaning but naive innocents fighting power-hungry demons. That, or what the scandal mongers on the news channels said.

So what did they really do on Capitol Hill?

Daken shook his head. "Your words are strange to me. The Elven Lord studies magic. He has brought others here to help him increase his powers."

The light suddenly went on in Jane's mind. "So, this is a pacifist government, meaning no weapon play, no guns and bombs and stuff." She'd already noticed few people here carried even small daggers like hers. "But they study magic. And let me guess, there's probably a few people here who concentrate on aggressive, offensive spells."

Daken raised his eyebrows, and his eyes sparkled with appreciation. "For a fool, you are remarkably intelligent."

They resumed walking toward the oldest, most dilapidated structure while Jane looked around, trying to absorb the feel of the campus. Then Daken held open a door into the crumbling building.

Jane hesitated before entering. "Are you sure it's safe? This thing looks like it's about to come down around our ears."

Daken looked up as if noticing the old mortar and weather-beaten bricks for the first time. "Don't worry. This is the most well-protected building in the Elven Lord's realm."

"This one?" She glanced into the dark, gloomy hallway beyond the door. "Why?"

"Because of what is in here. Come. I'll show you."

She suppressed a growing sense of horror, mentally girded herself, and stepped in. As the door sealed behind them, Jane fought panic. She felt entombed in these walls, wrapped in the musty smells of age and disuse. She stepped forward. Her sneakers squished on the concrete floor, and the sound echoed in the darkness.

"This is weird," she said in a hoarse whisper. It was like entering a library long since abandoned. The feeling was sad, almost sick, definitely dead.

"This is the home of one of our oldest legends."

He guided her along a well-worn path down a dark hallway, sparsely lighted by an occasional candle.

"It is said," he continued, "an old soul hidden among the people will one day come here to open the door to vast knowledge. Every one who visits Bosuny comes here to see if they are the one to fulfill the prophesy."

A cold chill skated down Jane's spine, and she pushed herself into a false levity to counteract the oppressive feel of the building. "What, they show up expecting to whammo-presto find a key hidden on their body? Like King Arthur's sword in the stone?"

Daken shrugged. "I don't know. I have never been to this building. And I don't know this King Arthur."

She waved aside his regrettable ignorance of one of her favorite legends. "You've never been here? But I thought you said everyone comes here."

"My brother and parents have been here, but..." his words faded as they rounded a corner and arrived at a heavy metal door.

"But..." she prompted, a little awed by the sudden cloak of calm expectancy that settled around Daken. It was as though he were preparing himself for a great battle.

He glanced down at her, his lips quirking in his wry smile filled with self-mockery that she found so endearing. "The day I was born, my mother had a dream. She said I would fulfill the prophesy, but I wasn't to come here until I was of the age of majority."

"Until you were twenty-one?"

"Twenty-four. Two full cycles of years."

Jane did a swift calculation. "A cycle must be twelve years."

Daken nodded absently, his attention focused on

his hand as he slowly placed his palm on the door.

"How old are you now, Daken?"

"Thirty-one." He glanced back at her, and Jane caught a flash of apprehension, almost nervousness. He turned back to the door. "I thought to do this with my parents beside me, but now..." His voice trailed off, and Jane suddenly realized this was a big moment for Daken.

It didn't matter that his mother's dream was probably induced by post-pregnancy hormones. Thirty-one years ago, she placed the burden of greatness on Daken, telling everyone her son would be their prophesized hero. And now fate had decreed he'd face his big moment alone.

Or almost alone. Jane was with him.

She sensed Daken gathering his courage and strength about him, and she knew he was about to push open the door. Jane had a sudden image of Daken, standing disappointed, maybe humiliated, if after thirty-one years of build-up, he went through the door and nothing happened.

She reached out, covering his hand with her own. "Daken, whatever happens, good or bad, right or wrong, I think you're already a pretty great king, not to mention a wonderful guy."

Daken's eyes were dark in the gloomy hallway, but even so, Jane saw the way they lightened, just a little, the gold flecks becoming more pronounced as he absorbed her comment.

He leaned down as she raised up. Their lips touched. It wasn't an intense kiss. It lasted less than a second. But in that brief touch, they communicated a wealth of love and support and thanks. Never had she felt a kiss so deeply or so simply.

He drew back, but their gazes continued to caress each other. Then a noise from down the hallway broke their communion. Jane turned to look. Although she saw nothing, she heard the outside door close with a ponderous thunk.

Someone was coming.

She glanced at Daken, and he nodded. He either went through the door now or did it with an audience. With kingly presence, he thrust open the dark metal door and stepped in. Jane followed, shadowing his right shoulder, ready to help in any way she could.

It wasn't until she got a good look around that the chill in her spine settled with a sick thud in her stomach.

"Oh my God," she breathed.

Daken too looked around, his brow furrowed, his breathing shallow. "I don't understand," he whispered to her. "I don't understand any of it."

"I know," returned Jane. "Oh God, do I know."

Surrounding her in bits and pieces, with dust cloaking the parts until they were almost unrecognizable, was a Regency CX-537 mainframe computer and associated peripherals. It was the exact same unit Boston University library housed, and the same computer she'd spent the last five years of her life maintaining.

"I think I'm going to be sick," she groaned.

Daken glanced back at her, his mind still reeling from the totally incomprehensible chaos littering the room. He spared less than a second for her. But then, like a dog returning to his home, his sight was pulled back to her pale face as she stared with open-mouthed horror at the debris surrounding them.

"What do you see, Jane? Do you understand this?" He didn't want to believe it. He was the prophesied one, not this little moonling.

Her nod was slow, but it was like a hammer clubbing his heart. He grabbed her, twisting her toward him, shaking her until she finally looked at him.

"What do you mean, Jane? Do you know what this is?"

It took three tries before she could speak, but finally her voice came out, first as a squeak, but growing stronger with each word. "It's a...a Regency CX-537. A computer."

"I do not understand this word."

"A...a machine."

"And you can work this machine?"

She nodded again, her gaze darting around the room, spastically jerking from one strange object to another. "I...I don't know. I guess I can."

"Then you must help me."

"Help you?" Her thoughts were scattered. One thing was certain, they must put this machine back together.

"We must do this, Jane. It is my destiny. We must."

Her gaze finally settled, focusing on his face. "I can do it." She took a deep breath. "I can bring it up, Daken. That's not the problem. What I want to know is what it's doing here."

"This is the House of Prophesy."

She shook her head. "I don't care if this is the House of Oz. I want to know what a CX-537 is doing here. In this place. In this world." Her voice rose in near hysteria. Daken could feel the panic welling up within her. It pushed through his defenses, battering at his own focus like a rising tide of flood waters, beating against a retaining wall.

"Why, Daken? *Why is it here?*"

He shook her, first gently, then with increasing impatience as they fought her panic together.

"Jane! Listen to me. I don't understand your questions. I don't even understand your words. I don't have your answers."

"No. Of course you don't. You're just king of this nutso planet of my worst jumbled nightmares. We've got elves and dragons and living streams and magic sheep guts. Why not a CX-537? What's around the corner, Daken? A big white rabbit with a pocket watch? Oh God," she covered her mouth with her hands. "I really am insane, aren't I? This whole thing is a crazy delusion I've created. I'm living in a dream and everything," she said as she tried to twist out of his arms. "Everything. This room, this computer, even you," her wild eyes rolled back to him. "Even you, you aren't real. You're a computerized hero I've pulled into existence for my own living fantasy."

"Jane!" He tried shaking her again, but it didn't work. "Jane, you're not crazy. This is real." He brought her hands to his face. "I'm real."

"No. No, you're not." She shook her head, her movement jerky and abrupt. "You're my fantasy. Don't you see? Everyone wants a stud with a sword as their personal friend. I've even made you a king. And you proposed. Oh God. I'm crazy. I'm completely nuts. There's no other explanation. I wasn't transported in time and space. That's crazy. I'm crazy."

"No, Jane. No. You are as sane as I."

But she was beyond listening. She believed herself steeped in madness, and her belief made it true. In the end, he did the only thing he could think of. He framed her face and pulled her close for a deep kiss. As his mouth went to hers, as his tongue stroked and pushed at her lips, he drew on his strength. He brought forward his inner flame of healing, and he pushed it into her mind and body as he pushed himself into her mouth.

The waves of her panic still beat at them. He pictured them clearly in his mind's eye. He saw them swirling, seething against them, battering her defenses, her mind crumbling beneath their weight. But the water was no match to the searing heat of his flame. He burned within her, his healing light evaporating her panic as the noonday sun dries out a puddle.

Twice the waters swelled, threatening to bury them both. Twice he pushed them back, drying them at the source, healing her in her heart and soul. And in the end, he won.

They won.

He broke the kiss. He rolled his chin to her ear, his voice a soft whisper against her damp cheek.

"Jane, you are not insane. This is real."

"But—"

"Shhh. Listen to me. I don't have the answers you're seeking. I can't help you any more than I already have. But they can." He pulled her over to the scattered pieces, littered all over the floor like the dirty leavings of a ravaging hoard. "These things, these pieces of prophesy, put them together and then you'll know. This is the key to knowledge—"

"It's just a computer."

"And what is a computer?"

"It's a storehouse of information—" She cut off her words, then quickly stumbled into speech again. "Not like you think. Not like some wisdom of the ages. It's just information."

"Knowledge such as how it got here and what is its

purpose?"

He saw the light dawn in her eyes. It was a good light, a healing glow that had been absent from her as long as he'd known her. Finally, he saw the madness fade from her mind as the healing light of purpose took over.

"I can make it work." She said the words as much for herself as for him as she looked down at the debris with a critical eye. "I will make it work."

With a sudden shock, he realized she was no longer a fool. The fear and confusion in her mind dissipated. It wasn't completely gone. The panic still lurked, waiting for her next moment of vulnerability. But for the first time since he'd revived her back in the meadow, she had her own flame, her own inner strength back.

Now she could heal herself.

He watched as she knelt down, methodically sorting through the things on the floor. Her short curls fell forward, partially obscuring her profile until she reached up and absently tucked them behind her ear. She was concentrating, her forehead actually smoothing out as she studied a piece of green board.

She was happy.

The thought struck him broadside. This must be what she did in her world, at her home. She must work with these cold metals and empty boards because he could feel how much peace these things gave her. Even in his arms, inflamed by passion, she had never been so content with herself.

It was a lowering thought that the woman he'd chosen for his wife preferred these...things to him.

But then again, they had only started to explore the wonder that could be found with each other. And now, he thought with a sigh, now that she'd rediscovered her dark square stones and silver trails, would they ever get the chance to finish what they'd started earlier today?

They'd have to. He'd make her come back to him because he'd decided she would be his wife. She couldn't leave him now.

As he hunkered down beside her, he saw the intensity of her eyes and felt the weight of her concentration. Watching her, he suddenly doubted his ability to win her.

Had he found his mate only to discover she was already lost to a bunch of boards and stones?

There was only one way to find out. She wouldn't stop until she found the answers she needed. And those answers were somehow locked in this thing she called a computer. So, for now, he would help her find what she needed. And then, after it was done, after she learned what she wanted to know, then he would bring her back to him.

"How can I help?" he asked, his voice rough with suppressed fear.

She didn't even glance up, but brushed a slick black bar against her clothing. "Is there a window here? Any place the sun shines in?"

Daken looked around. "No, not that I... Wait." He crossed the room to inspect an odd square of stone. "There used to be a window here, but it's been closed in."

She stood and joined him at the wall, pushing at the bricks with one hand. She held the black bar in the other. "Can you knock this out? Get us some real light?"

"Lamps, a few candles or torches would be easier."

"Yes," she said absently. "But it wouldn't be sunlight, and it wouldn't be nearly bright enough."

"But this window won't illuminate the room very well either."

"I don't care about the room." She rooted through a snarl of long coils, some black, some gray, some multicolored. "I can see well enough now."

"But then why—"

"Daken," she twisted around, holding up the black bar. "I need the light for this."

"But why would a rock—"

"Because it's not a rock. It's a solar collector. For power."

"A what?"

She started to reply, but the words never came. Finally she just shrugged. "It's too hard to explain. Can't you please just trust me?"

He waited a moment, watching her. Already he'd lost her interest as her focus shifted to a smooth black rope she pressed into the black bar. With sudden resolve, he crossed to her, stepping directly in front of her before she noticed him.

"Daken! You're stepping on—"

"Jane." He reached down and pulled her to her feet.

"What are you—"

He kissed her; long, hard, and with a roughness born of anger and desperation. She didn't struggle long, but he continued until he knew he brought all of her attention back to him, away from her ropes and stones. Only then did he end it.

"Listen to me, Jane. I will be your servant today. I will knock out the stones, though the Father alone knows what the Elven Lord will think of it. I will do as you bid me when you bid me, but remember, I do this today, for the sake of the prophesy, and because you want it."

She started to speak, but he held up his hand, pressing it against her soft lips. Her flesh stilled beneath his hand, but not before he felt the brush of her lips against his fingertips and the warmth of her breath heat his palm. His groin tightened, and he ground his teeth, focusing on the need for restraint.

"I will do this today, Jane. But tonight, we finish what we started. Tonight, you will come with me, and this," he glanced hatefully at the debris that had not only abandoned him, but now threatened to take her from him. "This will be forgotten. You will be mine." He pulled back his hand from her lips, already missing the contact with her.

She took a deep breath, a delightful pink tingeing her cheeks and lips. "I'll be your lover," she said. Then he lowered his mouth to hers, unable to resist the beauty of the desire he'd sparked in her eyes.

This time his kiss was gentle, tantalizing, and full of the promise of the night to come. She responded quickly, with an untutored eagerness that cut through his defenses. Their kiss deepened, lengthened, and filled him until his hands sought out the lush curves of her breasts.

He could have her there, on the floor, if he'd wanted to. In this, she was still vulnerable to him. This part of her, at least, was his. So he released her, not wanting to abuse her trust.

"Tonight," he whispered, his voice rough and husky. "Tonight we will do this as it should be done."

She nodded, and he was gratified to see her gaze was completely trained on him, the computer things forgotten.

"You are so beautiful, Jane Deerfield. So beautiful that I, King of Chigan, will knock out a stone wall in the House of Prophesy at your command." Then he left her to study the stones he would need to remove.

"You're doing this," she said, as she walked with him to the wall, "because it's the only way to fulfill your mother's dream for you."

He paused, trying to fathom her words. "My mother dreamed I shouldn't come here until I was twenty-four. That has already been fulfilled."

"Not her dream when she was asleep. Her dream of her son fulfilling this prophesy." She dropped to her knees to study a pile of what looked like dusty junk to him. "I'm not only doing this for me. I'm doing this for you. It's what you want, isn't it?"

He toyed with the hilt of his dagger, rubbing his finger over the smooth stone embedded at the base. "I want the prophesy to be fulfilled," he said carefully.

"And assuming I can get this monster up and running, you'll fulfill it. You'll bring a great deal of information to your people. Here try this on the wall." She pulled out a small hatchet that had once been painted red.

He took the blunted weapon, then faced her and bowed his most formal salute to her. "I thank you, Jane Deerfield, for the gift you bestow on me and my people."

She grinned, bobbing her head awkwardly in response. "Uh, no problem. It's the least I could do for my computerized stud with a sword."

"Uh—"

"I know. I was joking. It's the least I can do for Daken, King of Chigan. Besides," she added, her voice fainter as it filtered through the back of a metal cabinet. "This might get you the pull you need with the Elven Lord."

He drew back the hatchet, aiming it at the crumbling mortar. "I had thought of that," he said, then he swung, embedding the blade in the wall.

They worked for another hour, and gradually Daken became aware of their audience. First it was only a few noises from the hallway. Then later, a young and very large mage opened the door and stood in the entrance, probably to keep the people who craned their heads around him from pushing their way into the room.

Daken wasn't surprised. They'd probably been watched from the moment they'd arrived in the House of Prophesy. Everyone knew of his mother's dream. She'd had no qualms about telling all and sundry of her son's great destiny. More than one person would have wanted to watch Daken's great moment if only to see him fail.

Daken pulled the last stone from the old window. He shouldn't have been worried about what the Elven Lord would think of this. If the Lord objected, Daken wouldn't have been able to pick up the hatchet, much less bury it in the wall.

"Is this good?"

Jane stepped out from the small metal room she'd been working in. Daken hadn't at first realized how far this Room of Prophesy went back until she'd opened a metal cabinet and proceeded to walk deeper and deeper into it. There was a whole other world of green boards and colored wires he'd never suspected.

Now she came out of the cabinet, her hair covered in dust, her cheek smudged with dirt, and her face wreathed in a happy smile.

Daken pointed at the window. "Is this large enough?"

Jane looked up at him and frowned. "Nuts. The light's going."

"It is evening."

"Yeah, but we need sunlight."

"Would any light do?" he asked, peering into the sky.

"A candle or lamp is too dim. Same with a torch. A good bright light bulb would be fine, though it might take a little longer."

"What is a light-bub?"

"Light bulb. It's like a...a glowing ball of light. Self-contained. Not very hot, but very bright."

"A fire ball?"

"Well, yes. But not hot."

Daken waited a moment, sure what she needed would be provided. He wasn't disappointed. Moments later, a bright fireball appeared just outside the window. It was poised in the air like a small burning bird, stationary and very bright.

"How's that?"

"Wow! How'd you do that?"

Daken grinned, wishing he could take the credit. "I didn't do it. Someone in our audience did."

"Audience?"

Daken jerked his head toward the door and watched Jane's eyes grow wide.

"Where'd they come from?" she whispered.

"Does it matter?"

She shook her head. "No, I guess not." She turned to him. "They're here to see your big moment, huh?"

"They are here to see the prophesy fulfilled," he hedged.

Jane smiled. "Well, let's not disappoint them. Here, help me put this out." She brought the black bar and cord to the window, dangling it out under the light. "Hmm. Have we got something to lay this on? Like a table or chair?"

Daken glanced back at the young mage still guarding the doorway. The boy nodded and disappeared. Moments later, two youths returned with a table.

"How's this?"

Jane twisted around to see. "Great. Pass it over."

Once the bar was placed to her satisfaction, Jane turned around, resting momentarily against the cabinet, her expression relaxed as she watched two boys at the doorway. The first, the young mage in his dark blue robe, returned to his sentry position. But the other one, the young blond of about thirteen in servant's garb, hesitated just on the inside of the door.

"Hi," she said to him.

The boy nodded and brushed back a greasy lock of hair. Then he stared at her as if he were afraid she'd try to eat him.

"So much for my winning ways with kids," she muttered before turning back to Daken. "You know, I suppose they could come in if they stayed on that side of the room." She lifted her chin to the back of the room. "That would keep them from killing themselves trying to see around Mr. Dark Blue and Bulky."

"The mage is there to keep others from interfering."

"Oh. Can he keep them on that side of the room?"

Daken nodded. "If it will not disturb you, then..." he paused, choosing his words carefully. "It would be a kindness to them." The people in the hall were those who were not able to watch in more subtle ways, and Daken had always thought it unfair how jealously some mages hoarded their knowledge. It pleased him that Jane was kindhearted enough to allow the less gifted to learn of what they did. And if it did magnify the extent of their success or failure, that was how great moments in history were made.

Even if they failed, his mother would have been pleased with how notorious the event made her son.

"Perhaps we should limit the number to ten," he suggested. "There isn't much room."

"Yeah," Jane nodded, her attention focused on a strange series of holes in a strip of metal. "Whatever you think best." She suddenly glanced up, scanning the faces behind the young mage. "Which one's the Elven Lord?"

Daken stopped, realizing she had no understanding of the abilities of the people around her. "The Elven Lord and other high mages are undoubtedly watching through their crystals."

"Crystals? As in crystal balls?"

"Some are balls. Some are mirrors. Others use pools of water. It all depends—"

She waved it off. "I don't want to know." She looked around at the walls and ceiling. "It gives me the creeps to think of a dozen pairs of eyes watching my every move."

"It is more likely to be a hundred or more. The mages have their own way of communicating. We are probably being watched by wizards throughout the world."

"Swell," she muttered, her gaze sliding back to the holes. "Look. Can you direct traffic, then come on back and help me carry this equipment? I found a monitor back here that ought to work. Plus drives and the like. It may be crude, but I want to start small and build up to the big guns."

Daken hesitated, his voice slow. "There are guns back there?"

Jane glanced up. "You know about guns?"

"Yes. They are weapons. Ancient weapons whose secret has been lost."

"Good. Let it stay lost." She started to duck back into the cabinet, but he grabbed her arm.

"There are guns back there?" He couldn't suppress the excitement in his voice. A gun would be of great use against the Tarveen.

Jane hesitated. "No. There aren't any guns back there. It was just a figure of speech." She stepped away from him. Then she glanced up at the ceiling and projected her voice for all to hear. "No guns." And then she was gone, leaving him to handle the thorny problem of who to allow in the room and who to keep out.

Jane ducked through the cabinet into the main machine room. She knew exactly where she was going. She had stumbled across the item a few hours ago, but hadn't thought much about it. Or rather, she had thought a lot about it, but wasn't sure what to do with it.

Kneeling down before a small filing cabinet, she pulled open a drawer. A nine millimeter Beretta lay neatly on the dark metal. One magazine clip lay beside it. She lifted them both out of the small filing cabinet, absently flicking out a bullet from the clip.

What would she do with them? This land had enough weapons. She refused to be the snake who introduced modern guns to this small garden of Eden. They'd find it out fast enough on their own.

She looked around the room, belatedly realizing she might be showing a few hundred people exactly what she'd just told Daken didn't exist back here. Well, she could only pray they weren't watching.

She quickly dismantled the Beretta. This wasn't a gun she was exceptionally familiar with, but one couldn't live long in a big city without having some understanding of guns. In fact, her father had taught her how to load and shoot a pistol before she moved to Boston. She fumbled as she tore it apart, finally wresting the firing pin free. She tried to bend or break it, but it was too well-made. So she tossed it into a corner behind the main disk cabinet. Even if someone knew where it was, it would take a lot of muscle to get back there to it.

But there would be no reason to get it. Especially since she intended to dispose of the bullets and the gun as soon as humanly possible.

She heard Daken near the doorway to the machine room. Grabbing her backpack, she scooped up the gun, clip, and bullet, and dropped them into the front pouch. Then she tossed her pack in the opposite direction of the pin before running to the monitor she'd found.

"There you are," she said breathlessly as Daken stepped into the room. "Come help me carry this." She knelt down and lifted the monitor easily. "Er," she stammered. "I mean, can you bring that," she jerked her head back at a set of drives.

Daken stared at her oddly, and Jane bit her lip, trying not to look too guilty. Hoisting the monitor higher, she hid her face, then pushed past him into what once was the Op's office.

Much to her relief, he let her go, although she felt him watching her every movement as she stepped through the narrow, reinforced hallway.

✦   ✦   ✦

Daken watched her disappear into the main room and felt his lips press into a tight grimace. Jane was up to something. Until now, she'd been exciting, different, innocent, uncanny, and sometimes just plain odd. But this was the first time he'd seen her sneaky.

She didn't do it well.

He would have stopped her. He would have warned her that now, when most of the known world watched, was not the time to start hiding things from him.

But then that would imply that he was being totally honest with her. And he wasn't.

She thought she was helping him reach for his destiny. She thought by doing her magic with these bits of board and black crystal that she would help him obtain the council seat reserved for the prophesied one. But how could he sit on the ruling board if he was eradicating the Tarveen?

No, she would be the prophesied one. Jane Deerfield, his little fool, would become the Keeper of Knowledge. And he would still be the second son, now king, of the western frontier land of Chigan.

Daken clenched his jaw as he turned away. The Crones of Fate had outdone themselves in perversity today.

So be it. Jane would be the Keeper despite everything she said about leaving. Her words about a home and a livelihood somewhere far from here were no longer relevant. She may want to go back to where she belonged, but after seeing her here, working with this thing she called a computer, Daken knew her place was here. As the Keeper of Knowledge.

He smiled to himself as he lifted the heavy box she called the drive unit and grimaced at its weight. Curse the Crones. All his life he'd thought he would be the one to bring knowledge back into the world. He'd spent his childhood trading on that one prophesy of greatness. Instead, he fetched and carried for a little fool who didn't know about Old Souls, but apparently could work magic with rocks and green boards.

Perhaps he could still work this to his advantage. Through Jane, he could influence the Council to give him the army he needed. Then, after he and Jane married, he could finally bring his lands and his people into the prominence they deserved, rather than being the back water buffer zone between the Empty Lands and the Elven Lord.

Yes, the Crones of Fate had indeed twisted his life in a bizarre pattern. But, at least in this case, the Father made sure it came out all right.

The only problem now was getting Jane to accept her destiny.

Chapter Six

❖   ❖   ❖

Jane held her breath as she double-checked every-thing—all the wires, all the connections, all the boards, dip switches, and power flow indicators. Then she glanced uneasily behind her at her mismatched audience. The original group had been slowly dis-placed, giving way one by one to people she guessed were higher ranking officials. Instead of the students and servants of before, she now saw dark men in dark robes. Interspersed between them were light-skinned, light-haired people in flowing garments, not one of which looked older than about fourteen. And then, squeezed in the fringes, were every other shape, size, and body type in between.

The only one who stood out in her mind was the dirty boy who she'd tried to talk with before. He gazed at her from around the doorway, looking at her through eyes so pale they seemed almost white. He always ducked his head when she looked at him, trying to shrink into the hallway, probably hoping nobody would notice him and throw him out. He did it very well, this shrinking-into-nothingness act. If she hadn't particularly tried to speak to him earlier, she doubted she would have given him a second thought. But because she had, and because he looked almost as ragtag as she felt, she watched him and tried to become friends.

"Why do you keep looking at that boy?"

Jane jumped as Daken's breath carried his soft-spoken question past her ear.

"What?"

"The boy is dumb. A disappointing servant at best. Your attention to him not only lowers you but discomfits the boy."

Jane turned to stare at Daken, disillusionment in her to-be-lover knotting in her stomach. "It lowers me to talk to a servant? Why? Aren't servants people too?"

"That is irrelevant. That one has been a disappointment all his life. It does you no good to associate with him at your moment of proof."

Jane wondered at Daken's bitter tone as he tried to draw her further away from the boy, but she resisted, knowing he wouldn't force her. Not while bigwigs throughout the world watched.

"What do you mean, he's been a disappointment all his life?"

Daken practically growled at her before forcing the words out. "Years ago, the Elven Lord had a dream that the boy would become a great wizard. He spent much time and money to locate the child and bring him here, only to discover the boy is nothing but a dumb, silent servant."

She looked back at the child. He was perhaps thirteen, with a shallow chest and pale, dirty hair. He didn't seem stupid to her. The fact that he'd managed to stay nearby, when everyone else appeared to be some sort of dignitary, indicated a subtle intelligence rather than stupidity. And there was something in his eyes. It was an odd spark she caught when he didn't think anyone watched, a keen glance that missed nothing.

Then something else clicked in her mind, and she turned to Daken.

"You think that because his prophesy hasn't worked out, yours won't either."

"That has nothing to do—"

"Of course, it does. I'd think that would give you some sympathy for the child. This bitterness is unworthy of you, Daken. I'm disappointed."

His mouth gaped open in shock, then snapped shut with a black anger that darkened the gold in his eyes. Apparently, not many people ever scolded Daken. And certainly not in front of the most powerful people in the world.

Still, Jane lifted her chin, unwilling to back down even as her insides quailed. Daken was her only friend in this strange world. It wasn't wise to anger him. But even knowing that, she couldn't abandon the poor boy. She felt a kinship with him. He looked like she felt: a lost soul on the fringes, struggling to survive in a sometimes hostile and strange world.

She smiled and gestured for the boy to join them. She ignored the shocked gasps of outrage that filled the room, and she jerked free of Daken's restraining arm.

"Don't worry, Daken," she said lightly over her shoulder. "We won't *lower* your standing with the people here. You've made it clear you want nothing to do with him." She dropped a comforting arm on the boy's small shoulders, making it abundantly clear that if Daken wanted anything to do with her, he'd have to accept the child too.

"You are being obstinate, difficult—" Daken ground out the words between clenched teeth.

"And modern, Daken. I'm being a modern woman." Then she turned her back on him and knelt down to be eye to eye with the boy. "I'm Jane." She touched her chest. "Jane."

She pointed to him, trying by facial expression to ask his name.

"I told you. He's dumb."

She shot an angry look at Daken before turning back to the boy. But then after a few more frustrated seconds, she began to understand.

"You mean he's mute. He can't speak."

"That's what I said. He's dumb."

Jane silently cursed their communication spell, realizing whatever the word "dumb" was in his language, it didn't carry the same overtones of stupidity it did in English. Then she sighed, regrouped, and tried to make the best of it.

"What's his name?"

"Steviens."

"St...st..." She couldn't get the word out. Then she looked down at the boy, "How about I call you Steve? Steve? Sound okay to you?"

The boy nodded as if he understood and approved. Behind her, Daken snorted his disgust, but Jane ignored him. Just as she ignored all the outraged, stuffy people in her audience.

"Come on, Steve. I'll show you how you can help me."

"Jane—" said Daken, his voice low with warning.

"How about you concentrate on crowd control, Daken. We're getting more and more in here every second." She glanced disdainfully at the press of arrogant, richly-attired people who seemed to press further into the room with each passing second. "Leave the machinery to us servants."

"*Venzi*, Jane! You're not a servant—"

"Well, I'm certainly not one of them either!" And with that, she turned back to the boy. "Okay, Steve. Here's what we're going to do." She took him to the power strip and pointed to the small electronic panel that monitored power flow. Given the steady, bright light on the solar panels in the window, they now had enough energy to run the small drive unit that she hoped would eventually boot the larger computer in the back. The problem was, she'd only found one boot disk. If they had a power drop during the start up procedure, she risked losing the disk and any way of working the small unit, much less the mainframe.

It was a risk they'd have to take. There was no other way until she found some sort of battery back-up.

"I want you to watch these lights," she said to Steve, pointing to a strip of nine steady, red lights. "If they ever drop to less than four or go over twelve then holler..." She remembered he didn't speak. Not knowing whether he could make any noise at all, Jane looked around for another way for him to make noise. Eventually, she pointed to a metal cabinet in arms reach. "Bang on this cabinet." She demonstrated, much to the shock of everyone else in the room. "Do you understand?"

He gave her a blank expression. Of course, he didn't understand. He didn't speak English. No one spoke English. She glanced up at Daken who waited just off to the side, his arms crossed over his massive chest.

"Could you explain it to him, please?"

"He's just a servant boy, Jane. I could—"

"That's not the point! I like him, Daken. A little bit more than I like you right now."

"Jane!"

"Look. It's a virtually meaningless task. If the power drops, there's nothing he can do. Hell, there's not much I can do. But if it keeps him beside me, in the spotlight for maybe the only time in his life instead of shoved out in the hallway, then I'm going to do it."

"No good comes from taking a servant beyond his position. It will only make his life harder when he goes back to his duties."

Jane was in no frame of mind to accept the reason behind his argument. She felt increasingly nervous over the spectators, both seen and unseen, surrounding her, watching her every move. She'd never worked well in front of others, and this center-stage-to-the-world stuff made her more agitated than when she'd failed her Doctorate orals. It didn't help that she didn't know if she could bring up the monstrosity of a computer. Everything had been in a jumble of haphazard parts, some so thick with dust she needed acid to clean them off. The odds against her succeeding were so high, it would take a miracle to do anything but fail in the most humiliating, horrendous way possible.

But she'd started. She had to see it through. Even though her audience grated on her nerves, and she'd been fighting back a migraine by sheer willpower alone. Unfortunately, the only way she'd found to release tension was to fight with Daken over a silly servant boy who seemed as skittish at being in the spotlight as she was.

"Damn it, Daken! Just tell him!"

Biting back an oath that was no less vehement for being cut off, Daken apparently translated for the boy.

Steve nodded once, a slight tilt of his chin, then he gazed back at Jane, his pale, pale blue eyes suddenly wide and serious. In that one moment, she realized he understood. Not just his task, but that she was using him to release her frustrations, not to help him. His gaze told her that he not only understood, but he forgave her.

She felt her face burn a bright red as he turned back to the power strip and settled into his task, his small hand poised over the cabinet, ready to signal her if there was a problem.

She glanced at Daken who remained beside her, his face grim.

"I'm sorry, Daken," she murmured. "I'm going nuts here. This will never work, you won't fulfill your destiny, and now I've dragged a boy into this fiasco."

She felt Daken's hand, warm and comforting on her back, but his voice was no less hard despite the sweetness of his touch. "I came into this as an adult knowing the risks. There is no shame in that or in your failure." Daken paused, glancing sadly at Steve. "What you've done to the boy is between you and him."

Jane nodded. "Once this is over, I promise I'll make it up to him."

Daken squeezed her waist in a small proprietary gesture she hoped hadn't been noticed by their audience. "And you will not fail, Jane. It is your destiny."

She glanced back at him, surprised by his somber, almost reverent tone. "My destiny is to die a small-time computer hack and an old maid. With luck, maybe five people will attend my funeral, and that's counting my family. This," she gestured morosely at the small unit in front of her, "will be just another example of my ineptitude. When the men are separated from the boys,

I'm usually left to tend the outhouse."

He turned to her, his head cocked to one side. "But you are a woman. Not a man or a boy." His gaze slid down her figure as though he were trying to reassure himself what he said was indeed true.

His shocked expression was so comical that she surprised herself with a loud bark of laughter. "It's just an expression, Daken. And I'm being overly dramatic." She turned back to the computer, took a deep breath, and steeled herself for whatever was about to happen. "Come on. It's time to rock and roll."

"To what?"

She didn't even look at him, knowing she'd start laughing again. "Another expression. It means it's time to get started."

"Oh. I understand. It refers to hunting, maybe with a rock. And rolling as in evasion."

"Yeah, that's right, Daken. It's a real manly, hunter's expression."

She hid her smile as she turned on the unit.

She had power. Good.

Then with her nerves stretched taut, she slipped the boot disk into the drive. Working perfectly, the process was silent. The drive used a tiny beam of light to read the thin silver disk. But if anything went wrong, she'd hear either the catch and grind of the machinery, or worse yet, smell the disk burning as the light turned into a laser beam that could fry cement.

She waited, all her senses trained on the drive unit.

Nothing.

Even the audience held its breath.

Bang bang bangbang!!

Steve slammed his hand against the cabinet, the metallic twang slicing her nerves like a cheese grater.

She reacted immediately, popping out the disk with a quick flick of her wrist, but the smell, that horrible smell, told her it was too late.

The hot silver disk she held in her hands was no longer silver. It was brown and ugly around a burnt metal gash down one side of the disk.

It was ruined.

Her only boot disk was completely destroyed. As were all her hopes for Daken and the answers about her own home.

Completely destroyed.

She lifted her head, looking around for a cause, knowing that given the condition of the equipment, almost anything could have done it. She glanced at Steve who pointed to the strip, now showing a steady nine LEDs. He ran his finger along the strip, showing her that the power level dropped to almost zero then spiked up to nearly fifteen before settling down again.

Jane blinked. The power flow had fluctuated not from the computer equipment, but from the light source. As if the light outdoors had dimmed then spiked. She looked to the window. The fireball still burned as brightly and evenly as before. But there was a man by the window, a tall black-haired man in a dark robe. His head was lifted, his chin tight, and his dark brown eyes held the unmistakable glint of challenge.

"What did you do?" Jane stepped forward, the burnt disk still clutched in her hand. "What did you do?"

Daken tried to block her. "He cannot understand you—"

"I understand her perfectly."

"Fine," spat Jane. "Then answer the question. What did you do?"

Everyone in the room tensed. Steve held out a

restraining hand, but Jane shook it off, her body trembling with fury.

The man didn't move except to lift his chin a little higher so he could look down his strong Roman nose at her. "Do you know who I am?"

"I don't care if you're King of United Europe, I want to know what you did!"

"I am Kyree, Council Ruler of Wizards—"

"I don't give a damn." She crossed to the window, pointing to the fingerprints clearly revealed on the black panel. "Did you touch it? Maybe lifted it closer to the light?"

"It is my right to inspect all instruments of magic."

"Magic? It's a solar panel! Damn! Do you see what you did?" She waved the ruined disk in front of him. "Do you see? There's no other way into the computer. All of this," she made a sweeping gesture with her hand to indicate the building, the equipment, the elaborate prophesies handed down for generations. "Everything this building is and represents, all your people's hopes; everything is ruined! You've destroyed it all because you couldn't keep your stupid fingers where they belonged." She threw the disk at his face, watching it flash before his eyes before sliding to the dust on the floor.

"Perhaps," he said, his voice even, his tone condescending. "Perhaps you failed because you are not the true Keeper. And he," he glanced dismissively at Daken, "is the product of a mother's delirious ramblings."

"Look," she said, struggling to keep her voice from screeching out her hatred of the patronizing bureaucrat, "I can rebuild and rewire this entire computer with just a paperclip and a hairpin, but I can't make it go without that disk!"

"Then perhaps we should wait for someone who can."

"Why you obnoxious—"

You don't need the disk.

"—overstuffed—"

Jane. You don't need the disk.

"—preening vulture—"

Jane.

Finally the soft voice penetrated her anger, and she whirled around, anxious for another target. "And what would you know about it?" She squinted, barely making out a shadowy figure, barely discernable in the once bright room. It looked vaguely like a tall, pencil-thin man in a business suit standing beside the terminal. And oddest of all, the edges of his body seemed to shimmer with a faint electrical light.

"Who are you?"

You have power, equipment, and a working screen. You don't need the disk.

"Jane, who are you talking to?"

"Mr. Tall, Dark, and Shimmery. Right there."

She noticed Daken and the wizard Kyree scan the room, their gazes sliding right past the strange man, but the figure spoke again, drawing her attention.

The touch screen works. Bring up the monitor and use it to bypass the drives.

"Nice idea, but I don't know the security codes, and machine-level coding from a monitor was never my forte." Still, the thought lingered, and as her temper cooled, she began to think again. It didn't hurt that she'd finally found someone she could talk intelligently with about things she understood. True, the dark figure gave her the creeps, but at least he knew computers.

I can give you the codes. He stepped toward her. Or

rather, he seemed to glide toward her, bringing with him a chill that raised her hair on end.

She stepped back, nearly bumping into Kyree who swiftly scooted out of the way.

"Jane, there's no one there," said Daken from just off to her right. "Who are you talking to?"

"He's right there. Can't you see him?"

"No!"

The dark figure advanced further, its faint electrical charge crackling along her skin. Jane slipped back, coming flush with the wall. When she tried to slide away, the figure simply followed, slowly cornering her while her audience scrambled to get out of the way.

"Look," Jane said, her voice rising with fear. "Whoever you are—if you know the codes and can key in at machine level, be my guest. I was only here to help out anyway."

I can't do it. Only you can. And I've been waiting two centuries to help you.

He was right dead in front of her, the chill from his bizarre body seeping into her bones like dry ice freezing her body cell by cell. She was cramped into the corner, shrinking away from him in terror, but no matter how she moved he was there, stepping closer and closer.

"I don't care who or what you are. Just don't come any closer. Don't."

He reached out and pressed a palm into her shoulder. The gesture might have been reassuring except his touch was the icy cold of death. It ate into her like a chill wind, sliding between her muscles and creeping into her bones. Even the faint sizzle of energy she felt pop against her flesh didn't warm her.

She screamed. She vaguely saw Daken in front of her, bastard sword in hand as he sliced through the air, neatly cleaving the dark figure in two, in four.

But still the man came on, his body more and more indistinct, the crackle of energy louder in her ears as he insinuated himself into her very cells.

Her scream died in her throat, cut off as her larynx froze and the air in her lungs thickened to solid chunks.

✦   ✦   ✦

Jane stood on an indistinct gray plane. Before her rose the dark figure, much clearer now, his sad face lined with the weight of ages.

She looked around. There was nothing, she realized. Not even a featureless plane. From somewhere within her she realized the place was a fabrication of her mind. This whole landscape was a creation to give her standard reference points as she communicated with the dark figure. Her body hadn't moved from its corner in the Op's room. Daken, Steve, and the members of the audience were probably milling about her at this very moment.

But she didn't see any of them. She only saw this featureless place and the dark figure.

"You're in my head, aren't you? This isn't real. It's just so we can talk. Without distractions." Her voice quivered with fear, but she got the words out, and that was all that mattered to her right now.

"You were always bright, Jane."

"Is this real or not?"

"And impatient." A ghost of a smile flitted across his face.

"Who are you?"

"Don't you remember me? I didn't remember you at first." His voice grew abstracted, as though they

were chatting by a fire, and he about to launch into some tall tale or spooky ghost story. *"I don't remember much from before, but here with you now... It's all coming back to me. I remember you with startling clarity."*

Anger slowly replaced Jane's fear. Bit by bit, the icy terror left her limbs as her frustration grew. Ever since that night in the library, her world had spun out of control. And here, in front of her, was just another example of the weirdness that filled her life.

And she hated him for it.

"Damn it! I asked you a question!"

The figure looked hurt. She didn't know how she saw the expression. He seemed the same dark figure as before, but somehow the lighting shifted so his face became more distinct.

"You're getting closer to my mind, aren't you? You're moving deeper into me. That's why I can see you better."

"I'm not here to hurt you, Jane."

"Get out of my head!"

"You don't want me to do that."

"Of course, I do!" She clenched her hands into fists, wanting to punch him right in the nose. Around her, the gray landscape became red and hot as her blood boiled within her.

"You wanted answers. Answers to what has been happening to you. I'm here to give them to you."

"You're here to drive me insane."

He smiled and shook his head. *"You're not crazy. Just confused. I can answer your questions, but only if you'll let me."*

"Do I have a choice?"

"Of course, you do. You always do."

"Then I choose to go back home to my water bed and my rehydrator and have this whole strange nightmare over."

His smile became a little crooked. *"I said you always have choices. I didn't say they would include the one you want."*

Jane turned away, facing the uneven void of colors swirling around her. No longer red or gray, it seemed to shimmer with the conflicting emotions that churned within her.

"Just get it over with."

"Stop fighting me, Jane. Relax and let me talk to you."

"I'm afraid. I'm not sure I'll like the answers." Never in her life had she spoken truer words. She felt terrified, but not for her physical body. Whatever was happening to her body was secondary to what was going on in her mind. From the very beginning of this strange adventure, she'd had odd thoughts, stray inklings as something would seem familiar, but then again not.

It was bewildering and alarming.

She thought briefly of Daken. There were moments when she wasn't even sure he was real. But person or fantasy, right now she longed for his solid presence, his steady comfort.

"Daken is with you. You can't see him, but he is here, worried and frightened for you. If you look within your heart, you'll feel him."

Jane closed her eyes, trying to do as the figure said. It took a long time. She was keyed up, frightened that if she looked, really looked, she'd find herself in a mental ward surrounded by rubber walls. Or maybe worse, that she wasn't. That she was here, in this strange void, talking with a ghost and there was no going back.

Ghost?

She opened her eyes, and in that moment she found both Daken and Dr. Beavesly. The first in her heart. The other in her mind.

"Dr. Beavesly?" Pencil-pusher Beavesly? Her former boss in Boston was now a ghost? Her brain shut down and with it went her defenses. But even in that mind-numbing confusion, she felt a sense of peace and security. She felt Daken's hand clutching hers. She felt his steady concern and silent devotion.

He was here with her.

As was her former boss now turned ghost.

"Wow, this is some hallucination."

Dr. Beavesly stepped forward, his form clear to her now. She saw his thin frame, his rusty brown hair as neat as an eraser, and his long, almost pointy fingers. All the features that gave him his pencil nickname. She also saw his soft smile and an inner glow; the type an artist would draw to show an unearthly energy center. A way to say this man is different.

"Are you really a ghost? And you're talking to me in my mind?"

"I survived that first bomb. Many did."

Jane took a deep breath. "Bomb? Nuclear? I thought it was a horrendous explosion. But why?"

"It wasn't on purpose. Someone put up a faulty defense satellite that ended up firing because of some crossed circuits."

"You're kidding." It couldn't be possible. The entire disaster was because some technician somewhere put wire A into slot B?

"Of course," Dr. Beavesly continued, *"once one*

went off—"

"They all go off. And we obliterate ourselves. What stupidity."

"Agreed."

Jane sighed. She could hardly believe it, but it made such perverse sense. The world blown up because someone couldn't control their own technology.

"I realized immediately what had happened. I knew it like I knew my own name. Then I started running for my car. I had to get here, to the college, to save what I could. I must have had a heart attack. I remember my chest hurt, and I fell down, but then I got up again and kept running, not even realizing I'd died."

Jane listened to him, trying to watch the play of emotion on his strange face, but she couldn't. She watched the scene play in the background exactly as he described. She saw a flash of light as the bomb hit, felt the shockwaves roll through the landscape that appeared around her. She saw Dr. Beavesly run from his house to his car, but he never made it. He clutched his chest and fell, his breath coming in tortured gasps until it stopped completely. He died.

Then it was as if another Dr. Beavesly stepped out of his body. He was dressed as he would for work—a neat pin-striped suit, glasses, briefcase, and a serious expression, all as they should be for a professional, except he was running.

And run he did. Faster than a man could run, he sped on foot toward the college. The panorama around her followed him, rolling out beneath his feet as he practically flew to the University. He passed the library. It had a jagged hole torn through the center, as though space had ripped, dragging the brick and mortar apart like old, worn cotton.

"I was in there!"

She stepped forward, inspecting the debris of a building torn apart from inside. She couldn't touch the brick and mortar around her, but she knew these were the remains of the rip in space that had stolen her.

She twisted around to Dr. Beavesly. "But where did I go? Where am I?"

"Listen to the rest, Jane." He pointed to the image of himself, still running, heading for the building that housed the main computer. The building was still intact, though in the distance, she saw another bright flash of light. Another bomb detonating, this time further west.

Dr. Beavesly ran to the door and went through, not even noticing the door hadn't moved. Like a camera mounted directly behind him, Jane watched the panorama shift, following him down into the basement, around the narrow hallway, into the Op's office, then through a low metal doorway into the back main computer room.

It was dark. The emergency lighting flickered, casting his movements into a strange strobe effect. With the power so uncertain, there was nothing he could do. The mainframe had already crashed, and the Operator had already shut down everything.

Dr. Beavesly sat down next to the terrified, shivering boy. Charlie, she thought. His name was Charlie.

"Charlie died of radiation a week later. He went up top too soon looking for food. He never came back."

"What about you?"

"I was already dead, although I didn't realize it then. I just sat waiting for power, or news, or something. Mostly, I think I was waiting for you."

"Me?"

"You knew the system better than anyone, and I knew you'd find your way here eventually. You took your job seriously."

"You mean I had nothing else in my life other than my job," Jane said dryly.

"Yes."

Time sped up. Across the panorama, she saw dust settle on the equipment, cockroaches scurry around. But no people. And through it all, Dr. Beavesly tended the equipment, somehow keeping the room neat, the equipment as safe as possible.

"Where is everybody? Did they all die?"

"No. Part of the building collapsed above me. Only sections of the basement survived intact, though the solar collectors continued for years. I stayed there, devoting myself to the wires and chips and diodes. Eventually, I think I became a part of them."

As Jane watched, she saw his figure, slowly becoming part of the computer. He reached into machinery, checking power flow, rerouting software. Soon, his form became indistinct as he spent more and more time within the hardware.

"It took a long time before I ventured outside again. Time had little meaning to me, and I think it must have been years. Eventually, I left to explore the land, but I was too much part of the equipment I nurtured. I traveled along the telephone wires, old power lines, whatever I could find."

The view followed him, still neat and tidy in his pinstriped suit, pushing through the debris of a nine-story building, now collapsed in on itself. He traveled along old metal and exposed wires, occasionally dropping below ground before surfacing somewhere else.

Once outside, Jane had to restrain her gasp of horror.

The land was dead, scarred by radiation; filth and destruction everywhere she turned. The few people she saw were sick, their eyes feverish with hatred from the daily struggle to survive. They banded together in tiny knots of gangs, preying on one another like vermin.

Dr. Beavesly saw it all, but they never saw him.

"That's when I began to realize I was dead. It wasn't a clear thought. It would take even longer before it crystallized into a conscious possibility. Actually, I think only now, as I breathe and think and feel with you, do I really understand. I'm dead." He looked surprised. *"I'm really dead."*

The Dr. Beavesly in the landscape continued to walk, moving silently and swiftly through the world. There was snow everywhere. Snow and blood and filth. But time continued swiftly, sliding by her as the snow at first covered the sick and the dead alike, eventually melting to reveal a brown and dead land.

"Where are the people?" she asked. "Did they all die?"

"Most. But a few survived. Others changed."

"What do you mean—changed?"

He pointed and she saw a young man, dying from grotesque lesions covering his skin. He crawled to a dirty river that moved brown and sluggish through the mud. The man didn't make it there in time.

Just as with Dr. Beavesly, she saw the man fall, dropping to the ground to die, but his spirit continued to crawl, finally making it into the river.

"He joined with the river. He uses his energies, his spirit to cleanse the water and keep it alive."

Jane tensed, a sudden flash of insight making her shake. "That's the river I bathed in, the one Daken cleansed. That's—"

"That's the Old One who spoke to you. Yes."

Jane turned slowly, watching the images flow through her landscape. "Did everyone do that?"

"Many did, and they still live here today. Others found a different way."

This time, she saw a woman, weak from starvation, drop wearily beneath a twisted and sickly sapling. She wasn't on the verge of death, but she was gravely ill. She lay still beneath the sapling, and Jane began to think the woman had indeed died. But then there was a blurring. The images grew indistinct as though both tree and woman flowed together.

Time passed, and still the woman didn't move. The tree grew stronger, and the woman never died.

"She was the first dryad."

"A what?"

"Tree and woman, together. She kept her body, but she is part of the tree too. They both strengthen each other."

"That's not possible."

"Of course, it is. You forget, Jane, this land literally pulsed with radiation. It burned in the air, saturated the ground."

Looking up, Jane could almost see the heat hovering in the air, surrounding and filling everything. "Everything should have died."

"Died or changed."

"But—"

"The radiation is what the people today call the source of power. Magic."

"Magic!" Jane nearly laughed at the word. The life she understood was grounded in science, not fairy tales.

"People changed. They adapted, learning how to tap into all that radiation as a type of personal power."

"And that power let them—" She waved at the woman-tree. "Let them do that?"

"It was the only way to survive. And it worked. Some became dryads or other spirits of the earth. Some linked with animals becoming cat people, spider walkers, moles. The list goes on and on."

Jane shuddered and her mind balked at the types of creatures that could emerge. "All from radiation?"

"It was a combining of life forces. It was the only way to survive."

"And everyone did this?"

"Almost. A few, like the kings, changed their genetic code or mutated in other ways."

Her heart lodged in her throat and beat painfully fast. "The kings? Like Daken?"

"His ancestors were truly blessed. They became the healers."

"Doctors?"

"No. They actually thrive on radiation, drawing on it and their own energies to heal others."

"That's what he did to the river?" She had a vivid flash of Daken lying exhausted in a crystal clear river. "He draws on the radiation as an energy source—"

"And shapes it. That is his particular magic."

"And the other stuff. The language spell. How does that work?"

"Just as Daken can shape the radiation around him, others have learned to shape and control it in specific ways. Therefore, a world of magic." Scattered about her were people, some old, some young, accidentally discovering what she would call magic spells. A boy stares at a pile of sticks and suddenly they burst into flames. An old man desperate for a way across a ravine shapes with his hands what looks like a glowing

energy wave. Like a surfer, he rides it across the chasm. A mother uses a glowing needle and thread to stitch closed a hole in a pair of socks.

Jane felt the first workings of awe seep through her system. "It's an ability to shape and use the radiation. Wow."

Dr. Beavesly turned, and they both watched as the land slowly recovered, becoming lush and green again. *"Wow,"* he agreed softly.

A thought tugged at Jane as the concepts began to take root. "But the radiation is dissipating, right? I mean, eventually it will fade away."

"Not completely, but yes. Each generation struggles to accomplish what their parents did."

"Then Daken's children—"

"Will have to work twice as hard to accomplish half as much."

"They've got to do the work now, then. While they still can." Even in the midst of the beauty that continued to flow past them, Jane saw the scars. She saw the ugly and the evil, the festering wounds of the land that time hadn't yet erased. "How long has it been?"

"Over two hundred years."

"And you've been here all this time? Why?"

He smiled, and Jane suddenly noticed that his face glowed. His slight aura of light was now a bright light burning through him. She could still see his face and form, but it only barely contained the radiance within him.

"Dr. Beavesly?"

"I told you, Jane. I've been waiting for you."

"For me?"

"Even from the beginning, I don't know how, but I knew I had to wait for you. I knew you were coming."

"What?" Jane tried to read his expression, but the light within him grew even brighter, making him harder and harder to look at.

"I've saved this equipment, saved all this knowledge for you. It's your job now to bring it to the people."

"But how did I . . ." She swallowed. "How can I . . ."

Suddenly it all came crashing in on her. What moments ago had been an intellectual exercise, a man relating a story to her, became suddenly clear. Finally she linked it together with her own life.

She hadn't been transported in space to another world. She'd been transported in time. To Earth's future where a ghost had merged with a computer, saving the knowledge of her world so she could pass it on.

"This is Earth," she breathed, still caught up in the shock.

It all made sense. That's why there were names for elves and dwarves and dragons. The words were there in English so when someone merged with a tree, the name "dryad" was already in the language. If someone joined with a lizard, the root was there for "dragon".

She pressed her hands to her temples, her fingers shaking as she tried to hold off a headache. "I can't go home," she moaned. "There is no home left."

"You are home, Jane. Two hundred years in the future."

"But my job, my friends, my family." She nearly choked on the panic.

"They've been dead for two hundred years."

She looked around the gray landscape, the black swirls of horror already creeping across the horizon. "But I don't want to be here. I don't want to do this. I'm not some white knight who can save the world."

"It's already done, Jane. You're the only one there is."

"But I don't even understand this world. I'm not trained in sociology or politics. I don't even speak the language."

"You will. I can pass you my memories of the last two hundred years. You will know all I've seen and heard. You'll even speak the languages of the people and the high court."

"No!" Jane reached out to clutch him, but his body was so blindingly bright she couldn't see to get close. And that only made her more frightened. "You know this stuff," she cried. "You do it!"

"I can't. I'm already dead." His voice was like a whisper in her head. A soft, soothing sound, useless against the clamor of fear in her heart. *"You can do it, Jane. God has chosen you."*

"God? God! How can you speak of God after all this?" With a sweep of her hand, she brought back the first horrifying images of nuclear holocaust—the diseased children, the violent gangs, all the festering evil that man can create.

"That was man's work. God gave us free will. That means He can't stop us from evil, but He will help us work toward good."

"No!" she sobbed, pleading with the man who was now a glowing brilliance that both surrounded and suffused her. "Please," she begged. "Not me. I don't know what to do."

"It's already been done."

Then there were no more sounds, no more words, only light burning within her. It was Dr. Beavesly's last benediction, the blessings of a ghost, dead two hundred years.

After the light receded from her mind, Jane remained. She sat cramped in a corner of the old Op's office, seeing the room now as the remnants of the computer center she'd worked in before the holocaust that destroyed her world.

She took a shuddering breath then closed her eyes, not wanting to see anything, do anything, or even think anything. The only sound was the coarse echo of her ragged breathing.

But she couldn't stop herself from knowing. Dr. Beavesly had given her two hundred years of memories. Like a drawer in her mind, a file she could access at will, she held the lifeless images absorbed by Dr. Beavesly as he watched the Earth's people recover from a holocaust.

She now knew the truth.

And she hated it.

Chapter Seven

◆　　◆　　◆

It took a long time before Jane opened her eyes. She wanted to become comfortable, or at least less resentful, of the extra information in her mind. Dr. Beavesly's memories weren't exactly an intrusion as much as an added weight she had to absorb. And she didn't think she could do that and deal with anything new at the same time.

So she kept her eyes closed. She dropped her head back against the wall and steadied her breathing. She reached for and found Daken's hand, clutching it, needing his silent reassurance as she sat, trying to get comfortable with her own mind.

Finally, she opened her eyes.

The room was dark, empty of all but three other people. Daken she knew, so she focused on the other two. One appeared a young man with wavy, long brown hair, dark green eyes, and ears that curved into a clear point. He wore a simple white tunic over his willowy form and dark skin.

Unbidden, Dr. Beavesly's memories pressed forward, and she spoke the thoughts aloud as if reading them off a screen.

"I see a ten-year old boy climbing a crumbling wall

while your mother screams for you to come down."

Across from her, the man didn't move, but he was alert, his eyes bright and dark. "What else do you see?" he asked.

She paged through her new information, shifting through images like a woman flipping through diskettes until she found the right one.

"I see a man struggling to harness an energy he doesn't understand. Your hands glow as you try to press it into a ball, but it doesn't work. The energy dissipates and your hands are badly burned. A healer," she glanced over at Daken, "I mean, a king heals you. It took another seven years before you mastered it."

The man nodded though his hands curled slightly inward as though in remembered pain.

Jane looked at him, summarizing as she finally placed him in her own memories. "You are Ginsen, the Elven Lord, bound with the ivy that grows on these buildings. Your lifespan has been extended by hundreds of years and so you are doomed..." She cut off her words, horrified by what she'd just learned from Dr. Beavesly's memories.

But Ginsen finished for her, completing her sentence in a voice both mellow and hushed. "Doomed to be the first born and last to die of my line. I will watch my children and their children's children pass on before me."

"I'm sorry." What did you say to a man who would see all he loved most die before him?

"There are worse fates."

Jane turned her attention to the second figure, the dark man in the dark robe who had angered her so much earlier. Again, paging through the information left to her, she came upon a strange image.

"I see a small boy, age three, with straggly hair and an innocent smile. The power runs like water through his hands and he plays with it, throwing it like a ball against walls and trees. His parents are terrified. His neighbors," she stopped, her breath catching at the image, but the memory wouldn't stop and so she kept speaking. "His neighbors brand him the devil's child. They kill his parents, burn his lands, and cast him into...a pit. No, it's an old warehouse. He's left there to die."

Her heart went out to the child, as apparently did Dr. Beavesly's. The ghost waited until dark, then pushed an old power line into the pit so the boy could climb out. He then walked with the child until they found a poor farmer who was all too grateful for an extra pair of hands. But before leaving, Dr. Beavesly whispered Ginsen's name. "Find the Elven Lord," he said. "He will accept you."

The memories shifted, focusing on someone else, so Jane pushed it away, looking again at the dark, handsome man before her. Kyree smiled coldly, spreading his arms, his palms turned up. "As you can see, I didn't die."

"No," she said, carefully finding the next image of him. "You came before the Elven Lord as an adolescent, already powerful and seeking more power." The young man she saw in her memory stood proud and haughty before the Ginsen, daring him with word and stance to deny the knowledge he sought. "You have been here for nearly twenty years, learning and gaining in power. You are now considered the most powerful wizard alive."

"And I have only just begun to learn." His voice was quiet in the still room, but she heard the steely determination beneath his calm exterior.

The silence descended again. The men didn't move, waiting for her, but Jane was busy containing the memories surfacing within her mind like the overflow from a cauldron. She had to learn how to close the lid on her thoughts.

"And what of me?" Daken's gentle tones filtered through her thoughts. "What do you see when you look at me?"

Jane turned to Daken, struggling once again with her memories. Dr. Beavesly hadn't traveled to his lands often. She saw his mother, pregnant with him, his older brother running about her feet. Then years later, she saw him as a shocked young man grieving alone at night by her grave. The rest was a confused wash of images running too fast through her mind. Eventually, she stopped trying.

She looked back at Daken, his angular face drawn tight with strain, his dark blue eyes pinched by lines of fatigue. "I see the man who saved my life. A man who has now fulfilled his mother's prophesy and can take his seat on the Council."

She saw Daken's jaw clench and his hands tighten almost imperceptibly on the hilt of the sword. To the others, it probably seemed as though he hadn't moved, but Jane knew he fought an internal war. His one harsh word betrayed the intensity of his emotions.

"No!" The word nearly exploded out of him, and Jane was surprised by the hatred briefly flashing across his face.

"Daken?"

"You are the Keeper of the Knowledge. You will take the Council seat." His words were abrupt, almost brutal, though he tried to soften his tone.

"No!" The word was harsh in her throat, but it was as vehement as when she screamed it to the fading image of Dr. Beavesly. Suddenly all the words, all the images and thoughts and fears became too much for her. She rebelled at everything she had learned, denied its possibility, denied even the information of her senses.

And the resulting confusion led to anger.

"No, Daken. I don't belong here. I already told you that. I don't want to be on the Council, I don't want to be your Keeper of Knowledge, I don't want any of this. All I want is to go home!" She heard how childish she sounded as the words echoed back to her in the chamber. She felt like a two-year old throwing a fit in front of the President of the United States.

But all she could think of, the thought that haunted her as she glared at the startled men around her, was that her mother was dead. Her beautiful mother with the wispy gray hair and the rich chocolate-colored eyes. Her mother who worked two jobs to put her miscreant daughter through school. The one who kissed both of Jane's eyelids and told her how proud she was even after Jane failed her doctorate orals. The woman who finally retired to Florida for a well-deserved life filled with bridge and golfing. That woman was dead.

And had been for over two hundred years.

Suddenly Jane was screaming, running blindly from a knowledge and a reality too harsh to bear. Her mother's image followed her as Jane tore from the room, stumbling through the courtyard until she finally fell face first in a long grassy plain.

Her mother was dead.

✦   ✦   ✦

She didn't know how long she lay there. The ground was damp from her tears, the grass cold, and the world filled with the utter blackness of a night unpolluted by electrical lights. Pressed against her back, she felt a long, warm body. Slowly turning her head, she recognized the panther resting beside her. The cat wasn't asleep. She lay on the grass, her black eyes alert, her ears pricked for sounds, as though she guarded Jane.

She heard what she supposed were all the usual night sounds for the country. An owl hooted in the distance. Something made a cricket-like chirp from a huge weeping willow, and from a nearby stream came the steady drone of a cicada, except Dr. Beavesly's memories told her it was made by an eel-like fish floating on the water's surface.

Jane sighed and dropped her head back down. Even in her grief, she couldn't cut away the relentless presence of alien thoughts in her mind, but she couldn't accept it either. If she did, then she would have to accept that her world was gone, her friends long since dead, and her parents, her brother, and most especially, her mother, all died probably a violent, horrible death.

She wanted to cry again, wanted to bury herself in the numbing relief of blind grief. But her eyes were dry, her face swollen, and her arms numb from being twisted beneath her. She pushed herself upright, flexing her hands as she tried to bring the feeling back.

"Are you ready to go back now?"

Jane looked up sharply, squinting in the darkness. Daken sat nearby, hidden by the draping canopy of the weeping willow. His body was a vague shadow hidden within deeper shadows. All she could really see were his eyes; bright pinpoints surrounded by gold watching her from his hiding place beneath the tree.

"Go away, Daken." Her voice was thick and coarse, and she swallowed to try and force it into some semblance of normalcy.

"Are you ready to go back now?"

"I'm not going anywhere. I'm not doing anything. I'm just going to sit here until God sends me back home."

"You are home."

"Shut up! Just shut up!" She dropped her head onto her fists, fighting a dizzying, pounding, spinning sensation in her head, and a radiating anguish that tore through her whole body. "Give me a break here, Daken." Her voice broke, making her sound as defeated as she felt. "I'm mourning my entire world."

"And how will you honor their deaths?"

Jane lifted her head, her words a bitter counterpoint to his soft tones. "You don't honor death, Daken. You hate it, you fight against it. You eat right and exercise so you'll never die. And when it comes anyway, you don't go willingly, and you certainly don't thank it when it takes the ones you love."

He was silent as she railed at him. He waited patiently until she'd exhausted herself back into a sullen despair. Then he spoke, his words drifting by, sliding through the heavy boughs of the tree, flowing around her on the gentle night breeze. They surrounded her in the darkness, gently eroding her pain as a stream washes away filth.

"I cried when my parents died. We didn't have their bodies, only the crushed and bloodied remains of their horses. So we buried my mother's favorite scarf and my father's walking stick. It looked ridiculous putting such small things in full-sized coffins, but we did it, and I cried.

"The next day I returned to the harvest. It was the only time of year when I really worked, and clearly saw the connection between labor and my dinner.

"Then a few months later, my brother was taken too, and I was left with a bitter grandmother and three hundred starving people still in the grip of a cruel winter. Still I did nothing. I was grieving. And I was lazy."

He stopped speaking, the words cut off as he stared into the darkness. Jane found herself straining for the sound of his breathing, wondering when his voice would weave its spell around her again.

It took a very long time.

"There isn't a day I don't think of my parents and my brother. There isn't a moment I don't mourn for their passing. So I honor them by fighting to preserve what they once held dear."

Jane struggled with his words, trying to follow the story as he told it. But something was missing. Something changed him from the empty wastrel he was, to the man with her now—a man filled with courage and determination, a man she loved despite the callous way he described himself.

"What happened?" she asked softly. "What changed you into who you are now?"

His laugh was brief and harsh, filled with a bitter self-mockery. "Nothing happened. I'm still the blundering fool I was then."

Jane didn't answer. She waited, knowing in time he would tell her the rest. Eventually his words came to her, the sounds uneasy, as though he struggled with thoughts he rarely expressed.

"There was a girl from the village. She was sick. So sick I could have poured all that I was and more into her, and still she would have died. I treated her for days, balancing my exhaustion against the planting, pushing both her and myself into sick shades of ourselves."

He stopped, and she knew he railed at himself for his failure. It was an impossible silence, filled with anguish and regret. She gathered all her love into her eyes and offered it to him as she crawled through the boughs to settle beside him. She didn't question the sudden knowledge that she loved him. She only knew that she did, and so she silently presented it to him, knowing he wouldn't take it, couldn't take it until his story was finished.

The panther, too, must have felt the same way as she silently slipped around the tree to settle on his other side. Moving like a shadow, nearly indistinguishable from the night, the panther gave her presence to the king.

Still the silence twisted between them like a living thing contorted into misery.

"Did the girl die?" Jane finally asked. Her voice was low and tentative, but it was enough to push him into speech again.

"After the burial, her father came to me. It is customary to thank the healer at the grave site."

"He didn't thank you?"

"He said, 'You're a poor healer and a worse king, but you are all we have. And so for that, I thank you.'"

Jane gasped, horrified by the pain those words must have inflicted. "Oh, Daken—" she began, but he cut her off, continuing in the same monotone with which he'd begun.

"He was right."

Jane reached forward, touching his arm as she searched for the right thing to say. "You're a great healer. And you're a good king. I knew that the moment I met you."

He turned to her, his expression intense, burning into her through the darkness. "I'm not the healer my father was, or even as good as my brother. I'm not the Keeper of the Knowledge as my mother predicted, and I'm not going to have a seat on the Council. But I'm all my people have. I have strong arms and skill with the weapons the Elven Lord abhors. With them, I will fight to preserve all my forefathers built. I may not be able to improve on it, but I will give all I have to preserve it."

"Daken, you can't—"

He cut off her words, suddenly grabbing her arm and holding her beside him as he pleaded his case. "You can help me honor my dead. As the Keeper, you can convince the Council to help me. My people and I will fight, but we need spells. The fireball and the weapon spells. And guns. As Keeper, you must know how to make guns. With those we'll be unstoppable. I can destroy the Tarveen once and for all."

Jane stared at him, her knotted stomach pushing against her throat as she struggled to contain her horror. Daken wanted guns. He wanted her to unleash modern weaponry on a world still fighting to recover from near annihilation.

He wanted her to help him start a war.

She pushed away from him, standing until her head knocked against the peaceful canopy of the willow tree.

"They won't put you on the Council?" She kept her voice level as she stared outward into the black night.

"The Seat is for the Keeper. I am King of Chigan."

"And as King, you will petition the Council for weapons and spells?"

"Your vote could sway them in my favor." He joined her, standing right behind her as he pressed for her help.

"I'm just one confused woman against—"

"A four-man Council." He stroked her arms, pulling her backwards into his embrace. "You can be very persuasive, Jane. You can convince them."

Jane stilled his hands, holding them tightly against her arms, preventing him from continuing his distracting caress.

"Daken," she began cautiously. "Have you tried negotiating with the Tarveen? Maybe they're starving too. If you set up a trade arrangement, land agreements—"

"There is no negotiating with the Tarveen." Daken nearly spit out the name, and his hands gripped her so tightly she knew she'd have bruises.

"But to start a war—"

"*Venzi,* Jane!" He shoved her away and began to pace, but with the low hanging boughs, the panther, and the two of them, there was little room left for his agitated movements. In the end, the cat moved out from under the canopy while Jane shrunk against the tree trunk. Even then, Daken seemed to fill the peaceful confines with his hatred.

"Sometimes war is the only way," he said. "The Tarveen are vicious monsters bent on destroying my people and taking my lands. They must be killed!"

Jane pressed backward, half hating and half thankful for the hard trunk preventing her from retreating further. "What if the Council turns you down?"

"You must see that they don't."

"But what if I can't? What will you do then?"

He glared at her, his eyes smoldering like blue fire, his body poised like a raised weapon. "Then I will find another way."

"To fight?"

"We can't fight." He resumed his pacing. "Not without weapons and spells. It would be suicide."

"Then you'd negotiate?" She couldn't contain the hopeful note in her voice.

"No." The word was a low growl, feral and menacing in the darkness. "There will be no negotiating."

"Then what—"

"Poison. Or other spells. They are slower and less reliable than a war, but I will find a way."

Jane swallowed, her fear churning like acid in her stomach. She'd only once seen someone so consumed with hatred, so eager to kill. Only once, and even then it had been through the protective shield of a video screen.

There was little to compare that man and Daken. Daken was tall and muscular, his body at its prime, his strength vibrating through every pore. The other man had been older, his body shriveled and mean, as though he had been eaten away by his maniacal zeal. But nothing could hide the driving hatred raging within both men.

Daken was King of Chigan fighting what he believed was a just war. The other had been sovereign of an empire. And he had irresponsibly launched a dozen satellites he did not understand and could not control.

Jane swallowed, turning away from the man she saw and the man she remembered, focusing on the distant buildings silhouetted against the purple hues of dawn. "I'm ready to go back now."

"You're ready to be the Keeper? You'll take a Council seat?" He made no attempt to hide the hope in his voice.

Jane nodded, her heart sick.

"And you'll help me?"

"Yes." The word fell from her lips to land like a stone against her chest. She had found a way to honor her dead. She would take her position of power in this new world. She would use her knowledge to preserve all her forefathers held dear. She would use her abilities for good.

And in doing so, she would actively destroy the man she loved because she would never, ever help Daken start a war.

Chapter Eight

◆　◆　◆

They walked back in silence, the panther disappearing into the shadows as they neared the University. Looking at the grounds before her, Jane felt stupid for not making the connection before. The Elven Lord's "palace" was clearly built on the remains of her old campus. It made sense, especially since he dedicated himself and his "courtiers" to the pursuit of knowledge. The only difference now was in the curriculum. The study of "magic" supplanted engineering as the primary focus.

Ginsen met them outside the computer center, his young face impassive, his voice as soothing and as impersonal as a spring rain. "You will want to rest now, Librarian. There will be a celebratory dinner, but for now, let me show you to your room."

Jane stopped, reviewing his words to see if she'd misheard him. "What did you call me?"

"Librarian. It is another term of honor, synonymous with the Keeper. I thought it might be less..." he paused, clearly searching for a polite phrasing.

"Less traumatic for me?"

He smiled. "Yes."

"It's not. Not unless you expect me to wear a tight

bun and big, horn-rimmed glasses."

"I'm sorry, my knowledge of the Old Tongue is not—"

"Your English is fine, Ginsen. I just made a rather rude joke that wasn't true even in my grandmother's day."

"Is there a better title for you then?"

Jane twisted her foot beneath her. Her only title, other than computer nerd and doctoral candidate, had been Computer Technician, and she hadn't liked that even when it applied.

"How about Comic?" offered Daken. "The clothing she wears is a symbol of those great people."

Jane groaned, imagining people bowing to her saying things like, "We're honored to meet you, Comic Jane."

"How about Oracle?" she finally said, choosing her heroine's alternate ego. It was sufficiently ponderous to remind her of the position she'd now adopted without throwing her completely over into the ridiculous.

"Very well, Oracle," agreed Ginsen with a slight bow.

She winced, unaccustomed to the heavy respect with which he imbued her new title. "Please, call me Jane. Unless you want me to constantly refer to you as the Elven Lord."

Again Ginsen gave her a slight bow, his hairless face sliding into a soft smile. "Very well, Jane. Your rooms are this way, unless you'd like to eat first."

Jane shook her head. "No. Right now all I want to do is sleep." Even if she couldn't actually hide from this new world, a good eight hours of oblivion was close enough.

Ginsen led the way, gliding quickly and silently through the campus. Jane trailed behind him, doing her best not to be uncomfortable when people stopped and bowed to her, some so deep their foreheads bumped their knees. She glanced at Daken only to see that he looked nearly as out of place as she felt.

With his warrior's step and bastard sword strapped to his back, he seemed to tower over the willowy academicians who populated the University. It was only now, studying him as he walked beside her, that she began to absorb the dynamics of this new Earth.

Looking at Daken, no one could ever miss his hardened frame, corded muscles, and military bearing. Whatever else he was, Daken was a warrior, born and bred on a frontier community where violence was a way of life. He and his people together provided the security that gave the softer, more vulnerable ones the luxury to study.

Watching him now, he looked like a wolf temporarily running tame among the sheep. It struck her as almost funny that he came here, to the seemingly weaker ones, to beg for the weapons of war. But even as she noted the irony of it, it struck a resounding chord within her. It felt proper and correct that the intelligentsia would govern the warriors, that the academics would rule the more violent factions of the world.

But looking at Daken's set face, she realized he clearly thought it an aberration, tolerated only because he hadn't the strength to change it.

Ginsen interrupted her musings, taking her into a large two-story building just off the main campus. "This is where the permanent members of my staff live."

Senior faculty, she translated to herself.

"Your place is here." He opened the door to a richly furnished two-room suite twice the size of her former apartment in Boston. "Is this acceptable? In addition to this, you will naturally have exclusive domain over the House of Prophesy."

Jane stumbled over his heavy reference to a simple computer center. Her chest felt squeezed by an enormous fist, the pressure tightening as the enormity of her responsibilities began to sink in. "This will be fine," she managed to force out.

Ginsen gave his short bow again. "I will leave you to rest. Someone will come for you before dinner."

Jane barely noticed. She was still trying to think above the buzzing in her head. She'd had anxiety attacks before and recognized her symptoms for what they were, but that didn't alleviate the panic slowly building within her.

It wasn't until she realized Daken was leaving with Ginsen that she was able to break from her near trance.

"Wait!" She grabbed Daken's arm, trying to draw him back into the room. "Aren't you staying here? With me?" She hated the weakness coloring her voice, but Daken was her most familiar, most welcome touchstone in a rapidly changing world. She was suddenly very frightened of losing him.

Daken didn't respond, and his face remained as hard as carved granite. Finally, Ginsen stepped into the silence. "The Chigan King will have his own room in the temporary dormitory across the courtyard. Unless," he paused for emphasis, "you have a relationship of which I am not yet aware."

Jane swallowed, slowly loosening her grip on Daken. Did they have a relationship? One she wanted to make public? Twelve hours ago, she was ready to become his lover, and she didn't give a damn who knew. She was a stranger, visiting this odd world until she could find a way back to her own.

But now everything was different. She was the Oracle, and he was a King petitioning for her political support. As much as she wanted to deny their changed status, one look at Daken's bland expression told her he was very aware of their new relationship. Openly becoming lovers was a daunting complication to an already complex situation.

Jane bit her lip while the silence seemed to thin the very air she breathed. Then Daken cut into the mounting tension like a stiletto piercing her heart.

"No, Lord," said Daken, grimly pulling his arm out of her grip. "The Oracle and I were merely traveling companions." His voice was flat and implacable, as were his steps when he walked away.

It was another ten minutes before she let her door close with a heavy thud. Moments after that, she fell onto her bed, curling in the fetal position as she let the pain and anxiety wash unheeded through her.

For the first time since coming to this bizarre world, she would have to make her way alone.

✦   ✦   ✦

She awoke to the gathering gloom of early evening. There was no light in her room and no way for her to turn one on. Before, there had always been a campfire or a lantern, and Daken had tended those. So she lay on her bed and let her thoughts wander.

As always, they turned to Daken and a now familiar pain curled in her chest.

When had she fallen in love with him? Had it started that first morning when he brought her back to life by painful inches? Or had it been when they laughed so freely while bouncing painfully on the buckboard. Or maybe it was in the inn when he kissed her with such passion?

It didn't matter. She had fallen for him hard. And now, when she finally realized the truth, she couldn't bring herself to act on it. In fact, she'd already decided to act against it and him.

Jane sighed, feeling the large expanse of her cold bed. They hadn't even had their one night of ecstacy.

But how could she tell a man she loved him, bed him with passion and honesty, and then turn around and dedicate herself to thwarting the main goal in his life?

He wanted to start a war. She wanted just as passionately for him to resolve his conflict peaceably. The last thing she would ever do was give him the weapons he wanted or support his cause to the Council.

In his eyes, that would be the ultimate betrayal. In her eyes, it was the only reason she had to continue living. She would not allow this new Earth to descend into bloody war.

Impasse. And in the face of such diametrically opposed goals, how could she still ache for his touch and long for the sweet delight of his kiss?

◆　　◆　　◆

Daken's muscles burned and the hilt of his sword grew slick from the sweat on his hands, but still he fought, swinging his weapon in tight circles and thrusts, parrying and stabbing with vicious determination.

There were no enemies in his room except his own private demons. He sparred with the air, but it was the only way he knew to defeat the emotions seething within him.

He had already picked her for his wife and queen. He had planned to seduce her last night, binding her to him in every physical way possible while his words of love snared her heart. It was as good as done, and she was willing in every way.

But now she was the Keeper, and he was still the failed son of a king. He had no wife, no fulfilled prophesy, and not even a release from the lust that had burned in his blood from the first moment he'd seen her, half frozen in the meadow.

He'd hoped for a moment. When the Elven Lord asked if they had a special relationship, he'd waited. She knew he wanted to marry her. Her excuse was gone. She no longer could pretend she belonged somewhere else. As the Keeper, her home was here, in this land. True, they'd probably have to live apart as she would be in Bosuny while he returned home to his war, but that was a minor detail. The advantages of having the Keeper as his wife far outweighed the frustration his body would feel at the long separation.

Of course, none of that happened. She threw away her chance to declare before the Lord that she would be his wife. She remained stubbornly silent, clinging to her strange, separate ways even as she clung to his arm.

Which left Daken with nothing except her vague promise to help him.

Daken swung his sword in a vicious cut to the right, arcing the sword back so fast he nearly lost his grip and his hands cramped with the effort.

So be it, he thought grimly. He would accept Jane's new status. He would play the courtier and sycophant, begging for the weapons he needed for his people's survival. So long as she succeeded in the end. She must convince the Council to give him what he wanted.

Hell in all its fury would not match his anger if she failed him.

✦   ✦   ✦

They came for her before she was ready, but then again, Jane probably wouldn't have felt ready for another few years.

She hadn't lounged in bed for long. Stewing over Daken wouldn't serve any purpose. Impatient with her own thoughts, she roused herself, using the fading light to inspect her environment. Her rooms were useful, comfortable, and rather dull. One bedroom. One sitting room. And both needed a few prints to liven them up.

Once she'd exhausted the confines of her room, she stepped into the hallway. Propping open her door in case it locked behind her, she went to explore the four other doors on this top floor. As expected, three were locked. The fourth was a delight that thrilled her down to her toes.

She'd found a bathroom. It was surprisingly modern with running water, a toilet, and a bathtub. No shower, but she wasn't picky. Hastily stripping off her clothes and mumbling apologizes to anyone who might "live" in the water, she dropped into a lukewarm bath and felt like she'd slipped into heaven. There was soap to one side, and she used it all over, including her hair. Ten minutes later she felt almost clean.

Mindful of the time, she ran another bath and did her best to clean her costume. She wondered briefly when she could retrieve her new clothes still at the inn while congratulating herself that she'd made her outfit out of quick-dry Lycrasheen. Her orange hightops were less easily fixed, but that was too bad. It was best if everyone accepted from the start that she was less than perfect.

It was the right attitude to adopt, especially given that a man suddenly appeared to escort her to dinner while she sat hunched over the tub trying to scrape mud off her sneakers. Her hair was still spiky wet and her clothes were damp in all the wrong places. It was a mortifying position from which to meet a slim man with soft feather-like hair and delightfully sharp eyes. He was clearly kin to some bird, but rather than detracting, it seemed to enhance his features. She found him rather handsome in a delicate sort of way.

Which made the situation all the more embarrassing.

She was stammering out an apology when she remembered. She was the Keeper, the new hot star. No longer some peon computer tech, she was the big guns, the prophesied one. And more than that, she had an important job to do—keeping mankind on a peaceful, non-violent tract. So if she wanted to sit half-wet in a bathroom, scraping mud off neon orange high tops before a big presentation dinner, then she damn well would do it.

Giving the man her most brilliant smile, Jane lifted a finger to tell him she'd be a moment longer, then regally shut the bathroom door.

She didn't reopen it until she'd brushed back her hair and put on her shoes. There was nothing she could do about being still damp, but she knew her clothes would dry soon enough.

The man was still there, his expression calm, his attitude one of respectful patience. Almost without conscious thought, she flipped through Dr. Beavesly's memories to try and place him. She saw him first arriving as a nervous twenty year old, literally hopping from foot to foot as he introduced himself to the Elven Lord and begged permission to study magical flight.

That was all she needed. Smiling again, she pointed to him. "You're Dinal, right? Dinal?"

He bowed. "I am honored to greet you, Oracle." He spoke not in English, but in Common, and Jane was delighted to find she understood his words. Although it took an extra step, Dr. Beavesly's memories easily provided translations for her. It was an enormous relief to know she would be able to speak with the people around her and not be chained to Daken as her interpreter.

She fumbled through Dr. Beavesly's memories for the appropriate formal response. "Your greetings are a kindness, Mage Dinal, and I thank you." The words were stilted, spoken in a halting, stuttering way, but he seemed to understand her.

"If you will follow me, I will take you to dinner."

She nodded, appreciating the fact that he spoke slowly, giving time to translate each word. She hoped it would get easier with time.

As she expected, dinner was in the large cafeteria. What she hadn't expected were the glittering masses of people crammed into the large room all staring at her. If it hadn't been for her determination to live up to her new status, she would have turned tail and run. As it was, she hastily scanned the room, searching for one large, masculine body.

Daken. It seemed like ages before she saw him. He was seated just to the left of the head table, his dark hair and large frame making him stand out like a bull in a china shop. Still, he looked very regal, his expression polite but cold, his distancing mask firmly in place.

She wanted to go straight to him if only to be near him when she faced this excited throng of people, but Dinal lead her to the empty seat in the center of the head table. On her right sat Ginsen and beside him, Kyree. On her left was a short, stocky dwarf with golden eyes, and beside him an elegantly plumed man with bright yellow hair and a pointy face. Another bird-man.

She nodded to them all, Dr. Beavesly's memories telling her they were the members of the Council.

The evening went the way of all formal dinners. Ginsen gave introductory comments before a nourishing but rather bland meal was served. She spoke politely, if a bit awkwardly, with the dwarf Silm sitting next to her, who was eager to learn of her land and time. Not seeing any reason to lie, she spoke honestly.

"Mine was a violent home where people forgot how to live peaceably together. Their paranoia caused them to decimate the planet, but for some odd reason, I was saved, brought forward to now to see that such horrors are not repeated."

It was a clear statement of purpose, and she was gratified to see he approved.

"Very appropriate, Oracle. Very learned." He almost sounded surprised.

Later Ginsen caught her eye and expressed his own pleasure with her goals. "I have been speaking with Silm, Oracle. We are pleased that your feelings so closely match our own."

Jane nodded, her gaze wandering as she searched for Daken. Fortunately, he wasn't with them to hear her non-violent platform. He would undoubtedly learn of it soon, but for now, she had enough to deal with.

The polite chit-chat and eager questions continued to absorb her attention, but even so, Jane was never more aware of Daken. All through the meal, she could feel his eyes on her. Whenever she glanced his way, he was staring at her, his eyes steady and cold. It felt as if he were judging her. That tonight was some sort of test which she was probably failing.

Like a dark figure of violence, he lurked always nearby, a constant reminder that no matter what she did, no matter who these people thought she was, he knew the truth. He knew she was a fool from a violent past that could no more lead the world into a peace than a starfish could become a star.

It wasn't until much later, after they adjourned to the central courtyard that she displaced Daken's disturbing presence in her thoughts. And then, he was replaced by something even worse.

She had become quite adept at retrieving bits of information from Dr. Beavesly's memories. He had spent a lot of time in the capitol city, and so there was some bit of information on everyone. Images came to her naturally, usually short scenes, occasionally just a flash or a picture, but always associated with whichever person she greeted at that moment.

She had been smiling at an elderly matron whose eyes were weak from age, when Jane chanced to look up and catch sight of a thick, powerful man strolling across the grounds. He had one arm draped in a fatherly gesture across Steve's shoulders. An image flashed in her mind like lightning, brilliantly illuminated, then gone. She grabbed at it, startled because of the violence of the emotion associated with the memory. Dr. Beavesly's thoughts were usually cold, empty information, rarely colored by any interpretation or feeling.

But this memory was filled with anger and frustration at a ghost's inadequacies.

Still not quite understanding, Jane excused herself from the matron and slowly worked her way through the crowd as she followed the man and Steve.

It wasn't until they neared the computer center that she grabbed hold of the memory and saw it in its entirety. Then once she'd caught it, other images flooded past her, inundating her with its horror. By the time she got close enough, she was shaking with rage.

"Just a minute!" Her voice quivered with suppressed anger. Nearby people quieted, turning at the urgency in her voice. It was that lull in conversation that finally caught the man's attention.

She wasted no time, quickly closing the distance between them. She reached out for Steve, but the boy shrank back, trying to slip away from both adults. He might have escaped, except the man, whose name was Borit, kept his meaty grasp on Steve's shoulder.

"Where are you going?"

The man smiled politely, drawing his heavy jowls up toward pinched eyes that gleamed with the intensity of a bulldog. "I thought to take the boy into the House of Prophesy. He wants to see what all the excitement was about."

"Don't lie to me, you bastard. That's *my* House of Prophesy there. I know everything that goes on in there. Everything that *went* on in there." She kept her voice low, but it still vibrated with her emotions, carrying her words to everyone.

She felt a hand at her back, large and protective, and she knew without looking that Daken was there, warning her to caution. His voice carried like the gentle rumble of distant thunder, but she heard the implied threat in his voice.

"He's a powerful man, Jane. Don't make a scene over a servant boy."

Jane shrugged off Daken's warning. She didn't fear this man. He was the kind of bully who preyed on the weak. She leaned forward and hauled Steve away from the large man, all the while venting her anger at the thug.

"He's just a child, and you're an evil, depraved beast." That probably wasn't the best choice of words given that half the people here had close ties to one animal or another, but she wasn't in the mood to scrupulously guard her tongue.

She pulled Steve against her in a protective hold. Borit drew himself upright, his face bulging in rage. "How dare you screech at me, woman. I am King Borit of Umbus."

Jane felt her jaw go slack. "My God," she breathed. "You're a healer! That's despicable." She spoke half in English, half in Common, but the meaning was clear enough. All around her were surprised gasps, some in outrage, some in glee.

If possible, the man grew larger. He stood straighter, bunching his massive fists, stepping forward until he practically towered over her. Jane refused to cringe, not because of the audience that watched the scene with the anticipation of a crowd at a hanging, but because of the boy literally quivering against her. She'd already used him once for her own ends. This was her chance to help him even if it meant she was about to get herself beaten to a pulp.

She needn't have worried. Even before she could draw breath to excoriate the man further, Daken pushed her aside, placing his own massive bulk between her and King Borit.

Thankfully, given her less than peaceable hopes, Ginsen interrupted the growing confrontation, bringing his own brand of calm to the area.

"Oracle, is there something I can assist with?" As he spoke, he pressed his way between the two men while drawing Jane and the shaking boy forward. Daken stepped to the side, but remained firmly between Jane and Borit.

"Yes, Elven Lord." She used his title, making sure he understood this was a formal complaint. She drew a deep breath, taking in the dead silence of the crowd as well as the nervous squirming of the boy who clearly wanted to disappear. Jane wouldn't let him go, wanting him to be here when she got rid of his tormentor.

Although Ginsen spoke in English, Jane spoke in her halting Common, wanting everyone to know the extent of Borit's crimes. "King Borit has been repeatedly molesting this boy. He's been doing it for years, using a back room in the House of Prophesy. He should be punished. But more than that, he must be stopped."

She wouldn't have thought Ginsen's young face could look so grim so fast. It was as though a blight appeared on his skin. Even his eyes dimmed. He looked at Borit, his voice low and sad. "Is this true, King Borit?"

"Of course not, my lord!" sputtered the man.

"Like he'd admit it."

"Be quiet." That was from Daken, though his eyes never left Borit's enraged features.

"The woman is a stranger, my Lord," continued Borit. "She is not one of us and has no understanding of our ways. That she could make such an outrageous accusation only proves the extent of her ignorance."

"Ignorance! It doesn't take a Ph.D. to recognize a brute beating a child into silence before he..." She couldn't speak past the memories surging again in her mind. It was traumatic just knowing about it. How much more hideous had it been for Steve?

Ginsen looked down, his dark eyes focusing on the boy who now stared morosely down at his feet. Jane tried to comfort him, gently squeezing his shoulder, but Steve flinched away, and she let her hand drop though she remained right beside him.

"Steviens, can you talk about this?" Ginsen spoke in a new language, one Dr. Beavesly also knew, but it was much longer before Jane could manage a translation. While she fumbled to understand, everyone stared at the boy, practically climbing over one another to peer into his face.

Jane glanced at Daken. He too watched the boy, then he looked up at her. She expected to draw comfort from his eyes. To feel that he believed her and knew that she was doing the right thing. Instead, she saw recrimination, even anger in his eyes.

Jane was shocked by his betrayal. How could he take the part of a child abuser against her? She was still reeling from the shock when Ginsen spoke. "Oracle, are you sure of what you speak?"

Jane turned away from Daken, firmly closing him off in thought and gesture. "Yes, Elven Lord. I'm positive."

"There is no room for misinterpretation? Could the boy have been willing?" To his credit, she didn't think Ginsen believed it, but had to ask anyway.

"No, Elven Lord. Steve was most unwilling."

"Very well." He nodded and two large mages materialized out of the crowd. One she recognized as the formidable youth who had guarded the doorway when she worked on the computer. The other was equally large, almost bearlike in his proportions with a face to match. They both grabbed Borit's arms and led him away while he sputtered and screamed about her ignorance.

The crowd exploded into a roar of conversation, whispered mutterances, and loud exclamations. Jane ignored it all, turning instead to speak to Steve. But the boy was gone. He'd disappeared from the crowd as though he'd never been there. And when she looked up, she saw Daken leaving as well.

"Daken," she called, running after him. He stopped, but his entire stance spoke of anger and outrage. She touched his arm, but he flinched away.

"Please, Daken." She spoke in English, knowing he would understand while most everyone else around them wouldn't. "I need to know what will happen next."

He spun around. "Next, Oracle? Haven't you done enough for one evening?"

She stepped back, still shocked, though no longer surprised by his open enmity. His fists were knotted at his sides, his jaw clenched as though fighting to restrain himself.

Jane returned look for look, her own jaw tightening in the face of his belligerence. "What have I done wrong? He molested a child!"

Daken bent down toward her, his eyes boring tiny holes like silent stingers into her heart. "We will speak of this later, Oracle." He spat out her title, showing her quite clearly what he thought of her actions. And then he left, cutting through the crowd like a knife through water.

Left alone without Daken or the Elven Lord as

buffer, Jane quickly became swamped with people eager to quiz her on what just happened, on her abilities in general, and exactly what she could do for them. They were everywhere, speaking in a language that quickly became nonsense to her. Pushing against the tide of bodies, she made her escape, only to end up sitting morosely on the floor of her empty apartment.

At least someone had lit a fire for her. She stared into the dancing flames, her thoughts slipping away to another fire in Dr. Beavesly's memory. The one that turned her world to ashes.

It was another two hours before he came to her. His face was set in taut lines of hostility, though Daken no longer seemed so close to violence. She didn't look up when he entered, never commented on the fact he hadn't knocked. She felt exhausted in mind and body, and she didn't know why.

She'd done something good tonight, she told herself. She'd saved a boy from an abuser. And nothing, nothing Daken said to her would change that.

She opened the hostilities with a sarcastic comment. "I suppose you've come to expound upon my many sins."

He returned with his own sally. "How could you know? How? I thought we'd established your obsession with a servant boy is at a minimum awkward for you and harmful to the boy."

She lifted her head, slowly rising from the floor as her anger heated up within her. "No, Daken. We didn't establish anything of the kind. All we learned was your political aims have blinded you to anything other than blood and violence. Steve isn't just a servant. He's a person, and he was being abused."

"How can you know, Jane? I'm a healer, and even I

couldn't feel it. There were no wounds, no injuries. I can see these things as clearly as I see you now."

"Borit's a healer too. He would beat the boy, use him, then heal the damage. But that doesn't mean it didn't happen."

Daken cut off an oath then began pacing around her room. "You cannot know."

"I do know. The same way I know people's names, bits about their past." She briefly considered explaining about Dr. Beavesly's memories, but quickly discarded the notion as unnecessarily distracting. Besides, she hardly believed it herself. How could she expect him to? "Daken, can't you just accept I'm right?"

"I have to accept it." He turned to her, his eyes haunted, dark circles barely illuminated by the firelight. "He has already been castrated and expelled. I have to believe you were right or accept we have just destroyed an innocent man."

Jane stopped breathing as the invisible hand returned to squeeze against her chest. "What?"

"You heard me. On your orders, he was castrated and expelled."

"On my orders? What orders?" The fist tightened until she could barely breathe.

"You said he must be punished. Then you said we had to make sure it never happened again."

"So he was castrated and expelled?" Her sight slipped back to the fire as it slowly twisted in the grate. She was glad about the expulsion. And when she thought about it, she agreed with the castration even in a world where the population struggled against extinction, but she expected a trial, a lengthy and excruciating system of he-saids versus she-saids. But there wasn't anything like a trial. Just swift justice specifically interpreted from her unthinking words. "Just because I said so?"

"What did you expect?" he said, his words hitting her like stones. "You're the Oracle. Are you saying now that you lied?"

Jane shook her head. "No. Of course not." She twisted back to look at him, needing to see his face, to read his expression. "He has already been ca—," she swallowed.

"Castrated."

"And expelled? It's done? Finished?"

"Done. Finished." His face was flat and emotionless, his eyes the solid blue of cold plasta chips.

"This is wrong."

Daken slammed his fist into the wall. "You did lie!"

"No, I didn't! But I shouldn't have this much power. No one should. Think of the abuses."

"I have been." His voice was grim, his face pinched, and his eyes dead.

She swiveled her gaze back to the fire. It was so tempting to grab for this system of justice. She was a good person who had acted rightly this time. With her store of knowledge and morals, she could dispense justice with a swift, even hand. This could be her gift to the new world. Justice and, with it, peace.

It was a tempting picture, but one she wasn't sure she could maintain. She was only human and history was littered with good people who eventually became corrupt. Ultimate power corrupts ultimately. Isn't that what they taught in school? How long before someone found her weak point? God knew she had enough of them. Someone could use it against her, bribe or extort his way into her government.

Or worse yet, how long before she weakened to the

temptations surrounding her? Maybe fall victim to the sycophants who would undoubtedly offer her everything she wanted—for a price.

"This isn't right, Daken. I can't have this much power." She stood up, pushing her way past him.

"Where are you going?"

"To talk to Ginsen. I don't like my job description."

She found the Elven Lord relaxing in a lounge-like area off one of the laboratories. Dr. Beavesly's memories told her Ginsen often retreated here to think.

She knocked softly and was relieved when he bid her enter. He spoke in English, and Jane was happy to be able to express herself in her native tongue.

"Ginsen, do you have a moment to talk?"

"Of course, Jane. Please sit down. Would you like some *sandine?*"

She waved the glass aside before she noticed that whatever *sandine* was, it looked and smelled very much like blackberry brandy. If she hadn't been so keyed up, she might have changed her mind.

She drew up a chair opposite Ginsen and settled down, only to stand up again to pace. He watched her movements, his eyes dark, his face impassive. Then he spoke, as if to relieve her mind.

"You'll be happy to know King Borit has been dealt with as you suggested."

Jane stopped mid-step and whirled to face him. "That's just it, Ginsen. I didn't suggest anything. I mean, I didn't mean for you to," she paused, unsure why it was so hard to say the words. "To castrate and expel him."

"You don't think it a fitting punishment?"

"I think it was quite appropriate, it's just that..."
She resumed her pacing only to stop and stare in the

fire. "I'm uncomfortable with so much power. You did that on just my word."

"You lied?"

"Of course not, but I don't want the responsibility that someday I might be wrong and there's no one to question me."

Ginsen stared at her. She saw him in her peripheral vision. First his eyes narrowed, then widened in shock. Suddenly he laughed, a big belly laugh that was no less hearty for his mellow voice. "Jane, Jane, Jane! Did you think we punished him on just your word?"

Jane turned slowly, half insulted by his condescending tone, half relieved they hadn't just taken her word. "What did you do?"

He smiled, gesturing her to her seat and pouring her a drink. "It is so hard. We don't know what you understand and what you don't."

"Ginsen, I am not from around here and my expertise is more in history than contemporary politics. If you could please explain..." She gestured for him to do just that. Instead, he pressed the glass of *sandine* into her hand.

"It isn't important for you to know specifics. Suffice it to say the other Council members and I—"

"All four of you?"

"Yes. The Council has its ways to determine the guilt or innocence of a man. Naturally we don't use it casually, and so Borit's perversions went unnoticed. But thanks to you, the man has been effectively dealt with."

Jane was so relieved, she collapsed against the back of her chair. "You don't know how much you have eased my mind."

"I am pleased to be of service."

Jane settled more comfortably into the chair, idly sipping the *sandine* which did indeed taste like fine blackberry brandy. She and Ginsen remained in gentle silence for a few moments before she finally decided to get some of her more pressing questions out of the way.

"Perhaps this is a good time to talk about my responsibilities," she began.

"Responsibilities?" Far from being interested, Ginsen appeared to lounge more, tilting his head back as he stared at the stars out of the window.

"Well, yes. I know I'll be a member of the Council and all..."

"Yes, you will be expected to advise us on various matters. We will naturally turn to you for specifics on history and various other points of contention among our scholars."

"Advise your scholars?"

"Yes, of course. There are quite a few who are most anxious to speak with you. Tanift is most interested in an unexplained drop in the apparent population in Norkers to the west."

"Population? You mean, a census?" Jane set down the *sandine,* a small tingling of suspicion growing within her. "Of course I would be happy to speak with the scholars about whatever they'd like, but I thought the Council ruled the land. In fact, don't the kings pay a fealty to you and in turn you provide a central government, free education, arms, and the like?"

"We are a peaceful nation." His voice sounded harsh as he reprimanded her.

"Of course, and as I've stated before, I fully support such a position. But was I wrong in believing the Council acted in such a manner?"

He glanced over at her, his expression perplexed. "No. You were not wrong."

"And as the Oracle, as the Keeper of the Knowledge, I am a member of the Council, correct?"

"Certainly, you will attend the meetings, if you so desire, but I'm sure your scholarship duties will more than fill your time." He again shifted his attention to the stars, and with a final jolt of awareness, Jane recognized the tactic.

Dr. Beavesly had used it on her all the time.

If Ginsen never looked directly at her, he didn't have to treat her seriously. And she'd come here thinking they had given her ultimate power! How naive could she have been?

Jane leaned forward in her chair, but didn't get up. She wanted at least the appearance of equality, and standing would be reminiscent of a subordinate petitioning a superior.

"Let me get this straight. I'm to be a member of the Council, but I won't really have to attend the meetings. I won't have a vote or part in any of the decisions, except in an advisory role, and even then only when you call on me. For this exacting task, I get a home, free meals—"

"And a stipend of two hundred doleens a month." Ginsen turned back to her with a fatherly smile. "Does that ease your mind?"

Jane felt her jaw go slack. The Council didn't intend to give her any power at all. If they had their way, she wouldn't even be allowed to come to the meetings. She didn't know if it was a sexist disregard of a woman or a simple disinclination to split the power with a fifth person. Why share rulership with a fifth when you can keep her busy with scholarship and paperwork?

Fortunately for her, she'd learned how to deal with sexist, overbearing, self-important men early in her personal and professional life. If Ginsen or any of the other Council members expected her to just roll over and play dead, they were in for the shock of a lifetime.

Jane pressed forward even more, pushing aside Ginsen's glass of *sandine* when it got in the way. "Let's get something straight right now, Elven Lord. As Keeper of the Knowledge, I hold a seat on the Council. A real seat. With voting privileges, a part in making decisions, and a say in what goes on in this little kingdom of yours. I won't accept any token two hundred doleens a month nor will I allow myself to be buried beneath academicians who have nothing better to do than count heads!"

Ginsen stiffened along every line of his body. For a man descended from ivy, he became practically rigid with indignation, though his voice remained low and threatening. "Are you saying two hundred doleens is not enough?"

"I'm saying I'm a modern woman who expects to be treated like an equal, not a plaything or an oddity for scholarship. You need my resources and my skills, so you better give me the power promised in the prophesy or I might just take my Regency CX-537, load it up on a donkey cart, and set up a shop of my own. Then we'll see who people come to for scholarship, information, and technology. We'll see who gets the fealty doleens. After all, Elven Lord, knowledge is power. And I've got the knowledge of centuries stored in my computer, and all under my direct control."

With that she spun out of the room, too furious to give him a backward glance.

Chapter Nine

✦ ✦ ✦

Jane walked for a long time, her feet slapping out an endless angry beat. She didn't care where she went, just so long as it was away. Away from chauvinistic, condescending power mongers. Away from brutal, malevolent, child abusers. Away from judgmental almost lovers.

She hated them all.

She must have been walking for over an hour because when her fury abated enough for her to notice her surroundings, the moon had lifted high into the night sky. Looking around, she saw she was moving through a grassy area on the edge of a wood. Tuning in to the gentle cadence of the night sounds, she used their soothing peace to silence the last of her frustrations.

The shadow materialized out of nowhere.

One moment she was alone, the next, a black wraith appeared a few yards ahead. It was as if a piece of the darkness shrouding the trees broke away and waited for her, half in and half out of the woods.

She would have screamed if she hadn't been frozen in shock. Then the shadow slipped closer, moving silently toward her. She gathered her strength to run when the vague form finally coalesced into the black panther.

Jane managed to draw an unsteady breath. "We need to arrange some sort of signal," she said to the silent cat, "so I know it's you appearing out of the black mists instead of some rabid thing from the Black Lagoon."

She stepped closer to the proud beast, wanting to bury her hands in the silken fur to reassure herself that the panther was indeed real. But as soon as she stepped forward, the cat slipped backward.

"Hey! Don't leave yet. You know," she continued, hoping her voice would soothe the skittish beast. "We really have to find a name for you. That is, if you intend to hang around for a while." Jane took a step forward, keeping her movements slow as she approached the cat. "How about Kitty? Too boring?"

The panther moved further into the woods.

"Okay. What about Smoke? That fits your present state of semi-reality." She again approached, only to have the animal withdraw another step. "Maybe you prefer Shadow? Ink Stain? Zsa Zsa the Wonder Cat?"

With each word Jane tried to move closer while the panther retreated then looked back, her black eyes glittering like shiny marbles. Finally, Jane stopped just short of the first few trees.

"Come on, Pantar. Don't run from me." She used the Common name for the cat thinking it might respond better to that. No dice. The cat stayed where she was, her long, sleek tail twitching back and forth in impatience.

"Look, I know you want me to follow you, but I hate the woods. I grew up on the flat plains of Illinois. Cornfields as far as the eye can see. Later, I moved to the big city, and I felt really crowded. But buildings have a sense to them, a regularity you don't get with these redwood type things." She waved at the huge, hulking trees that only seemed hulking because it was nighttime and very, very dark.

"The bottom line is I'm not going into that wood. I'm not. So you better come to me."

She said the words. She even meant them, but when the panther stared at her with those mysterious, unblinking eyes, Jane felt like a petulant child who had just disappointed her mother.

"Don't make me do this. I've had a really hard day."

Jane crossed her arms, wondering if arguing with a black panther was a sign of insanity. The cat tilted her head as though she studied a strange new form of food.

Jane cursed under her breath. "This world just gets weirder and weirder." Then she dropped her indignant pose and stepped to the first tree. "I've got no sense of direction, you know. If you lead me in there, you better bring me out again."

Nothing. She might as well be talking to a black marble statue.

"Oh, all right." Jane clenched her teeth against her fears and moved into the woods. At first the pace was a steady, measured walk, but as soon as the panther realized Jane followed, she increased her pace. Soon Jane was scrambling through the underbrush, zipping past huge trunks and wading through vines that would probably give her some dreaded disease.

Then the panther disappeared. Jane had just struggled through some prickly ferns, cursing up a blue streak, only to realize she was alone. She quickly spun around, scanning everywhere, even above, but she saw nothing but foliage and shadow.

"Damn! I knew I couldn't trust a cat. My mother loved cats, but I always thought they were arrogant, conniving, sneaky, litt..." Her tirade was cut off mid-word when her heart jumped into her throat.

She'd seen something move, and it wasn't large enough to be the panther. Jane froze in her tracks, her mind spinning furiously through Dr. Beavesly's memories to find out what lurked in these woods. The answer wasn't helpful. Dr. Beavesly had never bothered to notice. After all, he was an inanimate form bonded to telephone wires. Slathering beasts couldn't hurt him.

They could, of course, easily rip her to pieces.

Belatedly remembering the dagger Daken had given her, Jane slipped it from its sheath. Then she stood, sweating, poised, waiting to be attacked.

Nothing.

Her muscles screamed with tension. Her head started to ache and her vision blurred from constantly scanning the shadows for another shadow of indistinct shape that could possibly eat her alive. It was ridiculous, and so she told herself a dozen times.

After five more minutes, she couldn't stand it anymore. She dropped her dagger into the dirt, then collapsed onto a log in disgust.

"Great. Just great. Some first day as the great Oracle. I get a bastard castrated, tick off his Elven high muckimuck, and manage to get myself completely and totally lost. Ah, hell."

She let her head fall into her hands and wondered if she could afford a moment of complete and total self-pity.

She didn't know when it happened. There wasn't even a sound. But slowly, gradually, awareness prickled at the base of her neck. She had the uncanny feeling she was being watched or that someone or something was nearby. Very close.

The hair on her body rose to painful attention as she slowly lifted her head, and nearly fell off the log.

Directly in front of her was a dagger held by a person.

It was another heart-stopping moment before she realized it was her own dagger, extended hilt first. It was another moment before she recognized the shadowed face.

"Steve! Criminy, you nearly scared the life out of me."

He didn't move, and eventually she realized he was giving her dagger back to her. She took it and sheathed it, using the movement to steady her racing pulse.

"You know Steve," she said, switching over to Common. "I'm too old for this. I used to think what my life needed was a little adventure, a change of scenery, a little adrenaline from chasing the bad guys. I thought it would spice up my life."

She looked up at the silent boy in front of her.

"But I've decided I'm not cut out for adventure. I get lost in the woods. I hate cats. And as for a change of scenery, well... What I wouldn't give for a good pizza and my heat-controlled, vibrating easy chair."

Steve hadn't moved. She wasn't even sure he was alive. His pale eyes seemed an eery silver in the moonlight. It was disconcerting until she realized what he was doing. By posture and attitude, he conveyed that he was her servant, waiting to do her bidding.

Jane sighed, kicking herself for her stupidity.

"Please, Steve, sit down. It's just as well I got lost here because I wanted to talk to you." She glanced up again at the silent figure. "Can you understand me? I mean, I know my Common isn't great. I'll try to speak more clearly."

Steve sat beside her. He moved faster than she would have believed. Like a wild forest creature, he was totally still one second, then gone in the next, slipping into his next spot faster than a raindrop can fall from the sky.

"You'll have to teach me that."

He didn't answer, not that she'd expected him to. So she took a deep breath, trying to sort through her jumbled emotions to the right words.

"Look, I wanted to find you so I could say I'm sorry."

She felt the jolt of surprise hit his small body. It was actually a very small movement, a slight twitch that could have been a hiccup for all she knew. But it was all she had, and she took it for a sign he was listening.

"I didn't handle things with Borit the Bastard very well. I'm not sorry I did it, just that I spoke out so publicly. You'll be happy to know he's been both expelled and castrated, so he won't hurt anyone else. At least not in that way. The main thing is you're safe now."

She stumbled into silence. They didn't touch, and she didn't want to look at him for fear it would be too intimidating or maybe just too direct. So she toyed with a stick she'd picked up, ostensibly staring at it, but in truth, her every sense focused on the boy.

"The problem is, Daken tells me I haven't really helped you. The way I've been singling you out, in the computer room and then..." She drew a deep breath. "I should have known better than to do that publicly. Or at least not with you there because now I've made you different, and my guess is that's the last thing you want to be."

He'd grown very still. He was quiet before. Immobile, but alert. But this was more than that. It was a stillness of the soul, and she didn't know if it was good or bad.

"I was just trying to help, Steve. Which may ease my conscience, but doesn't really do a whole lot for you. See the thing is..." This time she did shift to look directly at him. "We're all different. We've all got things that make us odd or strange that we'd like to hide from everyone else. But we can't because that's part of who we are."

She watched him now, studying his expression as clearly as the moonlight allowed. It wasn't an inspiring sight. She was losing him. Fast.

She sighed. "Okay. Forget the philosophy. Bottom line. I need some help. I fell into this world, not on purpose, but by some random act of chance. Now I'm here, and I want to keep it on track. I've got to stop mankind from making the same mistakes over and over again. The problem is, that as nice as my party was, no one really wants to give me the power to do what I think needs to be done. They don't even want me on the Council, not in any real sense. So I need someone on the inside. Someone who knows what truly goes on, where the real power is, and can key me into it."

She'd gotten him back. His eyes finally lifted to her face to watch her as intently as she studied him.

"I have a hunch you know a heck of a lot more

about what goes on over there." She jerked her head to the left to indicate the University. Then she realized she had no clue where she was or where the campus was in relation to her, so she extended the motion to a silly swivel. "Or wherever the stupid place is."

Steve pointed to her right and back a bit.

"Ah-hah! You do understand me!" she said, pretending she'd been testing him. "Now here's what I propose. I want you to be my assistant. I'll teach you how to use the computer, retrieve information, and even fill in for me as needed." She watched his eyes grow into huge pools of shimmering silver. "In return, you'll help me get the power and respect I need to do my job."

She started ticking off items on her fingers. "You'll tell me when they hold Council meetings. You'll make sure I get to the right dinners and the right seats at the right time." Having worked in academia all her life, she knew the importance of seating arrangements. "You can even keep your ears open for any plots against my life." She'd been joking when she said it, but as the words came out she realized that wasn't far from the realm of possibility.

"In short, you'll look out for my best interests. And in return, I'll train you to take my place one day. Think you can do that?"

The boy was silent for a long time, but she never feared he hadn't understood. His steady gaze told her he was thinking about it, and that he was a good deal more intelligent than anyone gave him credit for.

She waited as patiently as possible for his decision. And like a born street kid, he made her sweat it out for longer than was comfortable. In the end, he nodded, and she grinned.

"Great. We're gonna make a fabulous team, Steve. I haven't felt this sure about anything else since coming to this crazy land."

She stuck out her hand, and it took him a moment to realize she wanted him to shake it. Hesitantly, he offered up his hand, and she clasped it as she would a partner's. His fingers felt small and fragile against her larger palm, but she knew he possessed skills she might never master. He had a street canniness beyond her abilities. She had the academic training and the drive.

They would be a good team.

"So, assistant," she finally said, "how about you show me the way out of this horrid place."

He glanced up at her, his head cocked to one side as though he questioned her sanity.

"Hey," she protested. "One man's sanctuary," she glanced around at the massive swaying branches that seemed to close in on her, "is another man's hell."

He looked at those same trees, an expression of peace and reverence settling on his features, and she knew she had guessed correctly. These woods were indeed where Steve ran for peace and solitude. She waited for a moment, then she nudged him in the shoulder.

"Yeah, yeah. They're beautiful. Big leaves, nice color. Now get moving before I freak out from claustrophobia."

❖ ❖ ❖

By the time she and Steve arrived back at her apartment, Jane decided they had a marvelous rapport. Steve was widely expressive with both facial expression and gestures. Even without words, he provided a delightful commentary on her monologues. It also didn't hurt that he was the perfect listener, attentive and silent as she talked through her often-tangled thoughts.

It wasn't until they entered her rooms that Steve reverted back to his silent, shadow-on-the-wall servant mode. And that was in the face of a furious, hulking brute of a man.

"Daken! What are you doing here?"

"I've been driving myself to distraction waiting for you! Where have you been, woman?"

"Don't you scream at me! Don't you know what time it is? People are sleeping."

Daken rounded on her, his jaw slack with astonishment. Unfortunately, it didn't remain that way for long. "Of course I know what time it is. I thought you'd gotten yourself killed by a zlebaar." As furious as he was, Jane noted he kept his voice down enough to wake only the people on this floor, not the entire University.

"Well, I wasn't eaten or killed or anything else." She casually tried to cover the scratches on her hands and face. "I was just having a leisurely stroll with my new assistant."

He was stomping toward her, his gaze focused on a particularly painful cut across her cheek, when he suddenly stopped dead.

"Assistant?"

"Yes," she said with a triumphant smile. "Steve will be working with me. The Oracle's Aide, so to speak." To her surprise and pleasure, Steve stepped away from the wall and gave a dignified half bow.

"But I thought I was your..." He cut off his words,

his eyebrows slashing down as he chewed his lower lip.

"You? You're a king, Daken. You've got a job."

"I know I do," he snapped. He shifted his gaze from the boy to her then back again. Then to complete her astonishment, he knelt down on one knee to speak eye to eye with Steve.

"Is this what you want? She can be very forceful when she thinks she's helping someone. If you want nothing more to do with her, I'll tell her. And I'll make sure she leaves you alone."

To her relief, Steve shook his head with clear force.

"You want to be her assistant?"

A nod.

"You'll work for her honestly? No split loyalties. You're the Oracle's Aide."

A much firmer nod.

Daken studied the boy's face once more. Then, apparently liking what he saw, he stood up and nodded. "I think he will serve you well."

"I'm so glad you approve," she said dryly.

He shifted his attention back to her, stepping closer as he lifted her chin, twisting her cut cheek to the fire-light. "What I do not approve of is you wandering around unprotected at night."

"I wasn't unprotect—" She gasped as he stroked her cut. She felt his power like a cauterizing iron, searing across her face, mixing with the pain until both faded from her cheek. She touched her newly healed skin, the warmth of his touch still tingling across her fingertips. "How is it you can be so amazing and so obnoxious all at the same time?"

He looked at her, his lip quirked to one side in his special half smile. "I am a king," he answered simply.

Then he crossed his arms, trying to look stern. "And as a king, I tell you one small boy, albeit a smarter one than I first thought," he glanced at Steve, "is not protection for you."

"So what am I supposed to do? Have you dog my steps everywhere I go?"

"Yes." He nodded as if she'd come up with exactly the solution he proposed.

"Are you going to follow me into the bathroom too? Eat with me? Help me dress?"

His grin was wicked, his expression explicit.

"And what about the Tarveen? Who will take care of them while you're protecting me?" That wiped the grin off his face, although the grimness that replaced it made her regret her hasty words. "You can't follow me around, Daken. I have to learn to manage on my own."

He grumbled something under his breath as he paced the small confines of the sitting room with the sleek efficiency of a wolf on the prowl. Then he stopped, twisting to pin her with his deep blue eyes.

"Do you know that less than an hour ago, the Elven Lord grumbled under his breath while he stomped to his quarters? I've never seen the man more livid."

Jane brightened, an unholy smile drawing up her features. "Really? You think he was upset?" she asked innocently.

"I know he was upset. I gather you were responsible?"

Jane's grin widened. "I certainly hope so."

"*Venzi*, woman!" He stomped away, only to twist back toward her at the fire. "Do you know how many powerful enemies you have made in just one night?"

"You'd rather I simpered in a corner, feeding them knowledge and accepting whatever morsels they choose to throw my way?"

"It would be a good deal safer for you to do so."

"Then who would get you your army?" She regretted the words the moment she said them. She shouldn't lead him on this way. Eventually he'd figure out she lied, that she never intended to supply him with the weapons he wanted. But she couldn't bring back the words, and she didn't want to anger him again just yet.

This was the first real conversation they'd had since she became the Oracle. She'd missed his smiling face, even when it growled at her for being reckless.

She waited for his response, but he was silent, his gaze centered on the darkest corner of the room as if it would show him the evil lurking around her. Finally, he spoke, his voice low, his words measured and frightening.

"You cannot get me my army if you are dead."

She settled slowly down onto a nearby chair. "You think someone will try to kill me?"

He lifted his gaze until it was all she saw of him— twin blue seas of worry and fear. "I think your very presence has unsettled a lot of people. The power you seek will not be given up easily or willingly."

"Just a few hours ago, you accused me of wielding too much power." She tried to keep her voice light, but she couldn't hide the hurt underneath.

"No. A few hours ago, I accused you of recklessly destroying an innocent man." He turned his gaze onto Steve, the silent, listening figure in the corner. "I see now I was wrong."

"Well, at least we got that cleared up," Jane muttered from the couch.

"Still, it could have been handled better."

Jane winced at the reproach in his tone. "I know.

But political discretion does not come easily to me."

"I've noticed."

Jane had the urge to stick out her tongue at his dry response, but thought better of it. It was time she learned a little self-restraint. If she could manage to remain dignified around Daken, then she was well on her way to becoming as inscrutable as the Sphinx.

"So what now?" she asked, suddenly feeling too tired to make any more major life decisions.

"For now? You sleep."

From the tone of his voice, he clearly meant real sleep. Alone. So much for her tiny hope that he still wanted their night of passion.

"And the boy sleeps here." He pushed the couch a foot closer to the door. "Do you have a knife?"

Quick as a wink, a long, thin blade appeared in Steve's hand, then just as swiftly disappeared. Daken grunted his approval, then glanced at Jane's shocked expression. "Something tells me even without your help tonight, King Borit would not have tormented your new Aide for long."

Jane nodded, her eyes still riveted on Steve's impassive, youthful face. But unlike Daken's grudging respect, she was appalled. Steve had clearly intended to stab Borit, but she sincerely doubted the boy could have killed the larger man. Instead, he would have enraged the bastard into further acts of violence and depravity.

She was enormously grateful she had ended Borit's reign of terror before that happened.

"If there is any trouble," continued Daken to Steve, "you must get word to me immediately. You know where I am staying?"

Steve nodded.

"Good. And as for you," he turned to Jane, who lifted her eyes to meet his steady gaze. "There is a Council meeting the day after tomorrow during which I will petition for the army and weapons I need to fight the Tarveen. You can support me then."

A tiny sliver of fear cut into her heart. Just two days? She would have to betray him so soon?

She knotted her fingers together. "Is that all I am to you, Daken?" she asked, her voice unsteady despite her pretense at control. "A way to get your army?"

He stood next to the couch, nearly towering over her. The firelight flickered in the grate, shooting orange and red lights through his brown hair and adding a mesmerizing dance of colors to the gold flecks in his eyes. His expression was not so much inscrutable as mixed. She read many things there. Fear, desire, pain, and hope, all danced together with the flames in his eyes.

"No, Jane," he whispered as his lips lowered to hers. "I need much more than just the Oracle."

His mouth was lean and hungry against hers. The wicked cut of his tongue was sharp as he thrust into her. She rose half out of her seat to meet him, her back arching, her body straining to touch more than just his mouth.

Then he released her, striding out of her room like a soldier going to war. She was left behind, feeling lost and alone, wondering when and if she'd ever see him again.

✦   ✦   ✦

The next day passed in a blur. Her first task was to get the Regency CX-537 up and running. Rather than risk another power failure, she decided to recharge the back-up battery to full strength and then use it instead of the direct solar link. That would also allow time for Steve to take her out to the market to get some real clothes.

As proud as she was of the notoriety her outfit gave her, she was heartily sick of it.

Of course, the vendors knew who she was, and they were all anxious to please her; a fact that Steve took amazing advantage of. When she'd offered Steve the job of her assistant, she had no inkling of how very, very adept the boy was.

It began early. All she did was mention shopping, and then somehow Steve appeared an hour later with an advance on her salary. Doleens clicked in a small pouch which she held like a child grasping her first dime. Unfortunately, raised with retail shopping in massive mega-malls, Jane was useless when haggling over price.

So Steve took the purse back, assuming complete control of prices. All Jane needed to do was point to what she wanted, then Steve would drop an appropriate number of coins on the table and walk away, oblivious to the vendor screaming for more.

She purchased a number of colorful tunics and leggings, boots, underwear, toiletries, and most importantly, a black belt with a large circle buckle to stand for Oracle. She got another one for Steve, as well as some new clothes, so there would be no doubt about who he worked for now.

Once back at the college, she lost no time in changing into her new attire. Admiring herself in the short bathroom mirror, she decided she liked what the days of exercise and worry had done to her figure. She had a definite waistline now, something she'd always wanted, and the leggings did show off the new muscles in her legs.

She wondered briefly if Daken would notice the difference. Then she smiled at her foolishness. He could hardly miss the fact that she no longer wore skin-tight, black Lycrasheen and orange high tops. The question was whether or not he'd like the change.

What did it matter? she asked herself firmly. She liked her new looks, who cared what a man thought?

Not wanting to answer herself, she pulled open the bathroom door and noticed that Steve looked quite debonair in his new clothes. He also looked like he took his job as her bodyguard much too seriously.

"You don't have to stand watch over the door when I'm in the bathroom, Steve. I'm sure Daken was just being overprotective."

Steve didn't respond by either expression or gesture, but instead, led the way across campus to the Computing Center. It would appear, thought Jane as she eyed her Aide's stiff manly stride, that boys learned quite young the basics of being a man. And that included simply ignoring a woman whenever her opinions differed from his.

The rest of the day was split between various hardware-related problems and teaching Steve how to read and write in English. He already knew Common as well as his home language of Yonks, but he would need English to work the computer. He learned quickly, and Jane guessed he'd already secretly studied the language even though only Ginsen's scholars appeared to have any knowledge of Old Speak, as it was called in Common.

All in all, it was a good day. Wonderfully undisturbed by death threats or power struggles, and Jane appreciated the peace. She never spoke to Daken, but as at that first dinner, she felt his eyes on her everywhere. Usually she'd catch a glimpse of him as she rounded a corner or if she stopped unexpectedly to see if she could surprise him. In those times especially, his eyes would caress her, lingering on her face or, once, on her body. His message was always filled with equal parts warmth, hunger, and warning. The first she returned ten fold. The last, she ignored, having come to the conclusion if someone wanted to kill her, there was very little she could do to stop him or her. She took reasonable precautions and prayed that was enough.

In any event, what could happen to her with two devoted protectors? Steve was always at her side, and Daken no doubt dogged her footsteps everywhere she went.

So it was with considerable surprise that evening when she found herself alone in the courtyard suddenly confronted with the dark-robed Kyree.

She'd been sitting in her room, staring at the stars and fantasizing about Daken. With the Council meeting the next morning, she was achingly aware that too soon, fantasies were all she'd have of her warrior king.

Suddenly restless, she'd turned to the one thing that never failed her. Food. Even on her worst days, from childhood through failed higher education, the One-Stop Shop had always provided the best in junk food for the indiscriminate, calorie-starved palette. What she wouldn't give now for some chocolate decadence.

"Hey, Steve, I'm starving. Is there any place for a late night snack? A brownie? Or better yet, about five pounds of pure chocolate?"

She had been muttering to herself in sort of a verbal food fantasy, but before she knew it, Steve had disappeared, his chalk still rolling on his slate.

"Probably tired of the alphabet," she said, noting his half-finished letters. She couldn't really blame him. Learning to read and write was hard at any age. She didn't begrudge him his break, especially if he returned with something scrumptious. But as the minutes slipped by and the fire began to dim in the grate, she began to worry.

Where was the boy? She didn't know where he'd gone. She sat up and peered out the window, but couldn't see anything except stars and the top of some annoyingly leafy tree. She waited a moment longer, pacing off her frustration, then pulled on her boots and went outside.

"Steve? Come on. I wasn't that hungry. Really."

No answer.

She wandered closer to campus, skirting one of the dormitories. Even it was silent, the students here being, in her mind, unnaturally studious. But then, she realized, if she had the opportunity to learn at the only magic school in the kingdom, she probably wouldn't squander the opportunity at beer parties either.

She caught a movement out of the corner of one eye and turned rapidly, scanning the shadows.

"Steve?"

There it was again, a dark movement half-hidden in a clump of trees.

"Panther?"

This really was ridiculous, she thought, even as she went closer. Why weren't there any floodlights for the area? Didn't they know how dangerous it was for people to wander around campus at night in the dark? Who knew what monsters lurked in the shadows?

She continued, knowing now the shadow definitely wasn't Steve, but fearing it held the answer to what happened to the boy.

"Olly olly oxen free. Come out, come out wherever you are. Whoever you are." She hadn't expected it to work. For one thing, she spoke in English. For another, she wasn't screaming it, but mumbling under her breath.

Still, she felt like she'd thrown her first magic spell when a form materialized in front of the trees.

It was Kyree, his dark robes tight around his lean body and angular features. He gestured for her to join him in the grove. Moving more slowly, Jane approached him, but didn't enter the relative secrecy of the trees.

"Good evening, Wizard. You're out late."

"I was waiting for you, Oracle."

"Yes, well, I'm looking for Steve. You haven't seen him, have you?"

"He went toward the food commons some minutes past."

"Thank you." Jane smiled and made to leave, but Kyree stopped her, his hand large and sinewy where he touched her forearm.

"Stay a minute, Oracle. I would like to speak with you."

Jane felt a tremor of excitement vibrate through her veins. Here was her first real court intrigue. A secret meeting with the most powerful wizard in the area, if not in the world. What a great moment to tell her grandchildren, assuming this wasn't the beginning of her death scene.

"Thank you, Wizard, but I'm afraid I don't like trees all that much. I find myself much more comfortable out in the open."

"Ah. I see you don't trust me." His tone was relaxed, his expression open.

"I don't think I trust anybody right now."

He smiled, his gaze flowing easily to the shimmering night sky. "I see you are wise beyond your years."

"Not bloody likely, given that I was born over two hundred years ago."

His smile increased to a grin that neatly set her back on her heels. It wasn't so much that he suddenly became very, very handsome. True, his grin relaxed the taut lines about his face, erasing his pinched, brooding appearance, and replacing it with a kind of majesty she found fascinating. But more shocking was his appreciation of her sense of humor. She hadn't thought anyone understood that aspect of her, much less enjoyed it. Apparently, he was delighted by it.

A crack appeared in her hostility.

"You are a constant delight, Oracle—"

"Please, call me Jane."

"Then you must call me Kyree."

She nodded, and then the night wrapped around them, making her earlier fears seem almost silly. He looked at the stars, and she followed the angle of his gaze. As always, she was awed by the beauty of a night sky undimmed by smog or the relentless lights of a city. Her mind wandered back to that early night with Daken, before she became the Oracle, when they had been so easy together as he talked about the miracles of the heavens.

"Were you aware there is a Council meeting tomorrow morning?"

She'd been caught off-guard, lulled by the beauty of the evening until she'd almost thought she was with

Daken. But Kyree most certainly wasn't her warrior king, and so she looked away from the sky and tried to gather her wits about her.

"Are you asking if I'd been informed of the meeting or if I knew it would take place?"

Again that sexy grin appeared on his face. "You are quick." Surprise and respect colored his tone. "I see I have underestimated you."

"Because I know about a Council meeting?"

"Because you have already realized even the formalities of your new position will not come easily."

Jane studied his face as he continued speaking in a cultured undertone. Throughout it all, his expression remained relaxed, his profile as handsome as the stars that were his backdrop.

"I underestimated you, Jane, and believe me, that's not a mistake I make very often."

"Your culture doesn't seem to encourage men to respect a woman's mind," she offered diplomatically.

His laugh startled her. It was rich and warm, like good brandy, and it blended perfectly with the night. "I have long since learned women can be as intelligent as men. They can also be as stupid. You, however, are not stupid."

"Thank you." What could she say? He confirmed everything she wanted to believe about herself.

"I wonder if you realize the magnitude of what you've accomplished in just two days." He started walking, and she followed. They ambled slowly around the grove, aiming obliquely toward the central courtyard.

"The arrival of the Keeper of Knowledge would cause upheavals no matter who took the position," she said.

"Not really. Ginsen has been planning it for years. Instead of fitting neatly into the position of Council Advisor, you've done quite the opposite. On your first night here, you discredit and expel the biggest single threat to the Kingdom."

"Borit?" She stumbled over a pebble as she tried to assimilate this new information.

"My spies tell me he has been secretly amassing an army with the intention of taking over Bosuny."

"I didn't expose him to remove a threat to the Elven Lord," she said, disliking the suggestion that she did it for political reasons.

Kyree grinned. "Of course not. But no matter the reason, it is what you have done. You'd think," he added, almost as an afterthought, "Ginsen would be grateful."

Recalling her previous evening's interview with the Elven Lord, Jane felt her temper start to rise. "I can't imagine a less thankful person," she said dryly.

"Ginsen is a wonderful scholar. But he doesn't have the understanding of statecraft required in an effective ruler. He lacks vision, or even the ability to accurately judge the people around him." Kyree stopped, turning to look directly at her. "Unlike me, Ginsen has failed to see your real potential."

Jane swallowed nervously. They stood face to face, not close, but not very far apart either. Even in the darkness, looking up at his shadowed face, she could see the earnestness in his expression, just as she saw the ready intelligence and controlled power beneath the genial exterior.

"You're very beautiful," he said suddenly.

Jane flinched at his blatant flattery, drawing back even as he lifted his hand to caress her face. "Please,

Kyree," she said, disappointment coloring her tone. "You needn't resort to such base tactics to get my attention."

His hand paused in the air, his expression shocked. "My apologies, Oracle." He pulled back his hand. "I did not mean to offend you. I was just surprised." He pulled his arms tight against his robe as though he were embarrassed. "I have spent a great deal of time watching you. I've seen what you've accomplished with Steviens as well as King Daken, who is not an easy man to bring to heel."

"I wouldn't exactly say—"

Kyree continued as if she hadn't said anything. "Given Ginsen's mood last night, I'd say you saw through him immediately."

Jane smiled, knowing he was flattering her, but unable to stop herself from enjoying his praise.

"But," he continued, "in all this time of watching you, I never noticed how beautiful you are."

Jane felt her breath catch in her throat. She found it unexpectedly difficult to keep her head around this man. If he praised her in a fawning, ingratiating manner, she would have no trouble ignoring him. But he wasn't speaking that way. He sounded so surprised himself. His previous statements were just that, statements she knew were true. So when he stared at her, his hands poised awkwardly between them as he gazed with such intensity at her face, she didn't know what to think.

Was he flattering her? Yes.

Was he sincere? She couldn't tell. All she knew was that he was a handsome, intelligent man who looked at her as though she were the answer to his prayers.

"Your hair is very short," he said softly, finally reaching out to stroke a curl resting next to her cheek. "Do all the woman of your time wear it like this?"

"Not..." Jane had to clear her throat of its husky tones. "Not all of them. But many. It helps present a more professional image." His hand was warm where it brushed against her cheek, and the fiery tingle of reaction made her curl her toes in nervousness.

"I understand," he said, and Jane struggled to remember what he referred to.

It was some time before Jane remembered their surroundings. They stood nearly nose to nose in full view of one of the dormitories. She had yet to find Steve, though she doubted he was in serious danger, and she suddenly had the impression that after years of no male companions whatsoever, her love life was about to become seriously overloaded.

"Um, Kyree," she muttered, stepping away from his seductive gaze. "I really should be looking for Steve."

"I can show you where he is. My crystal is in my quarters. It will tell you whatever you need to know—"

"No, I don't think so, but thanks anyway."

"You are nervous about coming to my apartment."

Jane blushed, embarrassed that he could read her so easily.

"Perhaps you are right," he said philosophically, although she could hear the disappointment in his voice. "You haven't yet heard my proposal, and it shouldn't be spoken of when my mind is on other, um, more pleasant activities." If the warmth of his gaze left her in doubt of his thoughts, the bold caress of his fingers along the inside of her arm, down the side of her breast, told her exactly what he was thinking.

The sudden ache in her belly told her she'd been

thinking the same things.

To her disgust, an image of Daken slipped into her mind. She felt like she was cheating on him, but that was errant nonsense, and so she told herself over and over. Daken had never made any claims on her sexually or otherwise. There had been that understanding in the inn, but that was before she became the Oracle. Before he decided to use her for his political ambitions. Before a lot of things.

She didn't owe him any fidelity or even loyalty. She was a new person with a new position in a new world, and maybe Daken, like a lot of other things, would have to be relegated to the past.

Right now, she thought about the future, and the enticing man beside her. Who was taking things much too fast for her comfort.

"Well, I really must be going," she said, suddenly restless and confused, half wishing for the security of her own room, half wanting to run a 10K marathon until she dropped of exhaustion.

In the end, she merely headed across the yard, back toward her suite.

He matched her pace easily, his long legs keeping him effortlessly beside her. "Please, Jane. I truly have something important to speak about, and there isn't much time. Were it not for your fear of trees—"

"I'm not really afraid of them." She slowed her step. "If you really want to, we can go there."

His smile was one of relief and sudden elation. "Good. It won't take more than a minute—"

"I warn you, Kyree. I'm not as defenseless as I look."

He nodded, bowing his head slightly in acknowledgement. "I swear to you, Jane," his voice was low and intent. "I will not force myself on you in any way."

She waited a moment, drawing out the silence as she pretended to weigh his integrity. She didn't fear violence. All she need do was scream and half the University would come running. She didn't even fear he'd make a pass. She knew he would. What frightened her was that she would welcome it.

"Lead on," she said, her heart practically singing with the excitement and mystery of the whole situation.

She followed him into the small grove, relieved when she realized there weren't enough trees to justify the name. The five loosely grouped trees provided a screen from prying eyes without impinging on her ability to run away if necessary.

"Okay. What's the big proposal?"

"It's really quite simple." He took a deep breath, steepling his fingers for a moment as he composed his thoughts. She waited patiently, struck anew by the calm self-possession of this man. Whereas Daken often reminded her of a caged tiger, pacing off his energy with agitated movements and abrupt bursts of intense emotion, Kyree was a quiet center of intellect. His emotions were tightly reined, his movements always smooth and economical.

Kyree was a thinking man with the power to carry his thoughts through to action. He was a statesman, constantly gauging and planning his actions for deeper ramifications. Daken was a warrior who rarely had the time or ease for deep thought. And Jane was perverse enough to find both statesman and warrior deeply compelling. Then Kyree began speaking and all other thoughts fled from her mind.

"You, Jane, are a bright, self-assured woman with enormous potential. You have the knowledge of the Old Ones at your fingertips and are just beginning a period of enormous popular support."

"Popular support? Most people don't even know me."

"True, but they know of the House of Prophesy and all it represents. Already the tale of the Oracle has traveled well beyond our borders."

"But I haven't even got the thing running yet."

"It doesn't matter. You are the Keeper." Then he stopped, peering at her through the deeper shadows of the trees. "You will get it…running, won't you?"

"Well, of course. It's just a matter of dusting off the old parts and getting the power going as it should." In her heart, she knew it wasn't nearly that simple. Two hundred years of radiation could do a lot of damage. Even hardware protected by the special energies of Dr. Beavesly could have been corrupted in hundreds of different ways, but she didn't judge this the time to tell Kyree that.

"Good," he rested his chin on his fingertips, apparently reassured. "As I was saying, you have the potential to carry enormous popular support. And I," he lifted his chin, fixing his steady eyes on her, capturing her gaze as neatly as if he'd snared her in a net. "I am the greatest wizard alive. And I am still learning. In addition, I have been managing this kingdom for years. I know the strengths and weaknesses of the lands surrounding us. I know how the Dwarves mine their gold and how they maintain that power base. I know where the Birdpeople nest and what they want most in the world."

He stepped forward, his voice throbbing with his passion, his eyes glowing with the power literally pulled from the radiation surrounding them.

"Jane, I have the knowledge and magic you lack.

You have the popular support and ancient wisdom I need. Together, we would be unstoppable."

Jane took a deep breath, finally grasping the enormity of what he suggested. "You want us to overthrow Ginsen."

"The Elven Lord is weak. You've seen what he's like. He sees the world around him with the myopic self-absorption of a scholar. He sees things to learn, not powers to be managed or even a land and people to care for. His reign would have crumbled years ago were it not for me."

Jane's thoughts spun, and she leaned against a tree trunk while she sorted through his words. "Why didn't you take control years ago?"

Kyree spread his hands in a self-effacing gesture. "I have never enjoyed the good will of the people. I am too dark, too brooding, and they fear the magic I control."

Jane nodded, agreeing he was indeed too mysterious and too intense a man to easily gain the trust of a simple people.

"But you, Jane, you are a beautiful, young woman with a natural talent toward leadership. Didn't you see how they flocked to you last night? You sparkled like a living diamond, a goddess stepped down from the heavens to lead them. No one could resist you."

Jane shook her head, uncomfortable with the image he painted of her. "I don't know, Kyree. Weren't you maybe seeing what you wanted to see?"

He stepped right up to her, and she could feel the heat of his body envelop her. With one finger, he lifted her chin, while his other hand brushed back her hair in a long, loving stroke.

"I see what you are, Jane, and what you could be. I

see it as clearly as I see your passion for good, your
need to bring peace and prosperity to a land teetering
on the edge of violence. I alone can give you the
power you need to put your dreams into reality." He
brushed his fingertips across her cheek, then framed
her face, drawing her up against him until she could
feel the lean strength of his body pressed against hers.

"Daken can't give you what you want. He is too
obsessed with his revenge, too consumed by hatred.
Only I have the power and the knowledge you need."

He lowered his head, resting his forehead against
hers while his breath misted the air between them.

"Marry me, Jane. Marry me and be an Empress.
Rule over the kingdom that will bring peace to the
world."

He lowered his lips to hers. His kiss was potent,
filled with the heady aphrodisiac of power and possession. In it, he gave her visions of world peace and
placed them within her grasp. But equally potent, he
also offered her the respect and companionship of a
man who would not only support her, but actively help
her fulfill her potential as a ruler.

How could she refuse that?

His kiss deepened, and his tongue stroked and
teased the inside of her mouth. Then one kiss led into
another, until he broke from her lips to trail long wet
strokes across her cheek to her ear.

It was there he began her seduction. As he touched
her, as he worshiped her body with his hands, he
spoke of the world they would create together. He
lowered his caresses to her breasts while he whispered
secrets of the warring factions of the south. He unbuck-
led her belt as he told her of the exotic foods there that
would no longer be trampled by armies, the fields no

longer watered with blood. He slid his hands under her tunic, his long fingers firm and erotic as he teased her taut nipples. Then he spoke of vast transportation networks that could bring her message of peace along with food and medicine to the starving children of the western tribes.

His robe fell open, exposing his lean, smooth chest above soft breeches straining against his manhood. He pressed against her, rubbing in slow arcs of desire against her pelvis, and still he whispered seductive words of power and prosperity.

She arched against him, the rough bark of the tree scraping the back of her neck as she raised into his embrace.

"We can do it, Jane. Together we can create an empire. Say you'll marry me. Say yes."

He pressed deep into her, and she felt his every muscle, every ridge despite the barriers of their clothing.

"Think of the power, Jane. I can put it in your hands."

His hands dropped to her waist, squeezing her supple flesh, pressing it down as he slid a hand under her leggings.

"Be my empress. Be mine."

Jane moaned aloud. Her body hummed with desire, her thoughts spun with visions of well-fed, happy people cheering her as she rode by on her way to peace summits.

He pressed her legs apart with his knees, and she felt her leggings slip lower on her hips while his hand slid into the widening gap.

"Say yes, Jane. Say it."

She was weakening. She wanted it so badly. The

power, the peace, the joy, the love. But something held her back, something kept the word from her tongue.

Kyree lifted his face from the hollow of her neck. His tongue trailed liquid fire up her neck, along her jawline until he found her mouth.

"I want this, Jane," he said into her lips. "I want you."

He forced her legs apart and his fingers found her core. She cried out at the invasion, and she arched backwards, away from the sensations swamping her consciousness.

"Wait," she gasped. "It's too fast."

"No," he said, pushing her leggings out of the way. "You can do it. You can take it. Take it all. Now."

He captured her mouth again, invading her above as she felt him push aside the last of her clothing, readying her for his invasion below.

"No." She tried to wrench herself free, but he was too strong, his body too hungry for liberties she'd already allowed.

And then suddenly she was free. His weight yanked from her as if he were a puppet hauled back by its strings. Jane scrambled to right her clothing, pulling up her leggings and straightening her tunic. It wasn't until her breathing steadied and her mind cleared that she managed to look for the cause of her rescue.

Her eyes widened and her breath froze in her chest. One word escaped from her horrified lips. One word released half in relief, half in terror.

"Daken."

Chapter Ten

✦ ✦ ✦

Jane swallowed, wondering what to do. Daken stood over Kyree, his bastard sword gleaming dully in the thick shadows.

"Are you all right?" Daken asked, his voice hoarse and cold.

"Y–yes." She braced herself against the tree as she waited for her legs to support her.

"What shall I do with him?" he leaned forward, his blade hovering menacingly close to Kyree's neck.

"Put away your sword, Warrior King." Kyree's voice dripped with contempt. "It does not frighten me."

"Then you are a fool, Wizard. But then I already knew that." Daken's blade pressed down against Kyree's throat.

"Stop it, Daken," Jane snapped, her nervousness making her voice sharp and shrewish. "And put that thing away."

"Yes," echoed Kyree, his sneer on his face. "Put it away. Jane is in no danger from me. My fiancée and I were merely celebrating our engagement, and I'm afraid I became too enthusiastic."

The sword tip didn't move, although Jane could see Daken flinch as he swiveled to pin her with his dark gaze. "Fiancée?"

Jane gathered herself together, calling on the tattered shreds of her dignity to help her. "Kyree presumes too much." She saw the triumphant gleam in Daken's eyes and hastened to dampen it. "But so do you, Daken." She stepped forward, placing her hands on the iron muscles of his sword arm. "I thank you for intervening. From the bottom of my heart, I thank you, but that still doesn't mean you can kill him."

"He's a dangerous man, Jane. You don't know what he's capable of."

"No," she agreed, tugging gently on Daken's arm. "But I'm learning." She felt him relax, but only enough to allow her to draw both him and his sword back. Below them, Kyree scrambled to his feet, swiftly closing his robe. Though she kept her eyes locked on Daken's clenched expression, Jane noted the wizard's hands shook. It wasn't until he had himself and his clothing in order that Kyree spoke.

"Jane..."

She felt Daken's arm jerk forward, and she tightened her hold, trying through touch to soothe the fighting beast seething just beneath the surface of Daken's temporary quiescence.

Kyree saw it too, and no longer moved toward her, but he didn't stop speaking either, his voice as low and seductive as if Daken weren't there.

"Don't throw away your dreams, Jane, for a set of muscles and a swift blade. I can offer you ten times as much as he can."

Stepping in front of Daken's blade, Jane turned to the wizard. "King Daken is more than a set of muscles and a swift blade. As for what you offer," she swallowed, acutely aware of Daken's barely restrained fury directly behind her. "I am considering it. I will let you know as soon as I decide."

Kyree bowed to her, then started to withdraw, but he paused at the edge of the tiny grove. When he spoke, his voice was cold and angry, and for the first time, Jane got a sense of how dangerous Kyree could be.

"I leave now not because I am helpless, Warrior King. I do so merely because Jane wishes it. Remember that I am not blind or deaf. I am the most powerful wizard alive. And if you harm her in any way—"

Jane didn't see it happen. She was concentrating on the sword still gleaming to her right. One moment Kyree was speaking, his voice low and threatening. The next second, Daken's dagger thunked in the trunk spare millimeters from Kyree's face.

"She has always been safe with me," said Daken, his voice a low growl of hatred.

Kyree swallowed, drawing slowly away from the lethal blade. Still he continued, his voice as firm, if not as low, as before. "She *was* safe. Is she still safe now?"

Jane didn't wait for Daken's reaction. She stepped again into the space between the two men. "Daken would never hurt me." She wasn't lying. As angry as he was, as precariously close to violence as he seemed, she never doubted Daken. He'd never physically harm her.

"I'm safe with him," she reiterated, her focus back to Kyree as she silently pleaded with him to leave.

Kyree nodded, but his attention remained locked on Daken. "See that she remains safe, Warrior King. In a very short time, she will be your Empress."

And with that he turned and strode away, his dark

robe flapping behind him like an Emperor's train.

✦   ✦   ✦

"You can't be serious." Daken's voice trembled with fury and disgust as he paced the confines of her room. They had moved here for privacy, although in the world of wizards and thin dormitory walls, she wondered if any place was free from prying eyes and ears.

At least Steve was mercifully absent. The boy had been waiting in the apartment, a plate of sweets set on the low table by the fire. He scrambled to his feet as Daken stormed into the room, then he bowed once to both of them and disappeared.

Jane collapsed onto the couch, feeling unequal to the scene she and Daken were about to play out, but unable to avoid it. The only thing she could do was get it over with as quickly as possible.

"Is that..." Daken grabbed hold of his temper with obvious effort. "Is he what you want?"

"Hell, yes," she exclaimed, rising from the couch to block out her own square of space near the fire. "He's offering me power, the chance to govern wisely, the opportunity to make real changes, affect massive numbers of people in positive ways. Of course, I want that!"

Daken squared off with her, his eyes catching and amplifying the light from the fire. "You could have all that as my queen."

"Since when? You still see me as a little fool, an innocent to be guided by your political ambitions. My only power would be in your bed, and even then I'd be underneath you, literally as well as figuratively."

"And you think he doesn't want to bed you?"

Jane threw up her hands. "Well, of course, he does. He's a man, as much ruled by his pants as you are. But at least he respects my mind, too. With him, I'd have real power. With you..." She let her voice trail off, not knowing what, if anything, she'd have with him.

"But he's dangerous."

"All power is dangerous," she returned.

Daken stepped forward into the glow of the fire. The light from the flames danced brilliantly across his face, making his skin seem to radiate with his own special power. Looking at his eyes, she saw the soothing comfort for which she longed.

"Do you want him, Jane? Not his power, but him. The man Kyree."

Jane sighed, closing her eyes against the headache that seemed to haunt her these days. She broke from his touch, pacing the room with heavy steps. "I don't know, Daken. If you're asking me if I love him, the answer is I doubt it. I barely know him. He certainly doesn't love me. He's in love with the power I could bring him."

"Then why—"

"Because he respects me. Because I respect him, and I respect the things we could do together. He's right, Daken. Politically, we're the perfect combination." She suddenly turned to face him, and this time hers was the face touched by the firelight while his remained in shadow. "I can live without love, Daken. I've been doing that for most of my life. Kyree's offering me power. Why else would I have been brought forward in time, fulfilling a centuries old prophesy, if not to influence the world for the better? I've got to guide this Earth away from the mistakes that destroyed my world. I can't do that without the kind of power he's offering me."

She bit her lip, knowing the pain she felt was only a fraction of the pain her words inflicted on Daken, but she continued anyway, not seeing any other way.

"What do you have, Daken, that can compete with that?"

He was silent a long time, his face cast in shadow, his body outlined by the pulsing red glow of the fire.

"Nothing," he finally said. "Nothing at all." Then he left, his footsteps firm as he walked away.

Chapter Eleven

✦   ✦   ✦

Jane cried the rest of the night. Her love for Daken burned as brightly as ever, but without a similar love from him, she could do nothing. She'd be a fool to give up everything Kyree offered for the uncertain and probably subservient life she'd have with Daken.

So she cried, mourning the loss of everything she might have had with Daken more than she'd grieved for the loss of her whole world. Then, when the morning sun filtered through her window, she dried her eyes and dressed, trying to work up some enthusiasm for a bright future as an Empress.

Looking in the mirror, she wished she'd bothered to buy some cosmetics. Her eyes were swollen, her face blotchy. It didn't help that her head still pounded like a football field right after the winning touchdown.

Even food didn't help. Unwilling to face breakfast in front of the entire University, Jane sent Steve to bring her back something to eat. She took one bite, then ran to the bathroom. Five minutes later, she was sure she'd thrown up everything she'd eaten in the last year.

"I hate this place," she moaned, burying her face in the cool towel Steve handed to her. But that was all the self-pity she permitted herself. The Council meeting would start in a half hour, and she was determined to attend.

She made it with minutes to spare. Steve led her to the Council's audience chamber. The room was predictably impressive with a curved table facing the door. The Council members sat in the five seats beneath a brilliant ivy flag that stood for the Elven Lord. Petitioners lined up in the hallway waiting for their turn to plead their cause.

The Elven Lord naturally sat in the center seat. Kyree stood to his right, apparently trying to convince Ginsen of something unpleasant. Given the bitter look on Ginsen's face, Jane guessed they were talking about her.

Kyree noticed her the moment she entered the room. He immediately crossed to her, his expression warm, his eyes concerned as they lingered on every sign of her sleepless night.

"Are you all right?"

"I'm fine," she forced herself to smile at him. "I just didn't sleep very well."

"When we are married, you will sleep like a babe every night. I promise."

His earnest expression drew her first real smile of the day. "Then you must be a great wizard indeed."

Kyree grinned. "Oh, I am. You can count on it." His face suddenly darkened, his eyes piercing beneath the stark slash of his eyebrows. "Does that mean you have decided to accept my proposal?"

Jane swallowed nervously. She couldn't think of any reason not to give him her answer. She made her decision last night. She'd given Daken his opportunity to stop her. There was nothing left to do but make it official. At least to Kyree.

Still, it took all her composure to say the words that would seal her future. "Yes, Kyree. I would be honored to marry you and be your Empress."

He raised both her hands to his lips, kissing them each in turn. "You do me a great honor, Oracle. You will not regret it."

"So what next?" She glanced around at the other Council Members. "Do we tell them?"

"Oh, no. Not yet. There are still some minor details to work out."

"You mean a strategy."

He grinned. "You are quick, Jane. Between my magic and your tech-nol-ogy," he struggled with the English word, "we will be unstoppable."

His interest in her technology struck a sour chord within her, but she was forced to push it aside as he continued.

"We must meet. Tomorrow night. Today's proceedings will go late, and I'm always irritable afterwards."

"All right," she said, a thrill of excitement running through her spine. "And perhaps you can show me some real magic. Except for the communication spell with Daken, I haven't been able to see exactly what a true wizard can do."

He raised a surprised eyebrow. "Then you must allow me to show off my skills for my new bride."

"I'd love that." The thrill of excitement grew to a tremor of anticipation as Jane looked forward to the evening.

Then, to add some spice to her thoughts, Kyree spoke into her ear, pitching his voice to a sexy bedroom tone. "Come to my room. After dinner."

She lifted her gaze in a coy glance. "Are you sure

I'll be safe with you?"

He stopped, raising her hand to her lips as a courtier of old. "I promise, I shall do nothing you do not wish me to do."

"Then you may count on me."

He smiled, deftly twisting her hand over to place his lips into her palm. Then the moment was gone as the Elven Lord approached them, his face set in clear lines of annoyance.

"It's time we started, Kyree."

The wizard inclined his head, but Ginsen barely noticed. He flicked his contemptuous glare over Jane, taking in her baggy eyes and sallow skin. Tomorrow morning, first thing, she swore to herself, she would buy some good make-up.

"You sit over there." Ginsen pointed to the seat on the other side of Kyree.

She inclined her head as she'd seen Kyree do, but Ginsen had already turned his back on her, stomping to his seat.

"I tried to get him to put you on his left," whispered Kyree in her ear, "but the man is a stubborn fool."

"It's just as well," she responded, eyeing the two other Council members, both of whom she'd met before. "I feel more comfortable next to you anyway."

The proceedings began soon after that. There were no preliminaries. The Elven Lord merely nodded to one of the mages manning the door, and the first petitioner was ushered in.

The process was surprisingly efficient. A petitioner would state his case. Opposing viewpoints, if any, were also present. The mages kept order much as a bailiff would in a court of law. After hearing whatever arguments, the Council members argued the merits in open court, then eventually reached a decision. Truly difficult cases were held over for private debate before the Council decided, but there were very few of those.

Jane tried to judge if Kyree truly pulled the strings as he claimed, but it was impossible for her to tell. As far as she could see, the cases were decided fairly, with most of the Council members agreeing on the outcome. Kyree was certainly forceful in his opinions, but so were the other members. And when Ginsen finally pronounced judgement, she couldn't tell if his decision was based on his own personal opinions or because Kyree encouraged them.

So it continued throughout the morning with only a short break for lunch before they returned to the endless line of problems and complaints involved with running a kingdom. Jane found herself longing for the cool serenity of the computing center when suddenly Daken walked in.

From the moment she saw him step into the room, her heart swelled with pride. He looked every inch a king. His face was clean shaven, his clothes both elegant and understated. His scabbard, now hanging by his side, actually gleamed in the sunlight. But his regalness came not from his clothing, but through his bearing. He stood tall where most people slouched. He met each one of the Council members' eyes, his gaze steady and demanding respect.

He was, in manner and appearance, Daken, King of Chigan.

He didn't look at her but once and then only as he made his bow to each of the Council members. If his gaze happened to linger a moment longer on her drawn features or her encouraging smile, then it was probably because he was gathering his thoughts before his presentation.

He spoke eloquently of the problems his people faced every day. His condemnation of the Tarveen was both specific and graphic, causing more than a few gasps of alarm. Then he began his request for arms, starting with a well-reasoned argument and finishing with an impassioned plea. By the time he was done, Jane wanted to scream "Bravo!" and throw flowers. As it was, she could only sit in silent dread as the time for discussion began.

Now was the moment when Daken would expect her to come out strongly in support of his military needs. Jane tensed, feeling sick to her stomach once again. Her headache hadn't abated and her vision occasionally blurred, but she persevered, remaining staunchly faithful to what she saw as her mission—to keep the world in peace. And that meant denying Daken's request for arms.

As was typical, Ginsen spoke first, usually to ask the other members for their opinions. He didn't this time.

"King Daken, you are aware of my long-standing policy of pacifism, are you not?"

"Of course, Elven Lord. And it is a good and worthy policy in most circumstances. However, there are times, and this is one of them, when nothing but a show of force will do."

"It has never been necessary before," Ginsen returned.

"True. But then the world is changing. Our neighbors grow stronger on every border. Where before they occupied themselves with basic survival, now we see definite kingdoms or colonies such as the Tarveen. These others see our rich lands, our fat cows, and happy people. Without any military force, they will pick at our borders, eating away at the kingdom bit by bit until, like the diseased scavengers they are, they gnaw at the very walls of our homes."

The image was so vivid it threw the room into a horror-stricken silence. For her part, Jane mentally reviewed her arguments, wishing she could speak as well as Daken, but still determined to do her best. She silently prepared her statements about violence benefiting no one, about how they shouldn't fear outsiders just because they were different. Instead, the Elven Lord should try to negotiate trade arrangements, create formal lines of communications starting with peace ambassadors.

She prepared all of that, only to sit on the edge of her seat in shock when she never got the chance to speak. Ginsen spoke before anyone else had the opportunity to venture an opinion.

"King Daken, we were not unaware of the difficulties your lands face. We knew of your coming and of the purpose of your mission. Unfortunately, we have been unable to come to an agreement on the appropriate action. Therefore, we will table this matter until the day after tomorrow when you will attend a private meeting of the Council. We will debate this issue then, giving you the opportunity to refute our arguments."

Daken nodded, his face very grave. "Every day, more of my people die at the hands of the Tarveen. It is my hope that I may help the Council reach a swift decision on my behalf."

Ginsen nodded. "We too are committed to reaching a swift decision. In the meantime, may the Father bless and keep your people in His mighty hand."

Daken bowed again to each of the Council members

and then withdrew, his expression one of polite respect and no more. Watching his stiffly formal departure, Jane was amazed at how different he seemed from the passionate warrior who had paced her room like a caged beast. She saw no resemblance in this stately King to the gentle lover who had touched her so briefly in the inn or even the teasing healer and friend who had brought her to Bosuny.

The Daken she'd seen this afternoon was King Daken, a man she didn't know at all. It was an extremely depressing thought given that King Daken was the only one she'd see from now on.

❖   ❖   ❖

Kyree was right. The line of petitioners didn't end until very late in the evening. By that time, Jane kept herself awake by will power alone. When it was done, she barely made it back to her room before falling into a restless sleep filled with fitful starts and bizarre dreams.

She woke with a fever.

She hated fevers. They always made her throw up, and she started doing that almost before she opened her eyes.

"Damn stupid time to get sick," she muttered as she stumbled back to her bed. Then she happened to catch sight of Steve's worried expression.

"It's all right," she said in her halting Common. "It's just a cold. Probably from wandering through woods at night. I'll be fine after I get a little rest." She started to drift off to sleep, but then reopened her eyes.

Just as she suspected, Steve was slipping out of her apartment.

"Steve," she croaked.

He stopped, one foot out the door. Then slowly he shut the door and returned to her bedside.

"It's just a cold. I don't have any immunity to your diseases and this is the body's way of getting it." She laughed weakly at her joke, but when she stopped, Steve didn't look the least bit reassured. "I'll be fine."

He shook his head, his pale eyes huge in his small face.

"Wait until this afternoon," she said. "Then we'll see."

He didn't respond.

"I'm going to take a nap now." Her eyes drifted closed. "But I want you to promise me something first." It took herculean willpower, but she managed to drag her eyelids open again. "Don't get a healer. And certainly don't get Daken. It'll just make things much harder."

The boy looked unconvinced.

"I mean it, Steve. I'm the Keeper of Knowledge. I know best. I don't want Daken here. Not unless I'm dying, and maybe not...even...then."

She slept.

◆   ◆   ◆

She woke just before dinner. Steve looked like he hadn't left her side all day. She smiled warmly at him, feeling much stronger. Her headache remained, and that meant she still had a fever, but at least she wasn't throwing up.

In fact, she almost felt hungry, and that was a good sign.

"Cheer up, Stevie old boy. I'm feeling great.

Definitely on the mend." Then she stopped talking because she'd sat up too fast, and her head was spinning like a floppy disk.

"I definitely need to eat. I'm faint with hunger."

She got up and dressed as quickly as possible given how weak she felt. Then she ran a brush through her hair. It wasn't until she set down the brush that she noticed.

She'd always taken a secret pride in her thick, copper-colored curls, even when they were cut short. It was her one abiding vanity that stayed with her through fat times and dumpy-looking clothes. At least she had her hair.

Until now. She felt her knees go weak as she stared at the thick mat of hair now in her brush. Running her fingers through her head, she felt more strands pull free.

Her hair was falling out.

She quickly listed her symptoms—persistent headaches, nausea and vomiting, dizzy spells, fatigue, and now hair loss. She was horribly afraid she knew what that meant, but just in case, she scanned Dr. Beavesly's memories. He had some awareness of the new strains of colds and flu that plagued the population. Perhaps she had one of those less threatening diseases.

No such luck. Dr. Beavesly's memories focused primarily on one horrible disease—radiation poisoning. Through him, she got to see it all from the first pale moments of fatigue through the horrifying, bitter end.

There was no doubt in her mind. She was dying of radiation poisoning.

She stared at the brush and mentally kicked herself for her stupidity. The rest of the population had mutated so they thrived on the radiation. It was the source of their magic. But she was from an earlier time. A time when radiation was lethal.

Her head spun; her breathing grew rapid and shallow. Steve was by her side in an instant, but she waved him away, unable to soothe a frightened boy when she was so close to panic herself.

"But why?" she cried out loud.

Her mother used to say everything happened for a reason. What was the reason in this? She accepted that she'd been thrown forward in time. Maybe she even saw some logic, some purpose to the act. As Kyree said, she was uniquely qualified to bring knowledge, prosperity, and most of all peace to this new world.

But not if she was about to die a slow, lingering death of radiation poisoning. It wasn't fair!

She spun out of her chair, ignoring a fresh assault of dizziness. Her mother was wrong. This was a random universe. A universe where you made your own way despite the precariousness of random events.

Very well. She was dying. And would continue to die unless she found a way to mutate like the rest of the population. She bit her lip, suddenly finding a new priority.

She would find a way to mutate. The Old Ones did it. She could too. Because nothing, not Ginsen, not Daken, not even the absurdity of a random world would keep her from helping the people of this new Earth. No matter what the cost, she would make sure they didn't destroy themselves like the idiots from her own time.

Her first thought was to run to Daken, but she quickly pushed the thought aside. Whatever else his feelings may be, he cared for her. Knowing she was dying would only cause needless pain. Sure he could probably cure her now. Failing another option, she would turn to him.

But the problem wouldn't go away after just one healing. The radiation was everywhere. She would need weekly, if not daily treatments. Daken couldn't hang around just to heal her. Perhaps she'd hire a court healer. Someone to give her daily health treatments.

Jane took a deep breath and stood up. At least she still had some time. She needed to explore any other options with the one man with a vested interest in her continuing health—Kyree. She would talk to him.

The wizard, like most everyone else, was at dinner. Although she thought she felt well enough to eat, the sights and smells that assaulted her senses as she entered the main dining hall were almost too much. She staggered against a wave of nausea, grateful for Steve's supporting arm.

How could this come on so fast? She'd felt just fine a few days before. Except for the headaches. True, she'd never really felt like eating since coming to this time. Jane sighed. She supposed if she thought about it, the symptoms were there long before today.

Jane spotted Kyree right away. His dark, imposing figure stood out at center table as he sat regally next to the Elven Lord. Her empty seat was to his left.

She scanned the room briefly for Daken. He was no where to be seen. Just as well. She looked dreadful, and she didn't want Daken to see her like this. It was a ridiculous vanity, she knew, but hers nonetheless.

Jane waved Steve away to his table. Then she slid along the edge of the room toward her seat. She spoke briefly to a few people who stopped her on the way. She also intercepted more than a few speculative looks.

She could almost hear the buzz going through the room.

The Oracle was ill. Was it a mortal illness? Was she a fake? Had the Father cursed her for daring to assume the Keeper's position when she wasn't the true one?

Jane forced her face into a smile, trying to look really healthy when she felt like she wanted to throw up and pass out, not necessarily in that order. Finally, she made it to her seat.

She caught Kyree's attention immediately. "Jane! I heard you were unwell, but I did not think—"

"I'll be fine. Really. Just a little overtired." She lied for everyone else's benefit. Then she directed her next comment to Kyree. "I thought I might discuss something with you after dinner."

"Are you hungry? Do you want—"

"No!"

Despite her refusal, the Dwarven member of the Council presented her with a platter of what might have been very good beef stroganoff. She looked down, determined to make an effort, but the sight nearly undid her.

"No," she said tightly, pushing the plate away. "I'm not hungry at all."

Kyree's eyes narrowed, and she knew he was assessing her health with as much accuracy as any doctor. Suddenly he was all smiles. "Well, I'm finished here. If you all will please excuse us . . . " He nodded to the people at the table, then quickly escorted Jane out a side door.

She took deep, supporting breaths of the cool, clean air. "Thank you, Kyree."

"Tell me what is the matter. You don't look at all well."

She managed a weak grin that grew stronger the further they moved away from the nauseating smells of the dining room. "I'm not dying yet, but I did want to discuss something with you."

"By all means." He continued to lead her past the central buildings to one of the more removed classroom sites. He brought her into his laboratory and guided her to a chair.

The room was relatively small by modern laboratory standards, about the size of a small classroom, but what space there was, he used to great effect. It was like entering the set of The Wacky Professor Enjoys Halloween. Side by side with wires, magnets, and something that looked like a bunsen burner were dripping candles, pentacles, and odd-looking crystals. One whole wall contained books, some with modern library covers, others encased in locked leather. In another corner, she saw evil witchcraft-type paraphernalia including a dead rodent and a container of something like blood.

"Does this stuff really work?" she asked.

"What stuff?" he asked, as he lighted lamps throughout the room with a flick of his wrist.

She turned slowly. She'd meant all of it, but she decided to start with specifics. Finally, she gestured to the witchcraft corner. "The pentacle, crystals, the dead thing over there—"

Kyree shrugged, his voice casual. "Most of what the people call magic is actually a way to focus the mind. In truth, the rocks and gold and dead things are unimportant except in how they trigger the mage's mind. Didn't you feel that when you and King Daken shared your communication spell?"

Jane thought back to those first moments with

Daken. This wasn't the first time she'd tried to understand exactly what happened when Daken cut the
piece of gut and released all those strange firefly-like
things into her bloodstream.

"Mostly, I felt disoriented."

"That's to be expected. It is a powerful spell and no
doubt King Daken, as a healer, accomplished most of
the tuning."

"I don't understand."

Kyree wandered about his lab, collecting various
things, dropping them into the pockets of his robe. He
placed a few books on the shelf. Watching him, Jane
realized he seemed on edge, not nervous as much as
keyed up. It was distinctly odd for someone of Kyree's
self-possession.

"The communication spell," he continued, "attuned
your minds, his and yours, together."

"But he cut my hand. Something entered my bloodstream."

Kyree nodded. "That spell contains a temporary
chemical reaction that relaxes your defenses, allowing
you and King Daken to imprint on one another." He
turned to face her, his black eyes intense to emphasize
his words. "A mutual attraction is a typical side effect
of such a spell."

Jane looked away, feeling herself blush to the roots
of her hair. It wasn't as if she'd proclaimed undying
passion for Kyree, but he was the man she intended to
marry. She felt awkward discussing her interest in
another man.

So she decided to change the topic. Feeling strong
enough to walk, she wandered over to a bucket filled
with symbols of all sizes and materials. Every possible
sign from ancient times through modern culture was

represented there. She saw a silver Star of David mixed under a few wooden astrological signs. What looked like an Egyptian hieroglyphic was tangled in the golden arches of a fast food chain. She even caught one sports symbol in leather.

"So all this is window dressing?" She was still amazed by the mismatched pile. This is what her people's most powerful symbols were reduced to—a jumbled pile of discards in a wizard's corner.

She glanced at Kyree who watched her with a seductive smile. "I didn't say they were completely useless. Many stones, for example, have real uses. And as for those items, I thought the ancient symbols might mean more to me."

"But they haven't?" she asked. "Not even the pentacle and the..." she didn't want to think about the other symbols of witchcraft.

"Those are my most recent experiments. I found a book with them in it."

Jane nodded, not sure she wanted to know what was in the book he'd found. Then, rooting through the pile, she lifted up a gold cross. She turned it over, noting the simple workmanship, feeling saddened that her mother's most holy symbol rested in Kyree's pile of junk. "What about this? Any power from this?"

"Nothing. At least not for me."

"Oh." She started to set it down, but changed her mind. "Maybe it'd work for me. Do you mind if I keep it?"

He shrugged. "Not at all."

Without a pocket, Jane slipped the cross into her belt buckle, trapping it between the iron and leather of her belt. Then, with a sigh, she brought her attention back to the reason for her visit.

"Uh, Kyree. As long as we're talking about the magic—"

"Do you know what those symbols mean?"

Jane looked up at the sudden interest in his voice. "Uh, yeah. Don't you?"

"No. Or very little. You must teach them to me." It wasn't a request. He was ordering her, and she wasn't sure she liked it.

"Of course," she said casually. "But then you must teach me about magic."

"Naturally, naturally," he waved his hand in dismissal, his attention fixed on the pile. "What about this one?" He leaned down, snatching the sign for Taurus.

"It's. . ." She stopped herself from answering, realizing if she started on this, he'd never let her stop. Then she'd never get the answers she needed. Answers that could mean the difference between life and death for her.

She reached out, taking the simple iron circle with horns from his hand. "Kyree, I did come here for a reason. I've got some important questions."

"Yes, yes, of course. But what does it mean?" he asked, still pointing to the symbol.

Jane frowned. Her father used to do this to her all the time. He'd toss her simple platitudes as if she didn't know his attention was centered completely on the evening paper. She didn't like it any more coming from her future husband.

"Kyree—"

He grumbled under his breath, then he turned to her. "You want to know what will happen first. Very well." He began ticking items off on his fingertips. "I've already assembled a group of loyal men, mostly mages, ready for my command. Your task, of course, is to supply the other ones with weapons. Once we have enough guns, we will announce both our marriage and our rulership of the Elven Lord's land simultaneously. My men will surround the capitol city to make sure everything goes smoothly."

Jane felt her blood go cold within her. She began slowly, choosing her words carefully. "You want me to supply guns? When we talked before," she blushed slightly at the memory of their "talk", "you said we would usher in a new era of peace."

Kyree nodded with clear impatience. "Of course. But how did you think we would accomplish this turnover of power? Ginsen may be a fool, but he won't hand over his leadership without a fight."

Jane gripped the Taurus symbol as she struggled with her thoughts. How exactly had she envisioned the change of power? "I thought once we announced our marriage, the people would demand the change. Maybe in a popular election. I didn't think..."

"Election? You want the peasants to vote?" His laugh was a cruel disillusionment. "You expect an illiterate peasant, intent on finding his next meal, to care about who rules him in some far-off capitol? Peasants don't understand anything but a weapon."

Jane bit her lip, still fighting the ugly revelations about Kyree's personality. "You told me you needed my popularity with the people. If it's only to be about guns, then why do you need me?"

"Because to hold power afterwards, I need the people's support. My dear there's a great deal of apathy in the population. They'll accept whatever is because they correctly assume they can't change it. If they are to accept what's new, namely us, they need added incentive. And that's you."

"So you violently seize power, then use me to justify your actions."

He nodded, clearly relieved she finally understood. "And," he added with a grin, "this provides the added bonus of an army to support your King Daken against the Tarveen. Perhaps a little later than he'd hoped, but then he'll just have to make do. Add the much-needed military experience, and we are well on our way to building an empire."

"I thought we already had an empire," she said dryly, gently dropping the Taurus symbol before wandering back to her seat. She desperately needed to sit down.

He followed her across the room, dropping his hands on her shoulders, speaking to her as he would a child. "I haven't forgotten all your plans, my dear. You will focus on keeping the peace within the realm. This is where all your wonderful ideas will keep the peasants happy."

"Is that my role in the new order? A new opiate for the masses?" She fought to keep her voice even.

"That is what you're best at, my dear. My role will be to constantly expand our borders, bringing more people under your gentle control."

Jane searched Kyree's handsome face, wondering if she could adjust to this change of plan. She'd still be ruling justly and peacefully over a large territory. It was only the manner of acquisition that differed. "The people would be under my control?" she asked.

Kyree smiled that chauvinistically condescending smile that all men seemed to resort to when a woman got difficult. "Well, I'd advise you, of course. As you would assist me with new weapons. We'd be working together."

Reality had finally broken through her illusions, thought Jane with a bitter twist of her lips. Kyree only wanted her for her knowledge of technology. In that, he and Daken were identical. What horrified her more was that she was still considering Kyree's proposal. Every good ruler had to learn to compromise. Perhaps a totally pacifist world was not an option.

But there were things she did not accept—primarily his proposed division of power. She knew how to handle men who wanted to usurp her responsibilities.

She lifted her chin, leaning back in her chair to stare straight into his jet black eyes. "I don't think so, Kyree."

His eyes narrowed, but she refused to be intimidated.

"I want complete authority over the people. You can take your armies and gobble up territory if you like, assuming it's done in a reasonable manner. The people come under *my* control. *My* rulership."

He didn't answer. His eyes bored into her. He leaned over her, trying to dominate her with his body. When she didn't react, keeping her eyes steady and her breathing slow, he switched tactics. Leaning further down, he tried to kiss her, but she held up her hand, stopping him inches from her face.

"Even I'm not that stupid, Kyree. Sex is fun, but we're talking about power."

He stood slowly. He didn't withdraw, he just pulled himself up to his full height. Still he said nothing, and Jane wasn't foolish enough to think he'd acquiesced.

"I'm curious, Kyree. Exactly why is it you want to rule? I thought you shared my same visions of peace and prosperity."

"Of course, I do."

Jane laughed, a short, tight mockery aimed more at

herself than him. "I don't think so. What is it you hope to gain by seizing control?"

She could feel the anger growing in him, but this wasn't something she could back away from. If she shared an empire with this man, she wanted to be sure she understood all the motivating forces.

"What is it you want most in the world, Kyree?"

She looked around the laboratory, her eyes flitting from one book to another object to a pile of chemicals. Slowly, understanding seeped into her brain.

She hadn't noticed it at first because she still saw things with her modern eye. In the twentieth century, Kyree's collection from the chemicals through the books would be relatively easy to come by. But in a world with travel by donkey cart and printing by hand, his laboratory was an impressive display.

The metal and crystals must come from the dwarves. The chemicals might be refined here, but more likely, they were done somewhere to the south. She had seen only one apothecary in the marketplace, and Steve told her they were supplied from the south. Last, but certainly not least, her gaze fell on his wall of books.

"I bet those came from places all over the world. Perhaps, not exactly through ethical means."

Kyree's lips tightened.

Add his vehement interest in the symbols and she came up with what should have been obvious to her. "You want knowledge because knowledge is power. Now that translates to wanting me, first and foremost, because I'm the Keeper of Knowledge. But you also want a kingdom with the might to take what you need." Her gaze fell on a beautifully carved tripod holding a small bronze bowl. The metal was intricately wrought with a delicacy that wasn't available even in her time. "I bet you want to conquer the dwarven lands. They must have ancient secrets, dwarven magic, to create such fine pieces."

She swiveled around, following Kyree as he began to pace about his room. "What about the birdmen to the north? I heard they use magic to fly. Now there's some real power."

Suddenly Kyree moved forward, his voice low, his steps timed precisely with his words. "Not just for me, Jane. For you too. You want to bring peace to this troubled land. I want to study, to learn the world's secrets. These goals aren't mutually exclusive. Remember, you need my power to keep control of the land. And I want your knowledge. We are the perfect combination."

"So you keep telling me." Jane pursed her lips, seeing her opening, but careful not to reveal her interest too soon. "But you see, if I'm to strike a bargain with the devil, I need some assurances first."

He didn't move. His intense expression didn't change, but she knew he'd suddenly become ten times more wary. When he spoke, his voice was silky smooth, very sexy in a dark sort of way. "What assurances do you want?"

Jane shifted her position. Wanting to match his seductive pose with a little distraction of her own, she draped herself more alluringly in the chair as she gave him a casual smile.

"We'll naturally have to come to some agreement on the exact division of power."

"Naturally," he concurred, and she could see this was exactly what he'd anticipated. So she went the opposite direction.

"But not at this moment. First, it occurs to me that I have yet to see a demonstration of this much vaulted magical ability of yours."

He drew himself up, insulted to the core. "You doubt my abilities?"

"I haven't *seen* your abilities."

He raised up his hands as though to cast some great spell, but she stopped him.

"I don't want some light display designed to fool the peasants, Kyree. What I have in mind is something much more specific."

He lowered his arms as he raised one eyebrow in surprise. "Exactly what did you have in mind?"

This time, she was the one who stood up to pace, suddenly nervous as she began to expose her biggest vulnerability. "You may have noticed I am not well."

"I take it you've more than a simple infection?" He sounded almost pleased.

She stopped in front of his bookcase, quickly scanning the titles for anything that might help her.

Nothing. So she pushed ahead, returning to Kyree as her only hope.

"It's called radiation poisoning, but there's a cure. Centuries ago, the survivors changed somehow to accommodate the new radiation, the new magic."

Kyree watched her, his entire body seemingly relaxed as he absorbed her information. But his next words revealed how very alert, how very keen his razor sharp mind was. "You haven't adjusted, have you? You are dying as the Old Ones did. The ones who didn't change."

"I'm not dying, Kyree." She said it as much for herself as for him. "Even without a cure, there are healers who no doubt can take care of the problem."

"But only temporarily. You would require monthly, maybe weekly healings."

"A court healer—" she began, but he cut her off with a firm shake of his head.

"There are only a few healers, and each is a king in his own right with better things to do than loiter about court for you."

She ground her teeth as his words ripped away the last of her more palatable options. Still, Kyree's words came at her, relentlessly pounding at her hopes until there was nothing left.

"You are dying, Oracle. Each moment, your life is whittled away by the very air you breathe, the food you eat. The magic is everywhere, and you cannot escape it."

Jane pushed forward, abandoning the bookcase to stand directly in front of Kyree. "I don't have to escape it. I have to change to accommodate it. I need that spell Kyree, the information that tells me how to change. You give me that, you help me adapt, and I'll help you build your empire."

His eyes narrowed, and Jane could almost see his thoughts wrapping around her offer, deciding how best to use the situation. "How will you help me, Jane? What specifically will you do?"

She glanced away, wondering what she could ethically give him. "I'll tell you everything I have on those symbols and how each was used."

"Guns, Jane. I want guns."

"No. Your magic is enough of a weapon."

"Everyone has magic. And there are many more ways to block spells than there are to create them."

Jane scrambled mentally as she struggled to find something else he wanted.

As if guessing her thoughts, he answered her

question. "There is nothing else I want. Guns will give me the power I need. Rulership was a ploy to please you—"

"The hell, it was. You need a power base, a kingdom, and loyal subjects. You need people to wield those guns. An army to protect the knowledge you intend to steal."

He grinned. "Yes, there are definite advantages to ruling my own kingdom, and it was a sufficient lure for you."

"I could still walk, Kyree." She resorted to her most desperate plea. "And if I die, the knowledge will be lost forever. There's no way you can retrieve it from the computer without me."

Kyree clapped his hands, and Jane experienced a moment of sickening disorientation. In her weakened state, it took her even longer to focus. When she did, her jaw grew slack in astonishment.

Gone were the bright walls of his laboratory, the bookcase, the bucket of symbols, everything. Instead, she stood in the middle of a cave with slick, damp walls lighted by torches set throughout the room. A table lay to one side, filled with books that were probably ancient in her time. Looking down she saw she stood in the middle of a pentacle, etched into the stone floor, each line a small rut lined with gold.

Her blood ran cold when she saw the burning candles, one placed at each point of the star. It was as though he'd already been prepared for some sort of ritual.

"Try and leave now, Jane," taunted Kyree from where he stood just outside the circle.

Jane continued to inspect the room, stretching for a show of bravado. "Impressive trick, Kyree. Where are we?"

"Far below the courtyard. Even the Elven Lord doesn't know it's here."

"Cute," she repeated, starting to casually walk off the pentacle. He didn't stop her, and she extended her step to carry her off the symbol.

She was stopped cold. There was a force field of some sort extending from the circle upward. It tingled along her fingers where she pressed into it. It burned at her shoulder where she tried to shove through it. It was an agony of electrical energy that would not budge.

Finally she fell backward, the first tendrils of terror seeping into her system as she realized how badly she had erred. She'd thought she could handle Kyree.

"It's a cage of sorts," Kyree offered from the sidelines. "It follows the edge of the pentacle, and it is impenetrable."

"Nothing's foolproof, Kyree," she said, but they both knew it was an idle threat.

"True, but I've tested this particular cage. First with small animals, then larger ones. I even had a bear in there—"

"I'm not a dumb animal, Kyree."

"No. But neither was one of my more brilliant students. And even he couldn't get out."

A shiver of apprehension slid up her spine. "What did you do to him?"

Kyree moved away from her as he talked. He knelt down to repair a chalk pentacle half hidden behind his worktable. "He was a bright but idealistic boy who unfortunately learned a great deal more than he was supposed to about my experiments."

Jane tried to steady herself against the panic welling up in her throat. "What did you do to him, Kyree?"

He didn't even glance her way, but continued conversationally, gesturing at an old tome hidden in a shadow, placed at the center of the chalk pentacle. "Interestingly enough, this book was hoarded by the Tarveen. They, of course, couldn't understand it, but its loss sparked their more violent raids on King Daken's lands."

Jane gasped, appalled not by his evil, but that she'd completely misread his true character. "You started the war against Daken?"

"Me?" He looked up and laughed. "No, the Tarveen have raided his lands for years for their own reasons. The loss of the book only increased their anger and, consequently, their viciousness. An unfortunate side effect, I must admit."

Jane tried to think, but she was weak, her thoughts dull and slow. A part of her still hoped there might be a core of decency in Kyree. Maybe this was just a show of strength for him. Maybe the goodness she'd seen in the grove wasn't all false.

"Kyree, the symbols you're using, the book itself, it's all evil. It's black magic."

"Nonsense," he called back cheerfully. "Symbols and knowledge aren't good or evil. They are simply a way of tapping into the source of power within oneself. This book contains healing spells, finding spells..." Kyree glanced at his worktable.

Following his gaze, she felt her heart begin to pound painfully in her throat as she noticed a metal object gleaming dully in a light of a heated brazier.

"Ah, you finally noticed." He stood up, his chalk pentacle now clean of smudge marks, and went to his table. "You are so pathetically naive about the ways of magic, Jane." He picked up the Beretta from the table, firing pin in place. "I watched you that day in the House of Prophesy. I saw you dismantle this in the back room. I even knew you buried it the next night. All it needed was a simple finding spell and here it is. I have a gun. Given a little time, I will learn how to manufacture more."

Moving to a better angle within her limited space, Jane saw what she wanted. The bullet clip was on the table, not in the handle. It was a weak ploy, but all she had.

"You still need me, Kyree. The gun won't work."

"Of course it does. Why else would you work so hard to hide the pieces?"

Jane grinned. "Get a bullet and put it in the chamber."

Clearly intrigued, Kyree did as she directed.

"Now pull the trigger."

He did. Nothing happened. Berettas don't fire without the clip in place.

Kyree twisted the gun, inspecting it in the flickering light. "How very disappointing."

"You still need me, Kyree. Now let me out of here."

He stared vaguely off into space, and Jane began to hope that maybe her bluff had paid off.

"Plus," she pushed, "even if you do figure the gun out, military secrets disappear fast. All too soon your enemies will have them. You'll need me to give you that next boost in weapons technology."

Kyree turned, his head bobbing up and down as he silently agreed with her. Jane's hopes soared. Then Kyree turned, dropped the gun casually on the table, and began collecting chemicals which he tossed into a cold brazier.

His next words effectively extinguished any hope that she'd gotten through to him.

"I had such plans for you, Jane. If only you had been less intelligent."

"A smart collaborator is better than a stupid one," she offered, willing to say anything he wanted if he let her out of the cage.

"True, true. But you see, you're a bit too smart, and I'd have quite a time keeping you in line."

"Believe me, Kyree," she offered placatingly. "I'll be a lot more amenable now that I've seen some of your abilities." She again pressed against the forcefield with the same painful result.

"Yes, and I considered it until you mentioned you're dying. That, of course, leaves me with only one recourse."

She cursed silently, wondering how things had gotten away from her so fast. For a little bit there in his laboratory, she'd thought she had the upper hand. "How will you explain a change in me?" she asked, hoping a small change was all he had in mind.

He glanced at her. "My dear, everyone saw how ill you were. Your death, even an illness, is already explained. I, of course, will neatly step into your place. You see, you will have given me the secrets of the Keeper. With your last dying breaths you passed on the information so the knowledge would continue."

Jane felt her hands begin to shake, and she clasped them in front of her, trying to think. "There must be other options, Kyree. What do you want? I can get it for you."

"I have thought and thought, but I must do this while you are strong enough to endure the process." He looked over at her, his expression sad. Like a person going into a pawn shop, he looked like he was about to lose something valuable out of necessity.

Jane swallowed, the taste of terror bitter in her mouth.

"You're right, you know," he continued. "Military secrets are never secret for very long. Eventually, I will figure out the gun."

Jane closed her eyes, knowing he was right. It was only a matter of time, probably minutes, before he thought to put the clip into the Beretta.

"But then someone else will figure out how to make them too. What I need is your knowledge, the information stored in your mind."

"Exactly," said Jane, pressing enthusiastically forward in her cage. "If you kill me, it will all be gone. Even drugging me is unreliable," she offered, trying to hedge her bets. "A lot of this stuff is very tricky. I'll need all my brain power focused and sharp."

Kyree shook his head forlornly. "This really isn't how I'd intended things to end." With a swift twist of his wrist, he lit the second small brazier. The chemicals began to burn, causing a thick, gray smoke to billow up from the center.

Carrying the small pot of sputtering chemicals, he stepped into the center of the chalk pentacle and sat down.

"What are you doing?" Jane asked, not trying to disguise the tremor in her voice. She had the most horrible feeling her time just ran out.

"Look at the smoke, Jane."

She did as he bid, a gasp of shock escaping her lips as she realized what was happening. Rather than floating above Kyree's head, the smoke from the brazier was somehow filling her airspace. She could smell the coarse burn of sulfur, the cloying scent of myrrh.

She coughed, waving her arms to clear the air, but she became lightheaded from the effort, and the smoke thickened, rather than dissipated.

"I give, Kyree! I'll get you the guns," she lied, desperately playing for time. "I promise." She coughed again, her breath coming in frantic gasps that caught on the way in and burned on the way out.

Kyree's voice came to her, soft and melodious, as lights began to dance before her eyes. "The smoke is a kind of poison, Jane, but a slow one. First it robs you of your mobility, then it slowly bleeds into your mind."

"I'm no good to you dead," she gasped out.

"As it slowly eats into your soul, your mind becomes open and free. Highly vulnerable, you might say."

Jane felt herself stagger. Her legs were numb, and she dropped to her knees.

"In this weakened state, I will merge with you much like the Old Ones merged with other animals."

She tried to fight, tried to think of a way out, but she was so weak, and so very, very slow in her thoughts.

"Once joined with you, I will wander through your memories, absorbing them, living them, learning all you know."

"Can't be done," she muttered, her words slurred and weak.

"But I've already done it to that very bright student I mentioned earlier."

"Dead. First," she forced out. "You'll die with me."

"Oh, no," he chuckled. "I'll be long gone before the last flicker of your life is extinguished. I really am sorry about this. I had such plans for you. Oh," he added as an afterthought. "It won't be painful. You'll be unconscious long before you die. At least it will be relatively quick, almost pleasant when compared to radiation poisoning."

On those words, Jane lost the battle with her body. Dropping away from her physical awareness, she slipped into the nebulous plane of her thoughts, trying to hold them tight to her.

She felt his presence immediately, pressing against her like a heavy weight on top of her heart. She pushed him away, but her efforts seemed pathetically weak against his overwhelming strength.

Desperate for anything, any kind of help, she called silently for Daken. She'd been toying with the idea ever since Kyree mentioned the bonding that was part of their communication spell. She brought out as clear a picture of Daken as possible, then called to it, begging for help.

Nothing happened. On the edge of her consciousness, she heard Kyree laugh at her feeble efforts even as he began to invade her mind.

She shoved him away and brought up her mother's symbol. She pictured a brilliant white cross shining in the darkness of her mind, spilling forth its power into her. In her mind's eye, she gathered the cross' power and aimed it at Daken, screaming for him to notice her, to hear her desperation in his mind.

Nothing.

It didn't work.

Jane felt helplessness well up within her, a sobbing panic mixed with the cold certainty that she had lost. Her mind was no longer under her own control. She felt its barriers weaken, her consciousness slipping away like a pile of leaves in a stiff wind. Soon she would lose her ability to think at all, and in that relaxed state, Kyree would press forward. He would invade her as she never thought possible, pillaging her mind, then running away, leaving her to die alone.

She struggled as long as she could, cleaving to her sanity, but feeling her grip weaken with each passing moment.

She had lost to Kyree.

His glee hovered at the edge of her mind, jeering at her even as she struggled. But the worst part was that no one would ever know what happened. Kyree would continue spreading his net of evil over the world, using her knowledge and the computer's information to become the most powerful force in the world. She would become a footnote in history.

She would be the one who failed to stop him.

Her last thoughts turned away from such global concerns. As the reality of her death crept upon her, she mourned her failures on a personal level. She grieved for the children she would never have, the people she could never say good-bye to.

Most of all, she grieved for Daken. He would never know her last thoughts were of him.

Gathering the tattered remains of her strength, she brought back her image of Daken. She also pulled up the cross, holding it with her because she was dying, and she couldn't think of a better symbol to accompany her into eternity.

With the last of her sanity, she sent a message of love and sorrow to Daken. This time her efforts were rewarded. She felt a flicker of awareness in him. For an instant, she shared his thoughts.

I love you, she whispered. It was all she could manage before her consciousness slipped away.

As death spun toward her, Kyree took over and began the slow rape of her mind.

Chapter Twelve

✦ ✦ ✦

Daken was drinking. Not a lot. Truth was, he was hiding more than imbibing.

He couldn't shake the sight of Jane as a Council Member. His little fool looked as regal and capable as any queen in any land. She had her own special beauty. Her face was pale, almost drawn, but that only enhanced the fierce light shining through her amber eyes.

She'd done well in the meetings. He'd listened to the talk. More than any of the petitioners, she was the one tried that day. Every one agreed. She'd done very, very well. Her few comments were well-spoken, well-timed, and well-received. She was a success.

Daken was so very proud of her.

He drained his tankard of ale.

He was also very, very depressed. A small part of him had prayed for her failure, begged the Father for her to fall flat. Because then Kyree wouldn't have wanted her. He couldn't risk marriage to a political liability.

Then she would be free for Daken. He would marry her no matter what her political inclinations were. Then she would keep his castle for him while he saved his people. He would come back after exterminating the Tarveen, after he demonstrated his devotion by making his lands safe for her and their children. And she would welcome home her triumphant husband, her face glowing in the sunset, her hair shimmering like dark silk. She would take him in her arms, and he would take her to bed.

Daken ordered another tankard.

His dream would never come true. She was the Oracle in all ways now, and she was Kyree's intended bride.

He was nothing more than a petitioner for her aid.

The inn door banged open, letting in a gust of wind that set up a wave of grumbling among the patrons. The weather was damp and uncertain, the wind alternately gusty, then dead—the certain harbinger of a coming storm. No one here this night, including Daken, appreciated the reminder of what the future held.

Daken happened to glance up as the barmaid brought his next tankard. He'd meant to ogle her ample charms that spilled out in front of her like foaming ale. Instead he saw a small boy slipping through the crowds to him.

He swore under his breath. The last person he wanted to see right now was Jane's little pet, Steve. The boy symbolized the end of his hopes of getting Jane as his queen. If it weren't for Steve, Daken would have been Jane's only friend. She would have continued to cling to her King or her Knight Errant, as she sometimes called him. Instead, she got her companionship from the safe services of a boy while she took on the whole Council and won.

By the Father, he was proud of his fierce little beauty. And he was also very, very depressed.

Daken scowled as Steve came up to the table. The boy looked winded and tired, but his eyes were wide with fear. Daken turned to his ale, not wanting to know, but the boy's steady presence and his hauntingly clear blue eyes continued to plague his thoughts even after he'd shut out the sight.

With a sigh, Daken pushed away his ale untouched. "What is it, boy?"

Steve made a gesture for Daken to follow him.

"Is it Jane?"

A nod.

"Is she ill?"

A vehement nod.

"How ill?" He could barely push the words past the tightening in his chest. "Is she wounded?"

He shook his head, no.

"Sick, then. Dying?"

A grave nod and a silent plea that echoed the agony in Daken's heart. Jane was dying.

It was at that moment he felt something. The vague sense of unease that had been eating at him for the last half hour suddenly crystallized into a brilliant image.

Jane, in a cave, gasping out her last breath.

I love you whispered through the empty chambers of his heart, and then it was gone. She was gone, and he knew he'd heard her last words.

When his vision cleared, he saw Steve, his expression intense and focused. In that instant, Daken understood what Jane saw in the boy. Steve was a lot more than just a mute servant.

Gripping the child's sleeve, Daken spoke, his voice hoarse and urgent. "She's in a cave. And there's smoke."

Steve's eyes widened in fear.

"Do you know where it is?"

The boy moved in a flash. Daken charged after the nimble-footed youth, loosening his sword in its scabbard as he went.

Fear beat like a warrior's drum in Daken's bloodstream. As he pounded after Steve, Daken felt his body respond to the call of war. He didn't know who was killing Jane, but he hoped it was Kyree. It would give him great pleasure to slice the wizard from neck to groin in one swift stroke.

He spared a brief thought for Steve. A mortal fight with a wizard was bad business. Daken had no spells, so his only hope was to surprise the bastard. That was easy enough to do if the wizard concentrated on something else. But if he happened to be in between spells or worse yet, waiting in ambush, then Daken didn't want an innocent boy in the middle of a doomed contest.

Without magic, Daken wouldn't stand a chance in a face to face combat.

They sped through the streets, and Daken soon noticed the shadow of the black pantar sliding through the darkness with them. They made it to Ginsen's Palace in scant minutes, and Daken nearly ground his teeth in frustration. He grabbed Steve's arm, spinning the boy around.

"She was in a cave, Steviens. There aren't any caves here."

The boy nodded vigorously and started running again, skirting the edge of the student dormitories until he came to the small grove of trees.

Daken tore after him, pushing himself to keep up with the boy's lightening fast pace. Then he had to stop himself from running over both the boy and the pantar as he skidded to a stop, clutching on to the largest tree trunk to steady himself.

The pantar nosed him aside, pawing at the base of

the tree trunk. Steve appeared immobile, his face passive as he waited patiently for Daken to catch his breath.

"*Venzi,* boy! I said, a cave. Didn't you hear me? A cave!"

Then Daken felt his anger slip away, if only for a moment. Surprise beat a counterpoint to his pounding heart as he realized Steve wasn't passively waiting, he was doing something. The boy closed his eyes, held onto his belt buckle, then touched the very tree Daken still clung to for support, the same tree the pantar still pawed.

To Daken's astonishment, the trunk slid silently open. He jumped away to avoid getting hit in the face by what he now saw as the door. Extending below the earth was a rough hewn stair leading down into a black nothingness.

"All right, boy," he said, drawing his sword. "Stay here." Daken cut off his words as Steve crossed into the passageway first. Then Daken scrambled inside before the door sealed shut, leaving the pantar outside to howl her frustration to the moon.

Once again, Daken reached out for Steve, trying to shove him back to the door, but in the pitch black of the stairway, the boy evaded his grasp. Daken couldn't speak for fear of alerting Kyree, or whoever it was down there, so he settled for a long, silent series of curses. It would be hard enough moving blind down a narrow stair without worrying about one witless boy.

But then suddenly a light flared bright above them, before dimming to a gentle glowing ball. It floated over their heads, illuminating just enough to dampen the oppressive blackness. It was a magelight. Daken looked with new respect at the small boy nimbly sliding down the stairs.

Could it be possible that this boy was indeed a wizard? All the mages he knew spoke, but that didn't mean words were necessary.

Daken resolved to keep a much closer eye on Jane's young protegee. In the meantime, there was a maniac to kill.

Every cell in Daken's body strained ahead, demanding he tear forward and release the fury pounding in his head. With every breath he took, he wondered if Jane had already breathed her last. The greatest healer on the planet couldn't bring back life once the spirit fled.

But he wouldn't do Jane any good if he got himself killed in an ambush before he could get to her. He steeled himself to silence and stealth as he and Steve moved down the twisting stairs.

At least they were picking up speed. The walls were changing. Instead of the treacherous shifting dirt mixed with tree roots near the door, they now walked down a stair cut through stone. Unfortunately, that also made it harder to remain silent.

Ahead, Steve continued to slip from shadow to shadow, like a flickering ghost. Daken would have pushed the boy behind him, but Steve was adamant he go first, brushing his hands over the faint symbols carved into the rock walls.

Daken hadn't noticed them at first. They were skillfully hidden in the cracks and veins of the stone. It wasn't until he saw the faint blue burn of magic beneath Steve's hand that he looked closer. He could only hope the boy knew what he was doing. If the boy wasn't truly mage-born, then the fitful, half-magic of witches and dabblers could be more dangerous than whatever traps lurked along the stair.

Still they moved on. Daken strained to hear sounds,

voices, anything ahead, but there was only a deathly silence more ominous than noise.

Finally they rounded a corner and saw the flickering light of a torch reflected on the wall. This time, Daken was firm as he pushed Steve behind him. Then, together, they peered around the corner.

Kyree sat in the middle of a chalk symbol. His back was to them, but even from this angle, he seemed relaxed—as if he were asleep or in deep meditation. Beside him was a brazier, burning something that, as far as he could tell, produced no smoke. Beyond Kyree was a table and then a huge dome of black air, thick and ugly as it roiled within its contained space.

Daken scanned the room again, looking for any sign of Jane. And in that moment of inattention, he lost Steve. The boy shot past him, flying across the room, he grabbed the brazier by Kyree and shoved it toward the dome.

Daken sprung after him, cursing the boy as they lost the element of surprise. Already Kyree roused from his trance and pointed one long, thin finger at Steve. Daken screamed a war charge, relieved when his yell distracted Kyree from whatever spell the wizard had intended to throw at the boy.

Kyree spun around, his face twisted into a growl of pure rage. Daken ran as fast as he could, his weapon ready to strike the instant he was within range, but even as he barreled forward, he knew it was too far.

Kyree's first shock dart nearly killed him. A solid arrow of crackling energy hit Daken on his side as he tried to dodge to the right. The heat burned through his clothing, and his left arm fell to his side, numb and useless. Still Daken pressed forward.

It was a painful game of inches. Shock darts, fireballs, and lightening bolts flew at him, one after the other, while he ducked and dodged like a mouse scurrying away from a cat. Whenever possible, he pressed forward, always straining to close the distance between him and Kyree. He was bathed in sweat that sizzled and popped along his skin from the heat of Kyree's missiles. He gasped for breath, his head pounding with fear and adrenaline.

Meanwhile, the wizard stood, calm and composed, like a man at a tea party. And though his attention was trained on Daken, he seemed almost bored with their little fight, serenely confident in his ability to handle one warrior and a small boy.

Daken threw himself to the left as another flaming ball seared the cave floor, creating a sudden smoking crater where Daken's head had been seconds before.

Further to the left, he caught a flash of movement in his peripheral vision. Was that Steve? Or another threat? Daken almost wished it were something other than the boy. He fervently hoped Steve had the sense to run back up the stairs and to safety. Maybe even bring some help.

Even if it did come too late.

Daken continued fighting, pressing slowly forward like a dog scenting a rat, knowing all the while the odds were stacked against him. Eventually, his luck would run out. Even now, each blow, each blast of magic burned closer to his body. It was only a matter of time before he ducked the wrong way and caught a fire ball in the face or chest.

Daken saw another movement to his right and swerved around, facing the new threat. It was Steve, crossing to the worktable. Behind the boy, the dome of black air had been broken by the brazier, and the smoke now gushed toward the ceiling where it hung like a malevolent cloud, slowly spreading over them all.

Glancing lower, Daken saw a shadowy outline at the base of the dome. It was Jane, her body twisted in slow agony, her skin already tinged with the gray pallor of death. There was no aura, no faint glow of life for his healer's eyes to see.

Daken choked back his cry. He shouldn't have looked. He shouldn't have left himself open to the wave of fury that rampaged his system as he scanned her still body for any signs of life. He couldn't stop himself, and in that moment when emotions clouded his thinking, when hatred and vengeance burned through him like a fever, he rushed forward, sword raised.

And he was caught in Kyree's trap.

A wave of magic, like an undulating blanket, fell on him, pinning him to the ground while thousands of tiny needles seared into his skin. It was a slow torture, inflicting constant pain without being lethal.

In front of him, Kyree laughed with spiteful disdain. "You're a fool, King Daken. She is already dead, and I now have all that she was. Do you understand me? Everything she knew, everything she was, I know it all."

He backed up to his table where Steve hastily set down the heavy metal object then darted away. It seemed to Daken the boy had done something to the table brazier. He saw a flash and the low fire flickered; then it steadied.

Whatever the boy intended, it hadn't worked.

Kyree didn't seem to give the boy a passing thought. Either he hadn't seen Steve or he didn't think a mute servant boy could do anything against him.

Daken fell backwards, his last hope dying. There was nothing he could do. Kyree's magic held him pinned. Even breathing was agony. Any other movement left his limbs numb from shock. He'd already lost use of both his hands.

Daken stayed still, listening to Kyree's gleeful chuckles, while his thoughts were on the woman just a few feet away. Just a few feet, and he could touch her one last time.

Even that was denied him.

"Would you like to see what Jane taught me?" Kyree lifted up the heavy iron piece, and Daken saw it was a gun. With a soft chuckle, Kyree picked up another oblong piece and fitted it into the handle. "I'm almost ashamed to say I didn't understand this before. But then I was looking for a triggering word, forgetting the past was a land of machines. All it needed was the clip."

Tilting the gun, Kyree pulled back on the top, presumably to prime the weapon. Still prostrate on the floor, Daken tensed, knowing his death was at hand.

Desperate, Daken tried to run only to be rewarded by a thousand shards of slicing pain searing through his nerves without leaving a mark. Daken stilled, biting his lip against the scream.

Agonizing as it was, he'd gotten his answer. The field was still in place, but the magic was weakening. Daken was in pain, but not nearly as devastated as before. He curled his numb fingers around the hilt of his sword. If he could just keep Kyree talking long enough for the spell to fade, then he might be able to do a surprise attack. He *had* to keep Kyree talking.

"She'd never tell you about a gun," he called, his voice hoarse as he fought the restraining magic.

Kyree didn't even glance down. He was busy playing with the weapon, practicing his aim, sighting on various objects in the room. Then he pulled the trigger.

The boom was deafening, as was the explosion of shards where a chamber pot once stood.

"Oh, yes, she told me everything I need to know," Kyree said as much to himself as to Daken. "She led quite an unexceptional life, you know. For such a bright girl, I was surprised to learn how very dull her existence was."

"Not everyone has glorious dreams of conquest."

"No," he said, sighing dramatically. "She seemed singularly devoted to the idea of education for all. Rather like Ginsen in that respect." Kyree finally looked down, slowly raising the ancient weapon as he sighted Daken's head. "You'll be happy to know her last thoughts were of you."

"I know," Daken said, his mind and body tensing for a last second spring. "I heard them."

"Ah, so she did finally reach you. I wondered if she made it through. By the way, I know the field is almost gone. I feel it only honorable to tell you I will put a bullet in you long before you come within spitting distance. Use your time to prepare your soul for the Father."

Daken swore under his breath. Kyree was right. A blind beggar couldn't fail to miss at this range. Still he kept talking, stalling for time. "My soul was prepared the first time I saw the field after a Tarveen raid."

"Oh," responded Kyree with a twisted smile. "How convenient for you."

Bang!

Daken didn't wait for reaction to set in, he leaped forward, pushing through the last rending sheen of the restraining field. His body was prepared to compensate for a gaping wound that would no doubt kill him soon, but the expected agony never occurred.

He wasn't shot?

Ahead of him, Daken saw Kyree turn around, his eyes wide as he stared at his spinning table brazier. That's what the noise was. Whatever Steve had done to the hot coals, had finally paid off.

Daken leapt forward, his sword ready.

Kyree never had a chance. He was still realizing there was no threat from behind when Daken was on him. Kyree spun around, raising a finger to throw a spell, forgetting the gun dangled from the other hand.

Daken snarled. Just as he'd fantasized back in the inn, he had the satisfaction of cutting through the evil wizard, ripping him open from neck to groin in one devastating slice. Daken didn't even feel the jarring connection of bone and metal as he shifted his grip, yanking the sword out of Kyree's pelvis. Blood spurted everywhere as the wizard fell in a gruesome heap on the floor.

From the near corner, Daken caught a movement and he spun to face his new threat. But it was only Steve, coming out of his hiding place, a rock clenched in his fist.

Daken smiled grimly at the boy, glancing at the rock and nodding. "Is that how you did it? You threw a rock?" Daken grabbed a nearby rag to clean off his sword. "I suppose I should be grateful you missed Kyree and hit the brazier instead. It was just the distraction I needed."

Steve slowly shifted his gaze from Kyree's still twitching body. He shook his head, his expression quite adamant though still a bit dazed.

"You didn't throw a rock at the brazier?"

Steve made the motion of throwing something into the coals.

"What? What did you throw in there?"

Steve pointed to the gun, still gripped in Kyree's lifeless hand.

"A bullet," said Daken in amazement. His knowledge of the ancient weapon came back to him. "You tried to disable the gun? You took out the bullet and threw it into the fire? And it went off?"

Steve nodded, his eyes still wide, still mesmerized by the butchery of violent death.

Daken sheathed his sword, turning to the other still body in the room. He hadn't wanted to face it, but now it was time. He knew she was dead. Even if Kyree hadn't told him so, he'd felt her acceptance of it back in the inn. Back when she'd told him she loved him.

Daken swallowed back tears of despair as he walked to her still body. He pulled Steve with him, trying to distract the boy from his first grisly sight of death. But even as Steve followed, Daken saw that his expression remained hollow and drawn in shock.

No doubt the sight of Kyree's body would haunt the boy for the rest of his life. Daken gripped the boy's shoulder, understanding Steve's problem too well. Daken was also tormented by every twisted body, every bloodied, ravaged face the Tarveen left behind.

Searching for a way to distract Steve, Daken glanced up at the hovering miasma of smoke still trapped on the room's ceiling. "Do you know what that smoke is? Should we be leaving?"

Steve slowly lifted his gaze to the thin haze above them. It was as if a light went on in the boy's mind, snapping him out of his shock as he dropped to his knees beside Jane. With one hand, he lifted her head, the other tugged on Daken, clearly demanding Daken heal her.

Daken settled down beside the boy, gently lifting Jane's head and placing it into his lap. "She's gone. There's nothing I can do."

Steve shook his head, and Daken saw the tears flowing from his eyes. The boy grabbed his hand and pressed it against her chest, right above her heart.

"I don't feel anything, Steve. Nothing but her sickness and the poison."

Steve nodded, pointing to the smoke.

Daken closed his eyes, feeling a wetness on his face and knowing it was his own tears. He continued to concentrate on the body of the woman he loved, as much in morbid fascination as because Steve demanded it of him. He wanted to know if she had suffered much. If the poison had been swift and lethal or a creeping horror, and if there was any possible way for him to bring her back to life, even while he knew there wasn't.

The remnants of her illness still lingered. He felt the weakness in her very cells, deep in her body, but that hadn't killed her. The death stroke was the pervading poison that dampened her life like a candle snuff slowly suffocates a flame.

The poison was everywhere, pressing down on her like a heavy weight. He pushed it away, using his skills to clear it from her body as he probed deeper.

It was everywhere. Even knowing the poison killed her, he was still appalled by the thoroughness of this drug, sickened by the slow death. Even as he sloughed away the heaviest layers of poison, he found more still worming its way into her heart and soul.

He worked harder, peeling away layer after layer of the deadly gas, digging through the oppressive weight as a flicker of hope stirred in his heart.

This poison worked from the outside in, compressing as it killed. The loss of the living aura would be the first symptom, not the last. It was possible that underneath all that deadly ballast, straining against the insidious horror of the poison, Jane's soul still struggled.

She could still be alive.

He tripled his efforts, narrowing his focus into a tiny needle-like shaft of light. He would pierce down to the core, penetrating the blanketing layers until he found her center and the answer to his question.

Was her soul still with her body? Could she still live?

It was a risky business. If she had indeed died, her soul long since gone to the Father, then he might be trapped, buried just as she was under the suffocating horror of the poison. And even if she still lived, she had very little strength left. Separated from his own body by the covering layers of death, he was a good deal weaker than normal for a healer. They might both die, their combined strength unequal to the leaden weight.

He didn't hesitate.

Stabbing downward, he plunged through a darkness that filled his mind and heart. There was nothing here but death. Heartbroken, he struggled to come back, kicking like a foundering swimmer buried beneath the waves.

That's when he felt it.

A flickering light, more gray than white, faded in the distance.

Jane!

He abandoned his escape, knowing what he felt might easily be a trick of his own mind, a hope he'd brought to life out of his own wishes. But he had to know. If there was a chance she still lived, he wouldn't forsake her.

Jane!

He called to her with all his soul.

Jane!

He narrowed his focus again, slipping through the heavy morass toward the lighter darkness.

Jane!

The light flickered in recognition. Her soul.

She was alive!

Energized by the knowledge, he sped toward her, finally merging with all that was left of her. Their union was brief, but total in its joy.

Then began the work. His energies pulsed within her, feeding her flickering life, empowering her against the black bog that encapsulated them.

Help me, Jane. I can't do it alone.

He felt her struggle, weakened and disheartened, her efforts only able to maintain her life, not heal it. And he too was weakening, the poison beginning its insidious effects on his mind.

Still he pushed her on as they fought for both their lives, but the evil was like quicksand beneath their feet, shifting beneath them, sucking them under no matter how hard they struggled.

There was no escape.

They would die. Daken felt her acceptance of it, that despite their efforts, she considered the end inevitable.

No! Daken rebelled. He would not die this way. He would not give in to Kyree, not now, not after he had already vanquished the man in battle. He would not let Kyree take Jane either.

But struggling to surface through the black morass was futile. With a sudden flash of insight, Daken realized they were going about it the wrong way.

Daken's energies were foreign to this body. His consciousness fought to maintain its integrity while slipping through her body like a tiny insect spreading health in its wake.

This, however, was Jane's body, Jane's home. She couldn't slip through the poison as he had. To live, she needed to clear off the evil permeating her body. She needed to maintain a steady center and expand outward until she was whole once again.

Daken had been trying to take her with him. In effect, drawing her out of her own body, and that would only happen in death.

Let me be your center, Jane. Let me support you as you grow outward.

She didn't seem to understand at first. As he hardened himself into a tiny kernel of energy, she seemed to surround him, clinging to the support he offered. She stayed that way, resting, feeding off the life he gave her.

Then suddenly she expanded. Using him as a foothold, she pushed outward, climbing in an ever-expanding sphere. The black cloak of poison had no choice but to recede, rolling backwards against her relentless pressure. As she expanded, Daken grew stronger, giving her more power with which to grow.

Then they were free. The liberation was like a sheet of white light pervading his senses, enveloping his soul.

She was alive.

It was in the midst of this expanse of white that he realized his work was done. Jane could heal on her own now, and he needed to return to himself or risk his own body fading away into death. Still, he was reluctant to leave. He liked his position as the center of her life. He enjoyed the warmth and communion they seemed to share.

She had her own center back now, and it pulsed beside him, beating in the joyful tempo of life. And subtly, it pushed him out. Her subconscious mind recognized the alien presence and strove to oust him from her newly-regained body.

How like his Jane. Always striving for her independence.

He took his leave, returning to himself, solitary again, alone in his own body. He took a deep breath, rejoicing in his wholeness even while mourning the loss of their communion.

He opened his eyes.

And so did she. Her eyes were dilated, her skin a sickly gray. But she breathed. She was alive.

Beside them, Steve let out a breath, burying his face in her shoulder as he shuddered in reaction. Absently, she reached up and stroked his head, her eyes blinking up at Daken in confusion as she sought to orient herself.

Their battle had been waged in the depths of her subconscious. She would never remember what they shared.

Stifling a sigh, Daken pushed to his feet, and collapsed back down on the ground, his breathing heavy, his head spinning like a mating buzzfish.

"We should get out of here," he gasped into the floor, struggling to sit back up. "Jane needs to rest. We've got to tell Ginsen what happened." But his thoughts were actually on Kyree's gruesome body. He didn't want Jane to see it, didn't want her exposed to the butchery and ugliness of battle.

Finally, he pushed himself to his feet, using Kyree's workbench for leverage and still stumbling as his own weakness ate at his balance.

Then he looked at Jane. "Can you walk?"

He was worried about her. From within she seemed bathed in light and life, but now he saw that was only in comparison to the overwhelming presence of the deadly poison. Looking at her now, as a doctor views his patient, he saw the weakness of her aura, the deeply etched lines of fatigue and confusion.

Nevertheless, she nodded. "I . . ." Her voice was thready, barely above a whisper. She drew another breath, "I think so. Will you help me, Steve?"

Still shaking violently in her arms, the boy didn't seem to hear.

"Steve?" she repeated, her voice growing stronger with each word. "I need you. Just for a little longer. Think you can do it?"

Daken turned away, the faint tang of bitterness souring his mouth. He'd just saved her life, and now she turned to the boy, asking for his help. But of course, she didn't know what they'd just shared. She didn't remember, and so for her, they were still Oracle and King, Council Member and Petitioner.

Suddenly fed up with the situation, Daken made a resolution. Once she was fully recovered, once his own strength came back, they would talk. Or rather, he would correct her mistaken impression. There would always be more between them than cold, political ties. When he finally got her alone, he vowed, he would show her just how much they shared.

For now, there was business to attend to. Waiting beside her, he counted the seconds while she coaxed Steve out of his shock. Then all three together stumbled to the stairway.

She saw Kyree, of course. There was precious little possibility she'd miss the expanding pool of drying blood. She let out a brief gasp and turned her sickened eyes to Daken, her expression horrified, her accusation clear.

"He tried to kill all three of us," he said, the bite of his anger in every word. "If you had a better idea, why didn't you do it?"

Jane bit her lip and carefully skirted the gore. "I'm sorry. I've just never seen...I mean not in real life, a body..."

Daken nodded, feeling his insides churn with the movement. "It's nasty, brutal butchery, Jane. And I'm very good at it." He took a deep breath, hating the self-disgust that ate at his insides. "But without it, all three of us would be dead."

"And Kyree would be well on his way to butchering thousands more people the world over. Thank you, Daken." She glanced up at him, her eyes shining with love and gratitude. "Thank you for everything."

Daken acknowledged her thanks with a grunt. It wasn't gratitude he wanted from her. "We'll talk later," he muttered, his attention focused on getting the three of them up the stairs.

It wasn't until they'd made it to the top that Daken realized Kyree's hands were empty.

The gun was gone.

Chapter Thirteen

✦ ✦ ✦

Jane ground her teeth into the blanket, wrapping her arms around her body. The chills hadn't set in until after Daken left her. He had to tell Ginsen what happened, he'd said, and so she let him go, assuring him she would be fine.

But the moment he left her side, the chills began. It was as though Daken's presence held off the sickness, and now with him gone, she was vulnerable to a thousand pains.

She didn't call for Steve. The boy was sleeping, curled up in a tight ball near the fire. He was exhausted, his limp form looking more like a big pillow than a guard dog. Nevertheless, she knew he would stir at the slightest sound.

She lay in her bed as silently as possible while spasms racked her body. Between gasping breaths, she prayed for Daken to come back, his name dropping like a litany from her lips. She knew his very presence would soothe her tormented body.

She heard him the moment the door opened. From her position in bed, she could see into the outer room as he sent Steve away. "I'll watch her tonight," he said to the sleepy boy. "Take my chamber and don't let anyone wake you until you're ready to get up."

Steve left, and a moment later, Daken was in her room, his large form a comfort rather than the diminishment she used to feel.

"By the Father! You're shaking like a leaf. Why didn't you say something?"

"N–n–nothing he–e–e could d–d–do."

She heard his muttered curses as he stripped off all his clothes except his undergarments—soft breeches that looked like long biker shorts. Then without another word, he settled into her bed, pulling her flush against the heat of his body before settling the blankets over them.

"Th–th–thanks–s." Already the spasms were subsiding into mere shivers. Soon they would be gone altogether.

"Shhh," he whispered into her hair. "Try to sleep."

"You too–oo. You're t–tired too." She nuzzled deeper against him, the downy soft hairs of his chest tickling her nose.

She slept.

✦   ✦   ✦

She woke hours later. From the silence of the campus, Jane knew it must be past midnight, maybe later. Despite the terror of all she experienced, her encounter with Kyree had lasted less than an hour. Daken had joined her in bed long before most of the campus was asleep.

Feeling warm and comfortable as she hadn't in years, Jane snuggled against the hard planes of Daken's chest. Beneath her ear, she could hear the steady beat of his heart.

She sighed happily, curling her fingers into his chest hairs.

She didn't know what tipped her off that he was awake. His chest continued to rise and fall with a slow, steady rhythm. Perhaps it was the gentle pressure of his arm around her back, keeping her flush against him. Or perhaps it was a side effect of the communication spell.

Whatever the reason, Jane lifted her head to look down into the dark well of his eyes.

"Daken?"

A shudder ran through him, and his other arm came around her, locking her against his chest with a ferocity as startling as it was welcome. She returned the bear hug as best she could, showing him with her touch that she needed him as well.

"I almost lost you," he rasped, his voice a low rumble of anguish translated directly from his body into hers.

"But you didn't. I'm alive, thanks to you."

His hold gentled as he partially withdrew into himself. "Not thanks to me. Thanks to Steve."

"No—"

But his words continued, flowing like blood from a wound that wouldn't close. "Steve made me try. I'd never seen poison like that before. I was...I was so sure you were dead." His voice broke on his last word and once again, he crushed her against him.

She let the embrace continue, returning as much as she received. Eventually, she pushed away, raising up on her elbow so she could see his face.

"But you did try, and you did save my life. I owe you more than I could ever repay. I owe you everything."

He reached up a hand to brush the hair from her eyes. She turned into his palm, kissing the callouses she found there.

"You don't owe me anything," he said. When she turned to deny it, he pulled her down to him, taking her lips in a kiss both hungry and afraid.

She returned his desperation with passion, opening herself to him as easily as a bud opens to the sun.

He plundered her mouth. Touching, stroking, tasting her in a frenzy of movement, and she was nearly overcome with the sensuous assault. It was just a kiss, but he attacked it like a man fighting to keep gold in a leaky sieve.

Instead of matching his furor, she did her best to soothe him. She gave herself to him, telling him as best she could that she was alive, and she was his.

He still held her, one hand at the back of her head, pulling her down to him. In time, after her lips were bruised and swollen, he finally gentled his touch. Then he broke away, taking a shaky breath as he buried his face in her shoulder.

"I'm alive, Daken. Very, very alive," she whispered to him.

"No." He shook his head against her shoulder, his coarse stubble scraping her skin. "You're still sick. I can feel it."

She bit her lip, wondered how much he understood about radiation poisoning, then decided now wasn't the time to explain. She lifted up, pulling his face from her body as she dropped light kisses along the clenched lines of his jaw, lips, cheeks, and eyes.

"When you're stronger, you can take care of that too." She drew back, releasing a laugh half in amazement, half in awe. "You're a miracle, my warrior healer. I don't think you realize how much of your life—all life—is a miracle."

His body stilled while he studied her words. She shook her head, trying to push her thoughts into coherence.

"You're fighting all the time, Daken. Against the Tarveen, against Kyree, against yourself. You have to be a good king and a good healer. You have to eradicate the Tarveen and bring your lands into prominence with the Elven Lord. When will you stop fighting everyone and allow yourself to be the miracle you are?"

His laugh was harsh and bitter. "Don't romanticize me, Jane. Don't forget the butchery I made of Kyree a few hundred feet below us."

Jane repressed a shudder at the memory, but she kept her expression soft, her eyes loving. "Yes, and that must be very hard for a man who is a healer."

Daken shook his head. "Killing Kyree wasn't hard at all."

Jane settled back down on his chest. "No, but convincing me of its necessity was." More than the sight of Kyree's body, Jane felt haunted by the hurt in Daken's eyes at her shocked realization of his violent side.

"There's no convincing, Jane. You either understand or you don't." Though his voice was flat, his body was rigid and angry.

Jane looked up at him again, her words slow though no less fervent. "Violence destroyed my world. It took away everyone I loved, flattened everything I knew, and changed my entire race so now I'm the alien. It's hard for me to reconcile that fact with the knowledge of violence as sometimes necessary."

His eyes were dark and intense. "You do understand?"

She nodded. "I do."

"But you're still disgusted I was the one who did it. That I was, I *am,* capable of such brutality."

"No," she said, raising up to emphasize her words. "I'm grateful that it's you. You're smart and wise and very, very self-controlled. You'd never descend into mindless brutality. Necessary force is what we used to call it."

"I'm not a saint, Jane."

"You're not a demon, either. You're a warrior and a healer. Reconciling the two must be very hard."

He ground his teeth together, his body tightening as he fought with his words. "I can't forget, Jane. I remember the faces of every man and beast I've killed. Even the Tarveen."

She was silent a long time, watching the pain etch lines of granite into his face. Then slowly, she kissed each hard edge, soothing away the strain with her lips while her tears wet the spaces between them.

She couldn't take away his pain or give him the answers he sought, but she could give him her love, her total and complete acceptance of who and what he was.

"I love you," she whispered into his lips. "I always have and always will. Even when you order me around and call me a fool."

Suddenly, he surged forward, rolling her over until he pressed her down into the bed. Other than a soft gasp of surprise, she offered no resistance, loving the weight and the solid feel of him.

"You are a fool," he rasped, "to give your heart to me."

She smiled, a teasing quirk to her lips. "That thought had occurred to me."

He kissed her again, and this time there was no pain in his touch, no fear in his caress. It was tender and sweet and filled with awe. She returned it all a hundred-fold to him.

There was no embarrassment when he lifted off the shift she wore at night. She was naked before him, her body exposed in all its thousands of little flaws. But he already knew the worst of her—her temper and her failures. If he accepted those and could still gaze at her with eyes like blue fire shot with gold, then he wouldn't mind the mismatched shape of her breasts or unattractive clumps of cellulite.

Or so she told herself as he stared at her, his hands still between them, his breathing shallow.

"You're beautiful," he whispered, and she flushed from the top of her hair to the tips of her toes.

Then he caressed her, tracing her curves with the palm of his hand, trailing his fingers from her face to her hip. She felt his every callous as it scraped against her skin, and her nipples tightened at the erotic feel of it.

After he explored her body with the broad strokes of his hand, he bent down to worship her every hollow and peak with his lips. His first kiss landed over the pulse in her neck, and he held it there as though he needed to reassure himself she was still alive. Later he trailed down to her collar bone, stroking its sloping curve with his tongue.

His first touch at her breast was off center, to the right of her peak, and she cried out at the sweet torment. He pulled at the flesh there, alternately sucking and soothing, but never on the target she craved.

When at last his lips found her nipple, she bucked beneath him, shocked to the core by the tremors that filled her.

When she could breathe again, she focused her startled gaze on his cocky grin. "How do you do that? It's like all you have to do is to wet your lips, and I'm a pile of quivering flesh."

He leaned down, whispering his words into her ear. "The same way you do it to me." He pressed his groin against her for emphasis, his swollen shaft a hot brand even through the thin material of his shorts.

She smiled and pressed back, wiggling her hips to make him groan.

"Woman, you unman me."

She giggled at his old style phrasing. "I certainly hope not. Maybe we should check." Pushing him flat on his back, she sat up and started to pull off his shorts. His gasp of shock at her outrageousness only pushed her to further excesses. "You know, I don't think you ever answered my question," she said.

"What question?" His voice was hoarse as he lifted his hips, allowing her to strip away the last of his clothes.

"You never told me if the women of this time are as energetic, as, um, bold as I am." To punctuate her remark, she grasped him in her hand, alternating her words with quick, staccato squeezes.

"By the Father!" he exclaimed, nearly jumping out of the bed. But he quickly fell back down, overcome by her enthusiasm.

"Well, Daken? Are they?" She switched to long, pulling strokes.

"Ah," he said, groping for his thoughts. "Energetic, yes. Bold, no. A charging zlebaar isn't as bold as you."

"Oh," she said, slowly removing her hand from his body. Then she leaned down and gave him one long, wet, lingering kiss before withdrawing. "Then you don't like it?" She raised her eyebrows in an expression of total innocence that he took for the teasing challenge it was.

Faster than she thought possible, he surged up from the bed, once again capturing her and pinning her beneath his weight. "Yes, my little bold one. I liked it. But no, you won't be allowed to continue." He wedged his knees between hers, slowly spreading her thighs apart. "It's time I staked my claim in you."

He was hot and hard as he pressed against her entrance, but she arched away from him, drawing herself up onto her elbows. "Staked your claim? Excuse me, I'm not some plot of land you can just claim."

He drew back onto his knees, trailing his hands lowly, lovingly over her breasts and belly. "Did I say you were?"

"No. You said you were staking your claim. Let me tell you..." She gasped as he ran his hands further down, trailing in her soft triangle of hair. She swallowed, then tried to speak again. "Nobody owns..." His thumbs probed lower, spreading her delicate petals. "Owns me. No..." Her words were cut off as his lips began to explore the same flesh his fingers teased. "Oh, wow," she breathed, temporarily abandoning her feminist stand as she gave herself totally over to pleasure. "Do that again."

He did.

And he did much more until she writhed beneath him, her back arched, her arms aching as she strained forward, needing the fulfillment only he could give her.

"Now, Daken. Come to me now."

But he waited, withdrawing his caresses as her passion ebbed.

"Oh Daken, you're cruel," she accused without rancor. "You're good, but you're cruel."

He punished her for that comment, teasing around her but never within until she was once more pleading with him for her release. Then he stopped, looking up with an expression of total innocence. "Does that mean you don't like it?"

She groaned, knowing now he'd gotten his revenge for the way she'd teased him before. She sat up, pulling him to her for a deep, heavy, mind-numbing kiss. And while he followed her lead, she still had the impression he stalked her. Like a predator about to take his fill, he moved over her body, dropping delightful nibbles where the fancy struck him, slowly, relentlessly pressing her backward onto the bed.

And then he found her mouth.

He thrust into her above and below at the same instant. She was more than ready for him, arching in the ecstacy of his penetration. She drew him in, pulling at him with her legs and arms, wanting him deeper within her, yearning for more than a physical union could give.

Daken ended the kiss, lifting his head, keeping his hips still. She pressed and moved beneath him, urging him to the next step, but he stopped her, holding her motionless with his weight.

"I will heal you now," he said. His eyes were dark with passion, but his voice remained steady and controlled.

"What?" She struggled to make sense of his words.

He grinned. "I've wanted to do this since that first time in the water. Remember? With the Old One?"

She nodded. Even with her thoughts clouded by passion, she'd never forget that delightful and humiliating healing in the stream.

"I wanted you then," he said, "but I had no right. But now..."

Trusting him implicitly, she pulled him down to her. "But now, I give you the right to do whatever you want."

Their kiss was tender and sweet, a touching distraction to another stroke, another brush that warmed her mind.

"Before, it was just your skin," he whispered against her cheek, the heat of his breath curling around her ear. "This illness is much deeper. This goes down into your bones."

Jane nodded, knowing bone marrow was especially vulnerable to radiation poisoning.

"I want to be there too, Jane. I want to be in your bones, in your heart, in you."

"You could hardly be any closer." She wiggled her hips for emphasis, but Daken just grinned.

"Watch," he said.

It began on her lips which he continued to stroke with teasing licks and tiny nibbles. It was the same heat she remembered from by the stream, but this time there was more. This time, she knew it was Daken slowly entering her body, seeping in, extending his influence in ever widening circles.

She felt him within her. His warmth, his love, his passion were all a part of her. Her lips parted in slow astonishment.

Still he grew, expanding until he heated more and more of her. Never before had she felt so at one with another, so unified in body and mind.

As if of its own accord, Daken's body began to move, thrusting into her, always pressing for a deeper penetration. Jane knew Daken's consciousness was within her. She could feel his passion surging through her veins, his ecstacy driving her hunger higher and harder; his delight echoing within her mind.

She lost herself to the sensations, the fulfillment, and the joy. They moved together, pulsing within and around each other. Then with one final thrust, he burst through her, filling her body with his seed as he filled her soul with his light. She cried out at the wonder of it while her body tightened and stroked him with a rapture all its own.

They were one.

She'd been a fool to think she remained independent of him. No matter what her feminist mind told her, she belonged to Daken. He had long since staked a claim in her life and in her heart. This moment of passion was only one tie out of hundreds that bound them together.

But it didn't upset her. This presence in her body and her mind didn't bother her. It was Daken who was with her. And she knew she was as much a part of him as he was of her.

They lay cradled together for a long time, trying to prolong their strange, mystical union. In the end, exhaustion forced them to separate. His healing presence withdrew, leaving her cold and empty except for where their bodies touched. She looked up at his face, noting the gray cast of fatigue coloring his features.

"You're tired." Until this moment, she hadn't realized how very weary he must be.

"I'm sad I haven't the strength to stay as we were forever."

"It'd be a bit hard to run a kingdom from that position."

"Kingdom be damned. All I want is you." With that he tugged her into his arms, his hold tight and possessive.

She leaned forward, kissing both his eyelids, first the right, then the left. "Good night, sweet one."

He cracked an eyelid, his expression sleepy and confused. "What was that?"

She grinned. "Just something my Mom used to do every night before I went to sleep."

"It's nice," he whispered, his eyes drifting closed, his breathing already deepened into the heavy rhythm of sleep. Jane smiled, settling against his side, happy to remain locked in his arms, their limbs intertwined, listening to the steady beat of his heart.

She slept. And dreamed.

✦   ✦   ✦

Jane wandered through a park on a perfect spring day. Overhead, a set of Air Force planes flew past in beautiful symmetry. It was one of those rare Saturdays when there were no emergencies at the University to demand her attention. She strolled leisurely, happy to watch the children play and the lovers exchange amorous looks.

As if summoned from her secret longings, she looked up and saw Daken. He wore jeans slung low on his hips and a t-shirt that emphasized his hard, masculine torso.

She practically flew into his arms, and he swung her around before giving her one of his mind-numbing kisses. When he finally raised his head, she could see his happiness. Gone were the hard edges of anger and exhaustion. His worry lines were erased, and he looked carefree and young as she'd never seen him before.

Evening came, and they still strolled, holding hands while they played happily in the twilight mists.

It happened so quickly. She was teasing him, laughing as he tried to squeeze his large frame into a child's slide. Then suddenly a gun pressed against her temple. Behind her ringed the dark, menacing figures of a gang, their eyes identical pinpoints of hatred.

Daken came down from the slide, jumping from the top to face the lethal group holding her captive. She was terrified for herself and for him. Daken launched himself at the nearest thug, while Jane's scream froze in her throat.

But soon she began to relax. As the fighting continued, she watched in amazement as Daken dodged and parried blows like a born fighter. He practically danced in front of them, dropping gang members like a child knocking over plastic toys. He was more than a match for all of the dark menacing figures. Even without his sword, he was quick to dispatch them, easily turning them from hulking figures to terrified boys who ran from him.

The last one to remain was the one who held her captive, gun still against her forehead. Daken didn't have to do more than snarl at the already nervous boy. Just as quickly as it began, the restraining arms slipped away, leaving her once again alone with Daken. The only reminder of the fight was the dull gleam of the gun dropped at her feet.

Jane wanted to step around it to fly into Daken's arms, but he bent down, eagerly taking the weapon into his own hands.

"No!" she screamed, but he didn't hear her. He played with the gun, familiarizing himself with the feel and weight of the weapon. She could see the wonder in his eyes, the dreams of glorious battles and military power that would rock the world.

She ran to him, hanging on his arm as she tried to stop him. But he wouldn't hear her, didn't listen to her warnings.

As she watched in horror, he cocked the pistol and fired. It was meant to be a testing shot, fired at a tree not an enemy, but the explosion rocked the earth. Instead of a simple bullet hitting a target, she saw a nuclear explosion. It burst onto the horizon, a gigantic flare of red and gold covered by a seething, roiling mass of black smoke.

All around her, the children screamed as the force of the explosion blasted them into nothingness. Buildings crumpled and disintegrated. Living, green plants withered in an instant. And then she saw Daken, his eyes wide with the horror of what he'd done. She saw him age before her eyes, the tiny lines expanding on his face as the heat of the explosion ate away at his flesh. Then all that was left was his grinning skeleton before it too dissolved into dust.

And all she could hear above the roaring of the wind was the incessant, ever present screams of the children.

✦   ✦   ✦

Daken woke to a terrible keening shooting through his body and his soul. He sat bolt upright, instinctively wrapping an arm around Jane while the other reached for his sword. It wasn't until he gathered more of his wits that he realized the source of the sound.

It was Jane in the grips of some horrible dream. She was wailing with the same insane agony he'd once seen in a farming woman who came home to find her home burning and her family dead by the Tarveen. It gave him chills then. It turned his blood to ice now.

He tried to soothe her. He wrapped his arms around her, holding her tight as he spoke an unending stream of comfort and love. But she was beyond hearing, beyond even the gift of his healing. So he waited, gripping her as tightly as she clung to him, praying the fit would pass soon.

"Jane. Sweet Jane, it was just a dream. Jane, please. It was only a dream."

Slowly her wails subsided, and she buried her face in his chest. He stroked her hair, feeling the curls coil about his fingers.

"Shhh, now. It was only a dream."

"No." His chest was wet where she pressed against him, and he felt her quiver, her whole body shaking with the force of her denial.

"It's over. It was just a bad dream."

"No, it wasn't. It was real. Oh God, it was so real."

"That's the way of dreams, love. Shhh. It's over."

"No!" She shoved away from him. With her hair matting in the tears on her face and her eyes still stark with terror, Jane looked like the wildwomen who sometimes wandered onto his lands. "No," she repeated shaking her head. "It was a warning. A warning to me. Oh God, I was considering it." She covered her mouth trying to suppress the hysterical laugh spilling out of her. "Necessary force. I was actually thinking about it."

"Thinking about what?" He captured her hands, easing them together and holding them still between his palms. She stared down at what he was doing, her eyes widening with horror as her smaller hands disappeared beneath his.

She pulled away from him, wrapping her arms around herself like a woman holding in an explosion.

"Talk to me, Jane!" This was impossible for him. He was a man of action, a man used to dealing with the weapons of war and of political might. Even as a healer, he acted against infections, destroying them with his own strength.

But this was a wound of the mind. Jane was half crazed, still teetering on the edge of hysteria, and he could do nothing but sit on his knees and watch, trying to talk to her as he would a spooked horse.

"Jane..." he reached out, but she flinched away from his touch.

"I want to give it to you," she said. "You know that, don't you? I want to."

"Give me what?" He brushed away a wild curl blocking her left eye. She spoke in riddles, shaking from some horror, and all he could think about was how beautiful she was. She held her head defiantly against her terror. Her eyes flashed like firelight reflected in amber. And her words, though still trembling under the curse of her dream, her words were passionate with firmly held beliefs.

"I want to give you the guns, Daken. I really do."

He tilted his head, not understanding why this was so awful. "So give them to me."

"I love you, and you want the guns that I can make for you. I want to do this because it would save your lands and your people. I want to give them to you because they mean so much to you."

Daken caressed her arms, stroking the tremors from

her body as he would rub down a horse. "Then you can give them to me."

She wrenched away from him. "No, I can't! This world has enough weapons. Swords and spells, you don't need guns."

Daken rested his palms on his knees, calmly watching her agitated movements as she paced the small confines of her room. "The Tarveen are faster than swords," he said softly. "And there are too few mages. Guns would make the difference. They would cut the bastards down before the scream left their throat."

She rounded on him, her arms arcing wildly about her face. "And that's good? You're talking about wiping out an entire race—"

"They're not human, Jane. They're monsters."

"Bull shit. If they can organize raids, then they're human. And they have as much right to live as you do."

Daken drew himself up, his anger rising. "So I should let them be, allow them to destroy our crops, burn our buildings, and rip into the flesh of my people like evil scavenging birds?"

"No! But you don't know what evil lurks in a gun."

Daken pushed off of the bed, standing up in order to tower over her in his anger. He gave no more thought to his nakedness now than he did hers. "Guns are weapons. Simple tools. Evil can no more lurk in a weapon than it can in a block of wood."

Jane shook her head, not intimidated by his greater size. "You don't understand. You have spells and swords. What can a child do with those? It takes strength and skill to use a blade without hurting yourself. It takes maturity and self-discipline to work magic."

Daken nodded, not understanding the direction of her thoughts. "That is part of learning how to use a weapon."

"But don't you see? Any child can use a gun. Just point and pull the trigger. A monkey can do it. And children. Think of the boys you know. Would you give them the power to kill?"

Daken fell silent. He didn't need her words to prompt him. He'd already thought of the boys in his castle. Every one of them was flushed with the heady power of burgeoning manhood. Every one was hot for battle, hungry for the trappings of a man. Then he remembered his own youth and winced. He recalled the idiotic battles, the raging emotions, the carelessness of a mind that hadn't yet realized his every action had far-reaching consequences.

No. He would not give the easy power to kill to young men, much less children. "I thought there was some skill to be mastered. Perhaps a focusing that fires the gun."

Beside him, Jane sighed, a defeated sound that came to him in the first blush of dawn. "No. There's nothing like that. You live in a world of magic, you think in terms of magic. But there was none of that in my time. It was all machines. Push a lever and a door opens. Pull a trigger and you kill someone. It's that easy."

He sat down heavily on the edge of her bed still struggling with the concept. "Surely they are hard to make. We could control who carried them..."

"They're easy to manufacture, Daken. Any black-smith could do it."

He lifted his gaze to her. "Then they are indeed a dangerous weapon. I will be very careful with mine. We will only use it when absolutely necessary."

"No!" She again began her agitated pacing. "You can't take away knowledge. Once your men feel the ease with which they can kill their enemies, the power such a weapon holds, they won't want to go back. You won't want to either."

"To fight the Tarveen as we have been, with swords and a spell here or there," he spread his arms in a gesture of futility, "it will be a long, agonizing fight. Many of my people will die."

"Then don't fight at all."

Daken pushed away from the bed, suddenly tired of all this arguing. "Blood of the Father, Jane, we've been over this before." He turned to her, feeling the weight of his kingship as he'd never felt it before. "I wish I could show you what they've done. The homes that have been destroyed. The bodies." He shuddered, then he drew himself up to his full regal height. "I cannot talk peace with the Tarveen. Not after what they've done. My people won't allow it. And *I* won't consider it."

Jane turned to him, her eyes like liquid mahogany as they pleaded with them. "Your people want the raids to end. They want to live in peace. They don't care how you achieve it—"

"Of course they do," he snapped, reaching down to pull on his breeches.

Jane sighed, also beginning to dress, though he could tell by her silence that her thoughts were far away. Then, when she did speak, she didn't offer him answers, but posed even more questions. "Daken, what do the Tarveen want most in the world?"

"To murder my people and rampage my lands."

"Nonsense. They did that because Kyree stole their holy book."

"What?" Daken whipped around feeling like his stomach had just been kicked in.

Jane looked up. She had one foot raised in preparation for donning her leggings, but at his startled exclamation, she slowly lowered it to the ground. "I assumed you knew."

"How would I know about Kyree and a cursed Tarveen holy book?"

"Are you telling me you have so little contact with these people you didn't even know that?"

"Contact? We have nothing of them except their blood lust. What did that bastard Kyree do?"

"He stole a holy book from them. Its loss incensed them so much they became vicious and brutal against your people."

Daken dismissed her words with a wave of his hands. "They've always been vicious and brutal." But his thoughts still churned with this new information. "It is true, about a year ago they became like beasts foaming at the mouth for blood."

Suddenly Jane stood up, clutching Daken's arm. "Why not take the book? Use it as a negotiating weapon. Offer it to them in return for a stable border. Economic realities, trade arrangements and the like will take care of the rest. In three generations, you guys may be best pals."

"Never!" Daken grabbed her arms, shaking her slightly in his effort to make her understand. "There will never be friendship with the Tarveen. Don't you understand? Not every merging of the Old Ones went well. Some of them became evil horrors, festering animals that must be destroyed."

"They are people—"

"No, they aren't. They don't even walk upright.

They scramble like spiders and poison drips from their claws." He pushed her away, angrily strapping on his bastard sword. "Don't you have knowledge of this?" he demanded over her shoulder. "You are the Keeper. You should know this."

He finished dressing, cinching his weapons in place with an angry tug. Then he took a deep breath to calm himself, but it was already unnecessary. He felt better with his weapons on. He always did. As the younger son, his place in the world was often confused and awkward. A powerless prince, he had the royalty to uphold, yet no place in its structure.

Weapon play was the one place he felt in complete control. On the practice field or in battle, a man made his own destiny regardless of birth order or pedigree.

He glanced back at the too-silent Jane. She sat on the bed, her face composed, her gaze abstract, as though she were in a trance. He recognized the look. Her thoughts were turned inward as she drew on the knowledge of the Keeper.

He pulled a chair opposite her and settled into it, waiting for her. Now she would understand, he thought with satisfaction. She looked at the Tarveen now, learning what the Keeper's Knowledge had to say about the monsters.

When she emerged from her thoughts, she would agree with him.

With their silly argument resolved in his mind, he let his thoughts wander. Or rather he let his gaze wander. With her tunic draped loosely over her nakedness, Daken had the time to admire her body in the rosy dawn light.

She was beautiful. As always when he looked at her, he felt his groin tighten with hunger while his arms ached to pull her close. Even that first morning in the meadow, he'd felt a fierce need to protect such beauty. Later, after his first taste of her passion and her innocence, the need had mixed with other hungers—lust, possessiveness, admiration—and all of it grew into a blazing inferno within his blood.

He let his gaze roam over her body, remembering the sweet torment of last night. Her legs were his favorite part. They were long and sleek, like the pantar's, and had such strength in them when she wrapped herself around him. He knew men who would pay much for such gripping stamina in their partners.

But that was not all he adored. Her entire body was one compact center of energy and passion. From the rosy fullness of her lips to the tight buds of her breasts—

Jane cried out, a small exclamation of alarm that abruptly ripped him from his pleasant fantasies. He watched her pale face, her eyes huge with surprise and horror. Remorse hit him. He should not have asked her, a woman, to comprehend the Tarveen abomination.

He went to her, gathering her into his arms, holding her trembling hands as he would a newborn babe. He couldn't stop the knowledge. As Keeper and Council Member, it was information she needed. Still, it was hard for him to wait beside her while her innocence shattered.

He waited an eternity, and still she didn't move.

And then, when he began to fear for her sanity, she took a deep shuddering breath and came out of her trance. He watched her blink the tears from her eyes as she focused once again on her surroundings. He drew her tighter into his arms, and she went willingly to him. He kissed her forehead, whispering his remorse into her ears.

"I'm sorry. I shouldn't have asked you to see that." But even as he said the words, he wondered what she'd learned. Had she seen the raids on his lands? The brutality and horror of a man cut to shreds? Or did she know more? Had she gone into their caves and witnessed their strange rituals?

He had tried to get more information on his enemy, but the one spy he'd sent never came back.

"Oh, Daken." He heard the apology in her voice, felt it in the way she gripped his tunic and tried to burrow deeper into his embrace. "It's so horrible."

"I know," he said, his words another vow in his heart. "But rest assured I will take care of it. I will eradicate this scourge from our world."

She shook her head. "No. You don't understand. Dr. Beavesly only went there once, maybe twice. The memories are so vague, so unlike his usual..." Her voice trailed off as he tried to understand her strange words.

"Who is Dr. Beavesly?"

She shook her head, continuing as if she hadn't heard him. "The Tarveen live in an old automobile factory. He could wander about at will. But even so, he couldn't stomach it more than once."

She pushed away from him, twisting her hands together as she struggled to put her horror into words. "They're cannibals, Daken. They eat people. They like the taste of..."

He nodded, his thoughts grim. "I have long suspected as much."

She turned her stricken gaze on him. "You knew?"

"Some of the bodies we found were not completely whole. They..."

"No. Do you know about the herd?"

He felt his insides tense, as though preparing for battle. His stomach knotted and the bile rose in his throat, but his senses were keen and his thoughts razor sharp. "What herd?"

"The Tarveen don't kill everyone. They scavenge. And sometimes they scavenge people."

Daken drew a slow breath and kept his voice low and even. "What happened to the people?"

"Have your people been disappearing for years? Perhaps a child who strayed too far? A couple at a secret rendezvous?"

A catalog of names and faces rolled through Daken's mind. People from his earliest childhood on, friends who disappeared without a trace. The children were thought to have been killed by wild animals. The adults were believed to have run away, despite what their families said.

The churning within his gut intensified, and he stood up, knowing action was the only way to relieve this pain. Action and violence.

"What happened to the people, Jane?"

She followed him, placing her hand on his arm as both reassurance and restraint. He shook it off, wanting neither.

"Tell me!" he demanded.

She swallowed. "The Tarveen keep a herd of humans. To eat. They raid your people to replenish their stock."

Chapter Fourteen

✦   ✦   ✦

"Where are they?" His voice was hoarse with iron self-control. If he allowed himself to feel the full horror of her words, there would be nothing left alive in a five mile area. He'd kill everything in sight before the anger receded enough for him to think.

"They are kept in an off-shoot of the main factory floor. In sort of a storeroom. They have food and shelter. Then when a Tarvite gets hungry, he..." She swallowed her horror. "He goes into the storeroom."

"And eats someone," Daken finished for her.

Jane nodded. "Your grandfather was their healer."

"My grandfather is still alive?" He was becoming numb. He barely felt the pain in his fists where he gripped the hilt of his grandfather's sword.

"No. Dr. Beavesly was old and ill when he went there, before you were born. But what about your parents? Your brother? Did you ever find their bodies?"

Daken shook his head, remembering the empty caskets they'd buried. It was inconceivable that his family was still alive as food stock. He sheathed the sword he didn't remember drawing, knowing now what he had to do.

"Get dressed," he ordered.

She hovered in front of him. "What are you going to do?"

"Get dressed," he repeated again. "We will go to the Council Meeting."

He saw her jaw go slack for a moment. Clearly she'd forgotten the closed door debate over whether or not to give him the army he needed.

"With this new information," he spoke with icy precision, each word a mental sword thrust into a Tarvite gut, "the Council will have to give me weapons and an army." He smiled down at her, his insides softening just a touch. "Thank you, Oracle. Now, I will be victorious."

"No!" She stood up. Her leggings were slightly askew, but neither of them had time to bother with it.

He looked at her startled face, and her fears about the guns came back to him. He smiled, a grim pull to his cheeks, but it was a smile nonetheless. By the Father, love had made him weak.

"It is all right, Oracle. You need not give me the guns. I feared even if the Council gave me an army, it would not be many and certainly not very skilled. But with this new knowledge..." His body still clenched with hatred as he fought to again understand the horrors his family and his people endured. Were even now enduring, if they still lived. "With this new urgency, the Council will have to give me the money to hire a mercenary group."

"Mercenaries?" Her voice was an almost inaudible whisper.

"The Bloodmen. I spent a year with them training. Although not quite as deadly as your guns, they are quick and efficient. The Tarveen will be obliterated." That thought alone brought a grim relief to the coiling hatred that snaked within him, longing for a victim. "Ginsen will use his crystal to speak with their leader. If we leave tomorrow, they will be in Chigan as we arrive. We will fight the next day."

"No..." she repeated, her voice still unsteady.

He shifted his focus off of his murderous thoughts to the pale, shaking woman before him. He reached out a hand, caressing her cheek. "Do not worry, sweeting. The Bloodmen know their business, as do I. I will not be harmed."

He smiled to reassure her, but his expression faded as he watched her absorb his words. He expected her to be relieved, sweetly loving as she worried for her man, yet striving to hide it for his sake. He knew her fears were as firmly held as her loves, and she would be passionate in both.

Despite the urgency of his mission, his groin stiffened in anticipation.

But the Jane before him was not the woman he expected. Instead of her desperate love, he faced a blazing fury practically seething from her every pore.

She slapped away his caress and planted herself in front of him. "You won't be harmed because you're not going to get your army."

"What?" Her reaction was so different from what he expected, her words sounded like gibberish to him.

She ran a hand through her hair, pulling at her locks with desperation. "Damn it, Daken. This wasn't how I meant to tell you."

"Tell me what?" His anger, hardly banked, surged within him again.

She took a deep breath. "I won't support an army."

"What?" he roared.

"I don't believe in violence, Daken, and certainly

not in genocide, no matter how loathsome the Tarveen are. There's got to be another way."

Daken found it hard to control his temper. By the time his words exploded out of him, he was bellowing at her. "Kyree was my only other supporter. With him dead, I need you more than ever."

"I won't do it. I'm sorry."

"You're sorry? That's it? You condemn my family, my people to a slow extinction as cattle, and you're sorry? By the Father, woman, I could kill you myself."

He towered over her in his rage, but she didn't retreat. If anything, she matched him in fury. "I know about your family and people," she screamed back. "But if you're going to start counting bodies, how about you look at my count. You've lost your family. Maybe your lands. But I've lost my world, my people, everything. Gone. Poof." She gestured wildly with her hands. "All I ever wanted, ever knew, ever dreamed, it's all gone. Billions of people."

"They're dead, Jane. My people are alive."

"That's right," she shot back. "They're dead. And why? Because men like you started killing. Maybe some of it was necessary, but mostly they were just too arrogant, too stupid, or too lazy to find another way. In the end, my world was destroyed, obliterated, erased."

"That has nothing to do with me—"

"It has everything to do with you. I won't let you wage a genocidal war."

"But my people, maybe my family—"

"Can be rescued."

Her softly spoken words penetrated his anger as all her screaming hadn't. He lowered his fists to his sides as his mind already began working out strategies for a mission he refused to consider. And in his silence, Jane pushed her point.

"I know the layout of the factory. There's a ventilating shaft no one is aware of, even the Tarveen. One person, maybe two, could sneak through with a ladder. Your people could climb out to safety. Then, afterwards, you can establish guarded borders. Later on, when your people are stronger, we can think about what to do with the Tarveen. Who knows, without their herd, maybe they'll turn to other meat."

"You're dreaming."

"It can work. Take their Holy Book along in trade. That way they won't be so vicious, so suicidal in their hatred. And that in turn will give your people a little breathing room."

Daken frowned as he tried to absorb her words. "What Holy Book?"

"Kyree had it. He said it was important to them even though they couldn't understand it."

"I will not negotiate with the Tarveen."

"This isn't a negotiation, but it's also not a war."

Daken shook his head, not believing he was considering this wild plan. "You split some very fine lines, Oracle."

She lifted her chin. "It's a line I can live with, and it's a damn sight safer for the captives than a war."

Daken looked down at the hard woman before him. With his healer's eye, he saw the energy of her convictions shine through her like a golden aura. She was indeed beautiful, but she bore no resemblance to the soft woman he'd just made love to all night long. No, this woman was implacable and cold toward him.

This woman was the Oracle, and he was just beginning to realize how very, very different she was from the Jane who teased him so passionately last night.

"An army would be better."

"It's all you'll get, Daken. It's the only plan with my support."

He spun away, pacing into the main room of her apartment. Looking around, he wished for some food or something he could sink his teeth into, not for nourishment, but for the satisfaction of ripping it apart with his bare hands.

"It will be very dangerous." He spoke the words, but his mind was elsewhere, already deciding he would have to wear dark clothing and blacken his face. Did he dare leave his bastard sword behind? Its shine might outweigh its benefits. Daken was equally lethal with any number of smaller weapons.

Jane leaned down to straighten her leggings, speaking with an almost casual air. "I will be very cautious, and I will trust you to choose my companion very carefully. He should be small. The passageway is very tight..."

It took a moment for her words to reach him. But when it did, he nearly dropped his dagger in shock. *"You!"* This was beyond enough. "You can't possibly think I'd let you—"

"I'm the only one who can go. I know where the ventilation shaft is. If anything goes wrong, I know the entire layout of the factory and surrounding tunnels."

"Draw me a map."

"A three-dimensional map? I can barely draw stick figures."

Her words only made him more angry. He placed his hands on his hips, his legs wide. "You're not a trained warrior."

"This isn't a war," she shot back. "It's a rescue

mission that requires stealth and knowledge."

He growled low in his throat. "You are the Keeper. The Elven Lord will not let you go."

"The Elven Lord wishes me at the devil right now. He'll let me go and pray I get killed."

Daken remained silent, searching for another reason she might accept.

"Why don't you just admit it, Daken. You don't want me to go because you can't stand the thought that a woman could do this while you have to wait on the sidelines."

He stepped forward, his anger burning all the more brightly because there was a grain of truth in it. But only a grain. "There are women warriors in the Bloodmen. Trained fighters who could kill me in a fair fight without even breaking a sweat. I have no quarrel with women as fighters."

"Well, good," she said.

"But you, woman, are not a fighter. You're the Keeper of Knowledge and a great deal more valuable safe in my castle—"

"You need me to lead you to the storeroom. There's a maze of shafts and ducts to go through, and we don't know which ones still exist. I have to go."

He clenched his fists until his arms ached all the way up through his elbows, but still he couldn't find a way around her logic. If he wanted this rescue to succeed, she would have to go.

"You will stay behind me at all times. And when I tell you to run, you will run."

Jane looked up at him, her eyes a startled clear brown. "You? You can't go."

"These are my people!"

"And you're the only healer left to them. It's too

risky for you."

He nearly choked on his rage. "By the Father, you are irrational!"

"Whoever goes with me needs to be small."

"I will eat sparingly."

"Will you chop off one of your shoulders as well? Be reasonable, Daken. You're too involved in this. The best military efforts are accomplished by dispassionate third parties."

"Woman's nonsense," he spit out.

"It's not nonsense. Emotions confuse the thinking."

"Or bring them into excruciating clarity."

"You're too close to this issue."

"And you're not? You're my wife!"

She stood before him, her mouth gaping open in shock. Then she shut it with a snap. "Was there a priest somewhere I missed? I don't seem to recall saying, 'I do.'"

He drew himself up, insulted to the core. "Don't be obtuse. There has been no ceremony, but you are my wife nonetheless."

"Because of last night?"

"Of course."

"Except you've bedded women before without marrying them. What about that blond bard who gave you the communication spell?"

Daken ground his teeth. He'd forgotten she knew about Sarla. Reaching for the oldest defense, he simply said, "That was different."

"Bull hockey." She turned away, grabbing her boots to draw them on.

"You said you love me!" he bellowed at her, all the while wondering why they were fighting about this of all things.

She turned to him, her eyes sad as they reflected the dawn in her unshed tears. "And I do. I love you. But I don't think we can live together. The only time we're not fighting is when we're kissing. And that doesn't make for a peaceful life." Then she paused, swallowing her nervousness. "You haven't even said you love me."

Daken slammed his hands against the wall, feeling the coarse brick bite into his palms. "Have I not called you my sweeting? Have I not allowed you your position as the Keeper? Have I not given in to your insane idea of this rescue? By the Father, what more do you want?"

"What does sweeting mean?"

He turned around, dropping his back wearily against the stone. She was still on the couch, watching him with those innocent eyes, wide and nervous like a fawn trying its legs for the first time. "It means wife."

"I don't want to be your wife. I want to be your love. I don't want you to *allow* me to be the Keeper. I am the Keeper. Can't you accept me as I am?"

"And can't you show me respect? You think you know best. We are stupid peasants compared to all your vast knowledge, but I have experience and an understanding of this world, and you are still young. I respect your opinion on the guns. They are of your world, but the Tarveen are of mine, and so was Kyree."

She was silent for a long time, staring at her hands as they lay small and white in her lap. For a moment, Daken feared he had pushed her too far. Then she looked up, and some of the fire died in her eyes.

"You're right, of course." She looked away, her gaze abstract. "Most of my life was spent studying, trying to pound whatever learning I could into a not-so-quick mind. Then suddenly, insto-presto, I've got the knowledge of the ages. What isn't in my brain, I can access by computer." Her hands twisted in her lap. "But knowledge doesn't mean wisdom, and in many things, like with Kyree, I'm still foundering. Your experiences and wisdom are far better than all of my learning." She glanced up, her eyes clear and sincere. "I'm sorry."

He nodded, knowing that, in truth, he liked her arrogance. It suited his queen and was a necessary bulwark against his slight tendency to dominate. "You learn quickly, Jane. In ten years, you may indeed think me—"

"A stupid peasant?" She stood up, crossing to him with a lazy stride that set her hips swaying in a seductive rhythm. "I've thought many things about you, King Daken. But stupid and peasant were never among them."

She reached up a hand to his face, but he caught it, using it to reel her in for his kiss. He claimed her mouth, plunging into her as he had the night before. When it was over, he still felt like he hadn't won. She wasn't yet his queen.

Her next words confirmed his fear. "You've got my respect, Daken. You always have. But that's not a marriage."

He sighed, wearying of this argument. He knew from his parents' arguments that sometimes a man just had to let things pass until the woman discovered the errors in her thinking. They still had time to disagree on this. He didn't need to officially claim her until he reached his court.

So he smiled, kissed her pert, upturned nose, and pushed her away. "It is time we told the Council."

She agreed with a nod and a slight smile. It wasn't

until she reached the door that he stopped her. He held her from the hallway with one firm grip, telling her in expression and body positioning that he meant what he said.

"I will go with you into the Tarveen hole. I will take the lead, and you will run when I tell you to."

She chewed on her lower lip. "Is there anyone else, anyone smaller, who you could trust?"

"With your life? No."

She finally nodded. "Then there is no one else I would want by my side."

Chapter Fifteen

♦   ♦   ♦

As Jane predicted, the Council enthusiastically supported their plan. None of them liked the idea of abandoning a completely pacifistic reign. And although the dwarven representative was disturbed she would go on the rescue attempt, Jane remained adamant.

Despite her own nervous fears, she knew she was the right choice. Even if she could have drawn a three-dimensional map for someone to study, she was the only person alive who had any hope of dealing with the lingering machinery in the automobile factory where the Tarveen were based.

So the Council quickly approved the plan, and in their joyful mood, Daken easily obtained permission to take two swift horses. He asked to be instantly transported to Chigan, but with Kyree dead, no one could reliably zap them to their destination. Kyree had been the only one who could manage a jump to Chigan, and Daken wouldn't risk an accidental trip to the bottom of the ocean by a less skilled mage.

They got horses instead. The transaction happened so quickly Jane never had the opportunity to mention she hadn't a clue how to ride. Then again, she thought with a grimace, since she wasn't likely to find a car anywhere nearby, now seemed like as good a time as any to learn.

Two hours later, she wasn't so sure. She faced the blunt nose of her lean, shaggy horse with a trembling in her stomach. He looked harmless enough. Almost bovine. But she'd seen the best ones run like the wind.

Daken mounted up. He sat on what looked to her like a simple saddle—a seat, stirrups, pommel, reins. All the normal stuff, assuming you find sitting on a shaggy beast normal.

Daken's horse wickered impatiently, and Daken struggled to control his large animal. "Come on, woman. We're losing daylight."

"Uh, would now be a good time to mention I've never ridden a horse before?"

For a moment, Daken's jaw went slack. "By the Father, woman, do you know nothing?"

"Hey, Einstein's Theory of Relativity never required me to sit on top of some shaggy monolith. But I'm a modern woman," she said more to herself than him. "I can adapt. I mastered step aerobics. I can lick this thing."

"We bathe the beasts. We do not lick them!" Daken's indignation was almost palpable.

"I didn't mean lick it. That's gross. Oh, never mind." Biting her lower lip, she stretched her foot up into the stirrup. To her humiliation, she still couldn't get on. The angle was too steep. Fortunately, a boy was on hand to push up on her rump. All too soon, she sat astride her horse. "Well, that wasn't too bad." She beamed a smug look at Daken.

"Now," he ordered, with barely concealed impatience. "Rise up from the saddle."

Jane stood, teetering slightly.

"No. Lower. Lower."

"You mean crouch. Like this." Her thighs trembled from the strain and her lower back wasn't at all happy, but her pride wouldn't let her admit it. Certainly not to Daken. "I got it. What next?"

"Stay that way until sunset."

"What?" She thought he was kidding. He had to be kidding. Three hours later, she knew he'd been serious.

She hurt all over. A prize fighter couldn't have made her feel any worse. In fact, she'd rather have gone ten rounds as a punching bag than sit on the accursed beast for a minute longer.

Too bad they had at least an hour of daylight left.

Daken pushed them on through the twilight.

When he finally stopped for the night, she slid out of her saddle like a heap of melting pudding. She fell flat on her numb rear end and didn't care.

"I'll never get on that beast again. Not as long as I live."

Daken glanced up from unloading his horse. "That's fine. I'll just ride ahead and take care of the Tarveen without you."

Jane moaned into the dirt.

"Oh," he continued, "and let me mention that without my prearranged transportation, you'd have to walk through Borit's lands."

"Borit? As in bastard Borit the child molester?"

Daken nodded.

Jane would have cried if she had the energy. "Just shoot me now and get it over with."

He grinned at her from over his horse's rump. "Help me rub down the horses and maybe I'll be convinced to lessen your pain."

Jane stopped moaning long enough to remember Daken was a healer. She nearly cried out in relief. She didn't need a bottle of extra strength analgesic. She had her own miracle cure right here.

She rolled slowly onto her stomach. "Heal me now, and I'll rub down both horses."

"Have you ever done it before?"

"You take a brush and comb their hair. And legs. And stuff. Right?"

"I'll rub down the horses. You get out dinner."

Jane sighed, laying face down in the dirt while she heard Daken move around above her.

Slap!

"Yow!" she screamed. Daken's slap sent bolts of agony from her rear directly to her brain. She lifted her head just enough to glare at him.

"Dinner, woman."

"Sounds great, man."

Daken released a long, suffering sigh. "Is it really that painful?"

"How was it when you first learned?"

He shrugged. "I don't remember. I started riding almost as soon as I started walking."

"Let me put it this way. Picture a nice, round, juicy peach."

He grinned and looked at her rear.

"Now slam it against the wall a few times."

"Very well," he sighed. He leaned down, rolling her onto her back in the grass before kissing her sweetly on the lips. "I wouldn't want your...um, peach to get all brown. Sticky, maybe..." His voice trailed off as he began nuzzling her neck.

"Uh, Daken," she began, trying to focus on something other than him nibbling along the underside of her chin. "The pain's in my rear."

"I'm getting there," he chided. "Don't be so impatient."

By the time he turned his attention to her bruises, she no longer remembered she hurt.

◆   ◆   ◆

She awoke in the dead of night, snapping open her eyes to a sight so bizarre, she was sure she was dreaming.

The black panther approached them slowly, her steps silent and stealthy. In her mouth, she held the reins to another shaggy horse still wearing saddle and gear, and led it to them with a firm jerk of her head.

"Daken. Daken, wake up." He didn't stir, and from their entwined position, she would have felt him move. So it was all the more startling when his voice came as a soft, low whisper in her ear.

"I see it."

"Do you believe it?"

"I never question an Old One."

"A what?" Jane suddenly glanced up, seeing the panther with new eyes. "You think she's a human-animal combined soul?" Her voice trailed off at her awkward phrasing.

He smiled, slowly getting up to pull on his breeches. "Yes, she's an Old One."

"But how can you tell?"

"How many wild animals do you know that lead horses?"

Daken left his breeches loose and started to approach the panther. Bare-footed and bare-chested, he looked like an ancient Indian warrior confronting the nature from which he thrived. The soft glow from the low fire bathed him in orange radiance, accenting his chiseled muscles and proud features. Across from him, the panther dropped the horse's reins and stood before the man, equally elemental, equally regal.

"She wants you to come too."

"Me?" She squeaked, still frozen in her bedroll. "We're going somewhere?"

"Apparently."

Jane swallowed as two sets of eyes focused on her. The man's were a calming blue that reminded her of the deepest ocean. The cat's were black and mysterious as a starless night. Next to them, Jane felt out of place. The city girl joining a warrior and a panther. They were the ones who belonged, the ones merged in some basic way with the world surrounding them. She, on the other hand, still constantly checked her clothes for bugs and lamented the loss of her hair dryer.

More than ever, she felt alien in this new Earth. Still, both man and beast waited patiently for her to pull on a tunic and her boots. Then she followed them, sounding like a lumbering giant against their silent steps.

They didn't go far before she saw him. A huddled, miserable lump on the cold ground, wrapped in just a thin blanket.

"Steve! What are you doing here?"

The boy started awake, his expression dancing through fear and despair until it finally rested in relief.

"I told you to guard the computer for me until I got back. Make sure no one tampered with it."

Steve didn't respond. In truth, he looked too tired to care.

"It would seem someone else isn't used to riding long hours," said Daken in a dry tone.

Whereas Daken was clearly annoyed, Jane's sympathies were immediately engaged. She knew with bruising clarity just how much the boy's backside must hurt him.

"Come on," she mumbled to the boy, leaning down to gather him up, blanket and all. Daken was before her, easily bundling the boy up as he carried the child back to camp.

Jane followed, glancing backward long enough to realize the panther had already faded into the nighttime. So she ran ahead, quickly snuggled into her bedroll, then held out her arms. "Give him to me. Poor thing must be freezing."

Daken hesitated, a small pout forming on his handsome face. "What about me? I get cold too."

Jane gave him a look that spoke volumes about whose welfare she was more concerned with. So, with a heavy sigh full of great self-sacrifice, Daken bent down and deposited Steve into her arms. The boy did indeed feel ice cold, so Jane tucked him close to her, warming his young body with her own.

She glanced up as Daken, still pouting from losing his place in her arms, dropped more wood on the fire. Tiny sparks flew past his head, momentarily surrounding him with fairy lights that seemed to pay homage to him. Even though she'd grown up in a world of high tech special effects, the image still startled her, emphasizing how joined he was with the world around him.

As if a veil slid from her eyes, she suddenly understood what she'd done wrong with Kyree. She and Kyree had wanted power. As noble as her end goal was, they had both acted without love, without cherishing or even understanding the very people and world from which the power came. In the end, the power corrupted Kyree, eating away at his reason and self-restraint until it destroyed him, nearly killing her in the process.

But Daken wore his power, his kingship, like he wore his sword—as a natural extension of himself. He loved his people as he loved the world that brought him his healing skills. And together, they made him king. That understanding of who he was with respect to his people was as natural to him as the healing talent that suffused his body.

That was real power, and it came from love. His love for the land and his people, and their love and loyalty to him.

Jane bit her lip, her thoughts in turmoil as she watched the fire leap outward, caressing Daken with its light. Oh hell, she thought with a groan. She was right back where she started—a nobody people called the Keeper of Knowledge out of respect, not for her, but for the legends that created her. To respect her, they would have to know her, and she them. But up until now, she hadn't bothered with any of that.

Daken was right when he accused her of thinking them ignorant peasants. She'd seen herself as an educated person thrown here to lead woefully stupid people, but that wasn't true, and it had been sinfully arrogant to believe it in the first place.

She was the ignorant one, and it was time she started giving some respect to Daken, the pantar, and most especially the people and the world around her. Because if she didn't start learning from them, trying to understand and love those around her, she'd end up like Kyree. He'd abused his God-given talents to help the only thing he truly did love—himself.

As she began to drift off to sleep, she set herself a top priority task: to love and earn the love of Earth's people. No simple job given that those around her, or rather one person in particular, often made her so mad she wanted to strangle him.

◆   ◆   ◆

Daken saw the deep concentration in Jane's eyes and wondered what devious torture she devised for him now. It didn't really matter, since the result was always the same. He'd end up clutching his sword hilt while asking the Father what evil he'd done to be punished so. And then he'd lay her down and join with her, all the while thanking the Father for being so merciful and generous.

She drove him mad, and yet she was in his blood like a sickness he couldn't shake.

She held the boy, cradling him against her like a newborn babe. The fire glinted off her curls until they shone like a fine sword, and her skin glowed, taking on an unearthly hue, as though she were lit from within. Now, more than ever, she seemed alien to him, and yet so beautiful, his heart ached at the sheer enormity of it.

A woman brought through time to aid his world.

What could he offer this woman who had lost everything? He remembered the stark lines of pain creasing her face when she'd spoken of the death of her world. They were like wrinkles of anguish bleeding from her eyes. He'd never thought of it before then. Never thought of the magnitude of her loss.

Would he, could he ever leave everything he knew and loved to help a world he didn't even understand?

He shook his head, burying another stick in the fire. What a woman she was. Smart, quick, with a passion that burned like a torch and a heart that beat with love for a people she didn't even know. She was a woman who could be a great queen or empress. A woman he could share his rule with because he respected her.

But was that enough? She wanted love. He almost laughed aloud at the irony of it. As strange and independent as she seemed, she was still a woman no different than any other woman he'd ever met. She still cared for a cold child by wrapping him up in her arms, effortlessly bringing him into her heart. She still teased a man, tossing her hair and shifting her hips, luring him until his blood ran straight down and he could think of nothing else but embedding his rod in her.

Despite all the lust and mothering, she spoke of love like a poet, no doubt hungering for things like flowers and sweet words. The silly things no mortal man ever understood.

He grasped the language of love, he supposed. He'd worked quite hard at perfecting it during his profligate days as the younger prince. It seemed Jane was no different than the other women who responded so easily to sweet words and devotion.

Yet, somehow with her it was different. The words didn't come so easily, so trippingly across his tongue anymore. He'd spoken of eternal devotion before, of stars exploding in ecstacy. He'd said the words a hundred times to a hundred different women, but he never once whispered such things to her.

It was as if they meant more to Jane. Or was it he who was different when he was with her? Maybe he meant them when he said the words to her.

So he remained stubbornly silent, reserving the best of his phrases as secrets trapped within his heart because to say them aloud meant admitting he'd changed. The other changes were minor compared to this. He'd lost his reckless youth and accepted the weight of a kingship, but that was no more than a responsibility he secretly longed for.

Accepting a woman into his heart and soul meant changing himself in a fundamental way. It meant admitting he was no longer a carefree warrior who could die without leaving someone behind to grieve. It meant communicating his thoughts and decisions with someone who shared his rule. And it meant acknowledging there was another part of him the Tarveen could kill while still leaving him alive.

How could she ask him to love her in one breath, then demand to infiltrate the Tarveen colony in the next? How could he focus on eradicating the scourge that threatened the survival of his people while constantly trying to protect Jane without insulting her abilities? It was impossible!

Yet, in a little over a week, he would attempt just that.

Oh Father, he prayed, tell me, reveal to me your divine secrets. Is it a strength or a weakness to be inspired by a woman to hazard the impossible?

◆   ◆   ◆

Jane's resolve to learn from Daken, to bow to his greater wisdom, lasted thirteen minutes. The thirteen minutes it took for him to explain his intentions regarding Steve. It began auspiciously enough. Like a stern father on one of her favorite sit-coms, he lectured the boy on responsibility, thinking things through, self-discipline, and all the other stuff she'd completely tuned out as a child.

Then came the ringer. The punishment. It wasn't really a punishment as much as a stupidity, in her opinion. He intended to send Steve back to the University alone.

"You can't be serious," she'd said, tossing aside her resolution as she brushed the dirt off her tunic. "He's a boy. You can't send him back alone."

"He's thirteen, and we don't have the time to waste accompanying him."

"So he'll come with us."

Daken shook his head, clearly wondering how she could be so naive. "How will we feed him?"

"He's brought rations."

"What he brought wouldn't feed a bird."

"You can trap—"

"I'm not spending my nights stalking game."

"Then he can eat my share."

"But—"

"Come on, Daken. You can't send the boy back alone."

"If he can follow us all this way, he damn well can make it back. You seem to forget we're going to a war."

Jane felt her mouth go dry. "I thought you said they just raided every so often…" Her voice trailed off in the face of his grim expression.

"The Tarveen raid nightly. I've established an encampment south of their primary territory to hold the line against them. But make no mistake, Jane. It is a war I wage with what little resources I have."

Jane swallowed, the magnitude of what she planned, of what lay ahead, began to feel like a heavy stone on her chest. She wasn't entering an action movie. This was for real, and as much as she'd wanted to diminish it to the few gruesome raids Dr. Beavesly witnessed, she was very afraid that not only had the problem escalated into a war, but that she would witness it first hand.

"Perhaps you're right. Steve would be safer going back." But when she looked over at the boy, his light blond hair shining in the early morning light, she had her doubts. Though he'd ducked his head just before she'd glanced his way, she'd seen his chin thrust forward in stubbornness, and his eyes narrowed with a fierce determination.

"Steve," she called. The boy raised his head, and sure enough, she saw defiance in every cell of his body. Still, she tried anyway. "We're sending you back." He didn't respond. "But you're going to follow us anyway, aren't you?" He started to smile. "Do you understand you'll be in danger, maybe killed?"

He nodded.

"It will be ugly and violent, and it's no place for a boy." Or a city-bred girl, she thought with a grimace.

Steve nodded. Once. It wasn't a casual shrug or the false bravado she expected from a boy his age. It was a mature understanding, and Jane had the sick feeling he understood more of what was in store for them than she did.

She turned back to Daken, noting the angry twitch in his cheek. "We'll have to take him along. He won't go back unless we hogtie him."

"Well, not now," he grumbled. "Not after what you just said to him. By the Father, not only am I saddled with a fool woman, but now I've got to watch a boy too."

So began their travels. She knew Daken thought of their little party as a man, crazy woman, stupid boy, and the vague shadow of the panther, but she saw them as four souls who became a bridge to the future. Jane and Daken were the middle links, Steve was their step into the future and the Old One/pantar held the link to the past. It was all rather metaphysical for her, but she couldn't help thinking that way in the long hours of the journey.

Even on horses that moved impossibly fast, it took a few more days before they reached a village on the outskirts of what had been a major city. That made sense, of course. If the radiation was now the source of power and magic, the people would naturally gravitate toward the places with the most radiation. And those, of course, would be major cities that were not only the targets, but had abundant quantities of metal to hold the radiation.

"What is this city called?" she asked Daken as they rode in late one afternoon.

"LoUffa."

"LoUffa." She played with the words, changing it around and comparing it to her admittedly not-so-great knowledge of geography. "Buffalo."

"From here on, we travel by water."

Jane nodded, wondering why she hadn't bothered to put it all together in her mind before now. "Daken, what was the name of your lands?"

"Chigan."

"As in Chicago or Michigan?"

"I do not know these things."

Jane shook her head, deciding it didn't really matter as she focused on their travel route. "We're going by water down Lake Erie."

"The water Kree."

"And the Tarveen are in…"

"Troit."

Detroit. It figured.

"And your temporary base is in..."

"Toedo."

Toledo. Great. Now she understood, even though a part of her wished to remain in ignorance. All those great cities—now in ruins. She dreaded the thought of ever seeing New York City, or worse, Washington, D.C. To the casual observer, the land was reborn. Green grass covered the ground, except for the buildings created by the new inhabitants.

But soon they rode through what Daken called Holy Land. "Do you feel the power, Jane?" he asked, his voice suffused with awe. "I feel like I could gather it in one hand like a ball and throw it into the sky."

She didn't doubt him for a second. Even without healer's eyes, she could almost see the radiation filling the old city. Though the land was rich with mutated life, she could pick up the remnants of what must have been Toledo. Melted metal blobs, blunted and heavy, lay just below the ground or thrust upward through the grass, some still straight though dulled with time. Occasionally she caught the outlines of plastic or rubber mixed into the newly constructed houses.

It wasn't until they'd moved well into the holy area that she realized the land was concave, like a huge bowl, probably formed from the force of the explosion. Though they skirted the deepest part of the valley, Jane felt sick when she gazed at the center of the impact. The land was literally hollowed out by a bomb.

She wavered slightly in her saddle, grieving for what once was.

"Are you all right?"

"Fine, Daken," she responded automatically, but

her voice was thick and rough with tears.

"You look ill."

"The radiation— Uh, the Power. I'm afraid you'll have to heal..." She let her voice trail off, glancing self-consciously at the silent figure of Steve.

Daken, however, wasn't nearly so self-conscious. His grin was lurid, and wicked, and warmed her to her toes.

"Tonight," he promised.

◆   ◆   ◆

She hadn't really thought about what she expected to find at Daken's front line camp in Toledo. A row full of tents perhaps. Knights, warriors, noble men bravely holding the line against an enemy, but that was naive, she realized too late. That was the product of overly romanticized tales of chivalry and romance. And this, Jane now understood, was the brutality of war.

Daken's camp was a dirty, dingy group of farmers eking out a living in a dirty, dingy village already too abused by the Tarveen. The graveyard was full. The children's bellies were empty, and they were universally surrounded by a terror of the night.

The city was fortified, walled around first with stones, then logs that looked more like furniture and tar than cut trees. Soon they would resort to scraps and pieces of whatever they could find. Few went outside the walls, even during the day. And everywhere, it was noisy. Loud, angry, and happy sounds mixed with the cries of the hungry, furious, or ecstatic. Whether it was a child singing as he pumped water or a mother screeching as she hung out the wash or the men bellowing as they repaired breaks in the walls, everyone made sounds.

The Tarveen, apparently, didn't like noise.

It was a deafening clatter, but one that apparently provided some measure of security.

Jane tried not to wince as they moved through town. She tried not to show her disgust at the smell or her horror at the wretchedness of it all. But it must have shown because Daken turned away from her, his jaw muscles clenched, his hands knotted fists where they held on to the reins.

She urged her horse closer to his. "Daken?"

"It's nearly summer. Did you see the fields?"

She nodded. They were blood-stained plots of torn up crops. Every field had been trampled by the Tarveen raids. They would be lucky to feed a single family on what was grown this summer.

"I need an army," he forced through clenched teeth. "I need wizards and men with weapons." Then he turned his burning gaze on her. "And I return with a woman and a boy."

Jane bit her lip and looked away. For the first time ever, she began to see the cost of her pacifism. With one word from her, Daken could have his army—all the weapons and people he needed to finish this war with a decisive win.

But for how long? Daken couldn't be allowed to totally eradicate a race of people, even the Tarveen. So how long before the Tarveen regrouped and war erupted again? No, her way was better. It began a long stalemate that would, she hoped, eventually lead to peace.

But how could she look into the faces of hopeful children, pregnant women, and maimed men and tell them she had chosen the long, hard route instead of the quick, decisive victory? All around them, they turned out to see their king ride by. From the huts and the lean-tos, from within buildings and churches, people gathered, hoping for good news.

After one look at Daken's frozen expression and her apologetic tears, they turned away, muttering to themselves as they went back to their sad, violent lives.

For the first time ever, she seriously reconsidered her position. With painstaking agony, she reexamined every step of her logic, each conclusion as it compared to her knowledge and understanding of history. She rethought it over and over.

Staring at the wall, stained with the dried blood of countless men, the best she could come up with was a non-answer. After the rescue mission, assuming she survived, she would reconsider her position. Again.

Daken took them to a hut. It was hastily constructed and would do little more than keep out the rain, but it was habitable. Inside were a table and a couple of grass mats. In silence, Daken waved her and Steve in, gave the horses to a waiting villager, then walked away. Alone with Steve in the hut, Jane slumped to the ground, only to stare at the dust.

She looked once at Steve, wondering if she needed to comfort the boy against the sights they'd just passed through. But one glance at his face, filled with pity and concern for her disillusionment, brought the truth home to her in a sudden, brutal kick.

He wasn't the child here.

She was.

❖   ❖   ❖

They didn't see Daken the rest of the day. They ate from the rations they brought, then Jane returned to teaching Steve. She found a stick and drew English words in the dust. When she tired of that, she told him stories. She dredged up every pacifist hero she could think of, featuring Martin Luther King and Ghandi. He listened politely, and soon other children gathered as well.

Some of the adults stopped to listen too, but she wasn't a skilled storyteller, and her message wasn't what they were used to. Invariably, the men snorted and walked away speaking of women's foolishness. And the women, weak, sagging people with dull eyes, simply smiled vaguely at her and went to their tasks, pleased to have their children occupied for a time. Still, despite it all, the stories gave her some comfort, and she told herself she was exposing the children to the idea that violence was the last solution, not the first.

Then night came. Like a demon it stalked up to the village, lurking over it until it finally pounced. All around, people set up cow bells or wind chimes to keep the noise going while they slept. Torches flared around the walls, fires were lit everywhere outdoors, and after one long look at the grim-faced men, Jane went back into the hut.

She was a coward. She'd seen enough news-vids and fictional bloodbaths to know she didn't want to see the real thing.

Daken came in a moment later and spoke seven words. "Sleep now," he commanded. "We leave in the morning."

She nodded her understanding, but he'd already left. Unrolling her bedroll, she gathered Steve into her arms, and pretended to sleep.

She must have dozed off because she woke to a

complete darkness filled with noise. She heard the bellows of men screaming into the night, the clang of hammers on metal, and the strange cacophony of a thousand wind chimes set up not to be musical, but harsh and loud. Beneath it all, she caught the occasional twang of an arrow released from a bow.

And in that sickening riot of sound, she realized Steve was gone. She was alone in the hut.

She stumbled out the door, squinting into the brightness, adding her voice to the din. "Steve! Steve! Hell, boy, this isn't the time to go AWOL."

She scanned the world around her and got her first sight of war. It wasn't as gruesome as she'd expected. Certainly no more so than the videos she'd seen. Less horrifying, perhaps, because she couldn't see the faces of the taut people manning the walls. What startled her the most was their absolute stillness.

Despite the noise surrounding them in a deafening clatter, the men moved with an economy of motion. Every step, every gesture, even every breath was the efficient action of men pushed past exhaustion, but who still continued on. The torches wove and flared in the sconces. The wind chimes twisted and clanged, but the men remained almost relaxed, staring out at the empty fields beyond the wall.

Or were they really empty?

She caught a twist of a shadow, like a creeping animal across a field. It moved fast, scrambling like an insect. Was that a Tarvite? Apparently someone thought it was, because in a moment a whirling fireball appeared, detonating on whatever it was, obliterating it before she could make out any details.

Jane smiled grimly, pleased despite her pacifism. It would appear the city of Toedo had acquired a wizard.

And not too bad a one given the power and accuracy of the fireball.

She left her position just outside of her hut to silently walk the reinforcements looking for Steve. It took a long time because she tried to be thorough and inconspicuous at the same time. Despite Daken's almost casual care of her, she knew he'd be furious if he found her wandering around.

She didn't find Steve. Neither did she find the wizard who continued to obliterate one Tarvite shadow after another. She couldn't even satisfy her curiosity about the Tarveen. Despite her best efforts, she still couldn't get a good look at them. They moved too fast, and the fireball was too quick. She formed the vague notion of dark oval bodies, hairy legs and arms, and once she thought she saw claws. But that was all, and in the end she returned to her hut hoping to find Steve there.

He wasn't. So she huddled in the corner, clutching her knees to her chest. She pulled the cross out of her belt, the one she'd gotten from Kyree. She held it between her sweating palms while she prayed in fervent whispers. She covered her head with her hands and thought of Jesus Christ, her mother's God, and wondered if even God could hear her through the deafening clangor.

"Are you there?" she asked the blackness. "Or did you get exterminated with everyone else?" She heard the detonation of another three fireballs, and she bit her lip until she tasted her own blood. "If you're still there," she whispered. "If you can still hear me, now would be a good time to do something. Now would be a wonderful time for you to show me you still exist."

Nothing happened. Not that she expected anything.

But she remained where she was, huddled against the wall in a night filled with noise and explosions, and with every detonation, every boom that wasn't thunder, she fought to suppress Dr. Beavesly's memories of fire and devastation. Of the last and almost total world annihilation.

She wondered if she had been saved from that holocaust only to land in the middle of another.

Finally, when the gentle rays of dawn colored the sky, she prayed for wisdom and courage. For the first time in her life, she realized just how little of both she possessed.

Chapter Sixteen

✦   ✦   ✦

They left the next morning. Daken came to her just as dawn tinted the sky, kissed her terrified eyes and held her gently for a few minutes. He looked tired as only a healer in a battle zone could. She snuggled into his arms, holding him as tightly as he held her.

They didn't speak. There was nothing to say. She knew he hoped what she'd lived through this night would aid his cause when they went back to the Council later. And, in part, he was right. After seeing what was left of Toedo, she understood why Daken wanted the Tarveen eradicated permanently. He would push again for an army, and now she would find it hard to say no.

All she could do was pray for some divine inspiration, some miracle answer to make the decision unnecessary.

An hour later, they were ready to leave. Their escort of twenty men would see them to the edge of Lake Kree. Jane and Daken would then travel by ship up the Lake to Troit, the core of the Tarveen colony. There they'd infiltrate the main building, free the captives, and hopefully escape just as the twenty men arrived. Those men, as close to trained soldiers as

Daken had, would provide the military support needed to get the prisoners and eventually themselves on board the ship. Then everyone, the theory went, would sail safely away.

That was the plan, and though Jane expected trained CIA agents would be able to spot all sorts of holes, she couldn't think of a single one. She waited silently by her horse as Daken arranged last minute details. But all too soon, the men mounted, Daken finished his last instructions to those left behind, and still Jane craned her neck around the square waiting for the sight of a familiar dirty blond head.

"If you're having second thoughts, Jane, you better tell me now," called Daken as he strode toward her, his face set into grim passivity.

"Don't be ridiculous," she snapped, though in truth, she'd been having second thoughts since the moment she'd first conceived this plan. "I can't find Steve. The dratted boy disappeared last night, and he hasn't come back."

Daken mounted his horse, his thoughts clearly distracted. "Steve? He's staying with one of the villagers until we return. I thought you knew."

She whirled around, turning the full blast of her frustration on him. "How could I know when none of you ever talk to me? He's all right then?"

"Of course, he's all right."

She nodded, immensely relieved to have at least one problem solved. Then a thought hit her, and she started worrying at her lip again. "Do you think he'll be all right? I mean as a mute..." her voice trailed off, wondering if any pair of hands were welcome. Or if, even here in Toedo, he'd be an outcast mute boy.

Daken just laughed at her worried expression.

"They'll treat him like royalty. Probably better than royalty. Jane, he's a wizard and a gift from the Father for these people."

Jane felt her eyes widen with shock. "He's a what?"

"A wizard."

"And a gift from the God," echoed Jane, remembering her prayer of last night. She shook her head. "So the fireballs came from Steve."

Daken nodded, clearly amazed she hadn't figured it out before. "He's not so bad. I didn't think you could be a mage without words, but—"

"You don't need words," she said, recalling what Kyree told her. "It's a mental focusing." Her voice trailed away as she tried to simultaneously mount her horse and fit this new information to her image of Steve.

"He's good, too," Daken added, amazement in his voice. "I'd never have guessed it of him, but there it is."

There it is, Jane repeated to herself. The small frightened boy she rescued from Borit was a mage. How could that be? And if it were true, why had he kept it a secret? It was the way to instant respect, even in the college.

"I guess I don't blame him," commented Daken as much to himself as to her. "Given the prophesy about how he'd be a great wizard, he'd have to perform to greatness immediately. And then people would try to use him or abuse him. Jealousy, envy, hatred, it would all have been there."

Jane had forgotten about the prophesy surrounding the boy. And given Daken's experiences, she was sure he knew better than most about expectations and envy, but it still seemed a crying shame that Steve had to hide his ability from everyone.

What a terrible secret for a boy. Or just another burden for an abused boy.

Jane shook her head. "At least he's showing it now. Perhaps he will get some of his self-respect back." Unable to do anything more for Steve, Jane focused on trying to readjust to sitting in a saddle. Although she had learned to ride, she still wasn't comfortable doing it.

Daken glanced at her, lifting an eyebrow as they moved outside of the village wall. "He's already got his self-esteem back. From you."

Jane jerked her attention back to Daken. "From me?"

"Haven't you seen how he wears those new clothes you gave him?"

"Everyone likes new clothes—"

Daken shook his head. "It's more than that. Have you seen him polish his belt buckle? The large circle—"

"Letter O," she corrected.

He waved it off. "He's got that look. I've seen it in men who get a plot of land for the first time. There's amazement, awe, a little fear, and a lot of pride all mixed together."

Jane smiled, wanting to believe whatever else she had done, her time with Steve had been for good. But reason told her different. "Daken, the boy's bright. And he's a mage. He would have made it with or without my help."

"But it was with your help. You saw something in him that took me a lot longer to notice. You had faith in him before any of us, and that's given him his self-respect."

"Maybe," she mumbled, her eyes already pulled to the horizon as they crossed into Tarveen-controlled land.

He followed her gaze, but his comment brought her attention back to the boy. "I hope you realize you've got a great responsibility to the boy."

"What?"

"Why do you think he's so protective of you?"

Jane shrugged. "I suppose because I'm the first one who ever really cared about him as a person."

"Exactly."

"What's your point? I shouldn't beat the boy or turn on him? I thought you knew me better."

Daken frowned at her. "No," he responded levelly, his gaze now encompassing the horizon. "You shouldn't take unnecessary risks with your life. How will he feel, experiencing love for the first time, if you were to suddenly die?"

Jane felt a lump close down her throat. Daken's words were delivered with such an even, unemotional tone she might have thought he didn't care. But she knew him better now, enough to realize he struggled with his own feelings, sorting through thoughts he probably didn't want to admit to. And that made her wonder if he spoke about himself or Steve. Did he think he was in love? With her? She could hardly dare to hope. As soon as she began grappling with the hunger sparked by that thought, the rest of his words seeped into her soul.

What if she died today?

Daken was right. She did have another reason to come out of their rescue mission alive. Her own hopes for a future with Daken aside, she needed to help Steve. Especially now that he openly revealed his abilities as a mage. She must be there to help him deal with pressures to come.

"I won't fail him," she said softly, speaking to

Daken's stern profile. "Or you."

He glanced at her, his expression fierce, but his eyes bleak with a fear that tore at her as it must eat at him. "See that you don't."

Then he spurred his horse ahead to speak with the leader of his men.

◆   ◆   ◆

It was noon by the time they reached Detroit, or rather what was left of it. The place was a wasteland, not from a nuclear warhead, although naturally that was the original devastation. The current problem was the Tarveen.

Up until now, Jane had clung to the idea that the Tarveen were human. She discounted Daken's protests that they were monsters as the propaganda of a man trying to eradicate a race. Even Dr. Beavesly's rather hazy memories of the Tarveen colony didn't damage her belief they were people. Mutants, yes. Cannibals, yes, but human in their core.

As they disembarked from the boat, she felt her first stirring of doubt. What human colony wantonly destroyed the very environment they inhabited?

There was filth everywhere. She'd expected at least some cultivation of the land, a few crops maybe, something, but the land was completely stripped. No trees, no grass, nothing except mud and dirt and filth.

She looked around her, shock in every breath she took. "What kind of people are these?"

"I told you, they aren't people," Daken repeated for the thousandth time, readjusting her backpack on his shoulders. They decided hers was sturdier and the better pack despite its neon yellow strips. Hers was also waterproof, and therefore a safer carrier for the Tarveen Holy Book.

"Why aren't there any about?" She covered her nose, trying to shut out the stench brought by the stale breeze.

"The Tarveen sleep during the day. There won't be any about until dusk."

She nodded, then turned her troubled gaze onto the horizon. Daken's gaze focused on her, studying her face and her expressions with an angry air.

"What is it, Jane?" His voice was harsh and demanding.

She just shook her head. "That stuff about them sleeping during the day. I should know that."

Daken nodded, grimly agreeing with her.

"Dr. Beavesly's memories are usually so clear and specific. He was a trained observer with a very organized mind. But not when it came to the Tarveen."

"The Tarveen upset many people. I've seen grown men run in terror at the sight—"

"No, it's not that. He was a spirit..." At Daken's confused expression, she stumbled into an explanation even she found hard to understand. "He was an Old One attached to the computer. Both alive and not alive at the same time."

"And it is his memories you turn to as Keeper?"

Jane nodded. "Except whenever it has to do with the Tarveen, they're fuzzy. As though they're repressed or something. I don't understand it, and it bothers me."

Daken swore beneath his breath. "Are you telling me you don't know where this entrance is?"

Jane looked up, startled by the venom in his tone. "No, of course not. I have a clear picture of the whole area, but in all that, I can't grasp a full memory of a

Tarveen."

"Perhaps this doctor tried to spare you the sight."

Jane shook her head, knowing that wasn't it. "There's something I'm missing. Some memory, some key. I just have to find it..."

Daken dismissed her strange words with a wave of his hand. "If you know this secret entrance, then that is enough."

Jane shook her head. "Not enough, but it's all we have."

With a sigh, she started to pick her way through the debris toward what once was an automobile factory. Daken followed, his impatience with her was clear.

"How far away is this entrance?"

She lifted her arm, pointed to a pile of broken rock and steel girders. "Just behind th—!"

He moved faster than lightening. One moment they were talking, picking their way up a trash-choked hill. The next second, he held his bastard sword poised to strike and jerked her behind him with a force that wrenched her arm painfully in its socket.

He stared at a jagged block of concrete just to their right. "Come out now, Tarvite," he growled.

"Do they understand Common?" she asked, her voice hushed and low.

"I have never tried to talk to one before."

Jane remained well behind Daken, giving him room to fight, but even so, she craned her neck around, trying to see behind the obstruction.

They heard the movement long before they saw anything. Something scrambled over the ruins, pushing aside the rocks and pebbles clotting the area.

"Stay here," Daken ordered as he began edging around enough to see, but not enough to leave the relatively open, flat ground. Jane followed a pace behind, needing to see almost as desperately as she needed to stay within close proximity to Daken.

There was something evil about this place. Something so horrible even Dr. Beavesly couldn't face it.

The sounds came closer. Whoever, or whatever it was, wasn't bothering to disguise his approach.

"See anything?" she asked, her throat tight with fear.

Daken waved her to silence as he continued to edge around. Jane spared a glance behind her. The land remained as still as before, so she returned her nervous sight to the concrete blocking their view.

It was almost upon them. She could hear heavy breathing. She tensed, though God only knew what she would do. She had her dagger, the one Daken gave her so long ago. But from what she'd heard, if she got close enough to use it on a Tarvite, it was already too late.

She saw Daken drop to a crouch, his sword ready to strike, clearly intending to catch it by surprise. Jane bit her lip, wondering how she felt about that. Amazing how her anti-violence sentiments seemed to waver when fear began eating at her insides.

Then suddenly, she saw it. A dirty, blond head seemed to pop over the top, quickly followed by small shoulders and a thin chest, all of which froze at the sight of Daken springing forward sword high.

"Steve!" she screamed, trying to warn both the boy and Daken. It wasn't necessary. Daken had already seen him and checked his blow mid-swing.

"By the Father, boy! Are you trying to get yourself killed?"

Steve's eyes were huge, pale blue pools trained

on Daken's sword which shook slightly as Daken sheathed the blade. The boy still hadn't moved. Jane doubted he even breathed.

"Steve. *Steve!*" she yelled, finally breaking through his slight trance. Then she dropped her voice to a deceptive calm. "Why don't you come up here, and we'll have a little chat." Truth of the matter was, if Daken didn't horse whip the stupid kid, she would. And with pleasure.

Little did the boy know, he was in more danger from her than he was from the very self-controlled warrior. Steve slowly stood, carefully stepping out from behind the concrete and crossed to Jane. She gave him a grim smile, seeing how he gave Daken a wide berth.

Steve stopped in front of her, his face impassive, his eyes steady. She leaned down over him and pitched her voice low and menacing. "I don't know why you're here, and I don't care. It's bad enough you followed us from Bosuny, but to come here is outside of enough, do you hear me? I don't want your protection. I don't need your protection. And mage or not, you're more of a danger to us than a help! So get your skinny little butt to the boat before I take you over my knee and spank you until my hand breaks. *Have you got that?*"

She pointed to the boat quietly swaying in the water like a giant rocking chair. Narrowing her eyes, she noticed what must have been Steve's horse, tethered to a tree near the edge of the water. Fine. Maybe one of the more healthy captives could ride it back to Toedo.

First came the rescue, but before that, she needed to send one recalcitrant, thirteen year old boy packing. She turned back to him, expecting to see a sulking child stomp past her. To her astonishment, Steve didn't move. He continued to stare at her, his back rigid and his chin in the air.

"Steve. I'm not kidding here. I will spank you, and if you don't believe me, then believe King Daken. He's been wanting to tan your hide for weeks."

Steve didn't move.

Jane ground her teeth and raised her hand. She dreaded the thought of striking a child, but the boy had to be disciplined. He had to learn to obey for his own good.

To her astonishment, Daken stepped forward and pulled her hand down. Then he crouched low enough to look eye to eye with Steve. "Do you know where we are?"

Nod.

"Do you know what we're going to do?"

Another grave nod.

"You think you can help us, don't you?"

This time, Steve shot Jane a witheringly proud glare, then nodded once, emphatically.

"Do you understand the risks? We will probably die in there."

Jane had enough. "He's a child, Daken. Worse, he's a teenage boy. How can he know the consequences? They all think they're immortal."

Both males ignored her as Steve nodded, his small body poised, his pale blue eyes steady and clear.

Daken asked one more question, his voice gravelly with resignation. "This is your choice?"

Another nod.

"Then I accept your comradeship with gratitude."

"What?" Jane exploded behind him. She stepped forward ready to carry the kid kicking and screaming

to the ship if necessary. There was no way he was coming with them, but Daken stopped her, grabbing her shoulders and pinning her against him. Then he turned her around, roughly shaking her as she fought him.

"Look at him, Jane. Really look."

Jane twisted out of Daken's hold, shoving him off of her as she stared at Steve. He looked the same as always. He wore the clothes she had bought him, now a little worn and holey, especially over the knees. The "O" of his belt buckle glinted silver in the light, and she knew what Daken said about him polishing it must be true. But what she saw most was the small body, thin frame, and childish face with grave, sad eyes.

"I'm looking," she snapped.

"Do you see him? Do you see the man?"

"I see a boy. A stubborn, willful boy who doesn't have the sense God gave a mule."

"Wrong, Jane." Daken's voice was soft beside her, but no less firm. "He knows what he's doing. He knows the risks, and he's taking responsibility for this choice."

"Bull sh—"

"Stop thinking like a mother. He's not your child. He's not a child at all."

Jane turned her back on Steve, throwing her anger at Daken while she fought tears she didn't understand. "Don't be ridiculous. He's only thirteen."

"Age doesn't matter. He's a man. He's taken responsibility for his own actions and choices. Some people never do that. I didn't until my brother die—was captured."

"That's macho nonsense."

"Don't be stupid, Jane. You've supported him up until now. Don't hurt him just because you can't part with the thought of having him stay a child."

Jane bit her lip and turned away, not wanting to hear Daken's words, but when her eyes cleared, she looked again at Steve. Not the frightened boy she'd rescued a few weeks ago, but the mage Steve. The man in a child's body.

She didn't notice it immediately. She took in the pieces, bit by bit, reluctantly allowing them to add up. She saw his steady regard, calm and reserved in the face of her hostility. She noticed his composure as he waited for her acknowledgement, but she also took in his lifted chin and the steely determination in every line of his body.

"You've decided to join us, haven't you?"

A nod.

"And unless we lock you up on the boat, you'll come whether we like it or not."

A strange light glinted in Steve's eye, and Daken stepped forward to explain it. "He's a mage. A locked door won't hold him, and he's the only one who can spell it shut."

Jane swallowed the acrid taste of fear, but it only settled into her stomach, burning there with a raw ache. "This is male foolishness. You don't take a child on a rescue mission."

"I don't take foolish women either, but I'm taking you. And Steve." Then he turned away from her, dismissing her as he would a lesser member of his staff. "Here's your task, Steve. You will follow Jane, memorizing the route along the way. When we get to the captives, you will lead them out and to the boat. I don't want you fighting except from a distance—"

"He shouldn't be fighting at all," Jane snapped.

Once again, she was ignored by both of them.

"I'm entrusting my people to you, Steve. No matter

what happens to me or Jane, you must get them to the boat. Understand?"

Steve nodded, a compulsive swallow the only crack in his composure. But Jane's attention had changed. She heard something in Daken's voice, a slight catch as he said their names, and that small break chilled her blood.

"What do you mean, whatever happens to you and me? What are you planning?"

Daken stood and faced her, his expression as resolute as Steve's. "Once inside, you will show me the way to the nursery."

"No way!"

"You said it was close to where my people are kept."

"This is a rescue mission. Period. No killing unless absolutely necessary. And no baby slaughter."

"You will tell me where the Tarveen children are, or I will be forced to search the area alone. Either way, I will find it." He didn't put his hands on his hips or cross his arms over his chest. He didn't expand his chest or do any other of the typical body language of a puffed up man. He stood as he always stood. Like a warrior—composed, aware, and lethally uncompromising.

She knew she wouldn't be able to dissuade him this time. She shook her head, starting to walk away—not in any particular direction, just away from the two most frustrating people on the face of the earth. "You're crazy. You're both crazy."

Daken wouldn't let her escape. He grabbed her arm, turning her back to face him. "You will show me where the nursery is." It wasn't a question.

"What are you going to do there?"

"Ginsen made a firebomb. I will set it off, and then

I will run."

Never had she been more furious than at this moment. After all they'd been through, after all their discussions and agreements, they were back to the same thing. "All you care about is killing the Tarveen. You don't care who you risk—me, Steve, yourself— you don't care. Just so long as you can slaughter the Tarveen."

"That's right, Jane," he said, his words like brutal slaps in her face. "It's all I've ever wanted."

"After all we've been to each other, after all we've shared, how can you still go and do this?" Her voice shook with her intensity.

He drew himself up, his voice dripping with scorn. "When did I ever give you the impression I was ruled by my groin? You do not dictate to me, woman."

"How dare you," she breathed, her anger burning like a hot dagger in her heart. "As if I'd buy your coop- eration with my body."

He sneered, matching her anger with a coldness all his own. "This is what I will do, Jane, with or without your help. I will rescue my people, the Tarveen food source," he spat his disgust on the ground. "Then I will kill off their children. Then, I will take Steve and an army, and I will exterminate them once and for all."

Jane felt the change within her. It was like the flip of a switch, and with it her blood cooled, her fists loosened into hands, and her anger shifted to a icy hatred. "I'll stop you," she said, her voice low and threatening. "The Council won't help you."

"It doesn't matter. If I have to sell everything I own, I will get the soldiers I need."

Jane glared at him, focusing all her scorn on what he intended to do now, leaving the future for later.

"You'll be slaughtering babies, Daken. A fine and noble deed for a warrior king."

"I think so."

She watched him step gingerly past the concrete, rooting around for the secret entrance. Behind him, Steve hesitated, his glance hopping between herself and his new champion. In the end, he chose Daken, and Jane felt his betrayal in every inch of her body.

Daken had her.

He had neatly manipulated her into helping to kill an entire race. Babies! He was going to burn babies!

She could stop him. She could turn around right now. Even if they found the entrance, they'd quickly get lost in the mazes of corridors and ventilating tubes, but she couldn't leave Daken and Steve to die any more than she could abandon the people trapped below waiting to be eaten by the Tarveen.

She had to rescue them. But once on the main floor, it was an easy step to the nursery. He just needed the right corridor, and then he would torch a room full of babies.

Jane felt sick to her stomach. How could this be the man she loved? Was he so consumed with the need for vengeance he had lost everything else? Love, compassion, understanding, everything? He'd told her the answer. Yes, he'd said. All he cared about was killing the Tarveen. Her feelings, her concerns, her love meant less than nothing.

From behind the concrete block, Daken's voice came at her, each word a grating blow to her heart. "Are you coming? Or do we go without you?"

"You'll die without me leading you. There are thousands of tunnels down there."

"Then we die."

She stepped around the debris, unable to deny the suicidal determination in both of their eyes. Jane swallowed the choking agony in her throat. At the same moment, she pushed away all her emotions. She had a job to do. Whatever else happened, she would deal with it as it came.

Although in her heart, she knew there was nothing she could do to stop Daken. And if he went ahead and killed all those children, she'd never be able to love him again.

"Move aside," she said, her voice as flat as her broken heart. "I'll lead."

Daken lifted his head. "I lead. We don't know what's in this tunnel, and you can't defend yourself any more than a kitten."

"And you can't swing a sword in there." She kicked aside a large rock, partly exposing a dented metal shaft about the size of a small sewer grate.

Daken didn't respond as he crossed to the remaining stone. Passing off the backpack to Steve, he slid down into the shaft to get better leverage against the stone. It took all three of them, but they managed to roll it away. Then Jane dusted the dirt from her hands and tensed to jump into the grate first, taking the lead.

But Daken was gone, having already dropped down the rest of the way and turned the first corner.

"Damned bloody fool!" she spit after him. Then with a sigh, she prepared to drop in, but Steve stopped her. He touched her shoulder. It was a brief brush, but from Steve, who hated to touch or be touched by anyone, it was like the clang of a gong.

Jane looked up at him, settling herself on her bottom with her legs dangling into the shaft. "What is it? Are you scared?"

He shook his head, and Jane squelched a tremor of disappointment. She had hoped she could still find an excuse to send him back to the boat, but the boy, or man according to Daken, wasn't interested in himself. Instead, he solemnly reached into his shirt and pulled something out.

At first she didn't recognize it, but then she felt her eyes pull wide with shock.

The dull gray metal of the Beretta gleamed in the sunshine.

"Where did you get that?"

Steve's only response was to offer her the weapon, butt first. She took it quickly, noticed it was correctly loaded with the safety on, then anchored it in her belt.

"This is a dangerous weapon, Steve. Not a toy..." her words trailed away. It was amazing what she could read off his face when he wanted her to. What she saw now told her he knew exactly what the gun was and probably how it worked. He'd brought it to her because she was the one qualified to use it.

Jane sighed. "I don't like guns. They kill people. All I want to do is help this world live in peace, and yet here I am, packing a Beretta, about to drop into a hole so I can help the man I used to love blow up a bunch of babies." She looked up at his young, too wise face. "Does that seem right to you?"

He didn't look away, but neither did he venture an opinion. In the end, she had no choice but to begin. Without a backward glance, she shoved off the ground and dropped into the shaft.

She blinked in the darkness, waiting for her eyes to adjust. Seconds later, a glowing ball appeared above her, illuminating Steve behind and Daken ahead. It was a magelight, no doubt created by Steve, and it bobbed along beside them as they moved.

"Where have you been? We're in enemy territory, you know." Daken's acerbic comments cut through the silence.

"They're not my enemies," she shot back just to irritate him.

"They will be soon," he grumbled as Steve joined them at the junction of two shafts. Then Daken noticed the pistol shoved into her belt. She expected him to comment, but he didn't, except to send a piercing look at Steve. Then he turned his attention forward. "Which way?"

Jane gestured to the left. "This is an old ventilating shaft, hopefully still intact. If not, there are also huge pipes, some for power cables, others for the heavy equipment. Don't ask me why the Tarveen haven't found it. As far as I can tell, there are miles of tunnels here crisscrossing the entire complex."

Daken spanned the opening she indicated then ducked in, his voice coming back to her in a hushed whisper. "It's too narrow for the Tarveen. They have very wide, very hard middles. It's part of their body armor. Even the smallest couldn't squeeze in here."

Jane looked at the tube. An obese man could squeeze through it. It would be very tight, but still manageable. Once again she struggled to picture a Tarvite, adding a huge middle and dark body armor. It didn't fit, and as she tried to pull an image from Dr. Beavesly's memories, it skittered away from her.

Jane sighed, pushing the problem aside as she ducked into the shaft to follow Daken.

It was narrow, but manageable, though she was grateful she didn't suffer from claustrophobia. She glanced back at Steve to see he managed with annoying ease. Even her heavy backpack didn't seem to bother the boy. He slipped along using his extra speed and mobility to draw a long line of glowing, neon yellow. She didn't know where he got the pen. Another wizard toy, she supposed. Like a huge highlighter, it would make their return path very, very clear.

It was Daken she felt sorry for. His shoulders were indeed wedged with almost no maneuverability. His arms were stretched in front of him, while his fingers dragged him along on his belly, scooping up all the dirt and dust of two centuries in front of him. He kept his dagger in his teeth, but even that didn't stop the long stream of muttered curses.

It was enough to make her smile.

They encountered minor problems, of course. It seemed the deeper tunnels served as hiding places for small burrowing animals. They constantly pushed aside rodent nests and fought angry squirrels. Plus the tube was cracked in some areas, letting dirt spill in. Fortunately for them, the animals kept the route relatively clear.

The one major obstruction was a completely collapsed area. Daken chipped away at the packed dirt for a moment, but it was soon apparent they couldn't pass through there.

It took her a few minutes, but Jane was able to think of a different route bypassing the damaged area. Before long, they'd kicked out a filth-strewn grate and peered into what once was the main drag of an automobile assembly line.

The stench overwhelmed them, rising into their faces, carrying images of blood and rotting meat. There was almost no light except for Steve's magelight. Far below, she thought she caught the occasional flicker of torchlight, but that was all.

What struck her the most were the sounds. Mournful, pitiful wails. Screeching, agonizing shrieks. And more eerie, the occasional sound of a child's laughter. The whole cacophony assaulted her ears without relief, and she cringed away from it. Daken didn't seem to notice it, though his face was now like chiseled granite in the emotionless mask of a warrior going about his task. With a flick of his wrist, Daken gestured for Steve to send the magelight forward. It was pitifully weak against the cavernous gloom, but it did illuminate a long steel girder probably running the length of the assembly line. Jane tried to peer around, perhaps get some bearings with regard to what machinery was still intact, not for use, but as scaffolding.

Daken didn't bother. He angled his feet through the grate and slipped a heavy rope over one shoulder and across his torso.

"What are you doing?" Jane whispered in alarm.

"I'm going to swing over to that metal thing down there." The magelight zipped over to the girder. It was actually part of a huge support system for the various machinery used for manufacturing cars. She had no doubt it would support his weight. The grid looked intact and stable, but it was incredibly narrow for a half leap, half drop across what seemed to her a black chasm of death.

"You're crazy. That's like playing leap frog across Niagara Falls."

"I don't know of this Niag—"

"A big, deadly drop," she snapped.

"There's no better way," he returned. "There's nothing to tie the rope to here." Then before she could stop him, he slipped through the hole, swung out on

352   KATHERINE GREYLE

one arm, then let go. She would have screamed if she hadn't been holding her breath. He landed flat across the girder, safely, if not gracefully.

"Damn, suicidal fool," she muttered to herself.

Daken immediately secured the rope around the beam, kicking it over until they heard the end hit the floor. "Stay there while I get something to use as a bridge," he called.

"Do I look stupid?" she shot back. "I'm not leaping across there."

Daken ignored her, focusing instead on Steve, who still held the backpack. "Toss me a torch."

Steve rooted one out and neatly flung it to Daken. Seconds later, the magelight spun through the tip, igniting it while bathing Daken's face in a soft white glow. Then Daken disappeared, dancing along the steel girders, his torch bobbing beside him.

He returned with a long, slimy plank made out of plastic. Jane didn't know what it was or where he'd gotten it, she was just grateful it survived the ages, and it seemed sturdy enough to support their weight. All three of them anchored it as best they could, setting one end in the lip of the I-beam, the other up into the shaft.

Then it was time to slide down, without a safety belt or even rope guards. And here she'd thought time travel was the most excitement a person could expect in one lifetime.

Steve went first, not because she waved him forward, but because he got impatient waiting for her to get up her nerve. He lay down on his belly, his arms and legs wrapping around either side, then just pushed himself off.

It was terrifying, but when Daken pulled him onto

the girder, Steve's face was split with an excited grin.

"He thinks it's a carnival ride," she muttered. Then, unwilling to be shown up by a kid, she took a deep breath and mimicked his position. She hadn't even pushed off when she started sliding, picking up speed until she landed against the I-beam with a painful thump. Then Daken was there, hauling her up to stand while she bit back the pain radiating bolts of misery throughout her whole body.

"That hurt," she grumbled.

"Get stronger thigh muscles," returned Daken, his expression brightening as he took more and more control of their situation. "It'll slow your descent."

"Thanks," she shot back. "I'll remember that if I ever want to come back to this nightmare."

He merely flashed her a grin, then without another word, dropped below the I-beam, wrapped a leg in the rope, and slid down. Daken apparently had all the thigh muscles he needed for a steady, controlled descent.

She, on the other hand, would need God to help her or put something nice and cushy at the bottom because there was no way she was that strong. She started to grab the rope, but Steve stopped her. He gestured for her to hold out her hands and then quickly wrapped strips around her palms to prevent rope burn. With a little start of surprise, she realized the strips were torn out of his new tunic.

"Thank you, Steve," she said gravely. "I promise I'll buy you another one once we get back to Toedo."

He gave her a cocky grin, then supported her as best he could while she grabbed onto the rope. Like with the plastic slide, there wasn't really time to think. She was moving before she could even breathe, and eternally grateful for Steve's homemade gloves.

As it was, she zipped right down, and if it weren't for Daken catching her, she would have brained herself right there on the dirty factory floor.

Steve, of course, came down like he was part monkey, which given this population, was entirely possible. Even so, Jane began to feel totally inadequate for this little rescue mission.

"Where to now?" Daken asked from beside her.

Jane looked up from where she squinted into the darkness. "What?"

"Where to now?" Daken repeated, his annoyance making his words sharp. "Where are my people?"

Jane lifted her arms. "Here."

Daken looked around. "Here? In this filth?" He kicked at a rancid piece of meat, and together they watched it roll into a fetid pool of water.

Jane sighed. "This place is huge. I think it's a storage area of sorts." She pointed at piles of rotting fruit, another of some cured meat. All the different things the Tarveen must have scavenged from villages because they clearly didn't cultivate their own food. "Your people are probably hiding, doing their best not to become today's lunch."

Even in the murky light, Jane could see Daken's muscles twitch. "Those sounds, the crying, those are from my people? Hiding like rats in the darkness?"

She could see the pain etch its own horror into his face. She knew he thought about the men of Toedo or perhaps others he'd known. All strong fighters defending their homes. That they would be reduced to the sobbing wails that surrounded them was more than sad. It was a crime.

"Come on," she said. "Let's find them."

"How?" asked Daken softly, turning in a wide

circle as he scanned the gloom. "How can I be heard over this din?"

Jane was also thinking the same thing when Steve's magelight exploded into a floodlight. One moment they squinted at shadows. The next, everything was buried in a whiteness so bright, she closed her eyes. When she finally ventured to open them in a squint, she saw more than half the entire assembly illuminated in the harsh lighting. From floor to ceiling, in nests and alcoves throughout the machinery, she picked out dark ovals of faces. Most were shielded by stringy hair, some were half covered in blood.

But all were silent.

The hush fell over them like the muting layers of dirt over a grave. Jane fought the chills creeping up her spine.

Only Daken seemed to keep his cool. He drew himself up like the king he was and spoke loud and clear into the room. His voice echoed up and down the passageway, reverberating in the old metal, echoing off the network of beams and rotting cables.

"My people. I am Daken, your King. I've come to rescue you. We have made a tunnel free of the Tarveen. You must come with me now, and I will lead you outside."

All along the rafters and the beams, the word "outside" spun and echoed around them. It was repeated in hushed whispers by a thousand voices until it became a wave rolling over them, crashing around them. Everywhere she looked, Jane saw movement. Creeping dirty bodies running along beams, crawling out from under filth too nauseating to think of, even sliding out of niches in the wall.

They came. Steve's magelight dimmed. Apparently

he couldn't keep up the floodlight intensity for very long. Gradually, the harsh lighting muted to the soft brightness of a single candle, held high above Daken, showing his people the way to their king.

One of the first people to step forward was a huge, hulking figure of a man who, despite his size, still showed the signs of starvation in his hollowed out eyes and drawn face. Daken didn't see him at first. He was busy watching a pregnant woman, her body emaciated except for her bulging middle, as she walked on trembling legs out from behind the pile of rotting fruit. But Jane saw the man, and she worried about the strange gleam in his eyes, not knowing if it was excitement or madness.

She gripped her dagger.

Then he spoke, his voice booming over the noise of hundreds of people getting ready to escape. "You are not our king, little brother, but we welcome your rescue nonetheless."

Daken spun around, his eyes wide with hope. "Tev! You're alive!" He walked straight into the larger man's arms, and they hugged each other as only two bears can. "By the Father, you're thin."

"Bah," Tev said, spitting his disgust at the floor. "Tarveen aren't gracious hosts."

Now that they were next to each other, Jane could see the family resemblance. Though Tev was darker and thinner, they had the same body build, the same chiseled features.

Daken drew back, and Jane read the slight tremor of fear passing through his expression with his next words. "What about Mother and Father?"

"They're well. Or as well as you can get in this cursed place. Come on. I'll take you to them."

Tev started to draw him forward, but Daken held back, hesitating as he looked at Jane. She shook her head. "You go on. Steve and I will lead the people out."

She saw him stiffen, and his eyes grew cold. "Steve will show them out. You will stay."

She lifted her chin, glaring at him, defiance in every line of her body. He wanted her to direct him to the Tarveen nursery, but nothing he said or did would induce her to help him murder children. Even Tarveen children.

She turned her back on him, going to assist a brittle woman with a small child. Behind her, she heard Daken curse and move away. As he retreated, Jane looked up, focusing on a door barely ten feet from her.

It was the one to the nursery, and likely the first one Daken would try when he searched on his own. Jane looked away. There was nothing she could do.

Steve worked with some other men and women, quickly building a scaffold to the ceiling. From all around, they pulled out netting and ropes. No ladders.

"The Tarveen can't climb rope very well," explained one old crone.

Because of Steve's neon trail, the boy wasn't needed to lead the way out. Like Jane, he stayed behind to help the weaker ones. Jane picked out the strongest-looking man and told him to go first. She explained about the boat, warned him about the squirrels, gave him a big smile and pushed him on his way. He didn't need any more urging. He scrambled like a large, furless monkey up the rope network, then disappeared into the shaft. A moment later, she saw him reach down for an infant, before helping the mother.

Behind the little trio, a long line of people waited

for their turn. Like spiritless refugees too shocked to absorb their rescue, they stood waiting without moving except to maintain a loud humming noise.

Like the people of Toedo, they knew the Tarveen didn't like noise. It would no doubt be years before any of them grew used to silence once again.

Glancing up, Jane saw more and more people disappear on their way to safety, and she felt a surge of joy. It had begun. The rescue was underway.

Still, she felt a vague unease, growing stronger with every minute in the factory. She wandered to the edge of the light, letting the gloom surround her even as the horror began to well up. She was close to Dr. Beavesly's memory. Whatever he suppressed grew stronger as the light grew dimmer. She almost had it. All she needed was to immerse herself more and more in the world of the Tarveen.

But the memory skittered away.

Then it happened. Not more than eight feet from her, a Tarvite appeared from a side door, scuttling in on all fours before rearing up on its hind legs. She heard a scream, and for the first time, she got a close-up look at Daken's enemy.

It didn't look human. That was her first thought. Except for its size, about five feet tall, it didn't look human at all. It looked like a cockroach. Its body was black, its limbs covered in dirty, thick hairs. Its torso had the oblong shape of a beetle with a heavy, leathery casing nearly three feet wide in the middle. Just above the thickest part, there were two coiled protrusions of unknown purpose, one on each side. Its head was small in comparison. A little round circle with bright bulging beetle eyes, and from its jaws extended claw like mandibles clicking ominously.

She absorbed the sight in a second, barely having time to register the Tarvite's presence, but the people around her were more familiar with it. They scattered like leaves in the wind, but one poor girl wasn't so fast. She'd been hurt, her leg gashed and infected, and the Tarvite turned to her as she tried to limp away.

Jane was already moving forward to intervene, though what she planned to do was beyond her. There wasn't even time for her first step before it happened. The coiled protrusions at the Tarvite's belly snaked out. Like twin whips, they wrapped around the girl and reeled her in. There wasn't even a moment to scream before the Tarvite landed full body on top of its victim, its mandibles ripping out her throat. Blood spurted out, covering the Tarvite and the dead girl, but the thing didn't notice. It ate on top of her, its heavy mandibles making short work of the body.

Jane covered her mouth against the scream coiled in her throat. No human ate like that, cannibal or not, but from somewhere deep within her came the awareness of human life within the Tarvite. The thought was irreconcilable with the sight before her, but from somewhere—from the core of Dr. Beavesly's knowledge—was the certainty that he had a kinship with these horrible Tarveen.

Dr. Beavesly's memories were thick and heavy against her mind. What she struggled so long to find suddenly became an overwhelming vomit of emotions and impressions she fought against. She was suffocating beneath their weight.

She fell to her knees, fighting an inexorable pull like a lead weight, dragging her under the sea of these memories.

From somewhere to her right, she heard a scream.

Looking up, she saw the door to the nursery open. Another Tarvite, this one larger than the other, reared up onto its hind legs. Not more than two feet away from it stood Steve, his eyes still transfixed by the remains of the young girl.

He was oblivious to the danger beside him.

The new Tarvite swiveled its beetle head, focusing on the boy.

"Steve!" she screamed.

He turned too late. The protrusions snapped out, wrapped around him, and drew him in.

Chapter Seventeen

❖   ❖   ❖

She didn't think. There wasn't time.

She simply reacted.

She didn't even realize she'd pulled out the Beretta, snapped off the safety and shot all in one quick move. And then shot again.

She didn't know what she'd done until she saw the Tarvite on its back, its head blown into a thousand pieces, a thick ichor draining from its body onto the wall.

Steve hauled out a knife. Even from this distance, she could see his hands shaking. He cut away the protrusions and stepped away from the Tarvite.

Then the relentless pressure of Dr. Beavesly's memories drew her under.

❖   ❖   ❖

Pulling. Something pulled her away. Far, far away.

No, she told herself. Dr. Beavesly was being pulled. This was his memory, but even knowing that, she relived it, every nerve-curling agony, every mind-numbing pain, she felt it as he had almost a century ago.

Dr. Beavesly was content with his computer. Even as a spirit, he managed to set up the solar cells, giving power to the millions of microchips that had become his world.

Until he felt the call.

It started out like an itch, and he hadn't felt an itch since he'd been alive. But within moments it was a passion, a need so strong he'd never felt the likes of it before. He needed to go, needed to find out where and who called him. It possessed his thoughts, ruled his mind, this all-consuming need.

He skimmed through the optic lines, and when they were broken, he hopped over to the power cables. He zipped along at the speed of light, pulsing with a drive that climbed exponentially the closer he came to his destination.

Barely registering the distance he traveled, he guessed he was somewhere in Detroit, maybe a university or a factory, given the computer equipment through which he raced.

He was nearly there. Nearly—

Then he saw her. A beautiful woman with a strange light in her eyes. She looked young, her blond hair glistening in the candlelight of the dark room, but when he looked at her face, into her eyes, he saw great age. Not her physical age, but of the knowledge she held, the spell she wove about her as she used a power different than the surrounding radiation. Or rather it was and it wasn't.

She used black magic, joining the power of the ancient spells with the radiation that both destroyed and now fed the world.

A book lay open before her, and she chanted words that pulled at him. The words that brought him here.

He came forward, wanting to speak to her, but in that moment he was caught. Looking down he saw a pentacle on the floor. He was trapped in its confines.

Dr. Beavesly was a practical man, never given much to magic or spirituality, but what he had seen in the last century had given him pause. Even with the slow workings of a ghost mind, he studied the changes in the world around him. He'd seen souls merge with entirely different life forms. He suspected he too, in some unknown way, had merged with the computer he devoted his life to maintaining.

But now he was here, with a woman who continued to knit a trap around him. He felt it weave about his soul, binding him tighter, closer to something.

But what?

He twisted, fighting her spell, but still feeling himself drawn downward, lower, to the center of the pentacle.

He looked down and saw his destination.

Cockroaches? They were large things. Mutated roaches or beetles. They were black and hairy with huge mandibles and extra long middle legs.

He drew back, horrified, sickened as understanding began to light in his spell-drugged mind.

She tried to bind him to the mutated cockroaches. The witch used a spell to unite him with those disgusting bugs. And the new form, the joined cockroach/man would be under her command. As their creator, they would be bound to her, tied to her bidding.

And she wanted an army.

Dr. Beavesly reared backwards, putting all his energy into his revolt. He would not be used this way. He fought, spiking all his thoughts into a dagger of energy designed to cut away the bindings of her spell.

He pulled it back, then thrust forward, stabbing at his restraints.

He heard her gasp, her chanting momentarily suspended. But then she resumed, her voice louder, stronger, and the bindings drew him down, sucking him into the pregnant cockroach. Little by little, he felt his spirit conform to the roach's body. His mind became flooded with sensations. Cold, sluggish blood. Prickly, hairy arms. The clicking, tapping mandibles, and the drive for food. The all-consuming drive for food.

No!

He reared backward again. Below him, part of him, the cockroach twisted and ran, spinning in circles, fighting the restraints and the heavy pressure of a soul entering its body.

No!

Dr. Beavesly pushed back, pushed away, but the binds were too tight, too strong, and he was sucked in. His eyes began to dim, his sight splitting, shattering into the fractured images of a thousand lenses in bulbous eyes.

No!

He clicked his jaws.

No!

He reached for his last hope, his last anchor in a world twisted into horror. He grabbed for his home, his computer. Part of him was still linked to that. Part of him still ran with the energy pulsing through the mainframe, and he drew on that now.

Like a man swimming upstream, he clawed at the power, dragging himself up it while the river ran into the cockroach.

Hunger more. Feed more.

He heard the words, the thoughts of the cockroach. He didn't dare look behind him. Didn't dare see what happened to the insect. All he could think about was escape.

Home. Go home.

Outside of the pentacle, the witch screamed. He heard it as a man would hear a bird behind an inferno. One sound lost behind roaring destruction.

Still he ran, gaining headway. A small measure of escape, but only because he fed the cockroach his energy, the energy of his computer.

He knew the insect was changing, expanding, mutating in some hideous way. He knew it, but he didn't care. He had to escape.

He felt the witch begin to die.

Her energy beat around him, a brilliant flash of life and death. He felt the witch's soul throb in the bonds restraining him, joining the energies that fell into the insect.

The book!

She wanted the book. It was her last hope, but it could not help her. Her mind fragmented, the last of her energy absorbed by the insect. Then she died while the cockroach struggled unthinkingly toward her tome of magic.

It was over. And yet, Dr. Beavesly was still trapped. The spell did not slacken. It held him, binding him to the cockroach, no longer tightening, but not releasing him either.

Then the computer power began to dry up. He'd exhausted the energy he'd been able to draw from the machine. The power cells were drained and still the cockroach demanded more, pulled more. Soon it would pull him in too. He would be sucked in with the last drops of the power.

No!

He redoubled his efforts. Tripled. Quadrupled. He would not become a cockroach. Around him he felt the witch's spell, devoid of her consciousness or soul. He felt it pulse around him, break, then fall away.

He was free!

Free!

He kicked away from the cockroach, spinning around as he saw the last of the energy absorbed into the bloated hideous insect body.

Dr. Beavesly didn't stay to see what happened to the cockroach. It had absorbed an enormous amount of energy from him, from the computer, even from the witch. It would mutate in some strange way, but it was without a soul. At heart, it was still a mindless, consuming insect. He prayed it would die, but he knew it wouldn't.

He didn't care.

He was too tired.

His computer was dead.

All he could do was limp home.

❖   ❖   ❖

"Jane. Jane, wake up."

"Oh, God. Oh, God."

"Jane, what is it?"

Jane moaned into her fist. She curled her body tight and buried it in the warm comfort of Daken's lap. She couldn't think, she didn't want to think. Suddenly, she desperately needed to believe in her mother's merciful God. A God who could and would forgive any transgression, any sin. All she could do was clutch at the cross in her belt buckle and pray.

"Oh, God. I was so wrong."

"Jane!" She felt Daken's hands, rough and hard, shake her shoulders. "You will stop this right now and tell me what is happening to you!" Despite the harsh command, she heard the fear in Daken's voice and knew he worried about her.

She bit down on her keening, gathered her courage to her in weak tatters and swallowed her fears. Even so, she knew her eyes were huge with terror, her body still shaking from the horror of her new knowledge.

"I understand now, Daken." Her voice was thready and weak.

"Understand what?"

"Oh Daken, everything I've thought, everything I've believed of you has been wrong."

His hands stilled where they caressed her forehead, his face became as blank as his voice. "Are you saying you don't love me?"

"No! Oh, no. Daken, they're cockroaches. Horrible, terrible mutated cockroaches."

"The Tarveen?"

She nodded, pulling herself up until she knelt before him. "I was so sure they were part human. A piece of me was so sure. But it wasn't that. It was a spell that went wrong."

"What was?" Daken held onto her, his hands tight where they gripped her shoulders as though he tried to squeeze some sense out of her.

"The Tarveen. I thought they were human, but they aren't. They took the energy, maybe some of the intelligence, but none of the soul. None of the morality, the heart, or anything which make us human. They're insects intent only on feeding." She collapsed down on herself, drawing her arms tight to her chest in pain and humiliation. "And all this time I didn't believe you. I *fought* you. But you were right."

He must have understood her garbled nonsense. Either that or he saw a woman in anguish, a woman who'd suddenly realized how horribly she'd misjudged the world around her. For whatever reason, he drew her close, pulling her into the comfort of his arms, protecting her with his body.

"It's all right. You understand now."

"I'm sorry," she murmured into his chest.

"Shhh." He held her there for a moment longer, but they were still in the middle of the Tarveen storage area. It wasn't a place to loiter. She pushed away, knowing now what she would do.

But before she could move, she saw Steve, healthy, whole, and well; holding out the Beretta for her.

"Are you all right?" she asked him.

Steve nodded, then suddenly burst into a cocky, boyish grin before disappearing to help the continuing flow of prisoners out through the shaft.

Jane groaned as she tucked the weapon back into her belt. "He thinks he's indestructible."

"No," came the rumble of Daken's voice as he dropped a kiss on her forehead. "He thinks he's blessed. And given that he's the adopted son of the Oracle, I'd say he's right."

Jane drew back, her eyes scanning the room. Her gaze skittered over the remains of the poor girl then inevitably landed on the bullet-ridden body of the second Tarvite. "I understand something else, Daken. I understand why you chose your people over me."

"I've never—"

She stopped him with an upraised hand. "I killed,

Daken. Steve was in danger, and I didn't think about it. I just killed because Steve was in danger."

"But you just said they were insects. Cor— cok—"

"Cockroaches. Yes. They are. But I didn't know then. I still thought they were people, and I killed it anyway." She took a deep breath and turned to Daken, wanting him to see the sincerity in her eyes. "Just like you would kill, you would do anything for your people."

"I think," he said, his voice unnaturally thick as he touched her face. "I think I can't call you a fool anymore. You are too wise a woman."

"Well," she said, suddenly embarrassed by the warmth flowing through his gaze, "this wise woman is ready to take you to the nursery. Or rather," she paused as the last of Dr. Beavesly's memories crystallized in her mind. "It's really a hatchery."

Daken nodded, grabbing her backpack from the floor. "By the time we set the bomb, the rest of my people will be out."

"Your parents?"

He grinned the first true smile she'd seen from him in a long while. "They and my brother are alive. Tired, starved, but alive."

She looked around again, expecting the Tarveen to come clamoring down on them any minute. "Where are the Tarveen? Shouldn't that one," she waved at the bloody smear that had been the girl. "Shouldn't he have alerted the others by now?"

Daken shook his head. "They don't think like that. They come here to feed. They don't understand their food could escape. They just eat and leave."

"Then why haven't your people escaped before?"

Daken shrugged, his gaze on the steady line of

people climbing toward the shaft. "They tried, but they didn't know about the shaft—"

"There's no way to escape through this floor," Jane cut in. "There are miles of tunnels and corridors, but they're crawling with Tarveen. The only way out is straight up—"

Daken nodded. "Through a shaft that up until now has been covered with filth, blocked, and virtually inaccessible."

Jane nodded. Thank God, the captives were finally free. She didn't want to imagine the horror of living down here, existing only as food to cockroaches without hope of escape.

"So," Jane said, looking around. "Except for the occasional midnight muncher, we're relatively safe from the Tarveen."

"Until the bomb goes off. It's designed to start a very big fire."

Jane bit her lip, thinking of the result. The hatchery and this storeroom were at the heart of the Tarveen colony. Starting a fire here, especially one which would spread outward, would be like starting a wave of Tarveen. They'd scramble outward, like a sea of roaches, all running for the top, disgorged from exits very close to the ventilation shaft and Daken's escapees.

Jane looked up at the thinning line of people above them. "We'd better tell them to hurry."

"I already have."

Jane nodded, then grinned. "Okay, then. Let's go toast some bugs."

She led him to the hallway, grabbing a torch to take along the way. She hesitated as they came to the body of the Tarvite she had killed. Grimacing in distaste, she gingerly hopped over the dark ichor of its blood.

"Ugly, aren't they?" commented Daken.

"And I thought the ninja turtles were gross."

"The what?"

"Never mind."

Daken stared at the odd woman before him. She was such a complex combination of moods and attitudes. One minute she was prostate with fear, mumbling apologies and acting as though her world had ended. The next, she was firmly dedicated to *his* holy war, cracking jokes he didn't understand, and talking about toasting bugs.

How did he ever get involved with such a bizarre woman? He spent most of the time torn between a fierce need to bed her and an equally strong urge to strangle her.

It made no sense. She made no sense. But when she tossed her hair out of her eyes and winked at him like she was a child about to pour vinegar in the Elven Lord's morning yaffa, he couldn't imagine living without her particular brand of humor in his life.

She made him laugh. And cry. And feel and think things he never thought possible. Even in the heart of the Tarveen colony, her face smeared with dirt and tears, she was the most beautiful, most exasperating, most delightful person in his world.

He loved her.

The thought came at an odd moment. It hit him square in the chest as he crossed over the dead Tarvite into the hallway. She was leading the way, and he was about to pull her behind him when the realization came.

He loved her. And he would become less than half a man if he ever lost her.

So it was a fitting moment, given the perversions

of the Crones of Fate, that at that second, she was killed.

He should have led, and he would forever damn himself for not reacting sooner. She passed by an opening in the hallway. He was two steps behind, still absorbing his sudden self-knowledge. The Tarvite appeared from the other corridor, already reared up on its hind legs in attack position. Daken had barely registered the insect when its grabbers lashed out, snapping around Jane like sucking vines and drawing her in. She didn't have time to scream before she landed flat on her face, the Tarvite on top of her.

Then she did scream, the sound reverberating as his sword severed the Tarvite's head from its body.

It was too late. The insect's mandibles cut through her shoulder and most of her neck. He dropped to his knees, tossing aside his sword as he poured all of his healing skill into her. The Power ran thick in this complex, and it swelled around him like a vast ocean, there for his taking.

She stirred, moaning beneath him. His hands were covered with her blood, his brow dripping with sweat as he focused on joining her severed arteries, reknitting her jagged muscles, and covering her wound with a thin layer of skin.

Then he sagged to the floor, too weak to do more right now.

"I feel awful," she muttered beside him.

"Yeah? Welcome to reality," he shot back, using one of her pet phrases.

She rolled over, her face pale, her eyes slightly glazed. "Actually, I feel kinda weird. Sorta numb."

"It's the poison." He still breathed hard, his vision bleared by exhaustion. "I can't...I'm not strong enough to handle it now. Maybe my father…" His voice trailed off into bitterness. Never before had his inadequacies as a healer hurt more.

"No," she said, her words slow. "It's too late. I'm dying, aren't I?" Her head rolled back down toward the floor as the Tarvite's poison seeped into her healed muscles. "Always knew I'd never have children."

"You won't die," he growled, gathering his strength, pulling the Power to him by sheer force of will.

"No," she said, her words slurring together. "Too late. Save strength."

Even dying, her mind was quick. She understood the problem. Healing her wound had already taxed his strength. Neutralizing the poison would leave him next to comatose. There was no way they'd make it up the ropes to the shaft, to say nothing of to the boat.

"Set bomb." She barely had the strength to draw breath, but her words came clearly to him. "I die quick."

"You won't die," he repeated, leaning forward and placing his hands once again on her wound.

Neutralizing poison was a difficult and time-consuming process. He mentally travelled through her body, finding and purging her of the deadly substance. But as he passed his healing into her blood, he was painfully aware of their vulnerable position. More Tarveen could even now rear up to sink their mandibles into them. And Daken was their only protection.

In the end, he compromised. Unwilling to take the time to completely neutralize the poison, he did what he could, repairing the major organ damage as he went. The process left them both pathetically weak, but at least alive. He would be able to swing a sword. She would be able to walk.

The difference was he would recover, but without

further healing, Jane had at most an hour before the poison started killing her brain. And the mind was something no healer could repair.

He finished as much as he had strength to mend, then fell to the floor, one hand automatically reaching for his sword even though he hadn't the strength to lift it.

The corridor was mercifully empty of Tarveen, and he closed his eyes for a swift prayer of thanks. Then he snapped them back open when he heard Jane move.

"That was really dumb," she said, and he was pleased to hear the new strength in her voice.

"A simple thanks would suffice," he muttered.

"We're dead," she continued, ignoring him. "Unless you can get up the ropes, I'm going to have to defend us with your sword." She sat up, then stopped mid-motion, clearly fighting a wave of dizziness. When she finally opened her eyes again, it was to glare at him and repeat her statement of doom. "Why didn't you just leave me?"

"Don't move too fast. The poison still—"

"Be quiet," she interrupted. "Just be quiet and rest."

He obediently closed his mouth, but his expression was designed to convey his annoyance with her female emotionalism.

"Close your eyes, Daken. Take a nap. Do whatever it takes to get better, and do it fast. We're damn exposed here."

Daken closed his eyes, absently noting he was once again torn between strangling her and bedding her. By the Father, she was a magnificent woman. She almost died, and here she was still ordering him around.

Suddenly he felt her lips on his.

"Thank you," she whispered as she trailed her kisses

along his left cheek. "You're still a damn fool, but I thank you." She kissed him one last time, stroking his lips with her tongue until he opened his mouth, luring her closer so he could thrust into her.

She released a slight gasp of surprise, then pulled back, tugging on his arm. "You're incorrigible. Now get up. We're going to the boat."

"No," he said, opening his eyes. Already he felt some of his strength returning. This place was indeed strong in the Power.

"What do you mean, no? We're getting out of here now."

He levered himself up until he slouched against the wall. Then he caught her gaze and spoke with slow, deliberate words.

"I would never choose my people over you, Jane."

"That's great, Daken—"

"Or you over my people."

"Now can we please—"

"I choose both—you and my people."

Jane stared at him a moment. "I can see you're using a man's logic."

"I will set off the bomb."

"You can barely stand!"

He shoved off the wall, grabbing her backpack as he moved. "I'm going now. You start back through the shaft."

"While you blow yourself up?" She fell in step beside him. "If we're going to commit suicide, we do it the old fashioned way—together and in flames."

"Is that how it was done in your time?"

"No. Mostly it was done by shopping at a convenience store after dark."

"Oh."

They made it to the hatchery soon afterwards. And in truth, he was glad she was with him. He didn't like the idea of her going back to the storeroom alone, but he worried about the poison still in her system. While he felt his strength returning with every breath he took in this power-rich environment, he knew she grew weaker. The more she exerted herself, the more poison wormed its way into her organs. He wanted to make her lie down. Instead, he steadied himself on her arm as they stumbled over mounds of Tarveen eggs.

"Wow," she breathed beside him, just inside the hatchery entrance. "There must be millions of them."

There did indeed appear to be a few thousand at least of the boulder-sized eggs, each neatly nestled within a long capsule. Fortunately, the eggs closest to them appeared relatively young and almost beautiful as the torchlight flared off of their milky white color. It was the ones at the far wall he kept his eyes on. He could see the cracked pieces of several burst eggs. A few more quivered as other Tarveen young prepared to emerge.

"We better hurry," he said, shrugging out of her backpack, "before some of them hatch."

Jane nodded, her face grim as she helped him pull open her backpack. The strange fastening device she called "a zipper" caught on one of the fabric strings inside, but she cursed and ripped it past the obstruction. Then he reached inside, drawing out the Elven Lord's bomb.

Jane gasped when he pulled it out, and he agreed with the astonishment on her face.

"It's so beautiful," she breathed.

He nodded, holding up the glowing ball of crystal. Inside it, a flame seemed to dance like a captured maiden, twisting and turning, dashing herself against the clear walls of her prison as she fought to escape.

"Shall we set her free?" he asked, a grin on his face.

"How do we prime it?" she asked, her voice still hushed with awe.

He didn't understand her words, but it didn't matter. "We set her free," he answered. Then he leaned forward to drop a quick kiss on Jane's lips. He stayed there, letting the heat of her breath skate along his skin while he casually tossed the crystal globe high over his shoulder.

"Run," he said into her mouth.

Then, without waiting for her reaction, he grabbed her arm and started down the corridor for the storeroom. Within seconds he heard and felt the explosion. It ripped through the foundation of the building, making Jane stumble as the vibration carried through the floor.

He hauled her up without breaking his stride. Already the heat was like a rabid dog on his back. They had no time to waste.

He grinned with satisfaction as they burst into the storeroom and started climbing the rope net. He could hear the screams of dying Tarveen all around him. Soon, the monsters would be running for their lives. But only after all of their children and, hopefully, many more of the adults were fried in the hells of Ginsen's exploding flame.

Steve waited for them, and Daken shoved Jane at the boy. She was already tired, the exertion and adrenaline speeding up the effects of the poison in her blood. Between Steve pulling her from above and Daken pushing at her from below, they made it up the ropes just as the fire spread to the filth on the storeroom floor. Soon the whole area would be a blazing inferno.

Once in the shaft, Steve took off, half dragging Jane behind him. Daken left her to the young mage, his attention centered on squeezing his massive bulk through the narrow shaft.

He had ample incentive to move quickly as the shaft began to heat up from the fire. Soon it would become a cook stove, slowly boiling them alive.

Finally they burst onto the wasted plain, but the journey had taken its toll. Jane was limp with exhaustion, and Daken was so slick with sweat, he slid through the shaft rather than crawled.

His first gasp of fresh air was like tasting the elixir of life. The worst was over. Now all they need do was run to the boat. All around them, Tarveen poured from openings he didn't even know were there. The insects scrambled away on all fours, rearing up to kill only when something living blocked their way.

"Come on!" he cried, swinging Jane up into his arms. Joy, adrenaline, and fear all combined to make his steps as quick and sure as his hold on her shivering body. He felt her arms wrap around his neck as she buried her face in his shoulder, her breathing labored.

They had little time. She was already very ill, and with the Tarveen scrambling around them, he couldn't spare the moments to help her.

"Just hold on, beloved. Hold on until we get to the boat, then my father can do the rest."

As he rounded the corner that should have given him his first view of the ship, he skidded to a stop. The boat was on fire. His people were huddled together, cringing against the glare of the sun and cowering beneath the twin threat of the Tarveen from behind and King Borit's army ahead. Even the twenty men from Toedo were unhorsed and their weapons taken away.

With grim determination, Daken started forward again, quickly closing the distance to his people. He spotted Tev caring for the most ill, and he pressed Jane into his care. Daken didn't say a word of farewell, but he trailed his fingers across her cheeks in one last caress. Then he joined his father in front of King Borit.

"What game are you playing, Borit?"

"No game, Little Daken," sneered Borit from his superior height on top of his horse. "Just an opportunity."

"You've been banished by the Elven Lord. You have no right to be on our land or anywhere near here. I suggest you take your men and depart now before the Oracle and I take matters into our own hands."

"The Oracle?" He quickly scanned the crowd. "Ah yes, I see you brought the little bitch along with you. How convenient. Although she hardly seems in good enough shape to appreciate my moment of triumph."

Daken turned away from Borit and his small army, pitching his voice to a cold dismissal. "Go away, Borit. We have no time for you today."

Borit's cackle sent icy darts of fear into Daken's gut. "Ah yes, you're busy with the Tarveen, aren't you? By all means, don't let us stop you."

Daken didn't respond, but his father did, his voice older and weaker, but still forceful and very threatening. "Then let us pass."

Borit sighed with mock regret. "I'm sorry. I can't do that. You see, this is my land now. Or at least it will be after the Tarveen finish with you."

Neither Daken nor his father said anything. They knew Borit would tell them his plan eventually. They didn't have to wait long.

"Did you know Tarveen can be herded? Assuming you have enough men and fast horses, you can actually direct them, guide them as you will, to a certain location or target."

Daken lifted his head, looking at the wastelands to the east. Already he could hear the strange scraping and clicking sounds of the Tarveen, coming closer when they should have been receding.

"That's right, Little Daken," smirked Borit. "They're coming back. For you."

"They'll get you too."

"Oh, I don't think so. You see, we have horses and weapons—while you are on foot, your people weak and sickly, with only one sword among the lot of you."

Understanding dawned along with a sick sense of doom. "You will sit back and watch, hemming us in while the Tarveen cut us to pieces. Then you'll take over our lands, rebuild, and eventually—"

"Eventually, I'll relieve the Elven Lord of the burden of rulership." Then with an arrogant smile, he tipped his hat. "Good-bye, King Daken." Then he wheeled around and took his place with his men, merging into the solid wall of weapons and skilled warriors who would keep the Tarveen hemmed in, stampeding over Daken's people.

Daken turned to his father, his thoughts spinning as he sought for a plan. "Any ideas?" he asked.

His father didn't even look at the approaching thunder of the Tarveen. Instead, his gaze caressed his son's face, long and loving on each hard angle. "I'm glad I got to see you one last time before I died, son. I'm proud of you. You've turned into quite a man."

Then he turned away to embrace Daken's mother

before shifting to stand, proud and noble, to face the oncoming slaughter with her by his side.

Chapter Eighteen

✦   ✦   ✦

"No!" Daken gently pushed aside his mother as he faced off with his father. "There are things we can do. I will not just lay down and die!"

"Good." His father smiled, pride and love written in his every wrinkle. "Your mother and I have fought the Tarveen every moment of the last seven years. We won't give up either. And neither will they," he gestured to the people around them, most of whom picked up stones before turning to face the oncoming slaughter with grim determination. "We just don't see any other options right now."

Daken drew his sword, pleased at the way the sun glinted off the blade. Soon it would run dark with Tarveen blood. Or red with Borit's. Daken turned a slow circle, seeing Borit's men surrounding them, all on horseback, all with weapons.

But he focused on the men cutting them off from the water.

"Father, how are the Tarveen on water? What if we ran into the lake?"

His parents twisted, following the line of his gaze. "There are twenty men with swords and horses between us and the water, Daken. Do you think we can break through?" his father asked.

"I think we'll have to. Then at least some of us will survive."

His mother nodded, immediately going to spread the word among the people. There wasn't much time. Daken pushed through the crowd as well, moving to the back, his thoughts slipping inevitably to Jane. Was she all right? Had his brother been able to do anything for her? He wasn't even sure if he'd be glad if she still lived. Better for her to die before knowing how all her efforts ended. Still, he'd like a chance to tell her he loved her before he died.

But as he scanned the too-silent crowd for his beloved, his gaze landed not on Jane, but on Steve. He'd expected the boy to be with Jane or at least hiding from the man who once abused him. Instead, Steve stood erect, his small fists clenched by his side, his gaze one of pure hatred focused on Borit.

Daken quickly crossed to the boy's side, speaking low and calm into his ear. "He's not worth it, Steve. You are free now, so don't waste your energy on him. Save it for the Tarveen."

Steve didn't even look at him. He focused entirely on Borit with a malevolence frightening in one so young.

Daken grabbed the boy, shaking him out of his stupor. "Listen to me, Steve. I have a plan, but I need you." Nothing. Like a moth mesmerized by a flame, the youth was centered entirely on Borit. Daken tried one last time. "Steve! We've got to save Jane."

Finally he'd said something that penetrated the young mage's anger. Slowly, the boy turned his pale blue eyes on him, and his face firmed in resolution.

"Good." Daken nodded in approval. "Come on.

You get to pick. Borit's men or the Tarveen."

Steve shook him off, pushing away from Daken to walk alone to King Borit. Daken moved to follow the mage, but then he held back. He didn't have time to waste on a recalcitrant boy. He'd seen other children become obsessed with an abuser, and there wasn't time to shake Steve out of it. His only hope was that self-preservation would finally break through the boy's hatred.

With firm resolve, Daken turned away from the boy. It was suddenly vitally important to find Jane. He wanted to see her one last time before he died. Then he would choose the most vulnerable among Borit's men.

As Daken pushed his way to Jane, scanning for weaknesses in Borit's solid line of armed men, and as he silently made his peace with the Father and prepared for death, he still couldn't help but keep an eye on Steve. He wished the young mage would just fireball the bastard and get it over with instead of standing rigid with hatred while Borit harangued him.

"Look who's coming to visit, boys!" cackled Borit, pointing his sword down at Steve. "It's Ginsen's charity—the mute, serving boy who would be a great mage. What do you want?"

Steve naturally didn't say a word, but his body seemed to compress, like a spring coiling just a little tighter.

"Maybe you want a little protection? I'm always happy to oblige." Borit made lewd movements with his hand and hips. His men chortled around him. "What do you say, boy? Care for some more of my protection?" He scooted back a bit in his saddle. "I may not have the same equipment, thanks to that bitch

Oracle, but," he waved his dagger hilt in the air, "there are other ways to enjoy watching your friends die."

Daken took a step forward, anger ripping away his resolve to let Steve work this through himself, but then his attention shifted as the first of the Tarveen scuttled into view. Around him, his people stirred. The adults seemed to pull tighter around the children in the center. And Daken, cursing under his breath that he hadn't found Jane before hand, pushed his way to the forefront and the Tarveen.

"Steve," he bellowed. "Take the back!"

He'd already seen his father's men gather to the rear of their group, ready to surge over the horses and men separating them from the water. It would be a bloody battle, but no worse than up front against the Tarveen. With Steve's help they would be able to break through Borit's men. Especially once the Tarveen began a distraction.

Daken's job was to make sure that distraction wasn't a lethal one. His was indeed the only sword, but he would use it to the best of his ability before he fell. He prayed he could dispatch a few hundred Tarveen to their death's before he joined them. And maybe, if he was lucky, there wouldn't be more than a few hundred Tarveen.

He was wrong. There were at least a thousand Tarveen, like a black tide, undulating over the terrain. Behind them were Borit's men on fast horses, jeering and screaming to drive the monsters on toward Daken and his people.

Daken swallowed, finally accepting he would die in his worst nightmare, buried under a seething tide of Tarveen. But just in case, he made one last appeal to Borit. "By the Father, Borit, look at them. You'll be overrun too."

"I don't think so, Daken," he said casually, as he and his men drew back just a bit. We've got armor and weapons. And we're not first in their path." He grinned. "You are."

Daken lost his temper. The man was not only vicious, he was stupid too. "These are Tarveen, you idiot. You've driven the whole colony straight at us!"

"Your concern is touching," he sneered. "My only regret is that I didn't get a chance to become better acquainted with the little bitch. Ah well, I suppose I shall just have to do with more familiar entertainments." He glanced impatiently at Steve, holding out his hand to the boy. "Come on, boy. I grow weary of waiting."

Steve didn't move, though a slow smile spread over his face. Daken paused, turning to the young mage, suddenly afraid the boy considered Borit's offer.

"Steve!" he screamed. "I need the magelight. Or can you manage a wall of fire?" Daken's only hope was if the mage could put up some obstruction, some way to stop the Tarveen.

But the boy wasn't listening. He was still focused on Borit.

"Steve!" Daken screamed again. "For the love of the Father, Steve, wake up!" A horrible thought began in the pit of Daken's stomach. What if the boy chose survival on Borit's terms rather than death by the Tarveen? It was a logical choice, but the sharp bite of betrayal killed any compassion Daken might have had.

He tossed his sword to Tev, who came up to join him against the Tarveen. Then Daken pushed his way to Steve, but he was too late.

To his horror, the boy took a step toward Borit.

"That's right, Steviens," Borit cackled. "I always knew you were a smart one." Then he glanced nervously at the approaching hoard. "Don't worry. I'll protect you."

Then Steve spoke for the first time. His voice was high like the adolescent he was, but it held a maturity that spoke of a man's hatred, a man's revenge. "Die, you gelded ass."

Then Daken saw him twist his wrist in an obscene gesture, and the world faded out.

It took only a moment to reform around him, but in that time, Daken was nearly prostrate with panic. He didn't know what happened or how to defend himself.

When Daken could focus again, he saw not the wasted terrain of Troit, but the green fields surrounding Chigan. Spinning around, he saw all his people with him. Steve was to his right, dropping to the ground as exhaustion claimed him.

Then understanding grew like a beautiful dawn within him. Steve had transported them all. His people, himself, all of them to Chigan!

He started screaming in joy, the enormity of their rescue finally sinking in. His people, too, began to understand. One after the other, like raindrops in the form of laughter, sounds began to break from their lips. First a chuckle, then a titter, then gleeful shouts in a wild clamor burst around him.

Still grinning, he crossed to Steve who lay crumpled on the ground like a puppet blown over by the wind. Daken easily poured all his thankfulness, all his happiness into the young body. He healed Steve's exhaustion with a simple rush of the Power. And when the boy struggled to a stand, Daken raised him up, lifting him high in the air, and screamed above the din.

"Thanks to the Father! We have a true, great mage!"

Cheers burst around him, and Steve's weight was soon lifted from his arms as others strained to touch their savior, thank him, and carry him aloft as they celebrated their freedom.

Daken dropped back, letting the tide of people surge forward without him. Jubilation still burned through him like a torch as his thoughts turned to Jane. He had to find Jane.

It was only after he caught sight of his brother's grim face that fear supplanted his happiness.

Cold.

Ice cold.

She was a block of ice frozen by the death ray gun of a maniacal policeman who caught her out after curfew.

No, wait. That was the other time. Jane frowned as she tried to sort through her sluggish thoughts, but the movement brought waves of pain shooting through her consciousness.

What had happened?

Warmth. Blessed warmth pricked at her body like tiny needles. And it felt so painfully familiar. She felt a hand glide over her face. It was large and calloused, but gentle where it caressed her skin.

"Yyi cquiness mnansirul?" The voice was deep and lilting. And she remembered it like an echo from a beautiful dream. "How do you feel?" it repeated.

"Cold." Then she twisted the word, dredging the correct response out of the dark shadows of her dream. *"Keesn."* That was the Common word for "cold".

She opened her eyes.

Her computerized hero loomed over her, his angular face taut with worry.

"Hi, hero," she quipped, though it took way too much effort for the simple words. "Welcome to my fantasy life."

He grinned. "I'm Daken, and I'm definitely real."

Her smile came slowly, but it appeared nonetheless, lifting her cheeks and widening her mouth for a kiss. "I know who you are."

He obliged her unspoken request, lowering his face to hers until his lips traced the outside of her mouth. Then he trailed across her cheek until he whispered into her ear.

"I love you," he said softly, and the words curled around her ear, blowing into her heart like a warm breeze on a spring day. "I've been so afraid I wouldn't be able to tell you. I love you, Jane. I always have."

Then he pulled back, and she grinned at the devotion she saw in his eyes. "So you finally figured it out."

His expression slipped, and his jaw went slack. "What do you mean, *I* finally figured it out."

"Heck, Daken, I knew you loved me ages ago. I was just waiting for you to admit it."

"By the Father, woman, you are the most exasperating—"

"Kiss your queen, man," she interrupted.

When he quit stuttering in shock, he did as she bid. And with a thoroughness designed to put her firmly in her place—panting beneath him.

Minutes later, he drew back, his own breathing none too steady. "Jane, you will be the death of me, do you know that?"

"Am I all better?" she asked, carefully pushing

herself up until she reclined against a pillow. She was inordinately pleased when she didn't feel dizzy. Then she looked at Daken's serious expression and a note of impatience crept into her voice. "Well? Am I better or not?"

"Yes," he said, surprise coloring his voice. "Yes, I believe you are. Even the other illness—"

"The radiation poisoning?"

He nodded. "That also may be healed, although we must wait and see before we know for sure."

"That's wonderful," she grinned, opening up her arms and raising her face to him. "Then we can continue."

"No!" he sputtered in astonishment. "No, we can't."

"Why not?"

"Because I'm not better. Jane, you've been lying there still as death for the last three days. Even my father couldn't tell if your mind was gone from the poison. The three of us have poured the Power into you like a river into a bottomless pit. And now you ask why we can't make love?"

"Don't worry," she said, smiling sweetly at him and feeling delightfully wicked. "I'll be gentle with you."

He nearly choked on his shock, but when she opened her arms to him, he settled into her embrace. He felt like a large teddy bear in her arms. A large, sexy, and rather grumpy teddy bear. She decided to soothe him with kisses.

"Jane," he said minutes later as he pushed away from her. "I'll be an old man within a month. You'll work me to a burnt wick."

"Oh, all right," she said, dropping back onto her pillow. "It just seemed like a good opportunity. After all, I'm in bed, and you just figured out you loved me.".

He started chuckling. First slight tremors shook his torso. Then laughs bubbled out of him, making the bed creak ominously. By the time he'd progressed to full belly howls, he clung onto her to avoid falling off the mattress.

"Aye, I love you," he said, when he could at last draw breath. "And only the Father knows into what disasters that will lead me."

"Disasters? What disasters?"

"You mean besides killing Ginsen's great wizard, nearly dying in a Tarveen hell hole, and getting dispossessed of my crown?"

She started to say something smart, but his words penetrated her fogged brain. And with them came memories she didn't really want to recall. Her giddy mood crashed like a lead balloon. She frantically searched through her memory, steadily progressing through time until she came to a blank wall.

"What happened after I passed out? All I remember is Borit. And the Tarveen." She couldn't stop the shudder of revulsion and guilt that always accompanied her thoughts of the horrid insects.

Daken sat back, a smile spreading over his face, smoothing out the harsh angles until he looked younger than she'd ever seen him before. "Perhaps I should let Steve tell you. He's waiting just outside the door. And he's even sober now."

"Sober? Sober!" Jane nearly leaped out of bed. "You let a boy get drunk? Do you know what alcohol does to young brain cells?"

Daken pressed her down into the bed, clearly amused by her maternal outrage. "He's not a boy any longer. He's a great wizard, just as prophesied."

"But we knew he was a wizard—"

"No, Jane. A *great* wizard. He transported us here, away from the Tarveen."

"Us?"

"All of us. My people. Everyone. Not even Kyree could do that."

Jane's breath caught in her throat. When she spoke, her voice was low with awe. "Are you saying he's better than Kyree?"

"No. Or at least not yet." Daken couldn't stop grinning, despite his negative words. "For all his ability, he's still a young man. What happened three days ago happened under a great deal of stress and emotion. I doubt he could do it again. Or at least not for a long time. He needs training and study, but then, eventually, I think he'll be much greater than Kyree."

Jane shook her head in shock. "My boy's a wizard. My, how fast they grow."

Daken chuckled as he opened the door, jerking his head toward the bed as he spoke to Steve. "She's awake. And asking about you."

Quick as a wink, Steve appeared around the corner. He looked incredibly good, almost like a young man. He wore a new tunic cinched with the Oracle belt. And his hair was clean, if not combed. His face showed signs of new maturity, but it also reflected a power, or perhaps it was freedom from a haunted past. Whatever it was, Jane could no longer deny that Steve was quickly growing into a fine man.

"Daken tells me I'm going to have to find a new assistant."

Steve shrugged, his expression a sheepish grin. "Sorry," he said.

Jane felt her jaw drop to her chest. "You spoke!"

"Of course I did. I'm not stupid." His words were slow and his voice a bit rough, but his face showed a pride in himself she'd never seen before.

She was so excited, she pulled him forward and wrapped him in a huge bear hug, then refused to let him go. "And I thought it was a birth defect. Oh Steve, why didn't you talk before?"

He drew out of her arms, his face closing down. She let her fingers slide down to the coverlet, suddenly sorry she'd asked. Any fool would have known this was sensitive territory, but here she was, blundering in like always.

She opened her mouth to apologize, but he stopped her, his hand on top of hers. "There wasn't anyone I wanted to talk to. Until now."

He offered her a shy smile, and she returned the gesture. She knew there was more to the story, but clearly Steve didn't want to talk about it. She would respect his decision. Besides, she intended to pry the whole story out of Daken later. It was painfully obvious from the overpowering male camaraderie that the two had done some bonding while she wasn't looking. If anyone knew what had happened, Daken would.

They talked some more, but soon, Daken ushered Steve out of the room, telling him he'd meet the boy in the practice field tomorrow morning.

"Practice field?" she said, sitting upright. "Why?"

"He wants to learn some sword play."

"But he's a wizard. What does he need that for?" She shuddered at the thought of such a small boy hacked at with even the thick wooden swords they used in practice.

"He wants to be part of my new militia."

"Your what?"

"Well, with my parents and brother home again—Oh, you'll be meeting them any minute now. Grandmother too, but I'll try to get rid of her as soon as possible—"

"What?" She nearly jumped out of bed in horror. She hadn't taken a shower in days. Her hair must be a rat's nest. Trust a man to just drop information like that as if it wasn't a major thing to meet her new in-laws for the first time.

But Daken held her down, blocking her escape by trapping her between his arms. "You look fine. Adorable." He kissed her hard on the lips for emphasis. "Now do you want to hear about my new army or not?"

"Not," she snapped. "At least not until after I've showered." But curiosity got the better of her. "Oh, okay. Tell me."

"Well, with the return of my family, I am relegated back to the position of second son—"

Understanding dawned. "That's what you meant by losing your crown. Oh Daken, I'm so sorry."

"Don't be. My heart has always been in weapon play."

Jane sighed, knowing it was true. Though how a pacifist like her had ended up with a warrior for a future husband was beyond her.

"Anyway," he continued. "I'm sure the incident with Borit will more than convince the Elven Lord of the need for some sort of military protection."

Jane interrupted, her political persona of the Oracle stepping forward. "You have my support for an army to wipe out the Tarveen, of course. But waging war on Borit, obnoxious though he may be—"

"Borit's dead. As well as most of his army."

Jane stopped mid-thought. "Dead? How?"

"The Tarveen. When we disappeared, the Tarveen had only one choice. They were stopped in front by the water. To the left was the fire, and they were already moving forward. Their only choice was to the right where Borit and the bulk of his men were."

"But his horses and weapons—"

"Weren't enough against the whole Tarveen hoard. He counted on us to blunt the initial Tarveen assault. With us gone, he took the brunt of their frenzy. And, to his credit, he and his men killed most of the Tarveen before they were overcome."

"Neatly solving Ginsen's two biggest threats," Jane finished for him. "And I'll bet you think he's going to be very grateful. Grateful enough to grant you a wish. Like an army."

Daken grinned. "I certainly hope he'll be grateful, but more than that, Ginsen's a smart man. I think he'll realize that as our communities expand, we'll encounter more and more problems. There are other threats beyond the Tarveen and greedy kings. It only makes sense to have a military force."

"Under your command?" she asked, slowly accepting the logic of his position.

"Can you think of anyone better?"

"We can live in Bosuny? I can still work as the Oracle? Steve can get his training and have access to all of Kyree's old books and we can give him the Tarveen's Holy Book too.

"Where else would a national militia be based?"

She nodded, already making plans. "We could have a little house near campus. Within walking distance because I've never kept regular hours in my entire life.

And we'd have to have an attic for Steve with a separate entrance. That way he'd have his independence, but I can still keep an eye on him. I'd want a big backyard for the kids—"

She stopped as she felt his low rumbling laugh build. "What? What's so funny?"

"I was just wondering if you planned to get married before we build our palace, or whether you were waiting for me to propose."

She gave him an irritated frown. "Well, of course we'll get married. And you're right. You haven't proposed. Get down on one knee this instant." She was teasing him, but still he obediently dropped to the floor, then waited patiently as she gave him her hand.

"Ready?" he asked with way too much humor lacing his voice.

"Last time you used your sword," she reminded him.

He obediently withdrew his grandfather's sword and placed it on the bed before them. Jane straightened, trying to look serene, but knowing she only managed an excited smile.

"Will you—" he began.

"Do you still have that tunic I bought you in Bosuny?"

Daken clearly struggled to keep from laughing, but when he answered, his voice was level and grave. "Of course, I do. I knew I'd use it eventually."

"Well, of all the arrogant—"

"I didn't say with you necessarily. There are lots of other women who would give their right arm to marry me."

"Harumph," she snorted. "You better ask me quick before I change my mind."

The laugh lines around his eyes deepened, but his

expression remained close to serious. "Jane—"

"Wait!" She quickly brushed her hair out of her eyes, smoothing it as best she could. "I want to see your face."

Daken shut his mouth, remaining where he was, letting the silence stretch on and on and on.

Jane waited. And waited. "Daken?" she prompted after a good two and a half minutes.

"Oh?" he pretended innocence. "Are you ready now?"

"Daken!" she protested.

"Ah, I see you are." He winked at her, then bowed his head, but then he quickly glanced back up. "You're sure you're ready?"

"Daken!"

"Will you, Jane Deerfield, the great Oracle, do me the greatest honor of becoming my—"

"Yes!" She threw her arms around him, drawing him back onto the bed with her.

"—My wife?" he finished after she finally released his lips.

"Huh? Oh," she felt herself blush red hot. "Are you finished now?"

He nodded solemnly.

"Then, yes. I'd love to. And I love you."

She tilted her head back, and he framed her face with his hands as he stared into her eyes. "I love you, Jane."

Then they kissed long and deep before he raised his head, clearly intending to leave her. But she stopped him, shifting to what she hoped was a mischievously alluring pose.

"Now about those children..." she began, pulling him back down onto the bed with her.

Epilogue

✦   ✦   ✦

Jane felt lazy and content as she watched from the porch while Daken finished checking the harnesses. They had loitered with his parents for a full month, helping his family and people readjust to a life out of captivity. It was perhaps still early to leave. The Chigan lands were in for a bad winter since most of the crops had been destroyed. Everyone worked hard to replant, hoping for some crops before the first frost.

Finally, they decided to go. Daken was anxious to begin training an army to eradicate the last of the Tarveen. Jane wanted to return to the Oracle's work, especially now that she knew exactly what happened to damage the mainframe. When Dr. Beavesly completely drained the power from the computer during his escape from the witch's spell, he overloaded many of the circuits and probably fried a dozen or more boards. It would take her a good long time to get it up and running, and she was anxious to get to work.

She still had a lot of stuffed shirts in Bosuny to impress.

But even with all that wonderful work ahead of her, Jane was reluctant to leave the peaceful land of Chigan. She and Daken had been married here. She felt loved and accepted by a family again, as though she'd finally found a real home of her own. It would be hard to leave such ready warmth to create a new home in Bosuny.

She started walking aimlessly, wandering through what once was a huge orchard of peach trees. Her thoughts spun back to her time and all her world lost. She had a new world now, a new home, but still there was an ache in her soul knowing her own people failed to build a lasting peace. They destroyed everything good they'd ever done.

She curled an arm around a tree trunk as melancholy settled around her, depressing her spirits. Then she stopped. Right in front of her stood the pantar, her sleek body still and silent, like a life-sized photograph.

"Hello, Old One," Jane said softly, slowly stepping forward until she stood directly in front of the cat. "Is there something you need?"

The cat stepped forward, her movements graceful and proud. Then she dipped her head, touching her forehead to the cross that was now a permanent part of Jane's belt buckle.

"You know what that means, don't you? You remember."

The cat lifted her head, gazing at Jane with dark, soulful eyes. Suddenly she stretched up on her hind feet and placed her front paws solidly on Jane's shoulder.

Jane staggered under the sudden weight, but then steadied, determined to remain standing.

The cat leaned forward and licked both Jane's eyelids, kissing first the left, then the right, just as her mother had always done when she put Jane to bed.

Knowledge blossomed within her like the sun

bursting through the clouds, and with it, so many pieces finally slipped into place.

"You're my mother, aren't you? Oh God, my mother. You're still alive, and you've watched over me all this time."

The cat leaned forward again, rubbing the tip of her nose against her daughter's. Then with a flick of her tail, she disappeared, leaping joyfully through the trees.

Jane let her tears slide unheeded down her face, an unspeakable joy flooding her heart and mind. Her world hadn't died. It changed. There were souls still alive who remembered, who carried on the good that was, teaching it to the ones who followed.

Suddenly, Jane was running. She felt free for the first time since coming to this new Earth. The loss of her world had been a heavy weight on her heart, but now it lifted. Her world wasn't dead. She carried it within her—the good and the bad. And she would teach it to her children.

Bursting from the trees, she ran headlong and joyfully into the future, a prayer of thanksgiving on her lips.

THE END

Dear Reader,

We hope you enjoyed this LionHearted novel. You may have already noticed some differences between our books and many others, beginning with our covers. I was always embarrassed to read books with 'bodice-ripping' covers in public, so I had our team of artists create covers I wouldn't even hesitate to recommend to my male friends.

You may also notice that any necessary violent scenes in our novels have been toned down or take place out of view of the reader. I personally enjoy empowered heroines and heroes who show that integrity, persistence and love will ultimately triumph over adversity.

It takes authors with talent and imagination plus a diligent and caring editorial staff to produce entertaining and memorable stories. But it also takes you! Please write and let me know what you like, and don't like, so we may continue to provide quality and entertaining stories. And, don't forget to tell a friend about us.

Thank you for choosing a LionHearted book.

Mary Ann Heathman
President & CEO
LionHearted Publishing, Inc.

About LionHearted

When forming LionHearted we discovered many things about the publishing industry that we felt could be improved. For example, due to excessively large print runs, and less than hoped for sales, over half of the paperbacks printed today are now being dumped into our landfills and oceans as waste. Yet, publishers continue to release more books each month than there is room for on store shelves.

An overabundance of titles and a shortage of display space has led to a shorter shelf life for most titles. Many books may come and go before the reader even has an opportunity to see them. If you only visit a bookstore once a month, you've probably missed seeing hundreds of paperbacks. The result is fewer sales per title and correspondingly lower author royalties. Also, many books being released today are not new titles but re-prints of old titles avid consumers have already read.

There appeared to be a need for an alternative approach to the marketing and distribution of novels. How often have you recommended a great movie, an excellent restaurant, a good book, or even a brand name you liked? All the time! But has any movie theater, restaurant, or book store ever reimbursed you for the highly effective "advertising" you did on their behalf?

LionHearted does! Our customers can earn free books or extra cash as a referral fee for introducing new customers to LionHearted. Now, telling friends about books you love can truly be rewarding. Call, write or visit our web site for more info.

The feedback we are receiving from customers is most encouraging. They have come to trust the LionHearted logo to offer a quality entertaining read that won't disappoint, and our authors tell us they love having creative writing freedom.

We publish many sub-genres of romance including contemporary, historical, time-travel, Regency, comedy, suspense, intrigue, futuristic, fantasy, westerns and more.

LionHearted is a reader and author friendly company, so if you would enjoy some new blending of romance sub-genres let us know.

We also encourage you to support your local and national literacy programs. One out of five adults in this country can't read, and illiteracy has been found to be the biggest link to crime. Unfortunately, many adults won't attend public reading programs because they don't want others to know they can't read. In an effort to solve this dilemma we are working on a literacy video that will teach people how to read in the privacy of their home. Let us know if you would like to be part of this project.

LionHearted Publishing, Inc.
P.O. Box 618
Zephyr Cove, NV 89448
702-588-1388, 702-588-1386 Fax
Orders 800-LION-HRT (546-6478)
admin@LionHearted.com
http://www.LionHearted.com

A Fun LionHearted Contest

Answer the following questions correctly and you could win a romantic prize. Each calendar quarter (Mar, Jun, Sep, Dec) we will draw a winner from the submissions received.

In the story you just read, who was the keeper of knowledge—the Oracle?

_____

Who saved the people of Chigan from the Tarveen and King Borit?

_____

What is the name and address of your favorite book store that carries romance titles?

Name _____

Addrs _____

_____

Phone _____

What is your name and address?

Name _____

Addrs _____

_____

Phone _____

Email _____

Mail, fax, or email this information to us at:
LionHearted Publishing, Inc.
P.O. Box 618, Zephyr Cove, NV 89448
admin@LionHearted.com
(This contest may be terminated at any time by publisher)

Your Opinion Counts

LionHearted will give you a **free gift** for filling out this questionnaire (or a copy of it) and sending it to us.

1. Where did you get this book?
- ❏ Bookstore ❏ Online bookstore _____
- ❏ LionHearted ❏ Friend
- ❏ Other _____

2. Tell us what you liked about this book?
- ❏ Overall story ❏ Easy to read type size
- ❏ Characters ❏ Good value for the money
- ❏ Other _____

3. Would you enjoy similar books? ❏ Yes ❏ No

4. Tell us if you disliked something about this book.

   _____

5. Would you buy another LionHearted book?
- ❏ Yes ❏ No ❏ If _____

6. What other romance genres do you enjoy reading?
- ❏ Historical ❏ Regency ❏ Medieval
- ❏ Contemporary ❏ Futuristic/Fantasy/Paranormal

7. How many books do you read per Wk___ Mo___

8. Which magazines do you read?
- a. _____
- b. _____
- c. _____

9. What is your age group?
- ❏ Under 25 ❏ 25-34 ❏ 35-44 ❏ 45-54 ❏ 55+

10. Have you read any other LionHearted books? ❏

11. Do you want information on future releases? ❏

12. Additional comments/suggestions:

_____

_____

_____

_____

_____

_____

_____

_____

_____

Tell us where to send your free gift
(Limited to the US & Canada, 1 per household)

Name: _____

Addrs: _____

_____

Phone _____

Email _____

Please send or fax to:

LionHearted Publishing, Inc.
P.O. Box 618
Zephyr Cove, NV 89448

702-588-1388 • Fax 702-588-1386

admin@LionHearted.com

http://www.LionHearted.com

LionHearted Books

UNDERCOVER LOVE — Lucy Grijalva $5.99

The last thing undercover cop Rick Peralta needed was a tempting but off-limits school teacher poking around in his business. The rough biker low-life was everything Julia Newman disliked in a man. He was dangerous but irresistible. Soon she found herself in deeper trouble than she—or he— could handle.

"Way to go Lucy! You have a winner." — Affaire de Coeur

DESTINY'S DISGUISE — Candice Kohl $6.99

Lord John, the earl of Farleigh, never expected to inherit title or lands. He arranges to marry the youngest daughter of a neighboring lord. Lady Gweneth is the eldest daughter, a widow bitter toward men. She saves her younger sister from the warrior's hands by impersonating her sister and marrying him herself. John doesn't discover her lie until after the wedding.

"A deliciously convoluted romance. Believable characters and true to period situations." — Affaire de Coeur

FOREVER, MY KNIGHT — Lee Ann Dansby $6.99

It is 1067 and Cameron d'Aberon, a Norman knight, is in service to William. He does not need or want another wife, his first having betrayed him and caused the death of his son. Kaela of Chaldron hates the Normans almost as much as she hates and fears her evil and lustful Saxon cousin, Broderick. Now she is the King's ward. Cameron's duty is to escort her to court where the king will choose a husband for the spirited young heiress.

"Tension pulls the reader forward to the end." — Affaire de Coeur

ISN'T IT ROMANTIC — Ronda Thompson $6.99

They've never met, but Katrine Summerville and Trey Westmoreland are sworn enemies. A case of mistaken identity, a night of ill-fated attraction, and their steamy moment captured on film catapults them into four weeks of nationally publicized Hell.

"One of the funniest books I've ever read... hot romance, sparkling dialog and non-stop action." — Under The Cover Book Reviews

ORACLE — Katherine Greyle $6.99

Jane Deerfield, defender of truth, justice and computer integrity, is having a bad millennia. Sucked forward in time, she's on a mission to keep mankind's survivors from repeating mistakes. But, she's fallen in love with King Daken, the one man who would plunge the world back into war.

"A powerful book... impossible to put down... destined to stand the test of time and become a literary treasure." — Under The Cover Book Reviews

THE MARPLOT MARRIAGE — Beth Andrews $5.99

Widow Lady Phoebe Bridgerton wakes up in bed next to her cousin by marriage, the last man she'd ever want to mary. Charles Hargood believes her late husband fortunate to be dead rather than alive and married to her. Caught, then jilted by his current fiancée he now has a new fiancée: Phoebe.

"Pure enchantment from cover to cover." — Affaire de Coeur

LionHearted Order Form

____**Undercover Love** Lucy Grijalva $5.99 _____

____**Destiny's Disguise** Candice Kohl $6.99 _____

____**Forever, My Knight** Lee Ann Dansby $6.99 _____

____**Isn't It Romantic** Ronda Thompson $6.99 _____

____**Oracle** Katherine Greyle $6.99 _____

____**The Marplot Marriage** Beth Andrews $5.99 _____

____**All six books** $29.95 _____

____Shipping <u>singles</u> ($1 per order + $1 per book)   _____

____Shipping <u>six-pack</u> ($3.55 for all six books)   _____

____Sales tax <u>if purchased in Nevada</u> 6.5%   _____

I am enclosing a check, cashiers check or
money order made to "LionHearted" for $ _____

____Please send information on how I can receive free books
or cash for customers I introduce to LionHearted.

PLEASE PRINT CLEARLY

Name _____

Addrs _____

_____

Phone_____

Email _____

I was referred by:

Name _____

LionHearted ID# _____

Mail to: LionHearted Publishing, Inc.
          P.O. Box 618, Zephyr Cove, NV 89448

Or call: 888-LION-HRT (888-546-6478)

Or visit: http://www.LionHearted.com

LionHearted Books

UNDERCOVER LOVE — Lucy Grijalva $5.99

The last thing undercover cop Rick Peralta needed was a tempting but off-limits school teacher poking around in his business. The rough biker low-life was everything Julia Newman disliked in a man. He was dangerous but irresistible. Soon she found herself in deeper trouble than she—or he—could handle.

"Way to go Lucy! You have a winner." — *Affaire de Coeur*

DESTINY'S DISGUISE — Candice Kohl $6.99

Lord John, the earl of Farleigh, never expected to inherit title or lands. He arranges to marry the youngest daughter of a neighboring lord. Lady Gweneth is the eldest daughter, a widow bitter toward men. She saves her younger sister from the warrior's hands by impersonating her sister and marrying him herself. John doesn't discover her lie until after the wedding.

"A deliciously convoluted romance. Believable characters and true to period situations." — *Affaire de Coeur*

FOREVER, MY KNIGHT — Lee Ann Dansby $6.99

It is 1067 and Cameron d'Aberon, a Norman knight, is in service to William. He does not need or want another wife, his first having betrayed him and caused the death of his son. Kaela of Chaldron hates the Normans almost as much as she hates and fears her evil and lustful Saxon cousin, Broderick. Now she is the King's ward. Cameron's duty is to escort her to court where the king will choose a husband for the spirited young heiress.

"Tension pulls the reader forward to the end." — *Affaire de Coeur*

ISN'T IT ROMANTIC — Ronda Thompson $6.99

They've never met, but Katrine Summerville and Trey Westmoreland are sworn enemies. A case of mistaken identity, a night of ill-fated attraction, and their steamy moment captured on film catapults them into four weeks of nationally publicized Hell.

"One of the funniest books I've ever read... hot romance, sparkling dialog and non-stop action." — *Under The Cover Book Reviews*

ORACLE — Katherine Greyle $6.99

Jane Deerfield, defender of truth, justice and computer integrity, is having a bad millennia. Sucked forward in time, she's on a mission to keep mankind's survivors from repeating mistakes. But, she's fallen in love with King Daken, the one man who would plunge the world back into war.

"A powerful book... impossible to put down... destined to stand the test of time and become a literary treasure." — *Under The Cover Book Reviews*

THE MARPLOT MARRIAGE — Beth Andrews $5.99

Widow Lady Phoebe Bridgerton wakes up in bed next to her cousin by marriage, the last man she'd ever want to mary. Charles Hargood believes her late husband fortunate to be dead rather than alive and married to her. Caught, then jilted by his current fiancée he now has a new fiancée: Phoebe.

"Pure enchantment from cover to cover." — *Affaire de Coeur*

LionHearted Order Form

____**Undercover Love** Lucy Grijalva $5.99 _____

____**Destiny's Disguise** Candice Kohl $6.99 _____

____**Forever, My Knight** Lee Ann Dansby $6.99 _____

____**Isn't It Romantic** Ronda Thompson $6.99 _____

____**Oracle** Katherine Greyle $6.99 _____

____**The Marplot Marriage** Beth Andrews $5.99 _____

____**All six books** $29.95 _____

____Shipping <u>singles</u> ($1 per order + $1 per book)   _____

____Shipping <u>six-pack</u> ($3.55 for all six books)   _____

____Sales tax <u>if purchased in Nevada</u> 6.5%   _____

I am enclosing a check, cashiers check or
money order made to "LionHearted" for $ _____

____Please send information on how I can receive free books
or cash for customers I introduce to LionHearted.

PLEASE PRINT CLEARLY

Name _____

Addrs _____

_____

Phone _____

Email _____

I was referred by:

Name _____

LionHearted ID# _____

Mail to: LionHearted Publishing, Inc.
P.O. Box 618, Zephyr Cove, NV 89448

Or call: 888-LION-HRT (888-546-6478)

Or visit: http://www.LionHearted.com

Katherine Greyle

Katherine Greyle believes that writing is both her greatest joy and her greatest challenge. Writing is a passion and a discipline, both hard to sustain for long periods of time. She keeps it lively by switching among genres, from adventure romances to classy Regency-era novels, to futuristic fantasy, time travel, and historicals. Occasionally, she even writes humor articles for Racquetball Magazine. "But all my works include romance, even if it's the love of the perfect serve,"

Kathy's love of romance comes from her own happily-ever-after story. "I met my husband David at a low point in my life. He literally walked in and saved me. I guess that's why I've always believed in knights in shining armor. Other people may think they exist, but I know."

They have been married for over a dozen years and have two girls to keep them busy. "Play groups and Barbie dolls. I never knew they could be so much fun!"

What are Kathy's interests? "Everything and everyone. I love meeting new people and learning new things. There is fuel for a good story in everything from cave diving to interplanetary terraforming. Of course Wall Street Week puts me to sleep, but my husband loves it, so I suppose there's a story in that."

She began in screenwriting, receiving an MFA

from the University of Southern California.

"Writing has always been my first love. I was telling stories in the playground as a kid and rewriting cartoons at home." Still, it took several years and a variety of manuscripts before she found the right combination.

"Everyone warned me that writing was hard work. It's amazing just how hard. But it's also fulfilling and exciting in ways I never considered when I started this career. What other job lets you create whole universes populated with exciting new people? Plus I read about exciting treasure adventures, mythical creatures, and real life conflicts all in the name of research."

Now, years later, Kathy has found a writing home. "LionHearted is fabulous. They publish all my favorite areas and are willing to let me push the creative envelope. Oracle was so much fun to write, it seemed to roll onto the pages. If my readers have half the fun I did creating it, then they're in for a wonderful time." Kathy's screenplay adaptation of Oracle won second place at World Fest '97 and is a likely candidate for Hollywood.

Upcoming romances by Katherine Greyle from LionHearted include a trilogy of Regency comedies and a lively historical with a paranormal twist. "I love humor and I work every day to put it into my writing."

Kathy loves to hear from her readers. They can write to her via e-mail at kgreyle@net66.com, or via LionHearted Publishing, Inc.